Dax Zander
and
the Hand in the Moon

DAX ZANDER: SEA PATROL

Volume One:

DAX ZANDER
AND
THE HAND IN THE MOON

by
Noah Knox Marshall

Imagination Bay Press
Los Angeles, California

Published in the United States
Imagination Bay Press

Library of Congress Control Number: 2018966336
Marshall, Noah Knox
Dax Zander: Sea Patrol - Dax Zander and the Hand in the Moon

Book Design Consultant - Leah Rachel Murphy
Cover Illustration by Giorgio Grecu

www.daxzander.com

For Jim and Jean Elder,
who enriched my youth with warmth and joy,
and unceasingly affirmed great faith in my future.

CONTENTS

BEFORE EVERYTHING CHANGED

The Delvans had enjoyed a peaceful civilization for nearly 15,000 years. This was possible simply because almost nobody else in the universe knew of their existence. Sleek and graceful creatures, the Delvans inhabited the vast oceans of their planet, Delvus-3. This watery region – and all that thrived within it – was hidden from view by a thick outer layer of ice and mineralized fossils. On infrequent occasions, probes from several alien worlds had dug well into the upper boundaries of that frigid shell and found nothing to betray the rich, warm life fathoms below. Thus, scientists from these faraway places had written off Delvus-3 as little more than another enormous, interstellar ball of ice, from surface to core.

So for eons, these docile, sweet beasts, wondrously intelligent and dazzling to behold, had kept one another company in blissful isolation, nurturing their hidden paradise. As their culture evolved, so did their very talented *minds*. By the time the first Vikings had taken to exploring Earth's seas, the Delvans had a chance to watch up close, for they had cultivated their joined mental capacities to warp the fabric of space and matter, enabling the creation of 'bubble corridors' that carried their kind to any charted region without the aid of ships. And it proved a good thing they voyaged to Earth at the dawn of our modern era, for on that visit they also were reacquainted with their long-lost cousins, the orcas, who had migrated many epochs before and adapted to the heavier gravity with ease. A mystery to be sure, but they were family nonetheless.

Centuries later, these cousins would receive another visit, this time out of dire need: The Delvans had abruptly discovered they were no longer inhabiting their world unseen. The first of a new wave of far more efficient alien probes had found its way into a fissure on Delvus-3's icy outer shell, plunging deeper than any device had before. The instant its precise sensors touched salty water, rich with bacteria, everything changed forever, for the Delvans and for the galaxy.

And very shortly thereafter, for Earth.

Out Too Far

D ax would never admit the galley was his favorite part of the seabase, but right now, free-swimming a good fifteen meters below the waves and nearly two kilometers from home and lunch, the rumble in his gut was persistent and food was consuming his thoughts. A fit and hardy, thrill-seeking thirteen years of age, Dax spent a big chunk of his days eagerly exploring the realm immediately surrounding his family's undersea home. Mornings were mostly devoted to studies with tutors, both live and recorded, leaving the afternoons free for kayaking, free-swimming, or surveying some new cave amid the reefs. That is, unless he was lucky enough to be visiting Grampa Pat's house on the mainland – which meant many hours surfing the rolling turquoise swells off the Honolulu coast.

Today was Friday, and with the week's schoolwork completed the day before, he'd left for a swim just a little after nine – on a hasty (and now obviously inadequate) breakfast. Young men require protein nearly as much as they crave adventure, and yet his mother Dayna's preference for vegetarian selections meant her kitchen was stocked with what Dax liked to call 'Granny Chow' – not the kind of stuff that could keep his tummy satisfied for very long.

Among friends and loved ones, Dax's appetite was legendary. Amazed by his ability to put it away, the Zander family subjected the middle son to endless servings of cute and witty commentary along with his meals – or at least what his mother, father and brothers considered cute and witty. So he had grown adept at 'stealth snacking.' This consisted of hoarding packaged treats under his bed, or in the back of a closet he shared with his eight-year-old brother, Kai. He also used a few 'tuck away' spots in Shaw's room, as his older brother was studying marine biology at the University of Miami, and absent for months at a time. Unfortunately, Dax had lately been forced to keep restocking his supply,

3

as Kai's metabolism and passion for 'treasure hunting' were nearly equal to his own.

So today, without his usual backups, Dax was especially famished after hitching a one-way, eight-kilometer joyride astride a humpback whale, leaving him with a very long return swim home. Not to mention the thermal protection of his skinsuit was feeling increasingly less effective. Graphenex was a wonderfully flexible and insulatory material, but the sea wanted everything in it to be cold, and the chill was settling into his bones. He needed to get home. The integrated sonics in the lining of his suit had been playing mood music appropriate to the enigmatic vistas on his travels, but a boost in momentum would get him back sooner. He gently clenched a fist and glanced to his sleeve, where a glowing display appeared.

"Tunes," he said, and a menu scrolled up, featuring dozens of tracks. He selected one marked 'Dad Surf Mix Four' and the hard driving chords of Dick Dale and the Del Tones, still potent more than a century after they were recorded, fueled new vigor into his kicks.

Dax loved free-swimming – where the vast, dark expanse of the ocean was his to chart, free of any tethers. But plowing against ever-shifting currents, his legs had been steadily tiring, and the drive to explore had been replaced by hunger and fatigue. Happily, he didn't have to worry about asphyxiating; the outer membrane of his entire skinsuit served as an artificial gill, constantly extracting oxygen from the water. This in turn was mixed with diffused nitrogen and helium contained in his shoulder-mounted *N-packs*, regulated in varying proportions according to his depth at any given moment, so as to prevent any chance of decompression sickness. The pale green 'air systems go' pulsed comfortingly in the lower right portion of his mask.

Finally, a tiny blue light – one of their perimeter beacons – was visible, flashing in the distant, murky blackness, one and a half kilometers away. From that point, only another 300 meters to the compound. And THAT meant less than half an hour till he'd be enjoying a salad lovingly prepared by mom – followed by a pouch of smoked turkey jerky and three chocolate candy bars from his secret stash.

WHOOSH! Something big and dark shot past to his left. Stunned, he tried to get his bearings when another huge mass came so close he could feel its slippery, pebbled flesh roll against his shoulder. Without warning, there were multiple currents churning about him – dozens of creatures – so close he couldn't get a sense of what he'd stumbled into. A flash of large, sharp, ivory teeth sent his heart racing. Dax tightened his body and fully inverted, attempting to sink straight down out of reach, but he was yanked back with a hard, tight pain just above his left ankle. Reaching for it, he stared at the beast that had clamped its maw on his leg and was now dragging him effortlessly along, with no sense of up or down. He had to squint – the flurry of motion made it difficult at first to determine what had him – but he could tell from the bulbous snout and a lighter, triangular patch under the chin that he was the prisoner of a pilot whale.

The rapid spinning was like a lurching carousel ride – his body fluttering like a ribbon amid swirling torrents of bubbles, his leg exploding with pain. Amid columns of hazy light filtering from the surface, Dax could make out the graceful curves of many more cetaceans, each somewhere between four and six meters in length, their immense, curvy forms blending together like a ballet of milk and coffee. A few swooped near, seeming curious about their comrade's prize. With the light intensifying, Dax realized he was now being dragged *up*. Far from relieved, he could vividly imagine his immediate future as an oversized sardine, rabidly plucked apart by a pod of hungry pilot whales. Gently but firmly, he elbowed the side of the beast's head, hoping to be released. Instead, its jaws clamped down even tighter, so much so he cried out in pain – muffled under his mask.

Vertigo threatened to overwhelm him, his brain swirling into a fog from the dizzying spins; but Dax resisted, knowing if he passed out he might never regain consciousness. His thoughts instead coalesced into a focused search, flashing through all he'd learned of these creatures and their physiology. That huge dark eye and the surrounding tissue were vulnerable; if he jabbed it with the pointy edge of his free fin, the creature might be disoriented enough to release him. Then again, it might lash out with pain and rage, after which all bets were off. He knew it must have mistaken him for a squid or a large fish, as incidents of aggressive behavior against humans were incredibly rare. And Dax couldn't stomach the idea of blinding an otherwise innocent animal to buy his freedom, when a safer, more creative option might exist. If only he could speak whale . . .

Then that thing happened – a jolt of inspiration that sporadically seized his mind with the pulsing energy of a new idea. He couldn't reason with the whale; he couldn't speak or sing in any way that would communicate "let me go" – but he *could* surprise it. Confuse it. He could make *noise* and that might be just enough.

Dax quickly peeled down the jelly-like, form-fitting lower half of his facemask, careful not to suck in any water. He bit down on the wrist of his left sleeve, ripping the Graphenex from the underlayer, exposing two flat, slender filament strips. He did the same to his right wrist, and in seconds, his diagnostics gauge began to flash the sort of information about life support systems that made his stomach tighten up. Dax did his best to ignore the warning, concentrating on bringing his hands together. But the thrashing of his body against the current, an impending blackout and the pain in his ankle were all vying for his attention. Somehow, he found a single place of concentration and slammed his wrists against each other, so the bared cable contacts touched.

The shrieking feedback from that brief connection swept through his body and skinsuit at full volume, startling Dax with its sheer intensity. Fortunately, it *also* shocked the whale like some horrific, undersea alarm.

As Dax came free, he realized he'd taken a gulp of seawater. He clawed at his mask, bringing it up to self-seal again with a low-vacuum pop. He coughed a few times, but at least the air was flowing again. Suddenly, a horrible pain coursed through his ankle – nerves that had been mercifully cut off from sensation until a few seconds ago. The whale backed off, likely still dazed from the sonic battering ram the boy had improvised. Though he knew he should keep moving, Dax reached down to quickly rub his throbbing ankle, and immediately realized that was a big mistake. The whale looped down and came charging at him, clearly intent on reclaiming its prize. Its jaws opened wide, those thick pointy teeth shining dully amid a dark, hungry void. As it rushed toward him, a gentle face glimmered in his thoughts, calming and sweet, and Dax whispered her name, the single person his death would devastate most:

"Mom."

WHAM! A massive black object rammed the pilot whale off its course, the shockwave tumbling Dax back like a tiny strand of limp kelp. Righting himself, he was astonished at the figure hovering before him:

An *orca*. Majestic and regal in its swirling suit of black and white, it bobbed there for a few seconds, gazing at Dax as much as he was gazing back. Then it turned to the pilot whale it had just intercepted, as if annoyed. Evidently recognizing the boy had a formidable bodyguard, the other beast gave up to swiftly join its pod.

The orca, however, lingered, its graceful body slowly drifting around Dax, surveying him like an art collector reverently admiring a renowned sculpture. His heart still racing, Dax held still . . . hovering there, as the great creature circled around and faced him once again – its snout less than four meters from the boy's nose.

Not quite sure why, Dax silently mouthed, "Thank you."

The ocean was quiet – tiny noises echoing and floating through endless chambers. The orca released something like a sigh, unmistakably warm and genial, and then it did something remarkable:

It *bowed*.

Or at least it seemed to, as much as a great finned beast in the water can; its snout and posture seemed for a few quiet seconds to offer deference and respect to Dax the way a commoner would to a king. Awestruck, the boy acted on his first impulse; he bowed in kind, humbly, respectfully, sensing that something was transpiring beyond his fleeting comprehension, but . . . better to play along.

The orca straightened out, almost seeming to smile, though it was simply the graceful contours along its mouth affording that impression. It considered Dax a moment longer, and then peeled away without looking back. The boy stared after it wonderingly as it became a fading ghost in the murky forever, until it was finally and completely gone.

Suspended in the silent sea, Dax looked around. The pod of pilot whales had moved on. He was alone and alive – and the beacon was flashing slowly, dully, within his range of sight. Then his tummy rumbled, demanding nourishment. It was good to feel something other than the dull ache in his ankle, and within seconds, his appetite became a singular, all-important objective. Famished as he was, a salad for lunch, even followed with secret snacks, was going to leave him wanting. And as it was Friday, Mom would almost certainly be cooking up some kind of stew for dinner, loaded with nutritious veggies masquerading as meat. What he craved – no, what he *needed* – was a thick, juicy cheeseburger. Still massaging his leg, Dax chuckled softly, now grateful for the injury; he wasn't above leveraging bite marks to his advantage.

He pinched the torn edges of his skinsuit sleeves together, and they began to knit, self-sealing. His diagnostics gauge blinked and reset, revealing he had barely sixteen minutes of air mix left, as his improvised escape had wrought havoc with the N-pack diffusers. With a wounded ankle, his remaining swim could well take longer. Dax abruptly felt much colder.

Urgently motivated and trying not to think about the damage he might sustain or aggravate further in his ligaments, Dax kicked hard, heading for the beacon and the compound he had called home most of his life.

. . .

Seabase UDN-1 was ninety-one kilometers northeast of the island of Oahu and twenty-eight meters below the surface, permanently moored on a natural geographic plateau amid a series of rising and falling ridges in the North Pacific Ocean. Deep enough to evade detection from any spy satellite of its time, designed to blend in with the surrounding topography, it had been built to serve as one of the first outposts in the Undersea Defense Network in 2061 in the early days of the Inter-Oceanic Pirate Wars. Dozens of nations from four continents had agreed to pool and coordinate resources in an effort to quell what had become the world's worst series of offshore terrorist onslaughts, mobile and lightning fast, attacking cruise and cargo ships, private pleasure boats and even smaller military watercraft with surgical precision before disappearing to parts unknown like phantoms. What became clear was a need to counter the threat with equal speed and surprise. So when a talented military strategist, Lieutenant Commander Evan Zander, presented his audacious proposal for a network of distant offshore seabases, the plan found enthusiastic, near-unanimous approval. Loaded with tracking equipment, small, hidden fleets of amphibious vessels and a robust compliment of infantry and specialists, these outposts would serve as a 'first encounter' deep into international waters. From these camouflaged undersea compounds, trained militia could be deployed with a speed and level of force more appropriate to the threat than ever before. Four years into the operation, Evan Zander was living with his wife and two young sons on Oahu when he was awarded a rare, early promotion to the rank of captain. The modest officer's quarters at Seabase UDN-1 were expanded into a residential module capable of accommodating a family with children, as well as an occasional visiting dignitary. Vested with the authority and admonition to oversee a new and more vigorous offensive strategy, the captain, his wife, seven-year-old son Shaw and infant Dax – who could already swim far better than walk – finally left the mainland for good, moving into their exotic new residence in 2065.

The Undersea Defense Network had justified its enormous expense within about a decade. By 2070, under the captain's initiative and leadership, virtually all incidents of piracy in the waters monitored by UDN stations had subsided to little more than anecdotal skirmishes with impotent, treasure-hunting wannabes. When 'mission accomplished' was finally declared in 2071, it was a happy ending for the Allied Naval Corps, and while troop numbers were steadily reduced over the next few years, the seabases continued to receive top-flight maintenance – several converted to purposes of scientific research, others leased out to educational institutions. Two were now in the possession of wealthy private citizens known for their lavish lifestyles. Since the location of each base had been successfully kept secret throughout the wars, it didn't matter. As far as any would-be pirates were concerned, these military operations were still fully funded and a major deterrent to stirring up any new trouble.

From above, Seabase UDN-1 resembled a massive, squashed spider wearing many big shoes. The whole thing was a compound of several low-slung structures, some devoted to barracks and lifestyle quarters for those enlisted, once housing dozens, now nearly empty. A network of corridors ensured easy access to every section. There was a separate command residence for Captain Zander and his family, an engineering core that held all life support, a laboratory and recycling quadrant, launch bays for vessels large and small, and located a discreet distance away, the OSB's: Ordnance Storage Bunkers – essentially a huge garage for all sorts of weaponry and ammunition. Throughout the compound were over a dozen separate *diver lockout chambers*. These small, pressurized cabins provided swift, easy transitions between the ocean and the dry seabase interiors. They were located in the barracks, the Zander living quarters, corridor junctions and a few other stations.

Most of the shielding, structural supports and inner walls were composed of Graphenex, an amalgam of three 'new generation' materials that could be manufactured in varying formulations depending on their purpose. Lightweight, but incredibly strong and sturdy, these had come to be classified as GX-1, 2 and 3 – all perfectly suited to environments prone to extreme stress, gravity, heat or pressure. After extensive testing in the seabases, GX was being used almost exclusively for the newest structures on the moon and Mars. A slight tweak to the molecular matrix rendered the finished materials transparent – known as GX-3 – so the seabase was blessed with expansive windows providing amazing vistas to the sea outside. For Dax, all of it was simply 'home.'

Halfway past the barracks, his strokes slowed a bit as he peered inside, spotting the last two enlisted men occupying that section, Maz Turocek and Brooks McKinney. When Dax rapped on the windows with his knuckles, Maz grinned, offering a thumbs up, while Brooks remained engrossed in a book – *Cooking With Less* – printed on real paper, a loan from the captain's collection. Dax didn't share the nostalgia or affection some people held for printed paper, people like his dad, for instance. The shelves of his private office as well as the walls of their living room were stuffed with old books.

The gauge on his wrist indicated he had barely more than a minute of air-mix remaining. Still, he couldn't pass up such a perfect moment to tease Brooks and Maz. He aimed two fingers at them – this was how his com system knew to send his message – before actually speaking.

"You guys in the patrol unit ever, you know, *patrol* anymore?"

Brooks glanced up from his pages with a knowing smirk and made a gesture with his hand – almost as if to salute, but then shaking his palm right over his right eyebrow. Dax burst into laughter, but Maz yanked the book out of Brooks' hands and whapped the back of his head.

"That's the son of our C.O.!"

"Dax ain't a puppy anymore. He's laughed at worse."

He glanced out to the big window for affirmation, but a shrill tone had just warned Dax his N-packs were in the red zone – meaning he was soon to asphyxiate – and the boy was already kicking away, jetting frantically toward the airlock right outside his home.

Indestructible

Dax had been out of air mix for eight seconds when the lockout chamber sealed with a deep THUNK! He leaned back against the cylindrical walls as seawater was sucked away through the floor gratings. In seconds, the chamber was emptied, triggering a green signal light, and he loosened his form-fitting hood to take in new air, just in time. His shoulders drooped as he relaxed and the doors before him slid open, revealing the spacious central 'living room' of the Zander residence. Everything in here was designed to accommodate curves and concentric circles, intended for both ease of access and a comforting environment. No awkward, utilitarian angles or sharp corners to navigate. The living room itself was sunken, with warm colors and an exposed stone fireplace, evoking a vaguely western desert feel – an ironic counterpoint to the perpetual cold and darkness immediately outside the seabase walls. It worked well enough for Dax, even if the flames were a projected illusion; his buddies visiting from the mainland marveled that he lived in such a place, and deep down, so did he. Every time he saw that fire blazing, it gave him a smile, a sense of belonging to something special.

"That you, Dax?" his mother called. He swung around a partition on the main level to find her in the large kitchen preparing dinner. Right beside her was Wrigley, a small culinary robot dicing garlic lightning-quick into leaf-thin sections with a tiny, but very effective laser. Quickly taking in the colorful party on the countertops, Dax saw veggie, veggie, veggie, cultivated fungus, garlic bread and . . . veggie. His gut winced; now he wanted a burger more than anything.

"You're dripping all over everything, Dax."

But suddenly he lunged forward and hugged her tight, his brief scare of less than an hour ago reminding him of how very blessed he was to have her as a mom. Dayna Zander held degrees in structural and molecular physics as well as structural engineering, had consulted on the lunar station's early designs and had personally overseen revisions of master plans for every seabase off the coast of North America and the Pacific Islands. She loved a challenge and wasn't afraid to get her hands dirty. But like most moms, she hated a messy kitchen.

And now, despite her resolve to stay dry, her son was draped around her like a soggy blanket, his chin nestled on her shoulder.

"Just sharing a little kiss from the ocean, Mom. 'Hi' from all the finnies." He yawned dramatically. "Wow, I am worn out!"

Dayna Zander nodded, setting a big head of cauliflower down on the countertop. Immediately Dax felt her eyes scrutinizing him, head to toe. Though nervous, he laughed aloud, hoping dearly she wouldn't see through his game. She glanced over to the ample pile of garlic shavings, as Wrigley's shiny tentacles reached for another clove.

"That's plenty, Wrigley. Mushrooms, please."

Her mechanical helper was about the size and shape of a squash, but from within its core, several coils of articulated, magnetic beads could telescope in and out, appropriating built-in tools to mix, cut, sift and knead. It whooshed obediently across the counter, opened a container of fresh mushrooms and began chopping them to some internal rhythm.

"You think inside he's got some music goin'?" Dax asked as he opened the fridge.

"What are you doing?"

"Nothing." Dax shut the door.

"Dax Zander, you are not skipping out on lunch . . . *or* dinner tonight. I'm making a perfectly healthy, delicious meal – with sautéed mushrooms. You like mushrooms."

Wrigley perked up and paused, then slid a bowl full of chopped mushrooms toward her. She sighed. "See? Just for you. Thank you, Wrigley. Sleep now."

Wrigley chimed a tiny acknowledgment of her command, rolled up into an elegant ball the size of an orange and hopped into a small dish where it would lay dormant until needed again. Dax's mother tapped a panel on their storage cooler, and it ejected a small, sealed container. She shook it before placing it on the counter before him.

"Here's lunch. This will tide you over till dinner. But no sneaking out to eat with Maz and Brooks tonight. You – *and* Kai – are going to sit with us and —"

Dax peeled back his hood completely and an impossibly thick, layered mass of platinum blond hair erupted around his skull. He shook it out, picking up some limes to juggle.

"No! How many times have I found your hair in the salad! When are you going to cut all that mess!"

He grinned. His generous locks were typical of the Zander boys, though each male sported a different hue.

"Don't worry, Mom. Tonight, I'm actually gonna comb it. Just for you."

"Wow, such a favor. Thank you, darling. But you're still having dinner here."

It might have been Dax's imagination, but he could almost swear he'd heard a chuckle from Wrigley's dozing form in the corner. He popped open the lid of his lunch container: celery, mushrooms, a few scraggly objects he didn't quite recognize and some mixed nuts.

That pouch of turkey jerky was about to get devoured, and he would enjoy the mixed nuts, at least. But his gratitude for a mother who always had a meal waiting for him, though maybe a little on the theatrical side, was nonetheless sincere.

"Mom! Mommasita! Where am I gonna go? You're going to all this trouble and I'm gonna skip out on you and Dad and Kai? Besides, you haven't heard about my awesome close encounter today!"

He started to loosen the ankle sleeve on his skinsuit.

"I almost got—"

But his words rolled right through her.

"You're dripping on everything, on me, on tonight's food. Go change before your father sees you and gets even more . . ."

She tightened, pursing her lips as if to cut off a thought. Dax looked at her.

"What?"

"Please, honey, lose the skinsuit. You can take your meal to your room if you like. But please now, go dry off."

A crisp, baritone interrupted them both:

"We're underwater, Dayna. Things are always getting wet."

"Hey, Dad!"

At 1.9 meters, Evan Zander was the kind of man who stood tall in any room. His thick eyebrows and coarse mane of charcoal-black hair were dramatically offset by a jagged streak of white on each temple, a family trait passed down from his grandfathers. His sparkling gray-blue eyes appraised his son up and down without comment.

"Everything okay, Dad?"

The captain had cultivated a cool exterior for decades, necessary for the men serving under him to believe their commanding officer was undaunted in the face of unexpected threats. But Dax had a knack for 'reading' the tempos of others around him, including (and perhaps especially) his father. Evan had promised himself he'd never lie to his wife or children, but he was at this moment still processing some unexpected, unwelcome news from earlier in the day. Rather than fumble through it, he brandished a soft smile, squeezing his son's shoulder.

"There are some things in play. We'll talk later."

Dax shrugged casually, making his way past when his father leaned close and whispered.

"You're limping and the leg of your skinsuit is perforated."

In kind, Dax whispered his reply soft and fast.

"I don't wanna scare Mom."

Evan locked him in his gaze for a moment, then nodded once. Dax took this as permission to move on.

The two of them alone now in the kitchen, Evan came up behind his wife, wrapping his arms around her still-athletic waist as she continued to add spices to a vinaigrette. Giggling, she flicked half a mushroom up into the air, over her head, and as if they had practiced a thousand times, he lunged back and gobbled the morsel mid-fall.

"Yummy."

"His skinsuit was ruptured —" she began.

"I saw it."

"I'm trying not to baby him. He hates that."

"Yeah, he does. Besides, it's probably nothing. You know, he goes out for hours and it's always okay."

"There's always a first time."

"I'll talk to him. How are the tension trials on your new joists going?"

"Not joists – they're foundational supports. So far, one pylon can support three times the load of anything we've used before. And each component can be extracted on any site where there's an adequate supply of two principle simple elements. We just add a tiny touch of a hydrated bonding agent, which is nothing to transport dry."

"Wow." He was keeping up so far, as she hadn't yet trotted out the really complicated jargon. "So, let's say they want to build a mining community on an

14

asteroid," he postulated. "They melt down the raw materials, pump those into one of your 'cookers' and it spits out—"

"Whatever we want. But it's the way we emboss the components with seams. When you assemble pieces into their final form, there are these microscopic grooves spidering out between the coupled surfaces. We shoot the bonding compound directly into the seams, it spreads in a split-second and melts everything together like it's one solid unit. Incredibly strong."

Evan held her back a little and shook his head. She was many things to him, but her brilliance was such a casual, modest thing, it made her all the more irresistible.

"And all of that ultimately keeps people safe. You're amazing."

She made a happy noise as he nuzzled her neck. But something in his brief silence following gave her pause. She put down the knife and turned, facing him.

"So it's a done deal? They're doing it?"

Evan sighed, sitting back on a stool, reaching for a piece of broccoli. Dayna took his other hand solemnly.

"Well. Life is change," she offered.

He looked up, his brow wrinkled with care. She took a tiny, nervous breath.

"Okay. What was the title of Donald Duck's graduate physics thesis?"

Evan blinked, caught off guard. His wife had lately taken to trying out jokes on the family to prove she had a lighter side beyond theorems and formulas.

"Oh, honey," he said, shaking his head, "you're not good at this . . ."

"Quark-quark-quark!" she shot back, giggling.

He groaned, shaking his head, pulling her closer.

"Come on!" she pleaded earnestly, "that was funny!"

"Yes, it was. It was. Thank you." They laughed together and he seemed better. Funny or not, she did have a magical way of making him feel better when he truly needed it.

"You smell wonderful," he murmured, and they held each other for a bit longer.

. . .

Kai's jaw was practically on the floor. He was already *on* the floor, staring up close at Dax's series of bruises. In six places around his ankle, the skin had been slightly pierced, and a purplish-yellow discoloration was setting in. With one hand, Dax plucked selections from his lunch container to chew on; with the other he waved a small Lumifuser wand from their home first-aid kit over the wounds. Three levels of UV light and a thin layer of antibacterial spray disinfected the entire area; on his second pass, a fine mist coated his abrasions, foaming up into a clear rubbery goo, sealing the broken skin.

"How big was it!?"

"Oh, Kai, so huge," he said, crunching a mouthful of lemon-roasted cashews. "I mean . . . remember at Truckosaurus a couple of years ago, when we went to Gramma and Grampa Z's in New Mexico?"

"That big!"

"Well, almost. And he was beautiful, and there were dozens of 'em! I mean everywhere! And he was yankin' me up and down and all around and—"

"How much did you think you were gonna die?"

Dax chuckled. All adventures for this eight-year-old were gauged by how close to death, or perceived death, one would come.

"A lot. And then the orca came and . . . WHAM! Knocked that thing like a . . . like a . . . sonic hammer, boom! Knocked it crazy and then I was free."

"Whoa. That. Is. Unfreakitable."

Then, Kai's admiring eyes began to well up; he embraced his older brother impulsively, and with such surprising ferocity Dax thought he might bruise a rib.

"Don't do that again! I don't want you dead, Dax!"

"Hey, I'm not goin' anywhere. Relax, buddy. I'm okay."

He pulled Kai up and they sat facing each other on the edge of a bunk.

"But. We can't let this go to waste."

"Whattaya mean?"

Dax's voice dropped to a whisper.

"Wanna see Grampa Pat tonight?"

Kai squealed so loud Dax had to clamp a palm to his lips.

"Really?!"

"Shhh!"

Kai calmed and nodded, fidgety but silent.

"Mom's makin' her chef medley salad thingy for dinner."

Kai's face scrunched up, anticipating an abundance of healthy yuckiness.

"Again? With 'sparagus?"

"Yeah."

"Why does she make that stuff all the time?"

"It's good for you. But . . ."

Dax shifted his leg over to proudly display his wound.

16

"Kai, I got bit today. By a big ol' whale. I think that deserves a little time off, don't you?"

Kai nodded, fully in. He loved a good scheme, the kind that made him rub his chin like a villainous cartoon character, and his big brother knew his way around a good scheme.

. . .

"Mommy! Dax got bit! Dax got bit!"

Kai raced into the kitchen, out of breath, his mother and father still holding each other, enjoying what had been a quiet moment.

"What? Where?"

"Out there! He got bit by a whale!"

Evan rolled his eyes but didn't say a word, waiting for what was sure to be a passionate if not entirely impromptu drama. Silently, he counted off on his fingers: five, four, three, two . . .

Dax appeared in the kitchen again, leaning on an aluminum crutch. His mother jumped up, horrified.

"A whale! How could you not tell me before! What—"

"Well, I tried, but you were mad about all my hair and getting you wet—"

"A pilot whale!" Kai offered. "It thought he was food!"

"Guess I was in shock, Mom. Besides, I didn't wanna worry you. But then the spasms started—"

"Spasms . . ." Evan repeated, rubbing his jaw ruefully.

Dax sensed his dad was wise to his plan and could bust him at any moment, but all he had claimed was true – technically. The bite still throbbed, a little at least, and he wanted to believe his father was sympathetic, so he kept playing to his intended audience with all his heart.

"I guess. After I got bit all I wanted was to . . . get home. To you."

Evan simply stood back as Dayna knelt down and rolled up Dax's pant leg.

"Oh, my dear Lord," she whispered, tapping gently at the rubbery sealer on the wounds, ". . . and you've already dressed it."

"Yeah. Well. I didn't wanna bother you. And I was getting hair in the salad, so—"

"Oh, sweetheart . . ."

Dax caught a glance from his dad, who nevertheless crouched to take a look, tracing a finger up and down his shinbone.

"Did you put it through a diagnostic? Check for fractures?"

17

Dax glanced between them; he *should* have run his leg through the diagnostic scanner in his mom's lab, especially given this was a bite from a wild animal. But though spectacularly bruised, the pain had subsided to a tolerable, if annoying level by now.

"We were gonna do it at Grampa Pat's!"

Everyone looked at Kai. Dax gaped at his little brother incredulously; he chose *this* moment to improvise? Dax realized their scheme had been exposed. Perhaps terminally.

"At Grampa's . . . ?" Dayna remarked, standing up again.

"Well, he does volunteer at that clinic," Evan added.

"Dax," she said, "you didn't do all this simply to get out of dinner tonight?"

"Of course, Mom. I swam eight clicks out with a bunch of whales dressed like a sardine so one of them would bite me —"

The brows of both his parents furrowed, his mother's eyes sparking with indignation, and Dax knew he'd offered too much.

"*How* far!?"

"Eight clicks?" his dad chimed in, no longer amused. "Eight kilometers? Dax, that far out, you *are* bait."

"I can't believe you'd do something so dangerous!" his mother added, clearly angry.

"Mom! I'm out there all the time!"

"Not by yourself. Not free-swimming. What if it hadn't let you go? You just can't take off wherever you want without thinking!"

"Mom! I'm thirteen! I'll be fourteen in a few months! Nothing's gonna hurt me!"

His dad grunted in frustration.

"Indestructible, I suppose. The boundaries we set are for your protection, Dax."

"C'mon, Dad, you worry all the time. Have I ever gotten, you know, *severely* hurt?"

"Okay, that's enough," Dayna chimed in. "You can go think about this in your room. And, Kai, I'm on to you, too. So. Scoot."

"What'd I do?!" Kai whined.

"It's called conspiracy," she said dryly. "Scoot."

"Dad," Dax pleaded, now hobbling on his leg with an earnest bravado that would make the most passionate Shakespearean actor blush. "Seriously, wouldn't it be better if Grampa took a look at this at the clinic? I mean, you wanna trust my health to some old machine we've had sitting around here for years? 'Cause tomorrow my leg could be oozing goo . . ."

Over the years, Captain Zander had sat through countless creative excuses from hundreds of men and women under his command, most begging for an unscheduled weekend furlough. Dax was not going to sway him where so many others had failed, and the idea that one of his own sons would try to pull one over on him always tested his otherwise amiable mood.

"You said it yourself. You're indestructible."

Dax stared at both of them; his parents were in solidarity.

"But—"

"Go."

Skipping Out on Dinner

In their bedroom, Dax and Kai had been playing Super Scrabble on the floor for over an hour. Outside the big round window, a school of parrotfish glided by, a few staring in curiously before moving on. Like any small boy, Kai's attention was alternating between the game board, the window, and one of the books in his brother's collection.

"I'm still hungry," Dax muttered. "And 'tacklum' is not a word."

Kai bounced up and flipped around, squeezed his arm under his mattress and dug deep into the middle.

"Yes, it is, like when we're watchin' football and Dad yells, 'tacklum!'"

"No, that's . . . that's not a word. And you're getting triple word score on it so it's wrong three times over."

His little brother spun around again brandishing a bag of dried pineapple chunks. Dax reached in but Kai whisked it behind his back.

"Tacklum."

"Fine!"

Kai released his grip on the bag. Dax helped himself as his little brother turned his attention to the book, where, hovering above the pages, animated gunfighters faced each other down on a lonely, dusty street.

"Who are these guys?"

"Cowboys. It was a long time ago."

"How long ago?"

Dax blinked; he could just let his little brother learn from the book, but Shaw had almost always taken the time to answer *his* questions, and he wanted to be that considerate with Kai.

"Well this is 2077, so I think they first started calling them cowboys maybe two hundred and fifty years ago, but they lasted a long time."

"So they were really real?"

"Yeah. Remember when we visited the reservation Mom's grandparents came from? Those people lived in America way before people came from across the ocean."

"People went from Hawaii to Eye-wuh? Why?"

"No, Kai…"

Dax bounced up to the wall and swept a hand across it; a shimmering screen appeared.

"You said Dad de-tapped all our games and shows 'cause we're grounded."

"Yeah, he did, except our educational taps," he explained. Then, turning back to the screen, he articulated crisply:

"I need a simple map of North America, mid-eighteenth century."

The image onscreen changed instantly to reveal a large map, but barely a second later, a fiftyish Japanese woman blinked into view before it, wearing a pretty blue and white dress.

"Hello Dax, do you need assistance with something in geography?"

"Hi, Doctor Yokana. No, I'm okay, thanks. Trying to teach my brother Kailen about the early United States."

"Oh, excellent," she said, beaming kindly at Kai, who leaned over to his brother, whispering.

"Is that really her somewhere or is it only a synthie?"

"Hello, Kai," she said with a smile, "I'm here. I try to be available to all my students if I get a signal that they might need some help with their studies."

"Wow. Hi! Is it nice where you are?"

Doctor Yokana turned, apparently to look out a window.

"It's overcast here in Monterey," she observed, "perfect for working on my personal projects. Which I guess I'll go back to now. If you need anything, Dax, feel free to call."

"Thank you!" Dax said, and her image evaporated.

"She's nice," Kai observed.

"Yeah, you'd like her. She's a great teacher, and she makes robots just for fun."

Dax stepped up to the huge map, drawing a line through the breadth of the Atlantic Ocean, to the Eastern Seaboard of the continent.

"Way over here, past the ocean, is Europe – England, France, Germany – all those places. And hundreds of years ago, people came to all of this, looking to start a new life."

"Why? That looks really far."

"Well, they wanted more than what they had. Life was tough where they lived and they didn't get to do what they wanted."

"We don't get to do what we want all the time."

"Yeah, but we're kids. That's how things are. Someday, we'll get to do a lot more."

"I wanna fly on a dragon!"

Dax shook his head and rolled on, pulling his finger west across early America.

"So first everyone lived in this tiny section of land, but some got restless, and wanted to move to places where they could spread out."

"What's 'restless'?"

"Bored. Like when you've tried everything and want something different. Or better."

"Like an adventure."

Dax nodded; finally Kai was connecting.

"Yeah, an adventure. And the people who moved out West – a lot of them were called 'pioneers' but others were called cowboys, 'cause they looked after all the cows and horses. But it was a tough life, sometimes pretty scary. They were going places none of them had ever been."

"But," Kai pondered, "if it's not very scary, it's not gonna be a good adventure, right?"

"I guess not."

"So why do you have all these books about cowboys?"

"I just like the stories. They're exciting. Some of them did things that weren't right. But most of them, they were brave and decent. They did things nobody had ever done before, without any technology or electricity and almost no medicine, and they helped start all of this..."

He drew a big circle around the entire Western territory.

"Are there any cowboys today?"

"No, not like the ones in those days. But I guess the folks on Mars are kind of like them. And the people who just moved to Europa."

"Yeah, that's pretty brave. Would you be a cowboy?"

Dax grinned, picturing himself in a ten gallon hat, astride a majestic steed. Not a little impatient, Kai pressed further.

"Would you go to Europa?"

"Kai. Look at the wall."

22

Dax gestured over to row after row of illuminated shelves, inset in the wall, where scale models of glistening, vintage speedboats and classic racecars betrayed the common denominator of his aspirations: speed. Kai considered his brother's collection, thoughtfully tapping his chin.

"But you'd be going on a spaceship. And they go fast," he said, finally.

"Yeah, Kai, but you don't feel it. And it's such a long way. Guess how far," he pressed.

At a loss, Kai shrugged. Dax was still for a moment, reluctant to admit even *he* didn't know the exact number himself; the distance to Jupiter would have to suffice.

"About six hundred *million* kilometers, Kai! So far that you have to sleep for most of the trip. Who wants to sleep that long?"

"You said your friend Cody wants to be an astronaut," Kai answered.

Dax fell quiet, pushing himself up off the floor. "Yeah, he definitely wants to go to space," he said, moving toward his glowing collection of models. He'd assembled and painted several himself; the rest were gifts, mostly from Gramma and Grampa Zander, obtained in their trips around the world.

"You wouldn't go with him? You'd really rather race cars and boats and stuff?"

Dax didn't answer. Instead, he gingerly plucked a sleek model car from its berth in the middle of the center shelf, its metallic gold and red finish gleaming like hard fire. He held it up to catch the light until it was clear he had his brother's full attention.

"Kai, this is a 1963 Chevrolet Corvette. There are only a few thousand left in the whole world, and all of them were made over a hundred years ago. Someday I'm going to get on a track, and get inside one of these, and drive it, so fast. And it's going to be amazing. Rubber wheels on asphalt. My whole body feeling it as everything rushes by – no magnets, no vibration dampeners. I wanna go so fast it scares me."

"You wanna be scared?"

Dax chuckled, placing the model back in its place.

"Well, a little, sure . . . It's just a great feeling, whenever I get to go super-fast. On Earth, there are all kinds of places I can go to do that. And when I'm old enough, I will. Space might be great for some people, Kai – and I know Cody wants that more than anything – but for me, when I watch the NASA feeds, it all just looks so slow. And boring. Besides, if I went somewhere as far as Europa, I'd be leaving you and Mom and Dad. And Shaw . . . and Grampa Pat and . . .

everyone else, for a super long time. And just letting all that go . . . that's scarier than anything."

Kai seemed satisfied. He hunkered down, closing the book to look at the game board.

"Good. That was a test. I don't want you going away."

Dax sat on the floor again, placing a few new tiles to form 'repetitious.'

"That's not a word!"

"Look it up."

"You can't use words I don't know!"

"They're words you're *going* to know! It means when you do something over and over, like disagree with me, which you do all the time!"

"I do not! I am not reptshush!"

"See! You know it already!"

A DING! preceded their door whisking open by half a second.

They looked up to see their father's head in the doorway.

"Take the red skimmer to Grampa's," he said, matter-of-factly. "But it stays parked while you're there, no island-hopping. And unless we tell you otherwise, you're back here by three tomorrow afternoon."

Dax and Kai looked at each other, confused. It was 1:30; they'd been consigned to their room for barely ninety minutes. Their father was by no means a hard man, but he rarely reversed a decision when it came to discipline.

"I thought we were grounded."

"You have to be more careful, Dax. We put limits on the perimeter for a reason. I know the new skinsuits give you more freedom and I know you like to explore, but there are real predators out there who just see you as food – and you can't be free-swimming without protective gear. Especially when you're without a partner."

"Oh, Dad. You should see this."

Dax picked up his skinsuit from a rack where it had been hanging and showed his father the sleeves and telltale 'scars' on the cuffs.

"What happened?"

"That whale was dragging me all around, so I tore open two of the embedded systems and crossed them, hoping it would create some crazy feedback and scare it enough to let me go."

"Well, obviously it worked. How'd you even know to do that?"

24

"Dad, I *do* study. I wasn't positive the sonic feed would interact with the diagnostic lines, but it's all frequency, right? I figured, you throw it all in the blender and hope it explodes. I wanted to scare the whale without hurting it."

Evan felt at the torn sleeves in his hands, chuckling with a mix of bewilderment and pride not uncommon when it came to his middle son. Perhaps it was the stimulation of an ever-exotic, highly tactile and technologically-integrated home environment, the benefit of an exceptional lineup of teachers who had signed up for his interlinear and multimodal school sessions, or some good genes from his mother, but the net result was that Dax seemed to embrace technology in a way others missed. He was routinely consumed with a fiery sense of wonder, an insatiable curiosity that approached the sciences like a powerful language that could unlock secrets for every human being.

And yet, a nagging byproduct of all this unbridled curiosity was the long line of broken toys and prototype machinery Dax left in the wake of his impetuous and imaginative exploits. He was impulsive and reckless, a thrill-seeker who relished nearly any challenge in his path, but also had an unfortunate habit of not preparing properly (or at all) for potential risks.

In moments such as these, Dax resembled a ship without a rudder, its destination impossible to predict. As Evan was a man with deep appreciation for a good compass – both at sea and in life – his son's capricious explorations were a real test of the captain's restraint. For now, he kept reminding himself the boy was still thirteen; the world wouldn't demand he chart a course for a few years, at least. Perhaps before then, his son would discover his true north.

Dax's voice scattered his musings.

"You know, whoever's designing skinsuits should integrate a sonic alarm in the next model. And it would be smart if they split the channel with a strong white noise."

His father blinked. "White noise?"

"Like a counterbalance. So if and when that alarm activates, whoever's wearing the suit doesn't go deaf from the noise."

"Or you could just integrate frequency cancellation plugs into the hood."

Dax chuckled sheepishly; that *would* be simpler. "Maybe."

"That *is* a good idea, Son. Could save lives. Tap me a memo and I'll make sure it gets passed along."

Evan sighed, leaning forward on the boys' study desk, gazing out the window to the reef. For a few seconds he said nothing. Kai cuddled up to his

25

dad's side – just sort of hugged him around the waist and looked out, aping his father's forlorn, searching gaze. Evan rubbed the top of Kai's head. He had been blessed with good boys. Even Shaw, though at that age where young men regularly butt heads with their dads, was a noble, considerate and generous soul. And very much missed right now.

"Daddy, what's 'conspirussy'?"

It took Evan a moment to remember his wife had just thrown the word out.

"You know how you guys planned my birthday party last year and I was so surprised? I didn't know anything about it?"

"Uh huh. Your face was so funny!"

"Well, all of you plotting . . . that was a conspiracy. A nice one."

"Sometimes there's bad conspirussies?"

Their father nodded, soberly. Dax detected a hint of melancholy there.

"Dad, you okay?"

"Yeah. You guys should hurry and get packed."

. . .

Beside a sealed hatch, Dax gave his mom a hug. Part of him felt slightly guilty; she DID love to cook, and it wasn't her fault if those kale and asparagus medleys couldn't compete with Grampa's barbecued *anything*. She held out a bag and Dax could smell the sweet aroma of her almond-glazed banana bread. Now *there* was something at which she excelled. He took it gratefully and she kissed him.

"I suppose if you're going to earn a cheeseburger, that's the way to do it."

Evan swooped Kai up and swung him around once, then gave Dax a kiss on his forehead.

"Dad!" Dax muttered, blushing.

"Listen to Grampa Pat," his father directed, "and see if there's anything around his place that needs taking care of. Go on. We'll let him know you're on your way."

Dax nodded, as Kai gave his dad a salute, quickly and happily returned. The captain opened the portal and the boys headed down a wide, low-ceilinged corridor labeled: "TO SKIMMER BAY." Kai started skipping ahead.

"Kai, you gobie! Don't run!" Dax called, all too aware of his brother's clumsiness.

"I'm not a gobieeee!" he shouted, sprinting off like a jackrabbit.

26

As the portal closed again, Evan turned to Dayna and embraced her. She settled into his arms with delight.

"Oh, hello . . ." she giggled.

"So much for modeling good discipline," he mused. "The boys try to pull a fast one over on us and we give them a holiday."

"Well. It's like you said. We have some things to take care of, to discuss, and without them underfoot, it'll be a little easier to figure out plans."

He sighed. She always found a way to turn things around for the better.

"You know what, Dr. Zander . . . that can wait a while. After all. It looks like we have this entire undersea wonderland to ourselves."

"Not quite. There are two uniformed officers in the barracks."

"Y'know, I don't think they like salad, either."

She slapped him lightly on the cheek, and then they moved to the c-shaped sofa facing the fireplace. They stared into the flames for a while.

"Gonna miss this," he said, quietly.

She looked at him with a mixture of sadness and adoration, then curled up across his lap.

"Well, the Evan Zander I married could build a fire pretty much anywhere."

And just like that, the tension of the day began to melt away. The nagging feeling of having failed somehow – it had faded. He leaned down and kissed her, so very grateful.

. . .

The launch bay was large enough to hold eight vessels – each with a six-person compliment – and room to spare for general maintenance. Four silos surrounded the perimeter, any of which could be sealed and isolated, facilitating a single vessel's departure without a need to flood the overall space. Given its size, these days it felt quite forlorn, as most of the original vessels had been moved out. In Silo One, still docked and held in the grip of four suspension clamps just above the steel-mesh floor, were two submersible oceanic skimmers, identical but for the fact one was predominantly a deep yellow, the other bright red. They were designed primarily for above-water transport to and from the mainland, but a retractable, watertight hood permitted the vehicles to submerge and operate to depths of over sixty meters, three times the depth of the bay where they were kept secure.

The main cabin was the size of a family car, wrapped up in a burrito-like shell of longitudinal pontoons. Dax checked Kai's restraint straps and then buckled himself in. The sectional hood of Skimmer Red began to slide together out of the sidewalls, and Dax waited until he heard the familiar hiss that indicated they had a nice, safe seal.

"Flood skimmer bay," Dax called out, and the computer responded by opening several overhead vents, raining torrents of seawater on the roof. He glanced at Kai, who *loved* this part; he was ever hopeful some fish would flop or slide across the windows, maybe an octopus – and sometimes that sort of thing did happen. But the bubble screens outside, triggered in advance of any docking or departure, served as an effective deterrent to undersea creatures, so most of their pre-launches had largely been free of falling fish.

"You wanna punch us up?" Dax offered, swinging a navigation baton over to his brother. Exhilarated, Kai gripped it with both of his small hands, then bit his lower lip fiercely, knowing the launch required his full concentration. Actually, it didn't, as Dax had put the navigation system on automatic so that all Kai had to do was hit a single button. But why ruin the illusion? Kai gazed at a display overlaid with a softly glowing grid. Their destination was straight *up*.

"Three, two, one . . . Boom!"

Both boys enjoyed the surge upward as they shot through the roof of the docking bay. Once clear, Dax reached for the navigation stick. Kai leaned over to look out a side port; Seabase UDN-1 was getting smaller and smaller as they rose toward the surface.

"Nice goin'," Dax said, taking control.

Sunlight flooded the cabin as the skimmer broke from the surface amid frothy whitecaps, a few startled seagulls flitting hastily away at the sudden emergence of this brash red beast. As rivulets of seawater broke over the front and side ports, the boys shared big grins, both taking in the brilliance of a bright blue Hawaiian sky.

"Dax, look!" Kai pointed off to the horizon, where a humpback whale breached spectacularly, fully erupting into the air and belly-flopping with a fantastic splash.

Kai waited for more. The tail emerged for a last graceful splashdown, but that was it. Dax was thoughtful.

"October fifteenth. He's early. Way early. That's weird."

"When do they migrate?"

"Late December, through these waters. Maybe he's lost." Dax tapped the console and the roof began to retract.

He made a wide turn and glanced at the glowing topographical map floating before them above the navigational console. He traced a line toward a cove on Oahu's North Shore.

"Track topography and redirect to target coordinates at thirty-five knots. Suggested route. Recalculate."

The computer immediately redrew their route for more efficiency, with detours around some dark sections.

"What are those?" Kai asked, pointing them out.

"You know what they are: reefs and shoals. If it's low tide we have to avoid them."

The computer's calm, measured voice replied with confidence:

"Redirect complete. Estimated arrival, forty-six minutes."

Pleased, Dax reached for his dad's Ray Ban sunglasses, hanging off a small hook below the console.

"Alright . . ."

"Daddy looked sad."

"Yeah, maybe a little."

"You know why?"

"No idea. But he'll tell us when he's ready, I guess."

He offered a reassuring wink, tousling Kai's hair, as a warm tropical breeze lifted his own thick blond locks. He tugged at Kai's seat restraints one more time, just for good measure, then tapped a yellow button. Two turbines fired up in the rear pontoons, and with a pulsing whoosh of twin silent engines, they were on their way to Grampa's.

"It's so fast!" Kai exclaimed, waving as they rushed past a large sailboat.

"Yeah, but way too quiet," Dax said. "What good is fast if you can't feel it? It's like those shuttles in San Francisco."

"The really fast ones?"

Dax tore a generous chunk off the loaf of almond-glazed banana bread his mom had packed up. The sweet aroma drifted up to him, so delectable.

"Yeah. The lev-rails. They're for grannies with sore butts."

"I like it fast. And the way it hums."

"Well, I like that you're not getting seasick. I remember when we went up in that copter to the Big Island you ratched all over the glass."

Kai's hard glare made Dax laugh so hard he spat banana bread crumbs out on his brother.

"Gross! I did not!" Kai protested. "It wasn't all over!"

"It smelled sooo bad, Kai!"

Dax offered some bread to his brother, but Kai simply scowled and leaned out over the edge of the cabin.

"It was 'cause we went way up! I like fast stuff, just like you. I just don't like bein' high."

Dax busted out with another laugh but decided against further comment. In Kai's pouty silence, he focused instead on the skimmer's near-silent hum, moving along at a crisp, boring thirty-five knots. There was nearly no friction, almost no sense of movement. Sure, the ocean was rushing by all around them and there was that gentle bobbing glide along the waves, but the skimmer had been designed by some industrious engineer determined to take all the fun out of it. He or she had, over time, created the aquatic equivalent of shock absorbers, the pontoons constantly readjusting their ballast to accommodate for a ride that felt more like skimming along snow than rising and falling waves. Now Grampa's boat, *The Empress Lilly* – THAT was a ride. But by the time they had dinner and dessert, it was going to be getting dark, and the odds were low that Grampa would be up for an impromptu cruise out on his century-old Chris Craft runabout. Then again, they weren't heading back till tomorrow afternoon . . .

Dax's whole body tingled with anticipation. Somehow he knew they'd be opening the throttle on that sublime, vintage vessel soon. And somewhere before and after, with any luck, he'd be surfing some of the best swells in the world.

Grampa's Place

A trail of glittering sea spray in its wake, the skimmer barreled past what seemed an endless strand of colorful sailboats headed in all directions. Just ahead and to the stern, a small pod of dolphin broke through the sparkling waves; Dax was about to point them out, but Kai was still sulking.

"Seriously?"

"My ratch doesn't smell that bad."

"Kai, everyone's ratch stinks! That's why we try not to do it! Wasn't your fault! Don't take everything so frippin' personally."

"Fine."

Dax looked at their trip timer. Twenty-one minutes till they hit shore. Plenty of time.

"Call Shaw Zander. Dorm."

Kai bounced up in his seat.

"Yay! You think he'll be home?"

"Depends."

"On what?"

"On if he has a date. It's 7:00 on a Friday night in Miami."

A secondary image rose over the topographical map, hovering there, with one word – 'REACHING' – pulsing repeatedly. Then the word vanished, replaced by the half-opaque image of a disheveled, sun-soaked bedroom, where a bare-chested, barefoot young man was hopping into a pair of khakis.

"Hey, tark, I'm . . . I just have a few minu—"

Kai shoved his face over the console, shouting.

"Hey, Shaw! Are you naked!?"

"Hey, buddy Kailen, I thought Dax was calling—"

31

"I'm here! Zip up, nature-boy," Dax responded, as he took in Shaw's chaotic environs. There were photos and souvenirs from parties and cross-country trips their parents had likely never heard about, hanging fishnet bundles of laundry waiting to either be washed or folded, two surfboards hanging askew from the ceiling, and whatever was growing in that cloudy, oversized fish tank was probably going to crawl out and eat Miami someday.

Shaw slipped effortlessly into some flip-flops, his chest and square shoulders still exposed as he rubbed some gel into his short-cropped, golden brown hair. Kai looked confused.

"I thought you started working out."

Shaw leaned into the camera, his deep green eyes unmistakably taking an ego hit.

"Kai! I've *been* work—"

Dax laughed, proud of his young shadow. Now it was his turn.

"So Friday night, no date in sight, huh? You and Bardy just gonna sit home and play ZBox football, order a pizza?"

Shaw paused, getting a good look at Dax.

"Wow, still wearing the bird's nest, huh?"

"Ohh, that's a misfire, cadet! But, hey, you know if you wash some of that laundry hangin' over your head, girls might just *like* the way you smell."

Shaw responded with a fake falsetto laugh, and would've offered something more potently articulate had it not been for Kai sitting right there.

"Keeps dirty clothes off the floor. And for your information, I *do* have a date. Her name is Hayley, she's from Ireland, and we're doin' a late night dive off Key Largo after dinner."

"She's in your class, right?"

"Well, yeah. Why?"

"I told mom that God'd have to make it easy for you. So, go-go-go, big bro!"

Kai felt left out, as he couldn't think of anything exceptionally interesting to say. Being eight, however, that didn't last long.

"Dax got bit by a whale!"

"What!?"

"Yeah, a pilot whale," Dax explained. "I guess it thought I was tasty."

Shaw's jaw tightened as Dax proudly lifted up his shin for the onboard camera.

"How'd you provoke it?" Shaw asked tersely, "Pilot whales almost never attack hu—"

"Shaw!" Kai interrupted, "where's Bardy?!"

"Bard has a late class on Fridays, Kai. He's joining us later on the dive. Dax, did you go free-swimming without any protect—"

"Hey, hey, hey! I already got lectured today!" Dax protested.

"Good! Man, you can be stupid! And are you—" he glanced around to gauge their location. "Are you out now – on the *skimmer*? I swear, they let you get away with murder!"

"Oh, thank-you-Dax-for-calling-me! I'm so glad I have brothers who love me and miss me and want to talk to me when I'm so far away from home!"

Shaw bit back a retort, distracted by a 'ding' at his door.

"Come in!" he called, and then bent closer, his voice an urgent whisper. "Okay, fine . . . sorry. But, Dax! You do stuff like that all the time! And I can remember a few times when you dragged other people into your mess."

Dax shook his head.

"Well, it's always fun talkin' to ya, bro."

A pretty redhead stepped into view behind Shaw, dressed casually in jeans and an attractive cardigan sweater. Kai leaned in again.

"Are you Hayley? Hi, Hayley! Thanks for going out with my brother! He gets really lonely sometimes, sleeping under all his dirty clothes."

Dax doubled over cackling as Shaw's cheeks turned intensely red. Giggling, Hayley leaned close to wave into the lens.

"Who's that?"

"That's my little brother Kai," Shaw muttered, "and that bucket of parasitic beach moss is his science project."

"Beach . . . moss?" She leaned in, as Dax, with little affection for Shaw's brand of humor, offered two thumbs down for the effort.

"Yeah," Shaw nodded, "he just eats, hogs the surf and stinks up the sand."

"Oh, that's your other brother, isn't it? Hello, Dax."

"Hi, Hayley! So wait, Shaw . . . you actually *tell* people about us? We exist?"

"Well," Shaw smirked, "they gotta know who to contact in case I do something stupid . . . like get bit by a whale."

"A whale!" Hayley laughed innocently, "Fortunately cetaceans are very friendly, so the chances of something like that are pretty slim! But it's very sweet to meet you both."

"Look, we gotta go, Daxer. Kailen, buddy, you be good. We'll get you down here sometime and I'll take you up to Marvel World."

"Yayyy! Tell Bardy I said 'hi'!"

"Okay, will do."

The screen evaporated, revealing their position on the topographical map, but Dax no longer needed it, as the picturesque cove where Grampa's home was tucked away had become visible on the approaching horizon.

No doubt inspired by visions of a visit to the massive Orlando theme park, Kai started singing the theme to "Spiderman" and Dax gave him a glare.

"Stop. The only word you know in that song is 'Spiderman' and you just sing it over and over."

"Okay."

The computer piped up, almost cheerfully:

"Destination imminent. Would you like to switch to manual navigation?"

"Affirmative."

Dax and Kai shared a smile, excited to be here. Kai gave his brother a slight 'salute' and Dax took the stick, speaking aloud once again.

"Please indicate path, reroute avoiding shallows."

The topographical map now merged with their perspective out the front windscreen, so that Dax could steer clear of any dangerous reefs or anything else exposed by low tide. They powered forward at a moderate speed, and very soon they could see a large, tanned figure in a loose, linen shirt and a big floppy hat, waving from shore.

. . .

Patrick Derry Redtree never saw the ocean until a family vacation to San Francisco on his twelfth birthday, but five minutes at the helm of a charter fishing boat, courtesy of their generous captain, was all it took for him to fall in love with the sea. He enrolled in a college near the coast, and ever since had lived most of his life in or near to the water. Here, at the northernmost point of Oahu, he had resided the last twenty-six years, most of it with his beloved Maggie, who had left this world when Kai was five.

His modest but comfortable residence on Crozier Loop took up just a tiny footprint on a spreading coastline with a few wide coves to either side and magnificent forest preserves all around. The house itself resembled a collection of native wood bungalows facing a generous yard dotted with volcanic rocks, tiki totems and torches. A carpet of thick grass flowed like a lazy river up and down the terraced slopes throughout the backside of the property, weaving around clusters of palms and hearty shrubs that eventually gave way to crunchy white sand. The roof was wonderful; Grampa Pat had built a deck up there, complete with a brick fireplace and a small enclosed observatory. Since adding those improvements, it had become 'destination one' for neighborhood kids to gather with friends and parents, roast marshmallows and gaze at the stars. Not a small part of its appeal was that to get down, you had two choices: a curving slide or a fire pole. Of course, there was always the boring little spiral staircase that cut through the inside of the house, but few ever chose that route. Even with the increasing stiffness in his joints, Grampa was still taking the slide these days – though slowly. He'd given up on the fire pole a decade ago; landing was too tough on his ankles.

There was one other thing – or rather hundreds of them – that inspired and evoked the childlike curiosity of every visitor. Inside and out, his home was filled with breathtakingly beautiful pieces of blown glass: lanterns, twisting bottles, crystal-octopus chandeliers, and all sorts of objects d'art that were beyond any easy quantification. Upon his retirement, Patrick took a stab at the ancient art of glassblowing and took to it like a master, mostly to dazzle his wife and surround her with color. Years later, the legacy of his love was still glowing: the sunlight bouncing and funneling throughout his home, even on slightly overcast days, created real magic for anyone fortunate enough to soak it in.

With Maggie now gone, he had given the glassblowing a rest, far more enthused with writing a history of the United States Navy, specifically during the Pirate Wars, as it integrated its operations with the military forces of other nations. Naturally, of personal interest to Patrick was bringing special attention to his own son-in-law's game-changing leadership across the breadth of those campaigns, restoring peace to the waters surrounding North America and elsewhere. And out of a genuine desire to contribute to the community, he spent at least one day a week assisting as a nurse at the local clinic. Besides reminding him how blessed he was to be in good health, it helped break up his rhythms, preventing any creeping sense of monotony.

But any visit from his family, especially his grandsons, was more than enough to tear him away from his research and writing. And after getting the call from Evan and Dayna, he'd freshened up, trimmed the more scraggly bits on his closely-cropped white beard, and even made a quick run to the local market for some special groceries. He knew Dax would never *ask* him to go to the effort, but that was part of the fun – surprising the boys with a serving of his grilled, semi-famous honey-mint burgers, a savory blend that also included garlic and feta cheese.

He ambled up the long, freshly painted white dock, passing the boathouse that held one of his most prized possessions. Glancing at an old clock hanging on a post, he knew the boys were due any minute. Still, he couldn't help but take a peek inside. He pulled out his key and fumbled with a lock – an old world method of security, but he preferred it to a system that could be undone by something as simple and unpredictable as sunspots or an unscrupulous hacker using a common voice replicator.

The door creaked open with a rusty sigh, and he took a half-step inside. A gentle orange light flooded his face and his cheeks flushed with pleasure. Satisfied, he turned and shut the door again, then made his way to the end of the landing.

The skimmer was visible now, zipping out of the horizon at a good clip, Dax at the helm, Kai waving jubilantly. Grampa Pat laughed and waved back with matching enthusiasm.

The humming turbines powered down as Dax steered in to the side of the dock, the hull brushing against rubbery pylon bumpers as Grampa lassoed a mooring cleat and pulled it close.

"Grammmm-PA! Grampa!" Kai yelled, unbuckling his restraints.

"Kai," Dax called, "Don't go jumpin' at Grampa Pat . . ." But it was no use, as he was already climbing over Dax to get out of the skimmer. He bounced across the cushions to the edge and leapt for the dock, right into those big, strong arms. The sudden impact of all that weight hit the seventy-four-year-old vet about the way you'd expect, reminding him all too well how the years were having reverse effects on him and his youngest heir. Nevertheless, his footing was solid, and he caught Kai with a strong, wonderful hug – the kind only grandparents dare to give, so strong you forget the rest of the world and its many concerns, so safe and warm you think your heart will be happy forever.

Dax caught the gentle scent of flowers and coconut and sighed, so happy to be here. He looked out from the skimmer to the waves breaking on shore: there were some enticing blue swells out there, and he hadn't been on a board in weeks. But there was something more important on his mind; the waves could wait a while longer.

Still holding Kai, Grampa looked at Dax and laughed aloud.

"Stop daydreamin', Shags!" It was one of seemingly dozens of nicknames Grampa had concocted referring to his hair. Dax was secretly grateful that sometime in the last two years, his grandfather had at least stopped using more embarrassing nicknames like 'Goldilocks' and 'Sheep-Dawg' and, especially,

'Platty' – as in platinum. Dax was pretty sure if any of his buddies on the island heard that one, he'd be 'Platty Zander' forever.

"Hiya, Grampa!"

He hoisted two overnight bags onto the dock, hopped over the edge of the skimmer and hugged Grampa Pat's side.

Kai slipped down as Grampa put a knobby hand on each of their shoulders.

"I swear every time I see you, you're both taller. And Dax! That hair of yours! Your mom must be having fits! Looks like the jungles of Borneo landed on your head!"

Dax shrugged amiably. He knew it was more a compliment than an old man's chiding, as Grampa's own hair was fairly untended – thick and tangled in a few patches around his scalp, completely missing elsewhere.

"Thanks! Mom keeps asking me to cut it, and I keep telling her it keeps my brain warm."

Grampa burst out with a big guffaw.

"Attaboy! I was gonna take a walk down the beach to look for shells and old glass. Who wants to come along?"

Kai bounced up and down as if his legs were chubby bungee lines, barely tethering him to Earth.

"Grampa," Dax started a bit meekly, "would you mind if I—"

"Went to see Cody? Nah. Just be back for supper. Soon as your dad called, I rustled up some ground sirloin and sliced up some yams and bananas. Ya don't want to miss any a'that."

Dax's acute sense-memory kicked in with such potency, he nearly swooned; he could practically inhale the sweet aroma of Grampa's delectable burgers on the grill.

"No *way* I'm missing that!" And he meant it.

"Your scooter's in the garage, all juiced up," said Grampa, waving toward the beach house. "Tell Cody and his mom we said 'hello.' And wear a helmet, m'boy."

"Yessir!"

Dax offered a quick salute, grabbed their bags and set off for the house, its countless hanging glass ornaments welcoming him, a tinkling concert of rainbows in the midday sun.

"Bye, Dax! Tell Cody I hope he's all better!" Kai waved.

For a fleeting instant, Dax's face fell. Of course, Kai had no idea of the painful irony in what he'd just offered, and as he threw off his shoes to splash about in the frothy shoreline, Dax envied his blissful ignorance. Cody had been his best friend since both boys were six, but right now part of him didn't want to go over there at all. He dropped the bags on the back steps and walked around to the open garage. An array of tools was neatly on display amid shelves and many rows of hooks. Built into the cabinets were drawers holding countless rivets, buttons, screws and a thousand other tiny objects that might come in handy for some project, someday. A nifty air compressor in a dull aluminum case sat in one corner, two nylon tubes emerging from the side. Beside it were two vehicles of modest size: a red object, not quite two meters long, resembling a jet-powered toboggan with a still-shiny logo – 'SilverSled' - embossed on the side; and Dax's royal blue scooter, a handsome work of art that he, his father and Grampa had put together three years before. Running a hand down the seat, Dax smiled; not only had Grampa charged it up in anticipation of his visit, but he had also polished the flawless chrome and wiped down the finely-stitched upholstery. The boy unplugged the line that went straight up through the roof to one of several solar bowls, and sat on the cushy seat that somehow felt just as comfortable now as it did when his derriere was two years smaller.

Dax tapped at his sleeve.

"Call Kiri Vallabh."

There was a brief blip and a forty-ish, caramel-skinned beauty with long black hair appeared on the small screen, her eyes lighting up when she realized who was on the other end.

"Dax!" She instantly lowered her voice, which after decades in the States still hinted at her native India. "Are you on the island today?"

"Yes, ma'am. I was wondering . . . would it be okay to come over?"

She nodded enthusiastically.

"Cody will be so happy to see you."

"Okay, I'm at Grampa's on my scooter, leaving now."

"Oh, I'll bake cookies!"

"No, no, please don't go to any—"

But he could see she was already spinning into her kitchen as the connection ended. Dax revved up his scooter, then just idled there as he thought for a moment.

A wave of uncertainty swept over him. It had been two months since he'd last seen Cody on anything but a remote video feed, and it was easy to put on a good front for a conversation with that buffer of distance. Now, the realization sank in that the creeping infection in Cody's nervous system could have done a lot of damage in two months. And he couldn't let his friend see him affected by whatever might prove a shock.

For just a few seconds, he toyed with the idea of backing out, of sending an excuse. But he and his pal had made a pact never to lie to one another and never to avoid each other. So, he revved up the scooter again and puttered out to the street, because his visit would cheer his friend, and that alone made it the right thing to do.

Surprises

Kiri Vallabh stepped outside before Dax had his helmet off, and knowing he was about to get wrapped in those smooth, slender arms, the color of dark caramel, he didn't resist. As much as he thought of Cody as a third brother, Mrs. Vallabh considered him a second son.

"Dax! So wonderful to see you!"

"It's great to be here."

"Have you surfed yet?"

Dax grinned.

"Nope. Came here soon as Kai and I docked. How are you?"

Kiri's eyes were already moist, but she was a woman who had walked many painful paths, and with one blink, she composed herself gracefully.

"I am very well. Cody's father is still at work, but he should be home in a while. It was sweet of you to come here first. I know how you love your waves."

As she held the door open, he admired the beautiful silk print dress that flowed in layers off her arms and body.

"That's a dazzler! Did you design it?" Dax asked.

She blushed with genuine appreciation.

"I did, thank you! I've done six this year, but they've all sold well. This is an original I kept for myself."

They moved through the spacious great room, decorated in rich walnut panels, the whole space resonant with the music of two cascading waterfalls sculpted from slate, one at each end of the room. A small fire pit punctuated the middle, surrounded by plush sofas. Dax had shared many happy Christmases in this room, and played cards with the family countless nights.

"Well, someday, I'm buyin' one from you," he said confidently.

Kiri turned back with a raised eyebrow that made the boy blink.

"Oh! Not for me!" he exclaimed, "but you know . . . when I have a girlfriend or something. For her."

"When that day comes, my dear, I will design something *just* for her. But here, I want to show you something new in the den."

Passing through an archway, they entered an exotic, darker space showcasing artifacts, a small library, and dozens of precious raw stones and ores collected by Kiri and her husband on their amateur geologic expeditions. He knew this space well, but there was almost always something new to discover.

She led him through an array of pedestals and standalone display cases, some caught in beams from spotlights above, others from below. Rough-hewn samples of quartz, topaz and opal glistened in the cool darkness. They stopped before a softball-sized clump of jagged crystal, its craggy facets alternately purple and pale gold. Dax bent near, hypnotized by its beauty.

"Whoa," he whispered, and though it was a simple reflex, Kiri nodded in kind.

"I say that a lot when I look at this one. We ordered it last month, from a dig in Peru. It reminds me there are beautiful things waiting to be discovered, even in the darkest places, if we are patient. And strong."

She led him back to the hall, then paused, her voice low.

"Dax. He is weaker. He has a hard time getting to sleep and that robs his energy. I wanted to tell you so it wouldn't show so much on your face. It hurts Cody when people look at him a certain way, and I think it would hurt even more if he saw *you* grieving . . ."

Now she was beginning to shake. Dax teetered a little, unsure if comfort from a kid would be appreciated or even appropriate. He went with his gut and hugged her.

"It's okay, Mrs. Vallabh. Anything can happen, you know?"

"Thank you, Dax." She relaxed with a deep breath, took a half step back and smiled. Something about his matter-of-factness broke past her walls of dread and restored a few bricks of hope. Wiping a tear away, she nodded for him to move on.

"Go say 'hello.' I'll bring you boys cookies."

She started to go, but then instinctively turned around again to discover Dax was still there, hovering in the hallway, cupping something small in his hands.

"Dax?"

He turned, taking a bite out of what she now realized was an *onion*. Dax's face twisted in revulsion with the taste, his eyes squinching almost shut, trying to speak over the chunk getting mushed up in his mouth.

"Somesunk we do."

"Something you do?"

Dax shrugged, still chewing. "Ith weird, but . . ."

Though puzzled, she managed an awkward little wave for him to continue.

"Okay. Ouch. I'll bring you something cold to drink, too."

"Frankyoo!"

And he kept chewing, hating every second of it, onion juice dribbling off his lips, stinging his eyes. But this was a matter of honor.

. . .

'Cody' was not a traditional Indian name, but after a troubled phase of life half a world away, his parents wanted their firstborn to feel he was very much a part of their new one. So they purposely chose something that felt 'American.' His middle name, however, was 'Dahak,' meaning 'powerful.' And for most of Cody's first decade, he had indeed run strong and boldly. However, a month before his tenth birthday, his left leg fell asleep and began to twitch with rhythmic spasms, and this lasted long enough to where his mother felt it merited a visit to the doctor. That led to a string of specialists puzzling over a baffling erosion of fibers in his central nervous system, accelerating with no seeming predictable path. Cody's body had succumbed to an incredibly rare malady of the immune system for which, even in this day of unprecedented medicinal prevention and cures, there was no course of proven treatment. After two years of watching their son put through various medical trials and "cutting edge" therapy, with no reversal of his condition, Cody's parents finally listened to his pleas - and stopped.

They stopped searching for experts who would guess at a 'sure' answer. They stopped submitting him to probing exams and prescriptions of chemicals ingested and injected. Cody's personal physician, Alphonse Lautrec, was one of the most renowned doctors on the planet addressing rare illnesses of this sort. And when he reluctantly agreed to end what had become a grueling cycle, Cody knew the tide had not turned in his favor; but in a way, he was relieved.

Free from rigorous daily regimens of powerful drugs and experimental therapies, he looked at each day as an opportunity to learn, explore, and prove he wouldn't just roll over and quit. He reassured everyone he was fine using a glider – a contoured seat mounted on a multi-directional wheelbase – and that his lack of mobility was something he could live with. Though now a thirteen-year-old who still loved to read Greek mythology and invent his own fairy tales, Cody had managed to come to terms with the concept of his own death, and as much as he could accept it as inevitable and not to be feared he had done so. What *did* crush his spirit, whenever his thoughts drifted in that direction, was the cold reality that he would never realize his dream of someday exploring the stars. He had wanted to be an astronaut almost as long as he could remember, and abandoning that dream was the cruelest part of this whole thing.

So his parents had worked hard to make Cody comfortable this last year, filling their home with things that would excite his intellect or provide even a little exercise, as that seemed to be the sole effective deterrent, though modest, to the march of biological demons ravaging his body. They kept him in school until recently, when it became clear it was no longer feasible.

Dr. Lautrec, a man of extraordinary compassion and empathy, still visited to monitor his health, overall comfort and offer whatever 'natural' therapies he could that wouldn't cause additional stress to the boy. As the doctor had long since become a caring friend, they enjoyed a few laughs together as well. These days, Cody was exclusively at home, surrounded by games of all sorts, an endless supply of reading material and movies, and a few cleverly-designed devices that would challenge and stimulate his muscles whenever he was of a mind to work with them. Having a fairly disciplined nature, he used these to good therapeutic effect on a daily basis.

Naturally, Cody's bedroom had also been renovated to his tastes, as his parents knew he would spend an increasing amount of time there. They had torn out the barrier between his room and a guest room upstairs to create a soaring, loft-like environment, broke through one wall shared with a garage and added several large windows. By the time the work was finished, his had become the largest room in the house by far, and worlds less confining. Later on, Kiri painted that entire new back wall of 'Cody's Cave' in a mix of deep blues and purples, spattered with pale aqua and finally embedded with hundreds of tiny lights. Anytime the room darkened, a sensor would bring galaxies of stars to shimmering life, simulating a magnificent view of outer space and all but evaporating the boundary of that single wall. It set Cody's room apart with an environment specific to his love for astronomy and science fiction, as well as lending a sense of grandeur and mysteriousness to the whole area. On another level, his mother hoped it would remind him there were many other worlds he might yet discover.

A light sweat from exertion prickling the fibers of his warmup suit, Cody was stretched out over a large, inflatable pad the size and shape of his own body when Dax entered the room.

"What's scary is, this isn't even the weirdest thing I've caught you doing," Dax remarked, startling Cody.

"DAX!"

Caught off guard by the appearance of his best friend, Cody released the handgrips on the pad and the rubbery 'arms' snapped loudly back into their spring-loaded sockets, sending a shockwave that flipped him entirely over and onto his back.

Both boys guffawed with abandon as Dax reached down to help him up. But he was still shocked at two things – how little Cody could actually participate in lifting himself and how much weight his friend had lost. They embraced briefly, Dax careful not to squeeze too hard.

"I'm not gonna break, Dax."

Rather than respond with some awkward shrug that would inevitably lead to an even more awkward conversation, Dax took in a deep breath, opened his mouth and leaned forward, barely a few centimeters from Cody's nose.

And then Dax *belched*, intentionally putting everything he had into it. For good measure, he blew what was left of that onion in a hot, horrid breath across his friend's face.

Cody howled like a sick coyote, his face twisting in disgust.

"Noooo! That's not fair! I didn't know you were coming and I couldn't—"

He stopped and sniffed the air, but it was already gone. Frustrated, he gestured slightly with a finger and Dax enthusiastically breathed on him again. Reacting with nearly as much ferocity as the first time, Cody squeezed his eyes shut and then figured out the smell.

"RED ONION!"

"Huzzah! My bruvvah!"

And Dax bent forward to bump his chest against Cody's – always a capping point after their 'gross out' ritual. But Cody extended a hand to cushion the impact, his face falling somewhat for the first time.

"I can't. My ribs are kind of sore all the time now."

"Oh," Dax said simply, "well, it's a dumb thing anyway."

"Ninja Tap?"

Dax brightened, remembering. Once upon a time they came up with the idea that two ninjas might honor each other by tapping foreheads, as the rest of their bodies were lethal weapons. So Dax leaned forward, and ever so gently tapped Cody's hairline with that of his own.

"There's mouthwash in the bathroom," Cody coughed, fanning a hand over his nose.

. . .

Grampa Pat ambled along with a brisk stride, still nimble enough to keep up with his youngest grandson's bouncy steps, as the shoreline lapped at their ankles in swirling, bubbling ribbons. Although for Grampa this walk was a daily habit, he seldom had such welcomed, lively company. The boy paused to stare out at the horizon, shielding his eyes from the sun.

"Whatcha lookin' for, Kailen?"

"Whales. Dax got bit by one today."

Grampa Pat absorbed this, wondering if this were one of Kai's 'invented' stories.

"He did, huh? And still lived to tell the tale?"

"It was a pilot whale! Dax made a big noise with his . . . sonics. And scared it away. Mommy and Daddy were really mad at him."

Patrick slowed, placing a hand on Kai's shoulder to still the boy. This didn't have the frilly, raggedy edges of his typical imaginary adventures.

"Why were they mad, buddy?" he inquired in a sing-song voice.

"Because Dax went swimming way too far by himself, where they told him not to."

Grampa Pat sighed, nodding uneasily. *Dax the Reckless.* Now that felt like a familiar story. The old man watched as Kai pushed through the shallows to a sizeable boulder, climbed to its modest peak and turned to offer a bow. Happy there, he did a pirouette and took turns balancing on each foot. Grampa Pat held his breath, stifling the instinct to warn Kai of falling; he knew young ones craved their little victories and learning the risk for such was at least as important. And Kai loved to climb, whether it was up a rock, over a rope bridge or a trellis on the side of Grampa Pat's house. So the old fellow just waded out a short distance into the surf, about mid-chest, deep enough to let the gentle tide sway him back and forth, lifting him off his toes and then back down. As he floated there, watching, it became wonderfully clear why his grandson's balletic moves gave him such pleasure.

"Your Gramma Maggie was a dancer, you know."

Kai looked over, balancing on his belly atop the rock, pretending to swim just above the swirls of foam and mist.

"What kind of dancing?"

"Oh, when I met her, she was still in New York City. She was a Rockette!"

Kai's eyes tightened.

"Gramma was a rocket?! And they let you *marry* her?"

Grampa Pat laughed.

"A RockETTE. That's what they called the dancers at Radio City Music Hall. They were very special. Lots of girls auditioned, but your gramma was . . . a rare talent."

Kai noticed a large branch wedged down in a crack and reached to pull it out. It didn't come loose easily, but when it did he jumped up and waved it around triumphantly.

"There ya go, Arthur!"

"What?"

"Never mind. I'll read you the story tonight."

"Is Gramma why you do all the bottles and glass stuff?"

Grampa Pat sighed deeply. This little guy had his own brand of insight.

"That's why, Kai. She loved the colors."

"I bet she still does."

"I bet you're right."

Kai climbed down to where his feet dangled in the sloshing waves, repeatedly thrashing the water with his stick. But knowing the lad would never hurt so much as a guppy, Grampa Pat was curious.

"Whatcha doin' with the stick there, Kai?"

Kai beamed happily, stick brandished high.

"It's my magic sword, Grampa! I'm checkin' for surf-dragons. I whump 'em on the head and they turn from bad to good."

Grampa Pat laughed. Whenever Kai spoke, his jaw seemed to open impossibly wide, and the gap between his two front teeth always drew a laugh. He hoped the kid would never grow one iota taller.

"Surf-dragons! I don't think they come this close to shore!"

"I'm just warning 'em in case they try to hurt you before I can fix 'em."

Grampa's throat tightened a bit.

"Well, thank you very much, Sir Kailen."

Suddenly Kai lowered his sword, staring intently at something farther down the beach, beyond Grampa. He dropped the stick, hopped down with a huge splash and sprinted off, as Grampa Pat stared out, squinting. His thick legs striding out of the water, he flipped around the zoomers clipped to the back of his left ear.

The powerful lenses instantly activated, synching with his retina, magnifying in the direction he was staring. Kai was running up to a dark shape embedded in the surf. It looked like another large chunk of rock, but rounder, black and shiny.

"Grampa!"

He was already on his way, but hurrying as he was jostled the view through his zoomers.

"Magnify by five and enhance."

Immediately his view enlarged to the point where it became clear Kai was kneeling next to a breathing body in what looked like a black skinsuit, a red stain blotting the sand. Not good. Grampa Pat's pace accelerated into a very fast walk, but he had long ago given up running, especially on sand. He touched the side of his zoomers.

"Tap Dax."

Dax's face quickly materialized as a ghost-like image in his lenses, fully attentive. Grampa could see Cody behind him, assembling some kind of model racetrack.

"Grampa? Something wrong?"

"Real quick – did you take the scooter or the air-sled?"

"The scooter. Why?"

"Just wanted to check before I go back for it. Didn't mean to bother you and Cody. Say 'hi' for me."

It was on the tip of Dax's tongue to ask why the need for the air-sled, but Grampa was prone to spontaneous weirdness. It usually ended in fun, and he liked surprises.

"Okay. Mahalo."

Dax's face vanished just as Grampa Pat reached his grandson's side. Right away, he could see a gaping wound, probably a shark bite, revealing pink, raw, jagged flesh.

Kai's big round eyes turned up to him, shiny with tears.

"Grampa, he's hurt! We gotta do something!"

A citizen's duty was to call the authorities, but they could take a while, and Grampa Pat knew their bleeding friend might not make it. He looked back along the coastline they'd traversed; it was maybe 400 meters to the house. He bent down, flipping aside his lenses to look Kai in the eyes.

"Can I trust you to be a big boy and stay with our friend here? I'm going to go get the air-sled and I promise I'll be back fast as I can. He's still breathing, so that's a good thing."

Kai wiped his cheeks, sniffling.

"Okay."

"Okay." Grampa tore off his colorful Hawaiian shirt, folded it over a few times, then pressed it and Kai's hand against the wound.

"You hold this here and don't press down too hard or it will hurt him, okay? This will help clot the blood and slow down the flow."

Kai nodded again and Grampa started off, glancing back with a reassuring wave.

"I'll be fast!"

"You promise to make him better?"

"We're gonna give it our best, Kai!"

As Grampa's legs carried him back down the beach, anxiety gripped him in a cold wave. The worst thing in the world would be disappointing his grandson.

"God, we need you bad on this one. Help us help that little guy."

Feeling a bracing new surge in his legs, he marched with even brisker steps toward home.

Floating

Dax and his pal were busy constructing a new set of elevated highways for Cody's model maglev train. Of what seemed an endless supply of track sections, they had thus far arranged an impressively involved route, circumnavigating the entire room – under the bed and back up a steep, forty-degree slope to the big bay window.

Kiri Vallabh stepped in carrying a tray loaded with cookies, fruit, fresh naan, dips and two large cups of pineapple juice.

"I know you like naan, so I warmed some up for you, Dax."

"Hot-now!" both boys exclaimed, a common term to express enthusiastic approval, especially at unexpected treats.

"*Three* dips, Mum?" Cody observed, impressed.

"How often does Dax get to visit?"

"Hey, no complaints!" Dax enthused. "Hummus *and* apricot-cranberry tastiness? You are a collosaraptor in the kitchen, Mrs. Vallabh. Seriously."

She had a hard time keeping up with their colorful expressions; they seemed to change constantly. She was pretty sure, however, that 'colossaraptor' was intended as flattery. Still, the blank look on her face betrayed some uncertainty, as Cody just grinned, offering a translation.

"Like a giant dinosaur, Mom. You thrash and stomp all over anyone else's cooking."

"Yes! Oh, good. Good. Thank you, Dax."

Her eyes wandered about the room, following the left and right turns of the track, the gently curving arcs. If things remained this way, moving about could pose a challenge.

"I don't think Cody's ever covered this much territory with his train tracks."

"We used every last piece," Cody affirmed proudly.

Kiri bent to examine one length of track running *under* a handsome chessboard made of inlaid oak. The board itself was elevated only five centimeters above the track, supported by four stubby legs, and it was obvious there wasn't enough clearance for the train, were it to pass through.

"What happens when it gets here? Won't the train crash?" she asked.

Dax shot a knowing glance to Cody, who grabbed a small controller.

"Watch, Mom."

The model maglev train, a sleek engine with several attached compartments, started wending its way about the room, gliding effortlessly on a cushion of air above the long, smooth track. As it approached the chessboard, whose exquisitely carved pieces were frozen in some unfinished game, Kiri tensed up; this WAS going to be a train wreck. Dax made a small gesture to Cody, who responded by speeding up the train. Just before it reached the chessboard, as if lifted by some invisible hand, it rose higher above the track, skimming *over* the heads of the rooks, knights and other pieces left on the board. Exiting the boundaries of the table, it lowered again to its normal height.

"How did you do that!" she exclaimed.

Cody turned off the train as Dax knelt by the table.

"Look closer. See those chunks?"

Kiri angled her head to study the dark underside of the chessboard. Sure enough, a line of small objects had been taped there, connected with thin strips of conduit.

"Magnets?"

Cody nodded.

"We'll make an engineer out of you yet, Mom!"

"You stacked magnets so the train would rise higher over the chessboard?"

The boys offered matching grins, proud of their work.

"But . . . why not just move the chessboard out of the way?"

Dax and Cody looked at each other, sharing a shrug.

"This is way chewier, Mom."

Kiri blinked; another new word. She chuckled, remembering that 'being mom' now included deciphering the alien slang of her son's generation – so different from that of her own.

"Ohh . . . that means 'cool.' Of course. I agree. It is very 'chewy.'"

"We need a tunnel, a very long tunnel," Cody mumbled, looking around for the best place in the room for it. Tasting some of Kiri's homemade hummus, Dax nodded, his eyes drifting to the ceiling in response to the savory explosion on his tongue. They had already forgotten she was there, which didn't bother her a bit.

"You boys have fun."

Kiri lingered in the doorway a few seconds longer, the boys digging into the snacks with a ferocity as if they had not eaten in days. In truth, her cooking *was* that good, and Dax rarely had opportunity to enjoy authentic Indian dishes. He glanced up to catch her watching them, and subtly offered his own warm, reassuring nod.

After she left, Dax smothered a piece of naan with candied apricots and remarked, "Your mom's amazing."

Cody swallowed his food. "You mean she's strong. Yeah."

"Okay. But I just meant she cooks incredible stuff."

"No, you didn't. But it's okay, Dax. It's better that she's strong. Sometimes though, I wish she would just cry more. I think she needs to."

Dax chewed in silence. Cody was probably right; his mom would be better off having a good cry. What neither of them knew is that no mother that loving is that strong. She cried a lot.

Dax moved to retrieve his glass of pineapple juice, settling on the floor between Cody and his 'space wall.' When Cody looked up, he paused, staring at his friend in a moment of simple gratitude. In doing so, there seemed something odd and painterly about the pool of light within which Dax sat and his distance from the colorful, swirling nebula. Cody couldn't help but stare, a thought tapping at the back of his head. Naturally, Dax tried to ignore it, but after a few seconds Cody's gaze was unnerving.

"Okay. What?"

"Just a weird feeling."

"Like 'Hey I just ate a hairy pregnant spider' weird, or . . ."

"You belong in the stars, Dax."

"Okay," Dax smirked, "kinda far. And nowhere to surf. Besides, *you're* the astronaut."

"I wanted to be one," Cody said wistfully. "I really wanted to go to Saturn. See the rings up close."

"Maybe you will."

Cody rolled his eyes and Dax sighed, realizing it was an unconvincing remark.

"Okay, but . . . anything can happen," he offered, sincerely wishing that were true.

"Fine. Sure. It's something I *wanted*, Dax. But I have this feeling . . ." His head tilted slightly, as if newly seized by some profound, yet confusing thought. "Like it's something you're *supposed* to do."

"I would make the world's worst astronaut. Can you see me, floating around, a gazillion light years from Earth? I would —"

He almost said "die" and both boys knew it, but he corrected himself in mid-stride.

"—go crazy that far from water. Besides —"

"I know. You want to race cars. Cars and boats. I bet you'd even ride an ostrich."

Dax lit up at the thought. He'd never considered the possibility.

"Do they go fast?"

"Pretty fast, I think," Cody answered, stretching back along his bed. He considered his friend again from this very odd angle – Dax against the black wall and a sparkling, glittery array of stars. It just *looked* right. "You know there's water out there," he added, "We've already found moons and planetoids with entire oceans. And spaceships are fast, Dax," he said with a wink, "that's why they're called rockets."

"Still a crazy long trip to those places."

Cody sighed. Despite numerous prototypes, faster-than-light travel still had not advanced from theory to reality. It was the big, forbidding wall he had once dreamed of helping crash through. Still, he was convinced the restless spirit of humanity, the need to discover would drive humankind to pierce that barrier. Eventually.

"Won't be always," he said.

Dax nodded agreeably, reaching again for the tray. He had been snacking non-stop.

"Save me some grapes!" Cody said. Dax grabbed the last cluster and tossed them to Cody. He reached out to catch them, but in doing so rolled onto his side with a grimace.

"You okay?" Dax asked, wary of coming off like a mother hen.

"Yeah. Stupid bed," Cody groused. "It hates me."

"Your mom says you don't sleep too great."

Cody shifted himself higher up, resting his back against the wall.

"It's just hard to get to sleep. And if I wake up to go to the bathroom or something, then it's hard to get comfortable when I get back into bed."

"Why?"

Cody looked up, frustrated, but Dax pressed further.

"Come on, no secrets."

"Everything hurts, Dax," he admitted with a tired huff. "Not all the time, but sometimes. And I don't like taking pills for pain. They make me sleep too much."

"Oh," Dax replied, once again reminded that his friend's problems were a lot bigger and more constant than anything in his own world.

"Can we talk about something else?" Cody pleaded.

"Sure," Dax said, but his mind suddenly felt as if it were separating: one part enjoying snacks with Cody, the other going to work – a strange, slightly not-in-control condition he experienced whenever faced with a seemingly insurmountable dilemma. Even as he laughed at some joke Cody retold from a comedy show, it was as if a silent twin were cataloguing everything around him, both the tangible objects in the room and the abstract factoids Dax had absorbed in his various life-science studies, searching the entirety with one objective: to fix Cody's problem. Whether that meant helping him sleep or easing his pain without drugs, he knew this was going to dog his thought process until some solution worth trying presented itself. Then Cody's words bubbled up, finally drawing his full attention.

". . . and the reindeer said, 'That's why they call me Dancer.'"

Cody erupted with a giggle, silencing when Dax just stared back at him as if he had not heard a single word.

"Dancer, because . . ."

"Uhhh . . ."

Cody sighed, moving his maglev train across the tracks with his hand.

"See? You *should* be an astronaut. Total space cadet."

As Dax watched Cody with his train, the whole image sort of flashed, searing into his mind – as if his senses were taking a picture and processing it with multiple filters in an instant, each one a different idea incorporating just Cody, that train and those tracks . . .

And then he had it – what seemed a relatively simple solution. Dax looked at Cody's bed. He gazed at all the tracks, winding across, around, up and down throughout the room. They had all they needed. Maybe.

"Hey!" Cody called out, "You're zoning again."

Dax blinked; he could feel the hairs on his arms and neck standing up.

"I'm sorry. But . . ."

Then he giggled slightly, not quite sure where the idea came from that had just super-baked itself inside his head, but somehow he knew it was a good one.

"What is it?" Cody pressed, "You got an idea. What?"

Dax considered the mess they were about to make, and the fact that Cody would have to destroy his beloved train set. But it would be worth it. He moved to the door, closed it without a sound and locked it, lowering his voice conspiratorially, eyes dancing.

"Trust me."

. . .

The boys had been quiet a long time. Dananjay Vallabh, a slender, dark man with striking features, entered the kitchen to find Kiri pouring a marinade over a chicken. She lit up.

"You're home early! I'm glad."

From the freezer, she retrieved a tall bottle filled with something green and slushy and held it out. Dananjay's eyes twinkled with delight.

"Ohh, so am I!"

He popped the cap, dipped in a finger and tasted. Then dropped a tiny dab on her lips.

"Yum, yum, yum," he said, before giving her a kiss. "I feel stronger already. Thank you."

"Dax is here."

Dananjay was delighted.

"He's staying for dinner?"

"No, I don't think so."

"Oh, what a shame. Well, what are they up to?"

"Some secret project. They arranged the model train all over the room – so amazing. Then I guess they got bored and found something else to do. Dax ran to the store for some special wire. Nitinol, I think he called it. But he was back here pretty quickly."

Dananjay laughed.

"What in the world are they doing? Making batteries?"

She shrugged. "Let's go see."

But to their surprise, they found the bedroom door was locked. Dananjay glanced at his wife and both instinctively pressed their ears to the door. They heard excited whispering on the other side and the random sounds of furniture moving around.

"Cody? Dax? Would you please unlock the door?"

"In a minute, Mom!"

From the other side, Cody's not-so-silent hush-voice could be heard.

"My parents are goin' drone. They're not gonna like—"

"Cody!" Dananjay insisted firmly, "we are not going drone! But keeping secrets is unacceptable. Now, young man."

The door clicked and opened up a wedge, Dax's contrite expression greeting them first.

"Okay, first, please don't get mad at Cody. This was my idea."

"Dax. So good to see you. But we would like to come in. And we won't—"

Dax swung the door open, and Cody's parents sucked in air, beholding the mess. The maglev track that had so elegantly woven about the room was gone, but the track supports were strewn all over the floor, a few of them broken. Stripped lengths of wire added to the clutter, and Cody's mattress had been flopped up on its side against the wall, revealing a frame that now looked like some sort of art installation – chunks of wire-wrapped nuggets taped to its crisscrossing spring supports.

His parents were hovering on the brink between remembering their son was very ill and forgetting that fact utterly.

"What are you doing in here?" Cody's father asked.

"The mattress!" his mother exclaimed. "You cut holes in the mattress!"

"Just on one side," Cody corrected, forcing a chuckle.

His mother moved to the mattress, touching one of about three dozen holes cut into the underside. Each was stuffed with sections of the formerly stately maglev train, and all those holes were connected by strands of wire. As engineering efforts went, this had no aesthetic value at all.

"Dax, we are very glad to have you here, but you boys need to explain this. Now."

Happy to oblige, though slightly nervous, Dax stepped to one side of the mattress.

"Okay. We were almost done. Mr. Vallabh, would you help me flip this back?"

Dananjay grabbed one end, Dax the other. Cody moved to a space near the bay window while the two turned the mattress so that the ugly side faced down. It dropped neatly into the frame with a soft thump. Dax nodded to his friend.

"Cody."

And with some effort, his pal pulled himself up and swung around to plop onto the bed. He retracted his legs so they were clear of the edge and sat there, swami-like. Dax handed him the controller.

Cody snapped on the power, and as his parents watched in quiet awe, the mattress *lifted* ever-so-slightly, a few centimeters. He adjusted a dial that Dax had apparently added to the controller, and the mattress began to gently teeter toward the headboard, then back the other way, then from corner to corner. Cody leaned back on a pillow, beaming a confident Cheshire grin.

"This will help him sleep," his father whispered aloud, with unmistakable gratitude.

Cody released a soft sigh of bliss.

"It's like I'm floating."

Dax nodded, pretty pleased with himself.

"We should add some sound effects! I'll record some surf tonight at Grampa's!"

Kiri took Dax's cheeks into her two hands and kissed him.

"Thank you. Thank you, Dax. This is such a blessing."

"We should have thought of doing something like this before," Dananjay mused. "Such a simple, brilliant idea."

Dax blushed, pleased but not one to meander in the spotlight.

"Sorry about the mess. We were about to clean it up."

Cody's parents laughed, shaking their heads. His father sat on the bed and once again his eyes popped, enjoying the random sensation of floating. He looked at his wife.

"*We* need one of these!"

She dared not sit on it – Kiri was not exactly an early adopter of technology – but she did put one hand out to feel the rise and fall of the mattress. Dananjay, however, laid back and the bed started humming louder.

"Dad, go on a diet or get off my bed! You're gonna bust it!"

Everyone cackled at this, including Dax.

It was the first day in a long time that the Vallabh house had been so full of laughter.

The Hand in the Moon

It was a sublimely balmy night in South Florida, and Shaw thought himself pretty clever for asking Hayley on a 'non-date' composed of a group dinner and a late-night dive in the reefs off Key Largo. Just a casual first time out for the two of them, with three others to keep it light and simple – Shaw's roommate, Bardin Narn, and two of their mutual friends, Timme Elder and Cora Galantino. All were studying in the sciences, Bardy tackling a double major in propulsion physics and fluid mechanics, Timme and Cora in botanical hybridization and microbiology, respectively. Hayley, like Shaw, was pursuing a degree in marine biology; though at twenty-one she was a full year ahead of him in the program.

The illumination beads embedded in their skinsuits afforded a stunning view of the endless, meandering reefs and their countless colorful inhabitants. Ever the loner, Bardin swam close to the bottom, on a quest to find thermal vents from cracks in the ocean floor, while the rest swam two and two through a deep gulley surrounded by towers of lattice-like white coral.

Every so often Shaw would beckon Hayley to pause and let the others move on, showing her a particularly vivid group of anemones or some sunken object just barely detectable after decades of organic overgrowth. Her contoured facemask, though tinted a pale blue, obscured nothing of her sparkling, inquisitive eyes and a broad smile that sent a warm feeling all through him every time it flashed his way.

She touched his forearm and when she spoke, he heard her smooth voice perfectly through the com system they shared.

"Thank you. I've only been on one night dive and never here. It's amazing."

"You've never been to John Pennekamp?" he asked, referring to the national park composed of a sweeping territory of reefs.

She shook her head.

"Belize. And off the coast of Kauai."

"Nice. We used to kayak off Kauai as a family when I was young. Got my first taste of marine science there when I was eight. I'd tag along with the preservation teams, taking data on the reefs, how we could flourish."

"Yes, I know. And I read up about your dad's work, too."

Behind his mask, Shaw felt his face turning red. She knew a *lot* about him and his family. He knew next to nothing about her. Should he have done some research? Was he coming off as less than curious or appropriately resourceful? Though the suit helped regulate body temperature, he felt abruptly cold and awkward, off balance. He glanced around for Bardin, but his buddy was a good ten meters away, barely visible in the dark sea, waving his hand through a billowy cloud of sediment surging up from below.

"Oh, you did," he answered, "and here I never thought about people actually reading Mom's journals."

"Oh, I've been all through them. She makes you feel like you're there. I can't imagine waking up and looking out a window and seeing nothing but this—" she gestured around.

"Well, I gotta say, it never gets old. The tremors aren't fun. But my mom designed our seabase—"

"And all the newer ones follow her engineering protocols, from what I understand," Hayley added. "Word is the newest modules going up outside Olympus Mons are modeled after her undersea designs."

"Yeah. So I trust my mom, but it's not fun to feel yourself shaking and wondering – are those windows gonna crack today?"

"I'd say if they're assembling her stuff on Mars, nothing's apt to crack twenty or thirty meters underwater."

Shaw nodded, pleased that his family history had afforded some advance goodwill. Nothing wrong with that; he had struggled with his own self-confidence, growing up not merely in relative social isolation, but also in the shadow of parents recognized internationally as tops in their respective fields. For the first five years in the seabase, he'd had little opportunity to interact with other kids and establish his own distinctive identity. Later his parents decided to split his education between remote tutoring and actual extended stints on the mainland under Grandma and Grampa's watch. But he'd felt something of an adjustment gap ever since; as he entered adolescence, Shaw watched Dax make friends instantly and effortlessly, where for him it always seemed an awkward, or sometimes even an embarrassing, experience.

In fact, selecting a college so far from home was part of his well-considered plan to reboot his identity, and so far it had been working pretty well. Now nineteen, Shaw, purposely avoiding any mention of his last name for his first full semester, had come to discover that people liked him just for who he was. So he took a deep breath and reminded himself that Hayley's token bit of 'extra knowledge' about his family didn't mean he had any obligation to resemble a great scientist, much less a naval commander who had helped end a major war. Still, he could play that card to his advantage.

"Well, if you ever want to meet them, you're welcome to visit."

Behind the contoured facemask, her eyes popped.

"Oh, yeah? But where would I stay?"

Shaw felt that twinge in his gut telling him he might have overplayed his first move. *Don't be anxious. Be smooth. Smooth.*

"Well, uh, there's a . . . designated room for visitors in the officers' quarters. A tunnel connects that section to our part of the compound."

She laughed, teasing him.

"You'd make me sleep with the grunts? Shaw—" She stopped, squinting for an instant. "What's your middle name?"

"Oh, you don't want to know—" But he already knew there'd be no satisfying her until he shared. His voice dropped, reciting dutifully, no hiding his discomfort.

"Arronax."

She blinked, but didn't comment, waiting for more.

"All of us have middle names honoring famous explorers. Thing is, mine isn't a real guy; he's a character in that Jules Verne book, *Twenty Thousand Leagues*."

"Well, Shaw Arronax Zander. I'm very hurt. I don't even get the sofa? Or do people living on the ocean floor do without sofas?"

Her teasing hit the mark. Shaw was actually stammering.

"Oh, yeah, I just didn't – I was kinda kidding. I mean we have a sofa." He felt instantly adrift in a whirlpool of hormonal chaos. "You were serious? About . . . visiting?"

A shimmering school of parrotfish flitted by and both were briefly swept away with the stunning array of colors in motion. When they had all passed, Shaw caught her coy smirk.

"If invited, I would definitely think about it."

Shaw tingled with pleasure. So far, college was *fantastic*.

"Exactly what is Bardin doing?" she asked.

Shaw looked over. Hovering just above the thermal vent as clouds of soot flowed up and over his entire body, Bardin slowly changed his posture, as if practicing yoga stances; legs spread wide, then arms, then pulling together in a ball. In the haze, his skinsuit lights blended his form into the plumes of soot, like some eerie, oceanic merman painted in oils.

"It looks like he's testing his resistance to the current," Hayley suggested.

"Let's ask him," Shaw replied, aiming his hand in Bardin's direction and flicking his wrist. A tiny icon lit up, indicating Bardin could hear them now.

"Bardy! You showin' off? You look like you're showing off."

"Not quite, mate," Bardin interrupted on the com, "I'm testing a new suit, trying out positions to determine what body configuration is most responsive to a current's propulsion."

Hayley put her hands on her hips, in case any doubt remained that she'd been right.

"Sure you didn't just want a good tickle, Bardy?" Shaw teased.

Even from this far, they could catch his slightly annoyed glance.

"Off my yon, bro. I'm always thinking about how things move."

"Sorry!" Shaw offered, resisting a laugh. He turned to Hayley and shrugged an *'oops.'*

"Well, he *is* a physicist," Hayley mused. "They tend to wander off and observe curious things like that."

Shaw glanced up, remembering they had saved dessert for after their dive.

"Back to the boat? Still got coffee and Cora's key lime pie waiting back at the dock . . ."

She nodded enthusiastically.

"Coffee sounds perfect. Feeling just a nip in my toes."

Shaw tapped a relay on his sleeve and 'COM-ALL' lit up in soft yellow letters.

"Hey, guys! We're heading up. Ready to get back to shore and have some tastiness."

Ahead of them, Timmc and Cora turned around and began swimming back with thumbs up. Now holding out some sort of sensor device above the vent, Bardin glanced over and nodded, his thick Australian accent strong and clear over the com system.

"Oy, go on and I'll be topside in two minutes, mate."

Shaw bowed slightly to Hayley, a chivalrous if silly gesture. Chuckling, she kicked her flippers and began to ascend.

He let himself enjoy the view from below for just three seconds, then followed.

. . .

Dax took the long way back to Grampa Pat's, winding through neighborhoods and parks on his scooter, occasionally following the paths under the winding LIM tracks that ferried people all over the community. Installed a decade before, the beams for the L-Cab rails and their supports were embedded with a seeded organic mesh, similar to those used for topiary plants. So unlike the bare, rust-stained mass transit grid work of yesteryear, the supports and troughs now resembled soaring serpentine hedges, blooming with all sorts of native flowers, vines freely hanging down and drifting in the warm breeze. The linear induction system assured a nearly silent trip for those using it – especially great for anyone living near the tracks – while the overall design both nourished and paid homage to an Island culture rooted from antiquity in a love and respect for all living things.

Dax didn't take the long way back consciously; something deep inside was compelling him to be alone for a while – a breather – before sharing space with people again, even if they were family. The quiet hum of the scooter played like music against the dissonant jumble of thoughts racing through his mind about his friend, about his friend's family and how losing Cody would devastate them. He knew they would have trouble moving on because he was already feeling the loss, and he'd just spent several hours *laughing* with Cody.

Suddenly Dax realized he wasn't moving. He had pulled into a park and taken the scooter up a ramp to the platform of a small amphitheater. Homegrown bands and school ensembles played here occasionally. Right now, looking out across empty rows of terraced seats, it all seemed profoundly spartan and strangely silent – broken only slightly by a train of seven connected LIM cars whooshing across the tracks at the other end of the park.

It was then he felt the full force of the wave of sadness he had been holding back for some time with an imaginary wall. He and Cody had agreed to never keep secrets, and in that spirit he knew he now needed to reckon with the murky future he'd been avoiding – a future without his best friend.

And partly to honor his pal, partly because he was tired of fighting away these thoughts, he just let the wave crash down, sliding off the seat of his scooter to the hard, cold concrete floor. He removed his helmet. And he wept.

When his tears were spent, Dax Zander sat there for a while, still not feeling ready or right to ride home. How great it would be if he could simply jump into one of his dream cars, jam the accelerator and let the screaming motor drown out all these thoughts. But there was no car, so his mind kept running to that place that liked to fix things, that loved to dig into the sciences for solutions. Then he remembered that he was still just a kid, and that he hardly had the knowledge to fix anything genuinely important, much less a highly selective neurological illness. One thing Dax rarely lacked was confidence, but right now he felt completely ill-equipped and ineffectual, and he hated that feeling. He resented its insidious power.

So there was but one thing left to him, a single resort.

He stood, and looked out to the sky, which was beginning to burn with the warm tangerine hues and cool violets of yet another spectacular Hawaiian sunset. The clouds were ephemeral and wispy, incredibly delicate, miraculously glowing with the brilliance of a sun barely hovering over the horizon.

"The sun's almost gone," Dax whispered aloud, "and there's still so much light."

He was surprised to hear what felt like poetry rolling off his lips, as if it were written in the air and he was trying to make sense of it. They weren't important or special words, but something about their simplicity struck him as holding a sort of wisdom. So purposefully and clearly, he spoke them again.

"The sun's almost gone, but there's still light up there."

And this thought took his gaze upward.

A single star – actually the planet Venus – sparkled gently, high up in the northern sky. Dax didn't focus on it, but he smiled because it was so beautiful in its isolation. He took a breath, finally accepting that he couldn't solve every problem for those he loved. And knowing that science was probably not going to intervene on Cody's behalf, he gazed up, beyond the star to nowhere in particular, and spoke out loud, his words halting just a bit because it seemed such a silly thing to do. Then again, it was all he had left.

"You gotta do something. You have to do it. Because I can't. And . . ."

Dax's eyes gleamed with tears again – tears not so much for Cody, but for shame that he was unable to fix this thing and had resorted to what felt a lot like blackmail with the Almighty.

"And this isn't fair. It's not. So you either show me how it's fair, or you fix it."

His lungs felt hot, forcing him to take in another cleansing breath. He'd never asked for something so grand, so brazen, in all his life. And he wasn't sure anyone was truly listening.

"I'll do anything. I'll go anywhere. Just please fix my friend. I can't believe that you like it when things aren't fair. Please show me I'm not wrong."

He stood there a moment longer, in complete silence. Nothing felt any different.

A gentle, balmy breeze brought the smell of hibiscus to his nostrils, and that's when Dax started to feel like he could head back to Grampa's. He felt at his face and rubbed some of the moisture away, then donned his helmet.

In a few moments, he was puttering down the streets, occasionally taking shortcuts, for the first time since late morning excited about Grampa Pat's amazing honey-mint burgers.

. . .

Breaking through to the surface, Shaw pressed a sensor twice on the side of his hood, and with a faint hiss, his facemask separated along a thin seam in the middle, half sliding up above his eyes, the bottom slipping into a barely discernible pouch under his chin. Bobbing there next to Hayley, the fresh salt wind felt good against his skin. In like manner, she decoupled her mask and Shaw blinked, reaching at tears across her freckled cheeks.

"You're crying . . ."

She giggled.

"Oh, that's so embarrassing. It always happens to me when I'm in a pressurized environment. Just my eyes compensating or something. I always have to explain it."

"Naw. It's just your body telling you you're a human being, not a fish."

As they swam a few strokes for the sleek motorboat just a few meters away, she called back.

"That's rather odd, coming from a marine biologist!"

"I love the sea! We come from the sea! But we left it . . . It's not our home anymore."

He pushed back against the hull of the boat, cupping his hands for her feet as she climbed up and in.

"Y'do realize the irony in you, of all people, saying that."

63

Shaw loved the way she said "you" with that gentle Irish brogue. In a single move, he pulled himself up and flipped over the rail into one of the plushly contoured seats. He meant to impress with his athleticism, and from the look on her face, he had.

"Well, someone's been working out."

Practicing would have been the better word, specifically to impress her, but Shaw would never say that out loud. He just stretched his arms around a few times, as if his impressive display of acrobatics was a wholly spontaneous afterthought.

Then her eyes lifted, fixing on something beyond him, opening wide with an unblinking, incredulous gaze. A seriousness fell over her face with such weight, Shaw wondered if a huge wave were about to crash over them. He turned and saw nothing.

"What?"

"No, Shaw – *up*. Look up."

And then he saw it – the new moon, almost entirely dark against a night sky peppered with countless stars, but the moon as no one had ever seen it before. Shaw blinked, staring with utter bewilderment, and cocked his head, as if those few centimeters would somehow make more sense of what was hanging in orbit up there.

A second later Timme and Cora popped up out of the water, and immediately followed Shaw and Hayley's sightline.

"Wait – what's that?" Cora shouted.

"Yes!" Hayley called out. "Exactly! It's crazy!"

And they all stared up.

There, as if projected upon most of one hemisphere on the lunar surface, was an odd, curving shape, glowing a ghostly green.

"It looks like a dove," Cora observed.

"Or maybe . . . half a killer whale," Timme added.

"What do you think's causing it?" Hayley asked, her voice now hushed with the sort of awe people ordinarily used in cathedrals.

"I don't know," Shaw answered. "Maybe some kind of dust cloud catching the sun's light?"

"It looks too specific for that."

Timme pondered for a moment. "I bet it's some publicity stunt," he suggested. "Who has a logo like that? Could you fire a laser from earth and paint something like that on the moon?"

"Could the settlements be signaling us?"

For a brief few seconds, Shaw considered the question, but it made no sense.

"Naww… A big weird symbol? Why wouldn't they use normal channels?"

Then Bardin chimed in.

"You see that?" he called out, bobbing in the black sea. "That green hand?"

Shaw looked over at him, about to protest that it more resembled a dove, but then a thought hit him.

"If it was a publicity stunt, there'd be no mistaking the symbol for what it was."

He'd actually murmured this loud enough for Hayley to process it and finish the thought:

"But we all saw something different."

As it was difficult to pry their eyes away, the others got into the boat and there they sat for a few minutes, gazing at the moon, muttering thoughtfully. Shaw and Hayley, still in full dive gear, were especially transfixed, pondering what meaning there might be in this. Famished and pretty sure nothing was about to change up there, Bardy dug into the cooler for some snacks and threw them around – but the tangerine he tossed to Shaw just bounced off his pal's chest.

"Shawzee! Wake up!"

Shaw grinned, snatching up the tangerine now rolling away, then hopped up.

"I think I brought a macro."

He dug into his backpack and pulled out a small, rectangular scope. He flicked on the power and took a quick look through. The glowing image was larger, and it was clearly floating above the moon's dark, cratered surface, but it seemed there wasn't much else to discover. Shaw handed the device to Hayley. She nodded, but after a few seconds handed the macro back.

"Is that the strongest setting?"

Shaw shrugged.

"They're mostly just for hiking," he mumbled, slightly embarrassed, "I'm not . . . an astronomer."

Hayley cringed, clearly regretting her remark, but happily Cora chose just that moment to break the mood, turning around to them both with a playful lilt to her voice.

"Shaw, is it okay if I take the wheel back to port?"

Lost in thought, he nodded absently, moving up to the bow, staring up at the sky. Cora started the engine and steered the boat back to the tiny dock lights of Key Largo. Hayley, now wrapped in a big towel, sat beside Shaw on a padded seat atop the bow. She spoke quietly.

"Any ideas?"

"I think maybe, it's a message," Shaw suggested, "and I'd bet money it's not the whole thing."

"A message for who?"

Shaw looked at her, for the first time feeling a tight chill in his bones, and not from the wet cold of the sea.

"Maybe . . . for all of us."

Thirty-Seven Degrees

It was just past 5:30 p.m. when Dax glided into the garage. He hopped off the scooter and after setting it back in its berth, wiped it down with one of the soft towels always stuffed into the jar on the bench; Grampa was particular about keeping things clean. As he recoupled the scooter's charger, a drip-drip caught his ear and he noticed the puddle under the air-sled, recently used and still very wet.

It seemed odd that Grampa hadn't taken the time to dry the air-sled off – but Dax was soon distracted by his surfboard, perched amid several others in the corner of the garage. The Zanders – every last one – were very much of the traditional school when it came to surfing. A few decades before, self-powered boards had become popular. They could churn through some nasty swells while their inner stabilizers helped to avoid awkward tumbles. But Grampa and Mom had both insisted that each of the Zander boys (including her husband) try the 'old boards' – with no special enhancements – just to get a more tactile feel. Without exception, Evan and all three sons preferred them, much to her delight. They all owned 'selfers' as backups, but those boards were rarely touched, except by an occasional friend, just getting used to plying the waves.

Dax stepped clear of the garage and gazed out to shore to see how things were breaking. Compared to a few hours before, the tide had calmed.

"Junk," he muttered. Perhaps he'd just go to bed early and catch a few rides just before dawn. Kicking off his shoes, he headed into the house, making a beeline for the *lua*, as he had gulped down three of Kiri's kiwi-blueberry smoothies on top of about a liter of mango tea. On his way down the hall, he heard voices in the kitchen and figured Kai might be helping Grampa prepare food for the grill.

Dax stepped into the large bathroom, saturated in shades of orange and apricot, and had just locked the door when he heard a loud, rusty MOAN from the tub.

He froze, sucking in air, seeing something big and dark tumbling about behind the semi-opaque shower curtain. Then, it stilled. Never taking his eyes off the heaving mass, Dax reached behind himself, feeling for the door.

A dark, whiskered snout darted out from the bathtub and *snorted*. Dax yelped, high and shrill, surprising even himself. In kind, the creature responded with a throaty, plaintive wail, and Dax screamed again. Pulling the shower curtain down around itself like a shroud, the thing started to splosh over the edge of the tub as he grabbed the doorknob and quickly slipped out, slamming it shut.

BOOM! The animal thudded against the door, moaning again.

"GRAMPA! What's in the bathroom?!"

They came running, Grampa wearing an apron in the shape of a lobster, carrying a bag of what looked like tiny fish. He laughed; he hadn't seen Dax this terrified since the boy came face to face with his first moray eel at the age of seven.

"Oh, you're home! Shoulda put a sign on the —"

"That's Scrub!" Kai shouted indignantly. "Stay away from him, Dax! He's hurt!"

Dax stared at them like they were both completely crazy.

"Trank yourself, Kai. What is 'Scrub'?"

"You know what a seal looks like!" Kai insisted. "And stay away from him! Scrub's mine. I own him."

"You can't own a seal!" Dax replied.

Grampa sighed.

"Now, Kai, the marine authorities are gonna have to decide what to do with him. We talked about this."

"I was only gone a few hours," Dax observed. "When did you decide to go and adopt a whole seal?"

Kai squeezed past Dax to crack the door open, then knelt down as Scrub's big fuzzy head squeezed through and licked his cheek.

"Hey, boy. You okay?" Kai cooed. He giggled, the creature's whiskers tickling his face.

"Here, Kai," Grampa said, handing him the bag of sardines. "Scrub needs protein so he can heal faster."

68

Grampa put a hand on Dax's shoulder with a reassuring look that this was under control.

"We found him on the beach with a big bite in his side. Used the sled to bring him back. He's a pup, but still heavy enough where the bottom was grazing the sand most of the way."

Dax looked back at Kai, sitting on the floor with half of a not-so-tiny marine mammal plopped in his lap, happily gulping down fish.

"And there's nothing in the other bathroom, right?" he asked, already briskly moving to the far side of the house. Grampa Pat laughed.

"Just my Kraken!"

. . .

Dax wiped his hands on one of the stacked guest towels Grampa kept in the bathroom, then noticed his face in the round mirror, framed in pieces of colorful broken tiles.

"What?"

He leaned in closer. A pimple was nudging its way to the surface of his left cheek. Dax groaned, moving his hands up as if to pop it, and then huffed.

"No, Dax. Do it the right way."

He looked through the medicine cabinet and found a small box. Inside were several plastic swabs immersed in a pale green gel. He lifted one out, snapped the box shut, and then swabbed the gel across the pimple.

As he waited, the pimple receded and healed, leaving nothing but a bright pink mark, which he knew would soon fade away as well. Dax grinned.

"That's right! Don't mess with *my* face."

Realizing his hair was shooting off in all directions, he picked up a brush, gave it two or three casual strokes – enough to get it out of his eyes – and surrendered. His locks were quite beyond taming at this point, but whom exactly was he trying to impress?

Emerging from the bathroom, he nearly plowed into Grampa, who was carrying a bag of woodchips.

"Goin' all out with the burgers?"

"You know it, Platty Zander."

Dax scowled. "Really, Grampa?"

"Ha! Okay. 'Dax' it is, for the rest of the day, at least."

They headed to the backyard, where the grill was already smoking. Dax tilted up the grates as his grandfather poured and spread the woodchips on the lower level, just above a bed of piping hot ceramic stones.

"Grampa, you know how Kai is. He finds stuff that's broken and then he just declares it's his. If it's got a heartbeat, that just makes things worse."

"Sure. But your brother's got that nurturing instinct, like your mom. And he's definitely got a way with animals. You saw him with Scrub. They already bonded."

"Yeah, so when the marine authorities come here and try to take Scrub away, Kai's gonna cry for days."

Grampa chewed on this and nodded in agreement.

"Well, let's see if we can get him back to full specs. If he goes out to sea on his own, Kai might be sad, but he'll know that's where Scrub belongs."

"Maybe," Dax replied, "or he might do everything he can to make sure Scrub never wants to leave his side."

They glanced back through the patio doors to see Kai giggling with his whiskered friend. It snorted in his face and he laughed out loud.

"You want the truth?" Grampa offered wistfully, "I think every kid should have a pet at some point."

Dax nodded, wandering off without further comment. His grandfather chuckled; Dax didn't even realize he had a pet of his own.

. . .

The sun had almost fully dipped into the horizon as they enjoyed their last bites of Grampa's glorious burgers – hints of honey, fresh mint, garlic and feta cheese blended in choice ground sirloin, grilled in round portions nearly the size of baseballs. The tiki torches were already blazing, infusing the air with the sublime scent of coconut.

Grampa Pat emerged from the house with a tray of tall mugs filled to the top with icy, multi-colored confections.

"And now to wash it all down . . !" he announced proudly. Dax sat up, his eyes dancing.

"You made fizzmotics!? Grampa, I love you!"

Kai hopped up, just as big a fan, as his grandfather set all three mugs down.

"*Fizzmotic Whammers*, Daxer. Pineberry today."

Grampa had two variants of his frozen concoction. Sometimes he whipped up his 'Citrapricotic Fizzmotic Wow!' – principally incorporating citrus fruits and apricots. But tonight he had crafted his 'Pineberry Fizzmotic Whammer' – a mellower rhapsody of apple juice, raspberries and pineapple, crushed, frozen and blended. The tall mugs awaited his final touch: On a small plate were three thick, chalky tablets. He dropped one into each and upon hitting bottom they began to fizz, with tiny popping, crackling noises erupting through the layers of slushy goodness.

"Cheers!" Grampa said, hoisting his decanter high. Kai had to hold his with both hands, but all three clanked their mugs together and began to slurp with delight, their faces contorting goofily with the sensation of countless tiny, spearmint-infused explosions on their tongues.

"This is the best," Dax said, wishing his mom would take on some of his grandfather's more exotic recipes. "Thanks, Grampa."

Their grandfather nodded, then burped suddenly, at which everyone shared a good laugh.

"I may be getting up there, but I can still whip up a fun meal. And I've been saving a quart of ginger cream, so tomorrow maybe we'll do coconut root beers."

Suddenly the very-tanned face of Milo Keener, Grampa's next door neighbor, leaned over the eastern fence, a rustic, informal border composed of old seawall pylons, bamboo and stone.

"Hey, there, Patrick! Hope I'm not disturbing, but have you seen the news?"

Dax and Kai looked up and waved. Still hovering over the grill, Grampa saluted with his tongs, happy to see his friend.

"Milo! No, I haven't in a few hours. Got some corn coming off the fire here – want some?"

"No, thank you! But check the news, it's amazing! Gonna be an incredible show tonight!"

"Okay. Thanks, Milo!"

Kai jumped up, heading back inside the house.

"I'm gonna check on Scrub!"

"Okay," Dax replied, glancing at Grampa with concern. "Have you even called the Marine Authority yet?"

Grampa grunted casually, betraying his low regard for protocol.

"It's the law . . ." Dax reminded.

". . . and a waste of taxpayer money. We got it under control."

Dax was about to counter that the bathroom was going to smell like sardines for a very long time, but a light began to glow on his wrist, which meant a call was coming in. He swept a palm across his sleeve and Shaw's face materialized just above it, his expression projecting urgency of a sort that seemed extreme, even for Shaw, who wore intensity like a floppy, old hat.

"Dax! Is the moon up yet?"

Dax smirked.

"You know Grampa doesn't skinny dip anymore."

Despite his raised eyebrow, Grampa still chuckled.

Shaw was insistent.

"Can you see the moon yet? Have you seen the news?"

This got their attention, especially coming so soon after their neighbor's same words.

"No, it's just getting dark here," Dax answered. "Did it blow up?"

Shaw didn't even try to hide his exasperation.

"Just queue up the NASA feeds, okay?"

"Grampa—" Dax began, but Grampa Pat had heard everything.

"FRED!" Grampa called. "NASA Channels One, Two and Three."

A friendly, disembodied but distinctly laid-back voice answered back:

"Coming up, Patrick. Aloha, Dax!"

"Yozies, Fred!"

And then, a thin, crisp wall of mist rose up from a long slot in the ground, up to Grampa's height and perhaps two meters wide, then the whole thing came to life with a grayish-blue glow, not quite opaque.

Almost every household had some kind of Customized Personality Coordinator, or CPC, integrated into its basic systems. Grampa had named his 'Fred' after a favorite pet, and had reprogrammed it to feel more 'beach-friendly.'

"Does Fred still beat you at Battleship?" Dax asked.

"Uhh, we stopped playin' that one. But he still reminds me if I'm overcooking dinner or if I don't empty the dryer. Gettin' older, so that's helpful."

Three floating, televised images appeared, stacked one atop the other. The lowest was a serene, panoramic view of Earth apparently captured by a satellite in orbit. The other was a remote unit from the colony on Mars, itself split into four views: an enclosed greenhouse full of crops, two perspectives of the exterior landscape, and a room where some engineers were examining a generator, commenting on its efficiency.

But the image on top was stupefying.

"Do you see it now?" Shaw asked tensely.

"Uh huh," Dax muttered, awestruck.

There it was, just a day away from a complete new moon, but a great portion of its visible surface was marked by the same glowing, vaguely crescent-like shape in green.

Grampa leaned forward, as did Dax, who swiped again across his sleeve – but this time he made a gesture as if to 'throw' Shaw over to the other video feeds. Instantly, his elder brother's image was hovering exactly where the broadcast from Mars had been.

"It's on NASA One. How long's it been like that?"

"We were out diving and I think it was about 11:20 p.m. when we surfaced, and there it was. Reports I saw said it appeared at 3:15 a.m., Greenwich Time. So, 11:15 p.m. here in Miami. Happened right before we wrapped up our dive."

"Kai!" Dax called. No response. "KAI! Come out here!" he called again.

"I'm with my seal!"

Grampa spoke more softly, but then again, he didn't need to shout.

"Kailen, come on out here, buddy."

And a few seconds later he did, not stopping at the threshold of the patio door, but moving forward to the images onscreen, obviously puzzled with the moon but brightening at the sight of his eldest brother's face.

"Hi, Shaw."

"Hey, buddy."

"Who broke the moon?" Kai muttered quizzically. "Why's it look like that?"

Nobody had an answer. Without warning, Grampa's mist monitor grew a smaller side panel, blinking red, indicating an incoming urgent message.

"Had a feeling they'd be calling," Grampa chuckled. "Fred! Place the incoming call next to Shaw and network all conversations."

Evan and Dayna appeared in the panel alongside their son, their manner every bit as off-kilter as the rest of the family's. With their connections, if anyone was going to have the scoop on something of this nature, it was Mom and Dad. But at the moment, they looked positively scoop-less.

"We saw it," said Dax. "Do you know anything?"

"Your father and I have reached out," his mother answered, "but so far, it's a mystery to the whole world. The one thing we have confirmed is that there's a suspended field of micro-fine minerals holding orbit about 400 kilometers from the surface of the moon, and the image we're seeing is light reflected from that particle field. It stands out even more because we're in a new moon cycle."

Dax's eye wandered to the many pieces of stained glass hanging from the beams extending over the back porch.

Shaw had also been thinking about what could cause such a phenomenon. "But that shape – this isn't just some drifting dust cloud, is it?"

"We don't know, Son," Evan responded. "There are a host of telescopes, including three on the lunar surface, being repositioned right now to try to figure that out."

"It looks like half a whale," Kai observed, biting his lip thoughtfully.

"We're coming to Grampa's," Dayna added. "We'll see you boys in the morning."

"Wait . . . why?" Shaw asked. "Is something going on?"

Evan's brow tightened. He was not a good poker player, but he was a parent. Right now, he didn't want to hypothesize on what wasn't much more than a feeling in his gut.

"We don't know, and that's the truth. But this feels like something we should pay attention to, and your mother and I felt we should be with Dax and Kai, at least for the next few days."

"Should I come back?"

"I don't know if that's necessary, Son," Evan replied, with an air of casual pragmatism. "Might be better if you concentrated on your studies until we know—"

"Shaw! Yes! Come back, Shaw!" Kai chimed in. Dayna chuckled, glancing at Evan, who nodded, obviously giving up any resistance for her sake.

"Whatever you think is best, Shaw."

"Okay. I'll try to be there by tomorrow night," Shaw announced. "Maybe catch a tube from West Palm to San Fran. From there I can fly or maybe take a double-guller to the islands."

"See you soon, sweetheart," his mother responded. "Please don't stress about this now."

Dax laughed aloud. Everyone knew Shaw would fixate on this event, its possible causes and ramifications, like a dog with a very large, meaty bone. It was his way.

"Bye, Shaw!" Kai called.

"Seeya soon, sport." And then he blipped out of sight.

Evan and Dayna relaxed a bit; their family would be together for a while, and whatever other tensions were in play, this was a very evident comfort. Dax took a step toward the screen, floating there in mid-air.

"Dad. You really don't think this is anything bad, right?"

Evan and Dayna shared a quick look, and then his father broke a warm, reassuring smile.

"No. Just unexpected. But there are some other things going on we should discuss tomorrow."

"Some changes coming, honey," his mother added. "But nothing we can't handle. Alright?"

Dax didn't like the sound of that, but he covered well.

"Sure, Mom. Okay."

"We love you all. See you soon," Evan added, and then their feed vanished. The image of the moon, however, remained – that strange symbol plastered across it like the work of some interplanetary urban artist with an enormous can of fluorescent spray paint.

Then *that* flicked out, too; Grampa had turned off the monitor.

"We'll be able to see it with our own eyes soon enough. Let's play some cards."

"I'll get 'em!" Kai declared, running back into the house.

It took Kai a full ten minutes to return with cards, as he indulged a brief visit with his recuperating pet in the bathtub. Eventually the three were engaged in a ruthless game of Crazy Eights, as it was Kai's favorite, but that would do quite fine for a while.

The moon did rise a few hours later, and with it a strange dance of lime green dappling across a choppy black sea. Funny enough, after about thirty or forty minutes, they became used to it, only looking up now and again.

Sometime after Kai had become bored with cards and curled up under the warm glow of a tiki torch, Grampa turned to Dax, his voice quiet.

"How are things with Cody?" he asked.

Dax looked at his cards and laid them down. He had been so preoccupied with the moon rising in the evening sky, he'd let slip concerns about his friend. But now all those thoughts were back again, just as potent and just as heavy.

"We had a good time. But . . ."

"Do they think he'll get better?"

Dax looked over at him with such a pained expression, Grampa reached over and put a strong arm around his shoulders.

"Well, then, we just keep praying for miracles." He pointed up at the moon. "And they still happen, m'boy."

Something about the slight, craggy grin on Grampa's bronzed face sparked a needed lift to Dax's spirits. If any day was proof the unpredictable could happen, it was today. And then he realized, today was the exact day he needed that sort of reminder.

They went through a variety of games over the next few hours, as the moon ascended higher through the billowing clouds over the vast Pacific. Through round after round they glanced up to the sky again and again wonderingly, knowing they were seeing this with no chance of special effects or televised shenanigans. This 'hand in the moon' was real, but like the rest of the world, they could merely watch, wait and wonder what it might possibly mean.

A little past 1:00 a.m., Grampa stood to stretch, then gently touched Kai's brow, the lad asleep in a chair and just slightly snoring, blissfully oblivious to any real concerns about what might be happening up there. Probably time to get that one in a proper bed.

Just then, Dax jumped up, shouting, "Whoa! You see that?! Look! It flipped!"

Grampa blinked, as he had missed the change, but the image did look different.

"You sure?"

"Yeah! Check the feed!"

The burned-in copy at the bottom of the softly glowing, televised image was just now updating. Exactly fifteen minutes after one a.m., the shape had indeed shifted. *Rotated.*

"It turned," Dax clarified, "maybe forty-five degrees!"

Grampa shook his head, reading the words crawling across the screen.

"Not quite. Close, though. It rotated exactly thirty-seven degrees, clockwise . . . on its center point."

"Yay! It moved!" Kai cheered. Grampa and Dax glanced down; apparently, they'd woken him up.

"What's so great about that?" Dax asked.

Kai yawned. "I dunno. But if it moves, it could be *alive.*"

"Thirty-seven degrees," Dax muttered, puzzled. "That's kind of weird."

"Nothing about that thing *isn't* weird," Grampa added.

"Maybe it doesn't mean anything," Dax mused, as he stared up, half-hoping it would rotate again. "Or maybe we'll never know."

"Now that would be disappointing, don'tcha think? I bet this turns out to be something incredibly special."

He rubbed Dax's neck, then plucked Kai up and carried him into the house.

Dax watched them go, silently hoping Grampa was right.

But even if still a few months shy of his fourteenth birthday, he also knew that 'incredibly special' might not equal 'incredibly wonderful.' And that was enough to haunt his thoughts until his eyelids became heavy as bricks and he finally passed out.

Together

Grampa Pat was up well before Evan and Dayna arrived, dusting, changing linens and pulling a few items from the freezer to prepare later that day. Throughout his activity, he kept switching channels, listening to scientists and pundits speculate as to how a strangely rigid dust cloud had formed in orbit above our sole natural satellite. Or how it was keeping itself in a perfect position relative to the moon's revolution around Earth, visible from any point in the world where the moon could be spotted with the naked eye. Grampa frequently erupted with snorts and chuckles, convinced most of these people simply liked to hear themselves talk.

He was sprucing up the front of the house when Dax's parents docked. As they climbed the winding, wooden stairway from the beach and entered through the backyard, they discovered their middle son, snoozing in one of Grampa's large loungers, tangled up in his limbs like a blond vampire bat. The captain smiled as his wife swept a beetle from their son's ankle, then kissed his forehead, deciding to let him doze a while longer. It was barely 8:00 a.m.

"Lucky guy. He can still sleep just about anywhere."

They found Grampa in the kitchen, mixing several different types of fruit in a quietly churning blender. Dayna watched him for just a moment, his flesh dappled in countless hues of light from so many hanging pieces of glass, and she took deep pleasure in the thought that throughout her entire life, he had been her own sparkly, cuddly rainbow.

"Hello, Daddy," she said, wrapping her arms about his shoulders to kiss his cheek.

"Aloha, boys and girls!" Grampa whisper-called, wiping his hands on his apron and giving her a big bear hug. He tossed a kiwi to Evan who caught it high and winked. The more of the family present, the happier Grampa was. With any luck, Shaw would soon join them.

"Kai's in the avocado room, but he's got a guest in there, so no sudden moves."

Dayna's brow furrowed. "A guest?"

Grampa chuckled mysteriously. "Go on. Wake him up."

They headed down the hall with wary steps, accustomed to his eccentric and quite often corny pranks. Grampa chortled deeply, gleefully dropping some bananas into the blender.

Evan and Dayna opened the door to a room drenched in various shades of green, adorned with large plastic palm leaves of the sort you might find at a theme park. Several plastic monkeys served as hat racks, mirror holders and an overhead lighting fixture, currently off. It was a great refuge for a little boy, a room Grampa had originally fashioned for Shaw. He added the monkeys a few years later for Dax, as he was born in the last days of the Year of the Monkey.

A few tufts of Kai's hair were sticking out of a very lumpy pile of comforters and pillows. As Dayna reached out to tap his head, Scrub's snout appeared from under the covers, whiskers popping out like an antenna array. Then he snorted.

In the kitchen, Grampa heard her piercing scream, loud and clear. Enjoying a deep, throaty chuckle, he turned the blender back on and went back to preparing breakfast.

. . .

Dax's senses were healthy and acute in general, but where food was a factor they spiked considerably; the scent of French toast and crushed pineapple lured him from sleep like a genie from a newly-rubbed lamp. The warm morning breeze tickling his skin, he unfolded his gangly limbs and yawned; the sky was bright and the moon had traveled quite a distance around the world. Plopping his feet into his flip-flops, the straps closed on contact, around and over his toes.

Grampa's backyard monitor was off, but no matter; he knew there'd be a feed running the latest news in the kitchen's breakfast nook. He just followed his nose.

Dax was still rubbing sleep from his eyes when Grampa ran a leathery hand through his thick mane of hair.

"Mornin', Prince Yawning! You're too late; all the French toast is gone."

"Oh, ha ha. Like you wouldn't save any for—"

But his face fell, staring at the table, where a few crumbs and some powdered sugar were left on the serving plate. Kai was rabidly chewing around what looked like the last half slice, suspended off a fork and dripping with pineapple glaze.

"Grampa!" Dax moaned plaintively. "You didn't keep—"

Hands wrapped around him, making him jump. Someone kissed his cheek.

"Mom!"

"Hey, there, sweetie. How's that injury?"

He blushed, having completely forgotten to follow through on his excuse for coming inland in the first place. Fortunately, Grampa Pat came to the rescue.

"HA! Gotcha!" He spun around holding another plate stacked high with golden brown slices of savory, egg-soaked delight. "Go on, eat, you need carbs and protein if you wanna heal up right."

Dax locked eyes with Grampa, who just winked fast. The boy dropped into a chair and started serving himself.

"Yay, protein!"

Dayna looked between them, chagrined.

"You two aren't fooling anyone. What I would give for just one other girl in this family."

Dax had already stuffed his mouth, but he held no pretenses about talking while eating.

"Like girls are more honesh," he said, chewing ravenously.

His dad hurried in, a video feed hovering above his sleeve.

"Morocco beat Costa Rica, five to two," he declared.

Grampa was grateful for a reminder the world was still moving on as it had, in this case with the World Cup semifinals. Perhaps to underscore the sentiment, he punched the air with a big shout.

"Yayyy, Morocco!"

Everyone laughed; it was no secret Grampa had time for just one sport: baseball.

Evan's eyes darted to the plate of French toast, then to his middle son.

"Better leave me a couple a'those, if you know what's good for ya."

Dax picked up a knife and waved it like a buccaneer.

"Ye'll have to fight me for 'em, Captain!"

His dad grabbed his own knife and they clashed a few times. Dayna, sitting on an elevated stool, spun around quickly with a loud 'shhh!' – freezing them mid-duel. Immediately their attention turned to the series of small displays that hovered in the air, all emanating from her own portable device.

"Where's this coming from?" Grampa asked, leaning in to read the copy scrolling across the bottom of the screen. "Austria. Okay, they're a good ten hours or so ahead of us."

"Dad, please," she interrupted, her urgency even more insistent. "It changed again."

Evan grinned; he loved catching that intensity in her sparkling eyes; she had a mind that ran boldly to new questions, rather than shrink from them.

"How much, Mom?" Dax asked.

"Thirty degrees this time. Now it's sixty-seven degrees off its original position. Rotating on its center again. Happened at 9:15 a.m. our time, exactly sixteen hours after it appeared—"

"—and eight hours after the first rotation, right?" Dax queried. He fell still, muttering. "Thirty-seven, sixty-seven . . ."

Kai knew that far off look in his older brother, the kind that meant he'd be no fun for a while. He sighed and filled a bowl with milk.

"I'm gonna go feed Scrub."

He was halfway down the hall when Dayna realized her little boy thought he was going to be adopting a wild animal.

"Honey, please don't get too used to Scrub!" she called after him. "He's a living creature and needs to go back to the—"

But whatever was on her display proved so compelling, the word 'ocean' never arrived. She turned to Evan.

"There's . . . I don't know what you'd call it. A migration of particulate matter moving from all directions toward a small cloud that's been in orbit, holding position with the moon."

"Yeah, saw 'em tracking it," Grampa said. "So it's like iron shavings to a magnet?"

She shrugged; it was as good a description as any. Evan squinted at the image on screen, but didn't comment. He was a military strategist, not oriented to astrophysics. In situations where science ruled the road, he was happy to let Dayna drive. But it could be humbling on occasion; in situations where he had nothing to offer, he felt a little off his game.

Dax, like his mom, was in a similar fugue. Not even realizing it, he drew lines through the puddles of glaze on his plate, one after the other, staring off into space, figuring out a puzzle.

"Dax? Helloooo?" His Grampa poked his shoulder.

"Ninety-seven," Dax replied.

They all looked at him, curious.

"If it rotates again, and if someone's doing it on purpose, I bet it's gonna hit ninety-seven degrees, and it's gonna happen at 5:15 today. This afternoon."

"Prime numbers," his mother nodded, "perfectly spaced apart, each rotation ending in seven. Yes, that would mean someone was trying to make it an obvious pattern."

"I don't know if 'obvious' is the right word," Evan mused.

"How about 'intentional'?" Grampa asked, as he placed a mixing bowl in a drying rack by the sink.

One of the feeds switched to people camping out on towels, some waving large signs with short phrases in German, French and other languages.

Evan wasn't a scientist, but he knew human nature.

"They think it's the end," he mused aloud.

"Or at least a new beginning," Dayna added.

"Dad," Dax remarked with earnest enthusiasm, "*something's* happening."

His father nodded in agreement, though if ever they needed a small tonic of normalcy, it was now. At least something to keep the anxiety down until the next 'rotation.' He craned his neck to look out the window.

"Waves are goin' off."

Dax lit up.

"Let's go!"

His mother called after him as he dashed down the hall to grab his skinsuit.

"I don't know; that limp is pretty bad! Think you can handle it out there?"

There was a punctuated silence, and then Dax's shaggy-maned head angled back out from his room. He wore a sheepish, guilty sort of expression.

"I'm sorry. But I honestly did get bit by a whale, Mom. I did."

She tried to maintain a stern façade, but that plaintive, puppy dog look made her burst into laughter.

"Go. Go get your suit and get out there. Silly."

She kept laughing as he did a happy bounce and disappeared again.

"You would make a terrible warden," Evan teased. She giggled, then poured herself a cup of juice as he left to get dressed. Grampa Pat pushed a plate before her with a sliced banana and one piece of French toast.

"Y'know, you could always adopt a *girl*. Now wouldn't that make Kai mad!"

And they laughed together.

The sun was high enough now to catch dozens of hanging pieces of colored glass, the gentle wind causing several crystal mobiles to clink together in delicate music. They were bathed in an array of brilliant hues, the kitchen surfaces alive with patches of glowing splendor.

Dax raced by his mom, the seam in the back of his skinsuit still sealing itself as he bounded out the door. Bouncing and trailing along, his hair gleamed like a golden meteor. She watched him run out through the yard, grab his board and sprint across the sand. A few seconds later, her husband followed. And for a few minutes, her heart swelled so much she forgot all her anxiety about any impending changes, planned and unplanned, natural and manipulated. She even stopped wondering what would happen if the hand in the moon rotated again. Which of course, it would.

While Kai stayed inside, capturing images of Scrub wearing a variety of baseball caps, Dayna and her father parked some loungers on the beach and watched Evan and Dax as they weaved through the churning swells, occasionally hot-dogging, always hooting. Zander men and water equaled much hooting. And while her husband and middle son were out challenging the surf, others, thousands of kilometers away in places where the sun had already set, were standing outside their homes, gathered near their places of worship, camped out in fields and on beaches, sitting on their rooftops, just staring up, riveted on the sky. Waiting for whatever was next.

And for those so lucky as to see it when it happened, twenty-four hours after it originally appeared, the hand, or dove, or half-whale or whatever it might be, shifted abruptly – another thirty degrees – to ninety-seven degrees from its original orientation. Just as Dax had predicted.

After which, nothing happened at all. For a bit, anyway.

. . .

From San Francisco, Shaw had pulled a favor from a friend to catch free passage on a 'double-guller' – an extremely fast, high-capacity hovercraft, whose main, enclosed decks were suspended between two enormous, turbine-powered pontoons. It was a smooth ride unless you ventured out on deck, where the winds could be so strong you had to clip yourself to a tether. Technically, once the ship got up to full speed, you weren't allowed outside of the main enclosures unless you were part of the crew, and even then only in extreme situations. It was always an exhilarating ride, not as fast as a jet but far less expensive. Fortunately the gullers docked at Ka'a'Awa Point, so from there he was able to catch a quick elevated transit almost the entire remaining distance to Grampa's neighborhood. The route snaked through a lot of communities along the way, but the cabs were comfy and the ride smooth as glass. Shaw had been traveling for the better part of a day; he had indeed managed to book cross-country passage on a high-speed pneumatic tube-train, but his Miami route transitioned in Chicago and he had been restless the whole morning. So by now he was pretty tired. Happily there was but one other person in the L-Cab right now, an elderly woman reading a magazine on a rollup – a scroll-like reading device that retracted into a long, thin tube when not in use.

He glanced over anxiously, not wanting to distract her, but finally spoke up.

"I don't jump off till Turtle Bay, so I was gonna sleep."

The old woman shrugged good-naturedly.

"I might snore."

Chuckling lightly, she pointed to her ears. Shaw stared for a moment, then realized this was likely her way of letting him know she was deaf. He was intrigued; with so many fantastic advances in medicine and related tech, it was rare to meet a deaf person anymore.

"Oh, oh, sorry! Okay. Thank you."

Her sweet sparkle of appreciation brought his Gramma Redtree to mind, the first he'd thought of her in weeks. Rather than push the memory away, he closed his eyes and settled back across three seats, using his rolled backpack as a cushion.

His mind drifted to summer days when his grandmother taught him how to build good, sturdy sandcastles, never minding the mess they made together, the swirling surf nearby creeping into the moats they'd dug. A waterborne virus contracted at age fifty-two had rendered Gramma Redtree deaf until about eight years before she passed away, so as a toddler she'd taught him to sign. He thought it was an amazing way to communicate. Around Shaw's seventh birthday, she finally accepted genetically cultivated aural implants previously shunned for years on the grounds that she didn't want "laboratory vegetables tapping into my brain." Within days of the procedure, however, she was reveling in the rich, endless diversity of sounds she'd missed for so long – especially music. Shaw loved how she would linger on the back porch, listening to the tinkling music of Grampa's ever-increasing collection of blown and stained glass, dangling and bumping in the wind. Occasionally, through a window, he'd even catch them dancing ever-so-gently to some old song they both loved.

With her implants, signing was no longer needed to communicate, so Shaw's skills grew rusty. He took the high school classes for an easy 'A,' but those classes were very basic and he never followed them up with anything more comprehensive. So his competency in that language had become more and more creaky with time.

Shaw opened his eyes and sat up. The elderly lady was still there, by herself, reading. He grabbed his bag and stepped through the cab to a spot just opposite to where she sat. Catching her fleeting trace of anxiety, Shaw sat slowly, in a way that signaled he meant no harm or agitation. And then he did something that surprised the lady. Hoping he got it right, Shaw signed, *"Are you visiting friends or do you live here?"*

Clearly touched, her deeply wrinkled cheeks bloomed with a new lustrous pink. She signed back, *"I am going home to live with my daughter. And you?"*

Shaw had to think before his next attempt.

"My signing is not great. But I my family home go wash."

"You are quite good," she lied politely. *"Have you seen the moon?"*

"Yes. Mother are scientist, and I study to be one. Why I go to the piglets."

The lady giggled. Shaw thought about what he'd communicated and tried again. Apparently, this time he correctly signed *"going to the family home"* and they both shared a nod.

Her brow knit.

"What do you think the moon images mean?" she gestured.

"I'm not sure. Possibly explanation is a natural. Maybe weather."

"But why would it turn?" She made an extra, deliberate gesture, as if turning a crank.

Shaw tightened up; he hadn't keyed into any updates while traveling, so this was new to him. What *was* clear was that none of the experts had offered any serious answers; and in the face of global uncertainty, this particular lady seemed unsettled. Shaw felt obliged to offer some consolation. His signing was awkward but he managed.

"Anyone who do that to a moon could probably hurt us if they want to. So I don't think large reason to be big afraid."

It took the lady a moment to absorb what he was trying to say, but she seemed pleased, and maybe also a tiny bit amused that the boy was trying so hard.

"That's a good way to look at it."

"Yes, I am a tomato," Shaw signed.

The lady grinned, reaching out to place her hand on his.

"It was very nice of you to say 'hello.' Thank you."

For some reason, Shaw felt his throat tighten up, as if his grandmother, for one fleeting moment, were here in this cab with him again. He nodded gratefully.

"My pleasure," he said slowly, so she could read his lips.

His alarm pinged – he'd set it to sync with the train's scheduled stop two stations before Turtle Bay.

To his mild disappointment, the lady stood. This was her stop.

She nodded, then carefully stepped before the glass doors, which whooshed open. Shaw also stood to watch her go, hoping she wouldn't stumble, as her movements were slow. Once out, she turned around and gently blew him a kiss as the doors slid shut. Shaw waved a warm goodbye.

And until his next stop, he thought about her, wishing he'd shared a little more with this sweet stranger. Shaw contemplated things like this – random interactions with people, how he came across. His tendency to overcompensate for what he perceived as his poor social skills was often met with amusement from his friends, and far less-inhibited chiding from Dax – who seemed to relish pointing out every flaw in Shaw's appearance and especially any awkward overtures with girls. He knew Dax didn't mean to be truly hurtful, but sometimes Shaw sorely wanted to shove him out a seabase lockout chamber without an N-pack.

As the train slowed to his stop, Shaw stood up and stretched, slinging his backpack over one shoulder. The blurring landscape transformed into thick stands of palm trees and lush explosions of colorful flowers, sprawling tangles of green broken by clusters of tastefully designed homes and apartments. It wasn't all that unlike parts of Coral Gables, near school.

"Turtle Bay Station A," a voice droned through the cab. The doors opened and Shaw stepped out to the platform. A native Hawaiian at the exit turnstiles greeted him, her brilliant white smile in perfect contrast to her lustrous, copper-hued skin.

"Welcome to Turtle Bay. Visiting?" she asked.

"Oh, no," Shaw replied. "Well, I *am* visiting. But I'm coming home." Just as he wondered if he could possibly stammer anything more convoluted, he added, "This is my home," proving he could double down.

"Oh, great!" Her voice taking on that professional, metered enthusiasm of a museum guide. "Did you see the moon?"

Shaw perked up; a conversation with a pretty girl was always worth a few minutes. He wanted to reach Grampa's before dark, but he had nearly an hour till sunset.

"Yeah, crazy . . ."

Shaw wondered how he might impress her with the small amount of information he'd accessed before his trip, but also suspected that by now she might have learned more about the phenomenon than he. Then his eyes dropped to her hand, where the diamond ring on her finger sparkled prominently. His heart sank more than a little.

"It just turned again!" she gushed. "Two minutes ago! What do you think it means?"

A sudden disquiet took hold of Shaw. He checked the time: almost 5:20.

"You know," he said, hoisting his backpack, "I think it's too early to tell, but there's no reason for anyone to worry, right?" She nodded, offering a little wave as he headed off down the ramp. Despite his words, however, there was a cold, empty feeling in his gut, like the world was hiding secrets from him, and he very much wanted to get home to his family.

Pink

Complete Zander family gatherings had become rare since Shaw left for college, so Grampa had prepared a grand feast of cultivated prime rib, jumbo shrimp and lobster. The grill was smoking with two racks of those delicacies and several corncobs, adding an intoxicating fullness to the overall aroma.

Entering from the street, Shaw arrived to find the living room and bedrooms empty, though a ruckus from outside made it safe to assume everyone was already in the backyard. No sooner had he set down his backpack, than Dax slid down the pole from the roof to land just in front of him. Shaw jumped; Dax slapped his brother's chest playfully.

"Yozies. Got some sleepy crud right there . . ." He reached a finger to Shaw's eye, which was quickly swatted away.

"Hey!"

Dax laughed. "Use a mirror!"

"Use a comb!" Shaw shot back. "You look like a blond sheepdog!"

There was a precious second or two where they just glared at each other, as if waiting for the next creative insult. Dax broke first, flashing a broad grin, and Shaw's came an instant later.

"Fill me in on what's been going on with the moon, will ya? I feel like I missed a lot."

Dax summed it up for him, Shaw's brow knitting in typical fashion as he processed the three rotations, each eight hours apart, the last having happened just as he was getting off the L-Cab. His younger brother shared his frustration – none of them had come up with any revelations, either. He nudged Shaw encouragingly.

"It's good you're back," Dax offered. "They're all outside and Grampa's already burned off about half his eyebrows. And Kai's been dying to show you something."

Shaw threw an arm around his neck and they headed out.

His mother and father each gave him a kiss, after which Kai, who had been examining a large shell he'd uncovered earlier that morning, bounced up and charged him like a rocket. Shaw immediately caught and flipped him onto his shoulders for an exhilarating jog out to the shore, where he dropped to his knees so Kai could roll into the surf with an exuberant scream.

They laughed together for a minute, after which Kai shouted, "Shaw! I got a seal!"

"You what?"

"He's in the bathroom!"

Shaw's face wrinkled up, trying to decipher this. There was a cosmic event happening that had drawn their family together in one place, but Kai had somehow managed to sneak something else into the headlines.

"Seriously? You really got a seal?"

Kai nodded gleefully, the gap between his front two teeth prominent.

Skeptical, Shaw looked to Dax, who had just caught up, ankle deep in the frothy surf.

"Yup! Kailen really got a seal!" he affirmed, and then added carefully, "and he really wants to *keep* it."

Shaw absorbed this, a look passing between them.

"Kai, show me your new seal."

And his little brother led him by the hand back to Grampa's house.

"He's great! His name is Scrub! I think a shark bit him and Grampa and me found him and he loves me!"

Shaw glanced back to find Dax looking into the sky, above the setting sun – but the moon was not yet in sight. Kai pulled at his arm, leading him back.

Not long after, Dax, Kai and their dad were crowded in the bathroom, huddled behind Shaw as he examined Scrub's wound and dressing. They'd done a good job. He carefully reapplied the bandage and gently stroked the creature's pelt of short, slick fur, thinking.

"Obviously a pinniped," he mused, "but . . . Kai, my jacket's on the couch in the living room. In the biggest zippy pocket, there's a blue square thing. Could you bring it back here?"

Kai was already halfway down the hall. In no time he returned with a small device. Shaw activated the controls and rubbed it against Scrub's snout and mouth.

"What's that?" Kai asked.

"A portable flow cytometer. It can learn all kinds of stuff from Scrub's cells."

The captain laughed. "It's gonna flow right into Scrub's belly if you don't hold tight."

And sure enough, Scrub bit down on the edge.

"Hey!" Shaw exclaimed as his father and brothers laughed. He yanked it out and turned away so Scrub would no longer be tempted. "Just needed some saliva," he murmured, waiting for the unit to process the sample. In seconds, the screen began flashing a cascade of images, which Shaw shuttled through as his father spied over his shoulder, genuinely impressed.

"Now I know what that big charge on our account went for," Evan observed wryly. Shaw cringed slightly, but his father put a reassuring hand on his shoulder. "Don't worry about it. Anything you need for school is a legitimate expense. Besides, your mother's gotten me accustomed to pricey lab equipment. So what's the verdict?"

"California sea lion," Shaw read, rising to his feet. "Awful long way from home."

"Can I have a look?" Dax asked.

Shaw handed over the device. Dax scrolled through the information.

"They get bigger," Dax read. "A lot bigger. This one's a baby."

"He's *my* baby!" Kai declared.

"Well, Son . . ." Their father didn't have much after that, knowing if he did, the conversation would end with his youngest boy in tears and he already had some bad news to share a little later.

"Dad?" Shaw asked quietly, with a tone that inferred his father should do the tough thing and tell Kai he couldn't adopt a wild animal.

"I think Scrub needs rest and we're all bothering him," their father concluded.

Shaw smirked, whispering in his ear, "You ended a *war*, Dad, but a pair of big, brown, puppy dog eyes just took you down."

As if he'd not heard that at all, Evan loudly announced, "I'm hungry! Let's go eat!" and marched out of the bathroom, Kai skipping happily alongside.

"Fifty bucks says Mom and Dad let him keep it," Shaw said, watching them go.

Dax shook his head.

"You think I'm dumb enough to lose fifty bucks? Been away too long, bro."

Outside, they found an enticing spread ready on the family picnic table. They ate well, laughed and caught up on Shaw's latest collegiate exploits as the not-so-dark circle of the moon rose over the sea. Dessert turned out to be one of Grampa Pat's signature concoctions – toffee and caramel-dipped pineapple spears. The boys tucked theirs into ice cream and dug in with decadent gusto. Evan shared a nod with Dayna and pushed back from the table. He couldn't postpone this forever.

"Boys, your mom and I feel it's time to let you know we're in for a big change."

All three boys stopped chewing – briefly. Dax glanced over at Grampa, who avoided eye contact and looked down at the table.

"Is it because of the moon?" Kai asked.

"You're not getting a divorce, are you?!" Shaw asked, gravely.

Dax looked at him sideways.

"You *have* been away too long, Shaw."

"No, no. Nobody's getting divorced," Evan answered.

"We love each other more than ever, sweetheart," Dayna added. "Besides, we vowed to work things out even when we don't feel like working things out."

"That's right; we're a family," Evan said, "and we'll *always* be a family."

"And so?" Grampa asked, knowing the boys' hearts were now dangling off a cliff.

"The Navy no longer collects from the international fund to maintain the seabases. And it's been quite a few years since we've had to intervene in any incidents of piracy."

"They can't just shut them down!" Shaw insisted. "It's a perfect hub for marine research."

"They're kicking us out of our home?" Dax asked in dismay.

"No, Shaw, you're right about that. The entire compound will be converted into a science station. The location is unique given the varieties of sea life passing through the nearby abyssal. So it's a great spot to begin—"

"But I wanted to take Scrub there!" Kai exclaimed. "'Cause he could live outside in the water and come in through the lock-it chamber!"

"*Lockout* chamber, buddy," Dax corrected, putting an arm around Kai. "Had it all figured out, huh? Not a bad plan."

"Fortunately," Dayna said, "we have about six weeks before crews arrive to begin changes, and then about two more weeks until we'll have to move into a new home." She sighed, turning to her youngest. "Kai, we'll have to think for a while about . . . Scrub."

Kai folded his arms and glowered at her.

"Where ya thinkin' of goin'?" Grampa Pat asked.

"NASA has asked me to consider leading a task force to design and prep structures for the first colony on Europa."

Dax was impressed. "Whoa, Mom . . . that would be chewy!"

Shaw, however, was cheerlessly blunt.

"Wait. Are you seriously thinking of leaving here to join some off-world colonization effort?"

Dayna shared a look with her husband; no doubt a jaunt into space was enticing to both, but her calm demeanor put her eldest son's concerns to rest.

"They'll use cookers on Europa to build most of the components. My job is to make sure all the pieces are designed – here on Earth – to fit so that everything can be fabricated onsite using only raw materials mined on that moon, or Io, or maybe from Jupiter itself."

"So, Cape Canaveral? Florida?"

"Yay! We get to be near Shaw!" Kai cheered, though behind him, Shaw seemed queasy about that new possibility.

"No," Evan said, "it's looking like Houston."

Dax made the very same face as whenever presented with asparagus casserole for dinner.

"Ouch! Houston's always hot! Can't mom do her stuff from somewhere else? Maybe fly in once in a while?"

Dayna cringed. Secretly, she wasn't crazy about moving to Texas, either.

"Can you surf in Houston?" Kai asked.

"No Kai, you can't . . ." Shaw muttered.

"Actually," their mother chimed in, clearly proud to have foreseen the question, "there's a lot of coastline not all that far away and supposedly some good surfing on the gulf."

"What's a gulf?" Kai asked, provoking a snort from Shaw.

"Dad," Dax asked, "what about you? Are you retiring from the Navy? 'Cause what the heck are you gonna do in Houston?"

"I've had offers to write about my experiences in the Pirate Wars, maybe even for broadcast. I might work with your Grampa Pat on his version. I could teach.

But I can do that anywhere, and it's important to me that your mom is happy and challenged in her work."

The sobering 'realness' of it all was starting to hit Dax. This wasn't just a possibility – it was a big change his parents had been agonizing over for some time. Maybe he needed to study up on Houston, but what he was picturing was about as far away from coconuts, hitching rides with whales and shooting barrels with the Zander family dawn patrol as he could imagine.

"Texas!" Kai said, with a measure of disgust more than matching Dax's tone. "Can't we go anywhere else?"

"Well, we can visit Grampa any time we want. We can even visit the seabase," his father added with a familiar twinkle. "Rank has its privileges."

Shaw had been quiet for over a minute, squinting up at the sky. Dax followed his gaze, his head craning up.

"Okay, this is new," Shaw muttered.

They all turned and looked up at the moon, or rather the image emblazoned against it. The ghostly green was fading, changing rapidly into a glowing shade of magenta.

"Whoa!" Kai cried out, wide-eyed.

And then its transformation was complete – to an almost fluorescently vibrant *pink*.

"This time, it didn't rotate," Dax pointed out. "Fred, what time is it?" The familiar, friendly voice of Grampa's digital valet boomed out again from thin air:

"Aloha, Dax. It's 6:52 p.m., local time."

Everyone seemed bewildered by Fred's announcement.

"Didn't rotate a fourth time," Dayna mused, "but an hour and a half after the last rotation, it changes color. A clear pattern of change, but then it's abandoned. Why?"

"Hour and a half . . ." Dax muttered. His eyes squinched shut but quickly opened again, bright with the clarity of a new idea.

"*Not* an hour and a half!" he exclaimed. "The last rotation ended at 97 degrees! And then exactly ninety seven minutes *later*, it changes color! Mom!"

Dayna rubbed the goosebumps on her arm, the implications impossible to ignore.

"There's no way that's a coincidence," she agreed with a whisper.

Evan, Shaw and Grampa Pat were silent, overcome with awe. For his part, Kai didn't speak either – mostly because he was spooked at the abrupt shift in everyone's mood. Noticing this, Grampa rubbed his little head comfortingly.

"Whoever's doing this is very patient," he suggested, leaning back in his chair. "But I would bet real money that it won't be long before we get a much clearer message, now that they've got our attention."

Shaw leaned over to Dax, smirking, his voice low.

"You might not have to go to Texas after all, Daxer."

His brother's remark left Dax uneasy in a way he couldn't quite define.

And around the world, right now, he had a lot of company.

. . .

The next morning, Grampa set about giving everyone something to do. To his thinking, there was no more powerful tonic to chaos and uncertainty than routine. He didn't have to work hard on Evan and Dayna – they had been up since 5:00 a.m., communicating with their respective friends in the scientific and military communities, trying to absorb, collect and compare whatever information they could gather. With a six-hour time difference between Oahu and Washington, they were intent on keeping up with events as they might develop.

His grandsons were a tougher challenge. Fortunately, Kai had asked Shaw the night before to help him teach Scrub a few tricks, and while he sensed this was a ridiculous and pointless pursuit to pass the time, Shaw had admitted to a nagging feeling that days like this with his little brother were going to be increasingly rare, so he simply said "sure."

Grampa stuck his head into the avocado room, or the monkey room, depending on who was referring to it, where he had heard Dax stirring earlier.

"We may have to crack the doors on that boat house, Shags, and take *The Empress Lilly* for a sail."

Dax was in the top bunk, talking to Cody by video feed.

"Love to, Grampa. You name the time."

"Soon's I get the kitchen shipshape, m'boy. Aloha, Cody," Grampa said, slipping out.

"Hear that?" Dax asked. "*The Empress Lilly!* I hope he lets me drive!"

"Yeah, I heard," Cody laughed, "but Dax, if you don't cut your hair soon, you won't be able to steer. It's like you're wearing one of those scrubby palm trees from your Grampa's backyard. I mean, you could do dreads if you wanted to."

Dax yawned, nice and long. "Maybe I *should* do dreads. Unless you know a cute girl who cuts hair."

Cody smirked, but then his brow knit, casting his eyes in shadow.

"So what do you think it means? The moon?"

"I dunno," Dax answered. "I think we just have to wait for —"

Scrub's croaky barking filled the room as he and Kai burst in.

"Kai, keep your werewolf quiet. I'm talking to Cody!"

"'Lo-ha, Cody!" Kai shouted.

Cody laughed. Having no siblings, he was very fond of the boy.

"Aloha, Kai!"

Kai leaned into view, his eyes darting about to take in the stars and plasma nebulas painted on the wall behind Cody.

"Are you still sick? I like your galaxy!"

Dax darted an icy glare at the tyke, but it was lost on him as he was completely riveted on the video feed.

"Sorry . . ." Dax muttered.

But Cody didn't mind; he knew Kai was asking a real question, with no pretense at all.

"Yes, I am, Kai, but I hope to get better. It's good to see you."

"You will! I pray for you every night! Bye!" Kai shouted, then disappeared under the bunk, as Scrub pounced on him.

Both Dax and Cody were stunned.

"That's very nice of him."

"Yeah," Dax responded. "He's weird like that. I should go get breakfast."

"You haven't had breakfast yet! You're lazy as a tark!"

"Okay! BOINK!"

They laughed. 'Boink' had no real-world translation, but "We're *both* stupid and proud, goodbye!" came close. As an insult, it was a much more affectionate term than 'Tark' – the name of a tiny frog discovered in a Brazilian rainforest around 2060, having the distinction of crawling like a turtle and releasing a potently nauseating scent when threatened.

Cody waved as his feed blinked out. Dax sat there for a minute, thinking about a whole swirl of things. Then he slid off the top bunk and looked underneath, where Kai was rubbing Scrub's belly. The bandage had been redressed recently – probably Shaw.

"What?" Kai asked, as Dax's stare was hard to read.

"Nothin'," Dax responded. "Do you really pray for Cody every night?"

Kai shrugged, innocently. "Sure. Why wouldn't I?"

Dax rubbed the sleep from one eye and chuckled.

"Come here."

"Why?"

"'Cause I don't want to get Scrub's drool all over my face."

Kai pushed away from his bed and stood facing Dax, who leaned forward, wrapped his arms around him and hugged him tight.

"Hey!" Kai protested, punctuating every syllable. "Why are you hugging me?"

"Just because," Dax responded quietly. "'Cause you're a good guy."

"That's weird," Kai said. Dax laughed and gave him an even bigger squeeze, producing a yelp and a perplexed snort from Scrub. Releasing Kai, he caught the scent of scrambled eggs and oregano and darted out of the avocado-monkey room to take on the day.

His parents had already assembled an array of information sources on the back-porch feed, where Grampa had set up a buffet of delicacies for breakfast. Dax kissed his mom and hugged his dad from behind, lingering for a second to whisper in his ear.

"Dad, can we talk for a second?"

Evan hesitated briefly, then caught a look from Dayna that meant '*Go talk.*' So he stretched and stood up, snagging two pineapple spears and handing one to his son.

"Let's check the swells."

Walking barefoot toward the ocean, the wind gently buffeting their cheeks, Dax was quiet. He started to say something twice, and finally his dad stopped and sat in the sand. The rumbling, over-and-over-again whoosh of breaking waves was intoxicating. Dax sat beside him.

"Don't ever forget how blessed you are to have enjoyed all this, Son. I know it sounds crazy, but an awful lot of people never even get to *see* the ocean. For most of your life so far, you've lived like you're a part of it. You were practically born of the sea."

"Yeah."

"So, what are we not talking about?" his father prodded. "Worried about this big move?"

"It's not making me all happy inside, but I'm not worried about it." Dax fell mute briefly, then added softly, "I was thinking about Cody."

His father nodded. "He's not getting better, is he?"

"If we move I won't be able to just come and see him. At least nowhere near as often."

Evan nodded. He remembered how intense friendships were when he was a teenager. And somehow, in the course of growing up and growing apart, pain always followed.

"Dad, I don't know who else comes to see him besides Dr. Lautrec. And unless something changes, in six months—"

The boy's face flushed hot, his throat tightening up. Evan put an arm around Dax's shoulders, and that strong firm grip somehow absorbed both his fears and profound sadness and diminished their power. He found his voice again.

"Can I stay here? If Grampa's okay with it? Just until . . ."

"Until you've been the very best friend he could have," his father finished, perfectly.

Dax looked up with a quick, silent nod, his eyes shiny.

"Yeah, if your mom's okay with it. And she loves Cody, so I don't think you'll get any argument there."

Dax embraced his father, who ran a hand through his thick locks.

"But you're past due for a haircut, young man. Soon."

Dax laughed in surrender, revealing his gleaming, pearly teeth. He was mostly a smirking sort, but when he *really* smiled, it was bright and infectious.

"Deal."

Suddenly there was shouting; it was Dayna. And then it was Dayna *and* Shaw, screaming for their attention.

"Get back here! HURRY!"

October 17, 2077

Dax and his father sprinted all the way from the beach to Grampa's terrace, where they found everyone else staring in utter shock at a single newsfeed image coming from Canada.

The nervous anchor was an unfamiliar face, but they all recognized the main delegate hall of LAMIGA, the Legislative Assembly for Mediation, Intervention and Global Amity. This body had been established as a new alliance for international diplomacy when 62 countries disbanded from the United Nations as a result of the horrific terrorist waves of the early 2020's and the Pirate Wars that emerged in the decades following. This new body settled in Vancouver and had since absorbed most of the other nations who had held membership in the UN, which lost its authority, influence, and finally its funding in the course of two short years. Thus far, LAMIGA's efficacy as a force for peace proved substantially more pronounced than its New York predecessor, but that was also its mandate: to effectively resolve cultural and interstate disputes, and to be preemptive wherever possible in issues like hunger, natural disasters and pandemics. Evan had testified there on a few occasions, famously addressing the entire assembly at the end of the Pirate Wars with his summation of the costs, losses and victories. While generally its day-to-day business was not of much interest to the popular media, today would be quite the exception.

For there, onscreen, was the sweeping, curving auditorium where delegates from nearly two hundred nations regularly met; and on the elliptically-shaped stage, hovering just above the floor were three bright, swirling balls of water, each about four meters in diameter.

The nervous anchor read her copy with evident anxiety, her jittery eyes tracing the information back and forth on her teleprompter as if she were watching a ping-pong match.

"Just moments ago, these strange objects appeared here, forming out of thin air in the main hall of LAMIGA," she stated. "Delegates are still arriving. Some, present when the phenomena appeared, fled the hall immediately, but others have taken their seats with cautious curiosity, as security forces have entered to form a buffer between the stage and any onlookers. We now have the President of LAMIGA with us, David Ben Tayeb."

A tanned, husky man with coarse white hair appeared in an adjacent window on the screen, smiling but clearly distracted.

"President Tayeb, do you think this event has anything to do with the strange markings on the moon of late?"

Gracefully, her guest deflected with all the specificity of a broad paintbrush soaked in white paint.

"That, of course, is possible, but to speculate would be unwise at this—"

He spun around as the entire hall behind him flooded with what seemed a deep blue light. At the center, the floating 'aqua-spheres' glowed brightly for a few seconds. As they dimmed, no one spoke, for now those orbs of water hosted three graceful, colorful figures, though for the moment they were mere silhouettes.

"Holy poopbeans, Dad," Dax whispered in amazement. "Those are . . ." He blinked. "What *are* those?"

"It was them," Dayna whispered with astonishment.

When it was clear nobody understood what she meant, she glanced around. "The symbol on the moon. Look at them."

Onscreen, while the anchor babbled, the camera angles switched again and again, revealing what seemed oddly familiar and fantastically different all at once.

The three beings bore some resemblance to large dolphins, but with two dorsal fins each, not one. Bold markings swirled and wrapped elegantly about their bodies, reminiscent of the patterns on orcas, though instead of black and white, each had their own pairing of two colors – one dominant and slightly glowing, the other darker. Rather than inky black marbles, the large eyes of these creatures shone just enough to make them all the more mysterious.

"Look at their pectoral fins," Shaw observed. "They're articulated, almost like evolving arms."

Grampa was leaning so far toward the feed he looked like he was going to fall over.

"I never thought I'd see it in my lifetime," he cooed, with all the atavistic awe of a little boy. "We've searched and searched and finally been visited by intelligent life. Hot dog!"

"Can you swim in outer space?" Kai asked.

"No, buddy," Shaw answered. "Chances are they come from a world that's mostly ocean. Those water balls? My guess is they sent 'em ahead so they could breathe when they got here."

"But *how* did they get here?" Dayna asked aloud to no one in particular. "We would have tracked any incoming—" But she froze, as the alien in the middle, barely moving its mouth, somehow made itself heard – and according to the news anchor, the voice was simultaneously broadcasting across numerous frequencies in six different languages.

"We extend sincere salutations, humans of Earth."

"They speak English!" Kai shouted.

Dax leaned in, squinting at the screen.

"Is he shaking?" he muttered. "It looks like he's shaking."

"SHH!" came the response from everyone, except Kai.

"Doubtless you have seen the images in your moon, designed to gain your attention as an initial gesture of peace. If these efforts provoked fear, you have our sincerest apologies."

Everyone in the family admired their softly glimmering colors and the way their bodies simply bobbed in place, perfectly upright. Though alien and animalistic, there was a regal quality to these beings, and though it might have been the novelty of their appearance, it was nearly impossible to take your eyes off them.

"I am known as Yol Prevek," the enigmatic visitor continued. "I am the chosen delegate from a world regarded by our kind as 'Q'or', known to you as Delvus-3 in the large Magellanic Cloud System. To my left is Ke'Yol Vren, and this other is Yol Beyyos. For thousands of years, our civilization has flourished in isolation, but no longer. And this change in condition has provoked our aspirations to attain—"

And then the entire feed went *black*.

Every member of the Zander family, and Milo's unseen crew next door, screamed out in frustration.

"Fred!" Grampa Pat shouted, "reconnect!"

"There is nothing wrong with our connection, Patrick. The signal has been terminated at the broadcast source."

100

Dayna glanced at Evan. His slight nod affirmed whatever unspoken suspicions she had. This did not go unnoticed by Shaw, who sidled up next to Dax and growled, "Dad's D.C. buddies again. They don't want any outsiders at the party."

"How d'you know?" Dax asked in a hushed tone.

"Cause that's what they do, Daxer. That's what they always do." He stuffed his hands in his pockets and grew still, until both heard Grampa clear his throat just behind them. Certain he had been listening in, both boys braced themselves for a lecture.

Instead, Grampa just shook his head in bitter agreement.

"You're probably right, Shaw. Soon as the big dogs get to Washington, they end up acting like we can't think for ourselves and start doing it for us, whether we like it or not."

They turned to look for Dad – but he was already heading toward the beach, discretely squeezing his earlobe to activate the tiny audio tap implanted there. The boys saw this as a telltale sign he was about to make a very private call, as he almost always used the com unit on his sleeve. Grampa kept his voice low, so just the boys could hear.

"They're gonna swear those delegates to secrecy and the whole world's gonna have to wait to hear what our new friends had to say. But you fellas are lucky, 'cause your dad's gonna know an awful lot inside just a few minutes, and you're gonna know everything *he* does a few minutes after that."

They looked around. Their mother was ambling briskly up the staircase to the rooftop terrace, already in an urgent, whispered conversation. Out on the sand, his bare feet sloshed again and again with foam as he paced down the shore, their dad was also chatting intensely with someone, determined to get answers.

And though it took longer than a few minutes, both their parents indeed learned a lot more about *something*, but it turned out Grampa wasn't quite as correct where the rest of his prediction was concerned.

. . .

Within hours of the event in Vancouver, it was as if their parents had become strangers. Well into the evening, the captain and Dr. Zander had been on multiple calls but would not share with the family whom they had talked to. Shaw grew more and more irritated as the minutes and hours ticked by; his mom and dad had to tell them *something*, and obviously they knew a lot more than just 'something.' Every plea for them to share had been met with a response to the effect of, "I just can't say much right now," or, "None of the experts are very sure what's going on." An uneasy and – for Dax – agonizing silence endured for hours, until dinner, when Grampa dished out lasagna. It was Gramma Redtree's recipe and he was achingly faithful in replicating it. Dax loved Italian food more than any other sort, so this was a welcome distraction.

Grampa set Kai up at a little table on the sand, where he could eat outside with Scrub and the two could get as messy as they pleased. The sea lion, healing up well, had become the boy's nearly inseparable shadow, and tonight this would be useful, as Scrub would keep Kai happily distracted from the rest of the family and what Grampa expected to be a tumultuous conversation. So though the lad glanced over every once in a while, or begged everyone to watch as he fed Scrub a sardine, for the most part he was in his own little world.

Grampa waited patiently, till everyone was smiling again, savoring the luxuriant layers of cheese and long-marinating sauce. When it seemed he'd gained some good will via their taste buds, he set down his large mug of coconut root beer and cleared his throat.

"Dayna, Evan, your kids deserve to know that the world isn't going to end tomorrow. That much, at least."

Dax's father and mother stared back at Grampa Pat, then at each other, and finally Evan spoke.

"Nobody here can repeat what we share."

Dayna looked over at the fence separating them from the neighbors and gestured for him to speak softly. He nodded.

"Come on, Mom!" Shaw exclaimed. "You're worried about Mister Keener hearing?"

She shot him a look as their father continued, even more quietly.

"No, the world's not ending. Not tomorrow or as far as we know, at all." He paused, as though considering whether he was breaking some taboo, then went on. "The Delvans' next words were 'this change in condition has provoked our aspirations – to attain your friendship.'"

"Whoa!" Dax said, "Wait'll I tell—" and the look from his father was so penetrating he nearly choked on his own words. "Nobody. I won't tell anybody."

"Not even Cody," his mother added, to which Dax nodded obediently, if reluctantly.

"Dad, they actually said that?" Shaw asked. "They came all this way to be friends?"

"It's what they said."

Grampa was twirling cheese around and around on his fork, just listening and thinking.

"So what then *do* they want?" he asked, quietly.

A palpable chill fell over everyone, as if Grampa's question had thudded down on the table like a huge mallet. The evasive lack of eye contact from Dayna and Evan didn't help.

"They want to be our friends, Dad," Dayna offered, in an almost condescending tone.

"Uh huh," he replied. "Remember when you were six and you painted the toilet seat purple and I asked you if you did it? You looked just like you do now."

"It's the truth."

"But they *want* something."

Her lips pursed shut.

"Dad," Shaw pressed, "is there anything bad about what's happened that we should know? I know you can't share everything, but should we be worried?"

"We?" his father asked.

"Dad, you know what I mean. Is this planet in any danger?"

"We covered this, Shaw. The Delvans mean us no harm."

"Who decided we'd call them 'Delvans'?" Grampa Pat asked.

"Dad," Dayna answered haltingly, "we . . . can't say much more."

Dax caught the new tension in his grandfather's face, an expression betraying his sense that something was being withheld from them all. But for whatever reason, Grampa Pat wasn't pushing any further. Maybe that was what you did when you got older – you didn't push.

Dax, however, was thirteen.

"Honestly, Dad. What do they want? We're supposed to believe they came all this way to say, 'Hi, let's be friends?'"

Shaw turned to him, offering a subtle '*attaboy*' nod, which took Dax off-guard. Kudos from his big brother were rare. Their father, though, was not biting. Instead, he took a deep breath and pushed away from the table.

"Your mother and I have to head back. There's some business to organize, an engineering evaluation to determine what upgrades happen before the seabase is transitioned for other use, protocols to brush up on in advance of all that, and then . . ." His voice trailed off, which is when Dax, Shaw and Grampa knew he was making at least part of this up. Their mother picked up the slack.

"You know what? I heard a joke!"

Everyone just stared at her, including her husband. Even Kai perked up from the sandpit he and Scrub were digging, as a joke from his mom was a rare event.

"Mom," Shaw sighed incredulously, "now?"

"I wanna hear, Mommy!" Kai declared. She beamed with pleasure, clearing her throat.

"Why did the anemometer and the barometer call it quits?"

She looked about earnestly to their puzzled faces, Kai's especially registering confusion.

"What's a nammanometer?" he asked meekly. Grampa started to reply, but fell silent.

"A tool that measures wind speed, Kai," Shaw observed dryly, "especially *hot* winds."

Valiantly joining her flagging effort, Evan piped up, loud and jovial:

"I give up? Why did the anemometer and the barometer call it quits?"

"One was moving too fast," Dayna quipped, "and the other felt pressured!"

Mystified, Kai blinked and turned to rejoin Scrub in the sand.

"Oh, Mom," Dax chuckled sadly, shaking his head. But Shaw was anything but amused. He sat up, weary of games.

"Dad, Mom, come on, what's going on?" he implored, with a look to his parents that pleaded, '*I'm an adult now; respect me!*'

His father turned purposefully to Grampa Pat.

"It's okay if the boys stay with you for a few days, Patrick?"

Either unwilling or unable to mask disappointment in his daughter and son-in-law, Grampa Pat murmured a soft, "Sure thing. We'll be fine."

Dax observed the whole thing, trying to read between the lines, but there weren't any lines. It was more like a thick tangle of beached kelp, and that was even more frustrating.

Inside of an hour, their parents were heading back to the seabase, leaving a house full of uneasy souls. Grampa tried to engage the boys in some cards, but they were too distracted. Dax had started to toss things into the fire pit to see how they flashed and smoked, while Shaw took a number of calls from friends asking if he knew anything about what had transpired today. Hanging up after a call with Bardy, he groused out loud, kicking the stones under his feet.

"Of course I should know something. Why shouldn't I? My parents know every person on the continent with a lab coat or brass on their shoulders! You'd think they'd trust us a little!"

"It's probably not up to them, Shaw," Grampa chided. "They have their orders; I'll bet from the very top."

"But we're their kids! They've always trusted us before!"

"Shaw . . ." Dax interrupted, "aliens on Earth. Kinda new. Maybe it's for our own good."

Shaw was flustered.

"We shouldn't have anything to fear about the truth. They even took both skimmers, just to make it harder for us to go back without them picking us up. They've locked us out, Dax."

He got up and headed for the beach, his long legs kicking up sand with each step.

"Why's he so mad, Grampa?" Dax asked. "He's mad a lot lately."

"'Cause he's a grownup, Daxer. And your mom and dad aren't treating him like one."

"They didn't tell you anything, though, and you're . . ." He almost said "a lot older" but hit the brakes and re-thought before it came out, ". . . a grownup."

"You're absolutely right," Grampa responded.

Neither said anything for a minute, then the deep scowl on Grampa's face, all the fiercer in the glow of firelight, transformed into an inspired grin. He turned to Dax.

"Wanna take Miss Lilly out tomorrow? We kinda got interrupted today. You can even take the helm for a while."

Dax's buoyant expression matched his grandfather's, and then some.

"Yeah!"

"Okay. Help me straighten up and let's get some shuteye."

. . .

Grampa Pat quietly swept the paving stones around the patio, humming some little tune which Dax couldn't make out but which nevertheless made the old man's sweeping more of a dance than a chore. Wiping down the backyard dining table, Dax thought how the world had changed that day, how his parents had taken to behaving like strangers, and how it gave him the odd sense that he and his brothers were not currently welcome at their own home. For now, he was content to wait on better answers. Tomorrow he'd wear a captain's hat and maybe even get a few minutes at the helm of Grampa's most prized possession, one of the boy's favorite things to do in the world. He could practically feel the salt wind whipping at his cheeks already.

"I'll finish, Grampa. You cooked and washed stuff. I got it. Seriously."

Grampa didn't protest at all. He ruffled Dax's hair, very proud, then grabbed the last pineapple spear still on the table.

"Y'know. I'm gettin' kinda used to it."

"Oh, yeah?" Dax replied, aware Grampa meant his wild tangle of blond locks.

"Yeah, it's okay. It reminds me life has a lot more flavor with some 'wild' in it."

Patrick Redtree sauntered off into the house, the zip in his steps lighter than it had been most of the day. But for the soft crush of waves somewhat distant, it seemed too quiet for Dax.

"Fred! How 'bout some reggae?"

"Sure, Dax! Please let me know if the selections do not suit you."

But Fred had by now learned his taste in music quite well, and the buoyant, percussive melody flowing throughout the backyard met with Dax's hearty approval. His cleaning up took on a brisker pace, scooping up dishes and cups left over from dessert, his hips and lanky legs kicking generously to the rollicking beat.

Suddenly he realized Shaw was behind him, laughing.

"I should broadcast this everywhere."

Never breaking stride, Dax waved handfuls of mugs to the music.

"Go ahead, mon! I was born to d'islands, mon!"

Shaw shook his head, grabbing a couple of plates, and they started toward the kitchen.

"You are the weirdest ever."

Right on the beat, Dax swung his back leg to kick Shaw in the butt.

"You get to do that *once*," Shaw said, "and then I bury you up to your neck in the sand and we wait to see how high the tide gets."

"Sure, mon. I got gills in me ears, mon. You kin cover me with water and I'll breathe with me ears!"

Maybe it wasn't *that* funny, but Shaw laughed again. He spun around with his own leg and kicked his brother's rear. In doing so a plate slipped from his grasp, but Dax swerved around to snag it in the crook of his elbow.

"Whoa!" both brothers shouted, impressed.

"Easy on the crockery!" called Grampa's voice from inside.

Shaw's jaw was still hanging open.

"How did you—"

"I just saw your kick coming," Dax explained, "and from the other side of my brain I could see you losing your grip."

"*The other side of your brain?*" Shaw asked.

"It just happens to me . . ."

And then his eyes glazed over a bit, slowing mid-stride.

"Dax?"

"Shaw, we're so dumb."

"Speak for yourself, blondie. I read three books a week."

"All we did was get mad about everything. I bet there's a lot more we can learn. We just gotta go back and look again. At everything."

Shaw scowled, momentarily perplexed. Dax just grinned at him – intent on coaxing him to a new thought.

"Oh! You're a genius!"

Dax shrugged happily, resisting the impulse to agree.

"Fred! Enough music!" Dax called out. "Can you play back today's press conference footage from LAMIGA before the blackout?"

There was an odd beat of silence. Usually Fred's responses came right away. Finally:

"Access to retrieve that footage has been blocked from all public servers."

"Blocked?" Shaw responded, "What do you mean, Fred? Blocked where?"

"That data has been wiped from all public servers, throughout the planet."

Dax and Shaw gazed at each other in dead silence, spooked.

Observation & Inference

Exasperated, Dax paced in a little circle. "I can't believe they'd keep everyone from accessing the files! That's sort of an invasion of privacy or something."

"No," Shaw affirmed with a deep scowl, "it *is* an invasion of—"

But Fred piped up with an unexpected glint of hope.

"If I may elaborate, the footage in question was erased from all public servers with openly registered sockets. However, twelve years ago, your grandfather created an emergency redundant drive for backups of critical data, in the event of severe weather or tsunami. It is purposely unregistered. But Patrick had the password encrypted."

"Is that against the law?" Dax whispered to Shaw.

"Who cares?" his brother answered. "So, Fred, do you think you can crack the encryption and retrieve the footage?"

"As I was about to explain, Shaw, it took me a few seconds, but I have the password."

Dax and Shaw high-fived each other with a muted "yes!"

"Fred!" Dax said, "Please play the footage from LAMIGA until just before the Delvans arrive, and prepare to loop any of their stuff at one-quarter normal speed."

"Their stuff? I presume you mean any footage containing images of the visitors in question?"

Dax rolled his eyes.

"Come on, Fred . . ."

"Very well. I will display the 'stuff' you requested."

"I think Fred was trying to be funny," Shaw chuckled.

In the backyard, both brothers sat in the soft grass, watching the liquid orbs hovering in place above the LAMIGA stage, the surfaces undulating just slightly with tiny ripples, shimmering . . .

"The surface, where it borders with air. Is it glowing?" Dax asked. Shaw stood up and leaned into the image.

"Maybe. Could be a reflection of some stage lights. Fred! Pause playback. Were there multiple broadcast feeds for 3Sixty archiving?"

"Yes. They reside as five supplementary files, synchronous to this one. But this system does not facilitate simultaneous feeds from multiple angles."

"Grampa . . ." Shaw groaned. "Almost to the twenty-second century, and he doesn't have a 3D monitor?"

"He says 3Sixty gives him headaches."

Shaw sniffed. So much for getting a better look.

"Cody's got a 3Sixty system," Dax said. "He has to have it for when his doctor does a remote exam, but he's allowed to use it for games and movies and stuff."

"Okay," Shaw said, "but it's late and Cody's probably asleep by now. Can we—?"

He looked at the water orbs, intensely curious, and his eyes lit up.

"Fred. Can you switch every eighth of a second between feeds, one, two, three, four, five, six? So that we are seeing angles sequentially?"

"I'll attempt a version of what you request," Fred responded, in his smooth, diplomatic tone. "If you're not satisfied, please indicate how to adjust."

Then, the images flickered, like a very old movie, but they were treated to an amazing, constantly shifting perspective of the object. It was 'almost' three-dimensional in appearance, though technically a flat, projected image.

The water orbs did seem to shimmer consistently on all sides, subtle speckles of light holding in the volume.

"It's an energy field. Force field. But . . ."

Dax looked at his brother. "But?"

"Why use that? Why not broadcast from a ship, where they'd be safer?"

"The bubbles arrived before they showed up," Dax suggested. "Maybe it's safe. Maybe this is how they travel. Or they thought people would notice more if they came in person?"

"Or all of the above. I guess it beats having to go through two webs of satellites. But, Dax, this means . . ."

Shaw's flesh tingled at the possibility.

"This means they could have wormhole technology. They've figured out how to travel through cosmic strings. Or even *create* them to suit their needs. Or something like that."

Dax nodded.

"Yeah. Pretty chewy."

Shaw sat, absorbing this.

"Imagine traveling through space without even needing a ship."

For a moment, they didn't speak, as the footage kept flickering and turning before them. Shaw released a low, contemplative "hmm," pacing back and forth.

"I'd like to know what the composition of that liquid is, if it *is* liquid. Fred! Can you do a spectral analysis of the chemical content of the liquid based on the recorded image?"

"I'm sorry, Shaw. I would be merely guessing, and there are hundreds of possibilities as to its composition, assuming only chemicals currently known to us."

Shaw wasn't giving up. "Okay, let's see Larry, Moe and Curly again."

"Larry, Moe and Curly?"

Dax chuckled, more that his brother had relaxed so much he was making dumb jokes than at the pun itself.

"Fred," he instructed, "please move forward at quarter speed so we can see the aliens – the Delvans – beaming in and out."

"I'm not sure I comprehend your use of 'beaming', Dax."

Shaw laughed.

"So now we know Fred is not a *Stooges* or 'Star Trek' fan. Fred! Please incorporate the first few seconds of the transition from where no aliens are visible, to a few frames past where the visitors in their respective positions are *completely* visible. Let's loop that sequence."

And they watched, as very slowly, a core shape of energy about the same mass of each lifeform began to bubble and burn brightly within the connected orbs – soon replaced by a fully formed creature.

"They're so beautiful," Shaw whispered. Dax simply nodded in awestruck agreement. "Okay, no visible gills."

"So they probably breathe air, like mammals on Earth?" Dax asked.

"Can't assume anything based on what we know of our species here," Shaw answered. "We don't even know what 'air' might mean to them. Let's just observe and maybe it'll add up to something."

"Their color patterns are kind of like orcas, but prettier," Dax observed.

Shaw raised a thoughtful eyebrow.

"I know," Dax murmured, "they're not related to orcas."

"Hopefully they don't bite like orcas, either."

"It was a pilot whale."

"Oh, right," Shaw said, chewing his lower lip. "Well, who knows. The universe is full of mystery, and orcas have been here a lot longer than us. But it offers a baseline for comparison."

"Wait!" Dax exclaimed, pointing at the image excitedly. "Two tones! Each of them has two color tones."

"Yeah, good. And they all have two dorsal flukes. Like, an anterior and . . . not really posterior, but . . ." Shaw's voice faded out.

"Secondary?" Dax suggested. His brother nodded agreeably.

"They might not both be dorsals. One could be a reservoir for something."

"Like a camel's hump?" Dax asked.

"Yeah, but on our planet sea creatures have critical organs and other functioning tissue in all kinds of places."

Dax squinted, his head cocking back and forth.

"Maybe it just helps them stay that much more fixed on target. Like an extra fin on a longboard. Wait—"

He leaned in as close as he could to the flickering image.

"Fred," Dax requested, "freeze, enlarge by 400 percent and—"

Fred's voice interrupted him.

"Could you please indicate, by drawing a circle with your finger, which section you would care to prioritize?"

Dax did so, and instantly they were examining an enhanced look at that same part of the alien's anatomy, with surprising clarity. Instinctively, Shaw drew closer, already intrigued with what had drawn his brother's attention.

"What are those?" Shaw murmured wonderingly.

Along the leading edge of the front dorsal fin, from where it met the body up to the very tip, was a line of tiny slits. A few bore traces of something resembling a thick liquid.

"They're not gills. Too tiny to be of any use," Dax said.

"Well . . . yeah, that's a good guess. Look here and here, like little beads of oily goo, coming out of a few of those not-gills. Molecularly it has to be of a different substance than the liquid they're suspended in, otherwise it would dissolve immediately."

"So their bodies produce something on the dorsal fin, maybe the other fins – the parts of their body that cut through currents and help them steer," Dax added, his brow tightly knit.

Then, he brightened.

"Oily! Wax! It makes them faster! Slicker!"

"Maybe . . ." Shaw mused. "Most fish produce some kind of lubricant to protect them from predators, but it also makes their movements super-efficient. Marine mammals don't, but we're dealing with beings that have almost certainly been evolving a lot longer. They might have adopted traits from other species over time."

Dax sat back and grinned.

"I bet we already know more about them than Mom and Dad know," he remarked, proudly. Shaw was moving the image about now, studying sections of the aliens' anatomy.

"Their pectorals look kinda like arms," Shaw said with a little yawn, "but the extensions past the last major joint don't seem made for any real dexterity."

Dax shook his head.

"College messed you up. Why can't you just say, 'They don't have hands'?"

"Specificity's a tool of science, little brother. Every detail counts."

"Fine. Then another thing is, they're all different sizes. The dark one is the biggest."

"Well, that might have something to do with age," Shaw added, "or it might just be these are the three who showed up for this visit."

"All of their eyes glow," Dax observed. "Creepy but kinda cool, too."

"Creepy and cool are subjective descriptors, but, yeah, they glow. That might mean their native habitat is so dark they need to provide their own light."

Shaw abruptly stood, rolling his shoulders and stretching his arms to shake off fatigue, the time difference between Miami and Hawaii starting to hit home.

"Fred! Ramp playback to full speed and extend the loop to the end of the available clip, will you?"

"What is it?" Dax asked, searching the flickering projections intently.

"Watch."

And they did. As the images returned to normal speed, something became more obvious – a detail they'd somehow missed the first time in all the excitement.

Each of the creatures had a primary and secondary color in the elegant patterns sweeping across their bodies – and on each of those bodies, only one of

112

those colors glowed softly. Shaw's eyes tightened, scrutinizing every little change.

"Their eyes and bodies both emit their own light. I bet they live in a very deep place. No sunlight or ultraviolet light of any kind."

"That big one," Dax added, "his colors are darker but he's also not glowing as much."

"If bigger means older, maybe the potency of their bioluminescence is in inverse proportion to tissue mass. Or it just dulls with age. Their heads seem larger than orcas or any species of dolphin on Earth." He looked at Dax with a raised eyebrow. "A little like pilot whales. Or pygmy sperm whales. And then, that largest one – his head is way bigger in proportion to his body than the other two."

Dax yawned. "Yeah, he said his name was 'Prevek.' We should call Mom and Dad in the morning and tell them all the stuff we figured out."

"Let's wait. We're guessing at a lot. And so far, even if all our guesses are right, none of it tells us why they've come to Earth. Or how."

Shaw glanced back to see his brother, on his back, spread out on the grass.

"You're tired already? Wow."

Dax was already thinking how comfortable the hammock had been and how perfectly the warm night breeze was rolling through. Nevertheless . . .

"No way, Haole!" he laughed, despite Shaw knowing better.

"This is what science is all about, Dax. Observing. Observation and inference. Over and over again, until our eyes see something they didn't, all the times before."

"I know! I observe stuff all the time," Dax huffed, unwilling to concede on a rare night of doing anything interesting with his big brother. Still, he suspected it wouldn't be long before his eyelids betrayed him.

"Fred!" Dax called out, "can you have the Swisher make some coffee? With milk, agave, maybe some mint?"

Shaw raised an eyebrow; that *did* sound good.

"Fred, please make two, but instead of milk I'll have some of Grampa's hazelnut cream."

Fred sounded almost chipper.

"Your beverages will be piping hot, available in the kitchen approximately three minutes from now, gentlemen."

Dax giggled, the late hour perhaps unhinging his funny bone.

"Fred called us 'gentlemen.'"

113

"Yeah, because obviously he can't smell you," Shaw said, before turning his attention back to the recording. "Please slow the loop back to half-speed, Fred."

As the footage continued, hanging in the air like an apparition, they scrutinized it. With the help of a little coffee, they studied it well into the night, murmuring on and on. Learning.

. . .

A little after dawn, Grampa found both of them snoring in the backyard, the LAMIGA footage mystifyingly still looping in mid-air. Dax had somehow managed to roll into a bed of smooth stones under a broad redwood bench, while Shaw's body and half his face were pressed into the dewy grass.

"For cryin' out loud," Grampa muttered. "Fred, turn off the broadcast."

"Look, Shaw's got a bug!" Kai observed, pointing to the ladybug currently exploring the freckled valley between Shaw's shoulder blades.

Grampa let out a throaty cackle worthy of a pirate, leading the boy back inside. "Hey, ya wanna have some fun?"

Kai's head bobbed enthusiastically.

A few moments later an impromptu band concert of clamorous brass pots and pans roused Dax and Shaw from their slumber, played with vigorous glee by Kai and Grampa Pat, as Scrub's cold nose snuggled Dax's cheek. He pushed the creature away, moaning, not sure if the slick, stale drool on his arm was his or the animal's.

"Whyyyyyy?"

"You fellas are not spending another day staring at news clips, hypothesizing about the mating habits of our pretty alien visitors," Grampa declared. "After breakfast I'm gonna run to the doctor and once I get back, we're gonna get a little salt up our noses and some wind blowing through our hair. Maybe even catch a few fish."

"Doctor?" Dax yawned. "Are you okay?"

"Yeah, I get a checkup twice a year, mid-April and mid-October. You get older, you gotta keep track of things. Now get yourself in motion, m'boy! You too, Shaw! Come on, they've already had lunch in Miami!"

As if refusing to recognize their presences, Shaw spit some grass from his mouth, pushed up off the ground with a grunt and marched into the house. Dax finally poked halfway out from under the bench, squinting, the fiery blast of sunlight briefly obscuring anything else. He shook himself, while Grampa and Kai laughed and continued to pound on their makeshift drums.

"Not funny," he said, his tongue still so numb he slurred his words. "If there's a black hole of funny, you guys are way, wayyy inside."

At this, they howled even harder. Smacking his dry, sticky lips, Dax turned to the ocean – the pounding surf calling with a promise of renewal. Rolling onto his backside, he stretched with a grand yawn, then ambled across the sand to the water and dove in with a wild scream.

Grampa winked at his little companion.

"Mission accomplished, Kai. You too, Scrub. Now how about some waffles! Go ask Fred for the ingredients and start mixing!"

Kai shot back into the house, eager to play chef, Scrub close behind in a boisterous, up- and-down gallop. Grampa shook his head and headed for the boathouse. His daughter had saddled him with three boys fueled to the brim with energy and attitude and given him no idea as to how long they'd be in his care.

Just before stepping inside, he glanced out to the shoreline where Dax was body surfing, erupting from the waves like a dolphin with a radioactively-bright blond mane. Grampa's hearty chuckle shook his whole frame; he hadn't been this happy in a very long time. Entering the large, quiet boathouse, he found *The Empress Lilly* waiting for him, her sleek, lacquered wood hull gleaming in the hazy light that fell from windows all along the ceiling. He remembered how Maggie had resisted the idea of buying a vintage boat until she saw it with her own eyes. This particular model, dating back to 1964, was a classic even by collectible Chris-Craft standards, but had been modified by its original owner to afford more room for passengers and storage fore and aft. Though he was nervous about the expense, the rapt expression on her face affirmed his instincts. It was Maggie who named her, and she came up with something fairly obscure – a memory from her childhood trips to Disneyland. The name *The Empress Lilly* was fitting, at once regal and old fashioned. In the years since, they'd taken many moonlight cruises, surveying the islands from about a kilometer out, catching sight of whales breaching in the black and silver ocean. He'd always taken good care of her, but since Maggie's passing he had lavished even more attention to keeping this vessel pristine. Sharing it with his grandsons on a day like today – what better way to ensure that someday one of them would keep her sweet and shiny?

He sighed, his heart full.

"Hey, there, Lilly."

. . .

Several time zones away, in a small but elegantly appointed room, Dayna and Evan Zander sat patiently, the faint track of classical music oddly dissonant to their shared unrest. Her husband had been summoned to Washington many times, but she was more used to giving him a goodbye kiss and busying herself in the labs until his return, at which point Evan would take her to an expensive dinner on the mainland – his way of politely avoiding mention of any top-secret affairs that might have been discussed.

This time, however, was quite different: they had both been 'invited' with an urgency that demanded they board a late-night flight from Honolulu to Dulles International Airport.

Forty minutes had passed since their arrival. Boredom, fatigue and an itchy anxiety taking their toll, she surveyed the art nouveau plasterwork lining the domed ceiling. Looking around, Dayna was about to point out how the Georgian furniture was an awkward match, but she had a strong aversion to small talk. Her husband, meanwhile, was immersed in the pages of a thick, leather-bound book chronicling the life of the legendary Admiral Heihachiro Togo. Perhaps set on the table as a decorative element, it had likely not been opened in years.

"You've got to be wondering why he wanted *both* of us here," she finally said aloud.

"Easton knows us both pretty well, honey. You've impressed a lot of people in this town with your work on the new beam-cookers. Maybe they have a new opportunity for you."

Her brow darkened. She turned to him, her voice low.

"You don't think they're holding those aliens and want to . . ."

He saw the look on her face, and reached out to touch her hand.

"Want to what?"

"Evan, if they ask me to join some scientific team to slice them open and —"

"Dayna, no," he said with a quick laugh, "the military doesn't do that sort of thing." And then he caught her glare. "Well, not *anymore*. And you know Easton would never be a part of anything remotely close to that, much less ask you to be involved."

She sighed anxiously, but let it drop. Hopefully nothing sinister was afoot. They had known Easton Russell for years, long before his appointment by the President to chairman of the Joint Chiefs of Staff, even well before his promotion to general. Dayna knew Evan was right; he wasn't the sort who would lend his approval to the covert dissection of extraterrestrial visitors.

"Well," she said, "if nothing else, it will be nice to see him again."

Evan set the large book down with a deliberate thunk, so she'd be sure to remember the cover, punctuating his words with equal purpose.

"*That* is quite a fine book."

"And *that's* your 'Christmas hint' voice."

His bushy eyebrows shot up, feigning innocence, and she laughed.

"You and your heavy old books. You realize there's a strong chance now that I'll be rummaging shops from San Francisco to Portland, trying to find a copy for your collection."

"I like turning real pages. And this one – Togo was a brilliant, courageous man. He rose to an incredible challenge in Japan's history and rewrote—"

A Naval cadet in full dress entered the room and saluted.

"Captain Zander. Doctor. If you'd please come this way."

They stood. Evan saluted back and they followed the cadet into the next room, where he opened a door into an adjacent, much larger chamber. As they stepped inside, Dayna's breath halted for a nanosecond. She and Evan looked out across the room, stunned.

Their friend was indeed there, but he was by no means alone. Rising from around a circular mahogany table were his Joint Chiefs of Staff, several others whose blank demeanors and dark suits screamed 'covert intelligence,' and at least six uniformed guards. Quite simply, they were standing before the senior officer for every division of the military, the FBI, CIA and probably a few government agencies that were not supposed to exist.

In the center, his chest decorated in a broad array of colorful bars, badges and ribbons, was the chairman, General Russell, a broad shouldered man with a wiry thatch of dark hair turning silver at his temples and eyebrows. He stepped forward with a warm grin.

"Dayna! Evan. Welcome to the Pentagon."

Drifting

Since the month-long celebration of victory at the end of the pirate wars, Evan and Dayna had not been in the presence of this much military brass at one time. And the vibe of the room, while not gloomy or threatening, had thrown the two of them off balance.

"So, I guess this isn't about building a new transit hub on Mars," Dayna said, dryly.

Easton Russell's toothy smile broadened, but he took a step closer, lowering his voice.

"I should have prepared you. I'm sorry," he whispered, his tone both sincere and matter of fact. Evan suspected he'd been apologizing a lot lately. "But – trust me, everyone in this room is here because they deeply respect the two of you. Please, just for a little while, hear us out."

He took Dayna's hand in both of his and she seemed somewhat more at ease. Evan grinned appreciatively and the two men shook hands. The general turned to the others – three women and four men – serving as vice-chairman and the senior officers of the Army, Navy, Marines, Air Force, National Guard and finally NASA, which had been added twenty-six years prior. The Zanders were introduced to the chiefs at the table, and then all took their seats.

Admiral Arlene Landau spoke first. The starry crescent logo on her turquoise jacket, sharing space with several rows of medals, clearly identified her as the ranking commander of NASA's Outpost Missions, but she was no stranger.

"It's good to see you both again. I'm taking lead on this briefing, as it clearly falls under a first contact situation."

Evan's eyes darted to General Russell.

"So, this *is* about the visitors who appeared at LAMIGA? The Delvans?"

"I'm sorry, Evan," the chairman responded, "this whole event is unprecedented and we're scrambling to organize our intel and craft coherent policy. It was important to defer any inquiries until we had you in here with us."

"But why both of us?" Dayna asked. "I'm an engineer and a physicist. Unless I'm building some kind of aquarium for our visitors, I'm not sure why you wanted me to consult on a diplomatic affair. Especially one, no offense intended, that seems to have been dropped into the hands of military strategists."

Dayna felt Evan's hand fall on her knee, a silent but clear request to go easy. Though aware he admired her capacity to observe and swiftly assess all aspects of a situation, Evan had also winced in response to her blunt bedside manner more than once. But from the looks traded about the room, it was evident the chiefs seemed amused, even pleased, with her remark. General Ward Dowling, commandant of the Marine Corps, was around sixty, his rugged face seasoned by a few too many hours in the sun and mud and a lot of laughter with his family. Highly respected and to a fault nonpartisan in his service, he had a confident, articulate way of speaking, firm and reassuring.

"Technically, you're not here to consult, Dr. Zander—"

"Please, I prefer Dayna."

"How we hope to engage you, Dayna, transcends any mere consultation. Frankly, our world is about to change, and the Chairman has pointed out that while the qualities of competency necessary to meet the moment were not present in any single individual, the sum of that proven experience and know-how *did* exist in one unique and trustworthy *couple*."

Easton chimed in.

"Short version: a situation has presented itself with unique challenges. In forecasting potential hurdles, we identified several preparative needs. Among those, we're looking for a strong, respected military commander and a compatible science officer who not only thinks about what's next, but creates it. We're just extremely lucky those two people happened to marry one another."

The Zanders glanced at one another. Dayna gripped Evan's hand, still on her knee. He squeezed back and nodded. After a few seconds of silence, he looked at the array of uniformed commanders and asked the question plainly.

"Right now I think I speak for both of us when I say we're very confused. It sounds like you actually want us to meet these 'visitors.' How about you tell us everything?"

And over the next two hours, that's exactly what happened.

. . .

When Grampa returned from his checkup, he found Shaw and Kai building a three-dimensional puzzle out of tiny magnets; in this case, the Eiffel Tower. As Kai had never been to Paris, he kept adding wings to the sides, and being a good brother, Shaw let him.

"They should do that to the real one!" Grampa said, carrying in a bag of groceries.

Shaw relieved him of the bag, his voice low and just a little tense.

"Everything okay, Grampa?"

Patrick Redtree beamed warmly and hugged the boy's neck.

"I'm fine. A little stiffness in my joints, but no bigger issues. I'm about ready for us to cast off! Where's Daxer?"

"He fell asleep on the beach!" Kai offered, still adding more unsanctioned improvements to his French monument.

"Asleep? Well for cryin' out loud . . ."

He glanced out the window, expecting to catch Dax napping, horizontal in the sand. But he was in fact sitting up, staring out at the sea. Something about his stillness gave Grampa pause.

"Want me to call him in?" Shaw asked.

"No . . ." Grampa said, chewing his lip. "I'll go get him."

Shaw nodded amiably, returning to Kai's grand experiment.

"It doesn't look like the pictures," the lad observed. "Is that okay?"

"Well, you made something new, Kailen," Shaw affirmed. "If anyone wants to see the old boring one, it's still there. But you're almost out of pieces, buddy."

"That's okay," Kai replied. He reached into a box on the floor and lifted a large Godzilla puppet into view. "Now we can wreck it!"

Shaw laughed, sitting back to enjoy the show.

Out on the beach, Dax heard a familiar whistling-huffing sound and looked over his shoulder to see his grandfather approaching. The boy offered a half-hearted wave.

"If you're worried about my visit to the doctor, I came out with flying colors."

Dax sighed, relieved, but far from cheered. Grampa sat beside him.

"I'm glad," Dax said quietly. "That's banga good."

"Something else?" A slight chill swept over Grampa Pat. "Is Cody . . ."

"He's fine. Same. Far as I know."

There was a short silence, overcome slightly by the crashing waves. Patrick Redtree stared between the ocean and his grandson, completely at a loss.

120

"Why don'tcha come inside and have a snack before we —"

"I had a dream."

"Bad dream?"

Dax turned to look him full in the face, and Grampa saw a world of pain behind those eyes. Whatever the boy had experienced had shaken him deeply.

"Nightmare," he nodded, putting an arm around Dax. "I get it."

"Would you be mad if I didn't go today?"

"Well, I dunno, buddy; you've been itchin' to take Lilly out for a spin . . ."

"I feel like I should go over to Cody's. Today."

Grampa swallowed; this must have been some awful nightmare.

"Y'know whatever it was, most of the time, bad dreams are best forgotten. You're all wound up about this whole alien business – and that's the whole world right now – but . . ."

He sighed, those lost, lonely eyes pleading silently.

"Okay," Grampa said reassuringly. "There's a barbecue and a country fair downtown with lots of cartoons and a petting zoo. I'll take your brothers there. You enjoy your day with Cody and tomorrow we'll get our sea legs on proper."

Dax gave him a hug, grateful his grandfather hadn't taken his request too personally.

"Tomorrow for sure!" he promised.

A taxi arrived in half an hour to take the two brothers and Grampa downtown. Shaw shrugged off the change of plans without question, happy to spend time with Grampa and Kai, neither of whom he got to see enough these days.

The disturbing imagery of his dream still weighing heavy on his mind, Dax headed to the garage and grabbed Shaw's 'drifter' – basically a skateboard lined with induction coils designed to interface with public, maglev pathways. Years before, many cities had taken the plunge to embed existing walkways with electromagnetic bands, essentially creating a series of solar powered community tracks, polarized for maglev propulsion. In turn, a host of entrepreneurs had developed a diversity of affordable, 'floating' tech compatible with the new sidewalks. Devices like the drifter and Grampa's SilverSled – a much larger and sturdier piece of hardware – provided fun new 'cruising' options for young people, and greater mobility for the elderly.

Dax ambled to the front of the house and placed the drifter on the sidewalk, but pointing toward the street. After stepping aboard, he did a little 'hop' to turn it ninety degrees, so that the drifter was now pointing down the length of the sidewalk. In doing so, the coils aligned with the current just beneath, and he felt his whole body lurch up five or six centimeters, the board gently hovering in place. The sensation was not unlike surfing, though on much calmer swells. It took a second or two for Dax to get his balance, but when he felt confident in his stance, he pushed off with one foot and shot forward like a big, lanky hockey puck. Unlike Grampa's air-sled, whose powerful internal turbines provided forward momentum (as well as air-powered lift over any non-magnetic terrain), the drifter was a simple, reactive device, requiring the rider to provide a literal 'kick' every so often. Zipping along and above the curving paths, he inhaled the sweet floral scents as the wind buffeted his face and chest like an old friend. Here and there, time had taken its toll on a walkway, and the connection of embedded ribs had been broken – usually from a new driveway or overgrown tree roots or a careless utility crew. As Dax reached these places, he didn't slow down, welcoming a quick opportunity to 'jump' the impending breach in resistant current, enjoying a fleeting but potent adrenaline rush each time.

Human beings were the more troublesome obstacle, and Hawaiians were notoriously never in any particular hurry. So, while he would shout ahead and hope people strolling along would move, sometimes they'd just stare back at him like wild deer, frozen and confused. On three occasions he had to pivot unexpectedly to avoid slamming into a bewildered pedestrian, and, of course, as soon as his board crossed out of the sidewalk's current zone and into someone's yard – or worse, the street – he'd skid to a halt. Once along the way, he suffered a pretty embarrassing tumble, but a tall, thick patch of pampas grass cushioned his fall. A good thing, as he'd not worn any protective gear. The one time he had to swerve into the street there was no traffic, and he managed to hop off the board just in time, avoiding a bad spill into asphalt.

Despite a few awkward moments and mild abrasions, Dax enjoyed getting reacquainted with Turtle Bay's network of enhanced sidewalks, and with the drifter. It was surprisingly tactile, unpredictable and simple enough to permit him control – but not *complete* control. After all, life was no fun without at least a little element of chance.

Upon reaching Cody's block, Dax finally turned the drifter ninety degrees to slow his momentum, catch his breath and enjoy the last bit on foot. Slipping the board under his arm, he noticed a car he'd never seen before parked in front, the hood and fenders glistening in the dappled sunlight. Perfectly framed between two royal palms was a beautiful, gull-winged sporty marvel of engineering in a shimmering emerald green, with light teal accents and darkly tinted windows.

Dax circled the vehicle twice, checking out the clean lines, imagining how fast this thing could go. Then he noted the license plate: 'I KARE.' This must be Cody's doctor. For a moment he considered turning around to avoid interrupting his friend's treatment, but Kiri stepped out and called to him.

"Dax! Come on in!"

"Hi. Is Cody with his doctor? I didn't mean to bother —"

"Nonsense, Dax," she urged, "they're nearly done. He's always 200 percent better after your visits. And he's excited to do the hockey experience . . . game . . . thing."

Dax giggled. Kiri blushed, realizing she'd said it wrong.

"X-Pince, right?" she laughed, remembering, "they're called 'X-Pince' games now, yes?"

"Yeah."

"When I was a girl, they were called 'experiential games.'"

Dax nodded, though that seemed a much clumsier term. "Ah, okay. Chewy."

"If you don't mind waiting in the den until they're done, I'll bring you some juice."

"Thanks."

He stepped into the Vallabh's sunken den, with its real books, carved pacific island totems and the abundant gleaming geologic treasures on display. Moving through the specimens, Dax enjoyed how the carefully placed touches of spot lighting made them glint and sparkle.

"It's like a cave, isn't it?" someone said in the shadows behind him, her voice lyrical and soft. "Dark, but glowy. It's like you're surrounded with magic."

Dax turned to see the form of a teenage girl with olive colored skin and hair that looked incredibly soft, her long locks flowing with the colors of autumn. Her eyes were in shadow. He leaned forward, mystified and intrigued.

Kiri appeared just then with two glasses of juice, holding one out for each.

"Dax Zander, please meet Illone Lautrec. Pronounced 'eeYOHnay.' She comes to visit sometimes when her father is meeting with Cody."

"Hi," Dax managed. It was a start. The girl smiled.

"Kiri's teaching me how to cook."

She took a small step forward and Dax took a quick breath upon seeing her eyes – they shone with a deep, beautiful luster, somewhere between an azure blue and purple. He'd never seen such eyes in his life. Except on a few fish. But these eyes suited his tastes far better.

"Well, uhh . . ." he stammered, waiting for that brain of his to contribute to the moment, "you couldn't get a better teacher. She makes great stuff. With food. And I eat a lot of food."

Illone giggled, as Kiri stifled a chuckle, stepping away.

"I'll come check on you two in a few minutes."

For all of another twenty seconds, Dax just gazed at her, unaware of the silly grin plastered on his face.

"Don't you love these?" she asked, moving toward a few large, egg-shaped rocks at the back of the room.

Dax blinked; *do something.* He reached to the wall and touched a pad, raising the lights.

Immediately Illone stepped backwards, pulling down her hat to shield her eyes.

"Umm, could you please turn it back the way it was?"

"Illone, my apologies!" Kiri called out, appearing suddenly with a half-peeled avocado in hand. "Dax, we should've told you. Illone is very sensitive to light."

"Oh, wow . . . I'm sorry!" Dax blurted out, dimming the controls again.

"I'm okay, Kiri. Thanks. He didn't know."

Kiri caught her winsome look and nodded, retreating to her kitchen once more. Illone approached a freestanding shelving display loaded with several softly illuminated ores.

"No harm done, Dax. It happens. Light inside doesn't hurt unless it's very bright, but sometimes it can be uncomfortable."

"You sure?" This close, with the soft light perfectly catching her face, he found those eyes even more amazing. So much so, he swept the drape of hair out of his own. She giggled.

"How do you keep track of all that?"

"What?" he asked, utterly confused.

"That mop! You have crazy hair. It's like a big blond jungle on your head." She reached up to poke at it, playfully. "Are there monkeys in there? Any predator birds?"

When her finger grazed his forehead, he felt a strange but wonderful shudder throughout his body, evoking a spontaneous, goofy, high-pitched giggle. Horrified to hear this rolling off his lips, Dax instantly tried a different laugh, in a decidedly lower register.

Illone's eyebrows popped up as she bit her lip to suppress a laugh at his expense. Blushing, he dropped his head, but soon recovered with a cavalier shrug.

"That was my toucan," he improvised.

"I see," she smirked. "Guess I'll just have to take your word for it. Never been to the jungle." She reached up to tease a few of his locks as if thumbing through a book. "Till now."

In the dim light, they shared a smile. Despite a clumsy start, he'd made a new friend. But his reverie was rudely broken by a booming voice just behind him.

"Young man, do you have designs upon my daughter?"

"Daddy!"

Dax spun about to see a broad silhouette towering over him, a man with skin the hue of warm mahogany, graying curly hair and thick sideburns that curved around his jowls, ending right under his thick chin. He gazed down severely; the boy dared not utter a word.

"It's okay," Illone said, "he's just teasing you."

Then the giant cracked a dazzling grin, extending a hand.

"She's right, Dax. I'm joking. Call me Alfonse. I'm—"

"Cody's doctor. He says you're the best in the world."

"Well, I'm not sure who's done Cody more good. The way he talks about you, you're the best *friend* in the world."

Dax blushed, averting his eyes, only to catch those luminous purple-blue orbs a couple of meters away. She was still smiling. *Why was she still smiling?*

"Go on, he's waiting for you," Dr. Lautrec urged. "We're all wrapped up. And I promised Illone authentic Italian tonight."

"Nice to meet you, Dax," she said, taking her father's hand.

"Hope to see you again sometime," Dax replied. Then, thinking quickly, he said, "You know, Dr. Lautrec – we live in a seabase about ninety kilometers off the coast. It's not that hard to get down from the surface. If Illone—" He gulped, his throat noticeably dry, and corrected himself. "If you and Illone ever want to visit, I know my parents would love it. And it's pretty dark down there. Just artificial light and the little bit of the sun that reaches down to the reef."

"Well, thank you for the invitation, Dax. We both love marine life and will consider it." He walked toward the door. "Italian's calling, Illone. Got your hat on?"

"Yes, Daddy. I'm fine." She repositioned the hat on her head with a subtle tilt for Dax's approval. His timid smile broadened slightly.

"Bye," he said.

And she mouthed the same before stepping outside, her father already holding open the passenger's door of that incredible car. After making sure she was strapped in, Alfonse simply said "Giddyup!" and his car roared to life, then shot away down the road with that low-pitched hum all the hydrogen turbines made, though Dax was certain this one had a good bit more 'oomph' than most.

"Dax, are you here?" Cody called from down the hall, and duly summoned, the boy bounded back toward his friend's room, as the afterimages of Illone's eyes and that fantastic car jockeyed for space amid his thoughts.

Troubled Waters

They had been playing 'full dip' hockey in Cody's room for two hours, sitting on SwirlyStools in the middle of the room, sticks at the ready. The whirl of players whisking past and the puck banking in all directions was dizzying enough, but their own momentum – lunging just the slightest bit to the side or pivoting nimbly – was enhanced by the motion governors integrated into their seats, making the whole thing even more surreal.

He and Cody had each won a game, so a tie-breaker was a must. Dax grabbed a tray loaded with treats Kiri had left by the door, brought it back up to the bed and they snacked.

"Your mom is the best."

"Well, your mom is building stuff that's going to other planets."

"Yeah, she's pretty amazing, too."

"Did you meet Illone?"

Dax stopped chewing his sesame-crusted edamame, his cheeks flushing pink.

"Ha! I knew it! How stupid did you get with her?"

"Oh, man, I completely . . . my brain just—" He made a humming noise, like an electric motor. Cody laughed, all too familiar with the feeling.

"Those eyes – they're amazing."

"Yeah . . ." Both boys droned the word, remembering.

Cody sighed gently. "She's kinda sick too, though."

Dax turned to him, disturbed.

"Right now it's mostly sunlight," Cody explained. "It messes with her skin, her eyes too. But her eyes are better if she can keep the lighting low indoors. I don't think she goes outside much unless it's cloudy or nighttime. It's kinda sad. I feel so bad for her father. He lost his wife when Illone was little, and he can't

127

even take his daughter out to the park without worrying if her skin will start to blister."

"That *is* sad," Dax said quietly, feeling a rising tinge of anger for a world that had thrown all kinds of ugly spurs into the lives of otherwise decent people. "It's like everything's just getting worse lately."

"No, Dax. I think when you're a kid you just don't know about all the bad stuff going on. Grownups don't want you to have to think about any of it. And then you start to grow up and it's like, 'Oh. It's everywhere.'"

"Like the jokes and stuff we don't get till later on."

Just then it struck Cody how Dax kept staring at his enormous space mural, almost as if it were some kind of beast, looming there, ready to eat them.

"You okay, Dax? You seem weird today."

Dax was quiet for a moment. The nightmare had been weighing heavy on his mind. It had brought him here, though he wasn't quite sure why. He had to share.

"I had a dream about us. We were in space."

"Okay," Cody answered, seeming enthused already, "and?"

"We were floating around, tethered to some ship. There was a meteor a little ways off. We wanted to explore it, but the control guys in the ship said we shouldn't go out that far."

"But we went, right?"

Dax nodded. "We went out and still couldn't reach the meteor. And then our tethers stretched. And yours snapped."

Cody was silent, fascinated, but his friend seemed wrought with guilt.

"You started floating away," Dax continued, "and I couldn't get you back. The ship started pulling me in, and you floated off. This black hole opened up out of nowhere and . . ."

"I got sucked into a black hole? That would be amazing!"

"No! It wasn't! It was . . ." Dax fell quiet, remembering how he awoke on the beach crying out, grabbing at sand.

"Well, it didn't happen, you gobie," Cody chuckled softly. "Forget about it. I have bad dreams, too, sometimes. They're not real."

Dax looked up at him, pained.

"It felt real."

"But it *wasn't*. You know what's real?" Cody asked. "You. My awesome friend."

Dax's throat tightened, the words taking him off guard. With effort, Cody pushed off the bed and walked, very stiffly, to his dresser. A Chicago Cubs baseball cap hung just above on a hook. Cody lifted it off, sniffed it once, and then turned with an extended arm, offering it to Dax.

"What?" Dax asked, reluctant to take the cap.

"It's yours."

"Cody, you've had this your whole life."

"I know. It was my dad's, then it was mine, now it's yours."

Cody sat again, crumpling the hat in his hands. He smiled sweetly, his slightly crooked teeth bright and white against his dark pink lips.

"Just take it, Dax. Please? Knowing you have it will make me happy."

Cheeks burning, Dax looked away, blinking back hot tears pooling in his lower eyelids.

"If . . . If that's what you want. Okay."

Cody leaned over and hugged him suddenly, tight. Dax was wholly unprepared, but took that instant to quickly wipe his eyes. As much as Cody needed him to accept the gift, Dax felt it would pain his friend to see him breaking. So instead he grinned and pulled the cap down around his head, bouncing like a circus monkey with a newly-discovered prop. Cody laughed. That set the world right, for a few minutes at least. There followed a few quiet seconds, where Dax just turned the cap over and over in his hands, pretending to study it.

"Eww, you got sweat all in the brim."

"You can't wash it," Cody insisted. "Otherwise there's less of me."

"Yuck," Dax said, making a face. "Thanks for not giving me your socks." He glanced at

a bright blue scoreboard reading 1-1. "You ready to finish this?"

Taking to their SwirlyStools once more, each picked up a game wand and extended it to resemble a hockey stick.

Cody shouted out with glee, "Game on! Hot-now!"

"Hot-now!" Dax echoed, fully immersed and happily forgetting all else. A horde of heavily padded players zoomed and glided all around them as they commenced their final match.

. . .

The next morning, Dax and Shaw had hit the waves early, but were thoughtful enough to leave a note for Grampa Pat to let him know. So he set about his morning warm up – what he called yoga, though in reality it was stretching his various limbs to some mood music until something made him grunt – and then set to making breakfast. By 9:30, the sounds coming from the avocado-monkey room told him Kai was up and watching cartoons with Scrub. Surprisingly, he couldn't see any surfers within proximity of his beach when he squinted out the kitchen window, much less his grandsons. He had just finished preparing a stack of banana-stuffed French toast and was about to whip up a bowl of fresh ginger-honey butter when he heard shouting from somewhere outside.

"Fred, keep the toast warm," he instructed.

"I will keep the toast toasty, Patrick," Fred responded from somewhere. "And should I soften the butter?"

But Grampa had already left.

"Oh, who am I kidding?" Fred's voice sighed. "You never eat French toast without it." An intense spotlight flicked on, squarely hitting a bowl of chilled butter on the counter.

Seconds later, staring into his open garage, Grampa Pat found his two eldest grandsons in a shouting match.

"You don't respect anything!" Shaw bellowed, holding his drifter aloft, his face red-hot.

"What did I do?" Dax barked back. "When's the last time you even *used* it?"

"You should have asked! Look! You cracked it!"

He waved the thing mere centimeters from his brother's nose; Dax lunged back.

"Who declared war?" Grampa interrupted.

"He just takes things and doesn't ask!" Shaw replied. "And then he breaks stuff!"

"Shaw, that's not even a crack," Dax said, pointing out a small nick in the underside of the drifter. "Look, Grampa. That's a chip. And I don't even know if I did that."

"You took the drifter to Cody's?" his grandfather asked. Dax nodded.

"Without asking," Shaw added flatly.

"You were already gone!" Dax countered.

"How hard is it to call?" Shaw asked, exasperated. "But that's not you. You don't call, you don't ask! You just . . . go. You see something shiny, something fast and you jump."

Dax groaned in frustration. Slow to intervene, Grampa's eyes wandered about the garage, landing upon the untouched kneepads and helmet still hanging on their wall hooks.

"Grampa, tell him he's not Dad! Or Mom!"

"Well, you need to respect his things, Dax."

"Thanks, Grampa," Shaw said, relieved.

"But he never uses it anymore. Isn't it all just all of our stuff after a while?"

Grampa Pat took the drifter and hung it on the rack just below the safety gear.

"Well, I guess," he said slowly, "if you accept the responsibility that goes with that."

Dax's brow furrowed in confusion until his grandfather ran a finger through the dusty surface of the helmet, and the boy understood immediately, his cheeks flushing pink.

"You went drifting on those old sidewalks without any gear?" Shaw exclaimed. "Or pads, or anything? Not even a helmet?"

"I know how to take a fall, Shaw," Dax said defiantly. His brother shook his head.

"You're gonna kill yourself," he said, matter-of-factly. "It won't take a whale. You just never think about – anything. It's like you don't even care."

Dax sniffed, then laughed. Standing behind him, Grampa Pat wore a tired, forlorn expression. He set the helmet down on a shelf, his finger grazing across its surface.

"Boy, you're flesh and blood," he said plainly, "so you can bleed and you can break."

He hung the helmet on the rack and started back toward the kitchen.

"I made French toast," he muttered. "Come on, before it gets cold."

Apparently feeling vindicated, Shaw stared at his brother with a smug little grin – which completely fell away when Grampa stopped and turned around to face them both.

"It hurts to see you fight like this," he said, with an unmistakable air of disappointment. "You're going to need each other someday. And God forbid something does happen . . ." His voice trailed off; he shuffled one foot against the gravel between the garage and the backyard. "Be smarter. Start figuring out how to be strong for each other."

He blew out a long, heavy gust of air and continued inside. Dax dropped his head.

"Okay, I'm sorry, alright?" Dax said. "I won't take your dumb stuff anymore."

Shaw shook his head with a rueful laugh.

"Yeah, you will," he said, plucking the helmet up, "but next time, wear this. If I ever do need you someday, I don't want you damaged."

. . .

At breakfast, Grampa Pat announced that today they were definitely going out on the boat, and nobody would be skipping. This suited Kai just fine so long as Scrub could join, though Shaw and Dax weren't exactly thrilled at the prospect of a whole afternoon at sea, stuck shoulder-to-shoulder. They knew better than to argue with their grandfather, however, so less than two hours after their meal they were aboard *The Empress Lilly,* a few hundred meters parallel to shore, plying the glassy turquoise swells. Grampa was at the helm, positively chipper. Scrub swam alongside, lured by the occasional treat Kai would toss overboard. Occasionally the pinniped would dip beneath the surface for more than a minute or two, prompting Kai to lean far over the edge, anxiously scanning the water. Grampa kept reassuring him that his sea lion was just learning to feed again in the wild and this was a very healthy thing. Sure enough, Scrub always popped up again with a fierce snort, and while Kai was the only one who actually cheered audibly – each and every time – his brothers were also pleased. The pup had in just a few days become a part of the family and a frequent source of laughter.

It was taking every bit of Dax's self-control to avoid pestering his grandfather for the wheel. That did not keep him from repeatedly coming alongside and hovering, however. They had zoomed a half-dozen kilometers along the coastline when Shaw, who was wisely using the time to catch up on some studying, glanced over and caught the frustrated slump of Dax's shoulders. He beckoned his brother over. After rolling his eyes, Dax plunked down beside him.

"Why don't you stop being a pest?"

As he was within earshot, Grampa Pat had no choice but to hear their bickering.

"Why don't you leave me alone?"

"You think he's gonna let you drive this boat if you just hang on him like a lamprey?"

"I'm not a lamprey."

Shaw smirked, apparently about to make some kind of witty retort when the boat pulled hard to port, their speed picking up.

"Grampa?" Shaw asked.

"We always keep it close. Let's take it on the wild side. Right, Dax?"

Though surprised, Dax loved the fresh breeze and the rude thumpity-thump of the hull smashing against the breakers.

"Yeah! Let's go!" he shouted.

Shaw pretended to go back to his reading, but he knew his grandfather must have a reason for whatever it was he was doing.

They continued like this for quite a while, Kai increasingly distressed, looking for his pet.

"We lost Scrub! He won't find us if we're out here!"

"Don't worry, Kai, we'll catch back up to him. I promise."

"Okay," Kai sniffed, not a little unsure.

After about ten minutes, Grampa throttled down and the engine puttered gently until they were just chugging quietly in the water, rocking back and forth. He was staring off the bow so intently, Shaw and Dax stood and joined him at the wheel. Gazing in the same direction, they fell similarly silent.

"What's all that out there?" Kai said aloud. "Is that where we live?"

"Yeah," Shaw answered grimly, "it is, Kai."

Far out to sea, instead of a clear, endless horizon, there seemed to be a lot of intense activity. Several large, bulky gray boats were anchored there, as military helicopters soared overhead, crisscrossing in various directions. They watched as one chopper released a large, wrapped bundle into the ocean.

"What's all that?" Dax asked.

"Could be any number of things," Grampa mused, though not with any enthusiasm.

"That's an awful lot of people to turn our place into a museum," Shaw said dryly.

Dax's cheeks tightened. There was no question they were staring at the location of their seabase. And instinctively, all of them knew they had not been meant to see any of the activity presently swirling about their home.

Dax glanced up at his Grampa, who seemed especially troubled.

"Maybe we should go check things out," Shaw suggested, without much conviction.

Grampa Pat looked at him soberly. He tapped his finger against the wheel for a moment, as if seriously contemplating a closer look. Then shook his head.

"Well," he said, in a gravelly voice, "they're probably just building a new luxury wing for rich tourists. Some stupid waste of taxpayer money."

"You know, Grampa," Dax suggested casually, "we could just cruise by. I mean, it's Dad, you know? They're not gonna shoot at us or chase us away . . ."

But the hard look on his grandfather's face chilled him. Without a word, Grampa Pat opened the throttle and turned the boat around.

They moved at a moderate pace through the ocean, the sea spray misting them liberally, their hair and clothing now quite damp. The mood was dour; nobody spoke – even Kai. But from the way he was biting his lip, there was little doubt where his thoughts were centered.

After about ten minutes, the North Shore coastline again came into view. Grampa slowed *The Empress Lilly* and spun around so suddenly, Shaw and Dax jumped.

"Gosh! I forgot my promise! Here, Dax, take the wheel. But keep an eye on the grid for reefs. Don't take her close in without checkin' for shoals."

The boys stared at him, as if a gloomy Dr. Jekyll had turned into a clownish Mr. Hyde. Nevertheless, Dax seized his opportunity.

"Don't worry, Grampa! I got it!"

He bounded eagerly to the helm, his chest swelling with exhilaration as Grampa retreated to the rear section.

"Grampa, why?!" Shaw whispered. "Do you even *remember* this morning?"

His grandfather merely chuckled, retrieving some floppy objects from a cooler. He held one up, a translucent purple pouch the size of a small sub sandwich, filled with fruit juice.

"Relax. Kailen! Here, buddy, gotta stay hydrated!"

The lad bounced forward, catching the slippery juice pack with both hands. Grampa lowered his voice, elbowing Shaw gently.

"Watch this – he puts on a little show."

Kai used his front teeth to tear a hole in the top and guzzled down the contents in mere seconds. Then he lifted the emptied casing above his open jaw and dropped it like a proud circus sword swallower, chewing the thing to oblivion. Shaw and Grampa applauded, laughing.

"The skin's my favorite part!" the boy announced happily, bits of purple goo still sticking to his teeth. "It tastes like gummies!"

Grampa pulled out a big floppy straw hat with a broad brim, printed with brightly colored lizards and flowers. Fitting it snug over his head, he batted his eyes like a silent film star, looking absolutely ridiculous and reveling in it. Shaw gaped at him incredulously.

"Hush. It was your gramma's."

"And *she'd* be laughing if she saw you wearing it."

Grampa cracked a grin, handing Shaw a juice pack.

"She always did."

But the old man's attention was again fixed on Dax, and his posture at the wheel. Grampa studied the boy, who stared ahead, leaning forward, the sun whipping his bushy hair wildly as their speed picked up. The boat was taking on a little lift, just barely bouncing them off their seats as the gleaming hull smacked each oncoming wave.

"We're far enough out, boy," Grampa called to Dax, "so you can open up the throttle a little if you like. Just keep an eye on your depth."

Dax glanced back with a big thumbs up.

"Okay!"

"Grampa," Shaw asked, more than a little anxious, "what's goin' on?"

"You oughta maybe buckle in, m'boy," Grampa offered quietly, looking for the strap under his own seat as the motor began to growl with liberated passion.

"Dax, easy, man!" Shaw called.

"Don't get all droney on my yon, bro!" Dax barked back. Shaw could yell all he wanted. Nothing could take this moment away – the salty spray of the sea, the torrents of wind ripping through his hair, the vibrating current from the engines surging all the way up to his shoulders. It was perfect. And the horizon, endless.

Grampa turned to the bow, where Kai was dutifully watching for Scrub.

"Kai, buddy, come on back here and sit with us."

"I don't see him yet!" he said, plaintively.

"He'll show up soon. We're pretty close. Scrub knows these waters better than us."

The lad trotted over obediently and sat between them. Grampa put his arm securely over Kai's shoulders, and catching this, Shaw gave him a look. Grampa returned it with a sort of sober nod, latching a small seat restraint over his lap. Shaw hesitated, then followed suit.

"Gettin' a little close to the shoals, Dax," Grampa noted. "You checkin' your gauges?"

With a swagger befitting a pirate, Dax offered a cocky glance over his shoulder.

"Grampa, c'mon! It's me!"

"Don't look back here, tark!" Shaw snapped.

Dax huffed but turned around, and instantly his whole body stiffened, eyeing the patchy maze of dark masses ahead, just beneath the waves. He eased up on the throttle, pulling the boat hard to starboard so forcefully that Grampa's grip on Kai's shoulder nearly shook loose, then tightened like a vice. Shaw reached for a support handle along the inside of the hull to keep from sliding off the seat. The boat's momentum kept them powering forward as Dax caught sight of the warning sensor just inside the helm, flashing bright red. He pulled the wheel as hard as he could to the right, grunting with the effort.

"HOLD ON!" he cried out, but it was too late.

A painful, gut-wrenching crunch jerked them all forward as the boat collided with something big and rough. Kai screamed, starting to tumble forward, but the twin forces of his restraint and Grampa's thick arm kept him from going far.

For a few seconds, there was just the grinding of The Empress Lilly's hull against the shoals, as the waves toyed with it like a predator would an injured animal. Rattled but unharmed, Shaw fumbled with the snaps on his restraints in a panic.

"Dax! Where are you!?" he called out.

Grampa craned his head to look around the helm. His grandson was nowhere to be seen.

Messy Kisses

Kai squirmed out of his grandfather's arms, slipped out of his restraints and ran to the bow, coming to Shaw's side. He was leaning over Dax, who on impact had been thrown into a cubbyhole in the forward section and was now groaning, clutching his bloody knee.

"Is he okay?" Grampa called, just now untangling his restraint from Kai's empty one.

"Yeah, he'll live to kill us another day," Shaw answered, reaching down to examine the knee injury. Dax swatted his hand away.

"Oww! Leave it!"

But Shaw persisted, delicately feeling around the joint and the two small cuts.

"His knee's bleeding!" Kai shouted, very close to Shaw's ear.

"Kai! Please . . . get us the first aid kit, okay?"

And he bounced off to the back of the boat.

"I'm sorry, Shaw," Dax said ruefully, catching his big brother's grim demeanor.

"It's not *my* pride and joy you drove into the rocks."

Dax winced; that hurt a lot more than his knee. Just behind Shaw, Grampa's face lurched into view. He wore a blank expression, betraying neither judgment nor relief, and then he was gone again. There was the sound of the engine dying – apparently Grampa had just switched it off – but the scent of burning oil remained pungent. Motors had long since turned to cleaner fuel systems, running on super batteries, hydrogen plasma or other compounds, but oil and silicon-based additives were still common lubricants. In a situation such as this, the superheated odor was a likely sign that some lines had been perforated.

His face hot with shame, Dax looked back at Grampa, who was at the stern, gazing down, looking for any damage. The whole boat was listing, though they had no way of yet knowing if that was because they were taking on water or were simply perched on some rocks. Kai handed the first aid kit to Shaw and ran to the starboard side of the boat, looking over the edge.

"What did you do, Dax?!"

Dax winced, trying to sit up.

"Hold still!" Shaw snapped, applying a protective gel patch over the wound. As soon as it was on, Dax moved to Kai's side to get a look. Grampa and Shaw joined them, staring down into the water. Even above the sloshing current, there were deep scratches visible in the previously pristine hull. Alongside and all around, they were surrounded by shallow reefs.

"You okay, boy?" Grampa asked. Dax nodded sheepishly.

"You said you were checking the grid," Shaw scolded.

"Grampa, I didn't mean to—"

But the grave look in his grandfather's eyes stilled him. Overwhelmed with guilt, Dax looked around and without warning, flipped himself over the rail, into the water.

"Hey!" his grandfather shouted, but the boy was already submerged, small bubbles trailing up from his darting form.

"He's gonna cut his feet on those rocks . . ." Grampa muttered anxiously.

From above, they saw his form hover in one spot for a moment, then move a few meters down the hull, until he finally surfaced. Water was drizzling down the golden locks clinging to his face, but that didn't camouflage the redness in his eyes.

"I really messed her up, Grampa. I'm sorry. I'm so sorry."

Shaw glared at him. He pushed away from the rail, returning to his seat in silence. Kai, however, spoke up.

"Are we gonna sink, Grampa?"

"I don't know, Kai. Dax, is the gash deep?"

"No, just . . . long. There's one spot though, cut about two centimeters into the hull. You got any foam?"

"Shaw," Grampa called back, "under your seat there's a couple of . . ."

Before he could finish, Shaw tossed over two red canisters. Grampa dropped one to Dax.

"Gotta twist the nozzle and pop it before the jet—"

"I know how to—" And then Dax caught himself. "Yes, sir," he corrected, meekly, and dropped beneath the waves again.

Grampa squinted, trying to see past the surface, but the glare was too strong. He relaxed somewhat, rubbing Kai's little shoulders.

"You knew he was gonna do that, didn't you?" Shaw asked plainly. "Why didn't you stop him before he ran into the shoals? You love this boat."

His grandfather turned with a gentle, sad smile, his voice soft.

"And I loved it just as much when I let you do the same thing."

Shaw's eyes popped.

"I never ran your boat into the—"

He stilled, remembering something. "Oh. Wow."

"Let's hope Kai doesn't make it a trifecta someday."

"Is that a disease?" Kai asked.

Grampa Pat just tousled his hair affectionately.

. . .

Underwater, Dax had identified two points where the reef had gouged the boat deep enough to cause serious trouble. He stripped the seal off the can's pointy nozzle, turned it to activate the release mechanism and then began shooting a stream of foam into the first rupture. It expanded on contact, sealing up against any leaks. Dax pulled out the nozzle, popped up to suck in some air for just a split second, then submerged again to fill the second gouge. The results were garish and ugly against the once-perfectly polished hull, but they would prevent any further leakage for the journey back to the boathouse.

No sooner had he surfaced but Scrub bounced alongside him, nuzzling his neck.

"Scrub!" Kai shouted happily, "You're back!"

Dax was far less enthused.

"Get your whiskers off me, you hairy dragon!"

"He likes you, Dax!"

Scrub licked Dax's face and he half-laughed, half-cried.

"Okay. Okay, Scrub. Good boy."

Deep down he was grateful for the kiss, as if it were a small but messy sign from the universe that he had been forgiven. Climbing back into the boat, Dax laid the can down and sat quietly in the rear section, across from Shaw, avoiding eye contact.

"We can get back now?" Grampa asked.

139

Dax nodded penitently. His grandfather looked over the instrument panel and hit a button, flushing coolant through the lines. The system cycled, then pinged aloud to signal the self-check was complete.

"Okay, engine's rebooted and there's no damage there."

The boys were quiet, so he throttled forward and gradually turned the boat around.

Grampa checked the topographical grid carefully, steering them away from the reefs lest he ruin the other side of the hull. Once they were clear, he took a brief look back. Dax was bent over, staring at his toes, glum.

"Dax. Can you hand me my hat, buddy?"

"Huh?" The boy looked up, a little lost, then glanced around and saw the hat. He hadn't noticed it earlier, while busy at the wheel, but now it struck him as a ridiculously big and floppy thing, as an unexpected giggle erupted in his belly. Feeling unworthy of laughter, he stifled that impulse, grabbed the hat and swung it over. Grampa reached for it *slowly*, forcing Dax to watch as he very carefully positioned it on his head and cocked it to one side with a dainty tap, as his grandsons stared on in shocked amazement.

Finally, Dax cracked with a loud snort, and Grampa did a little curtsey, which got Kai cackling. Dax's eyes got moist, his heart filled with a dawning awareness of what the old fellow was doing, just for him. Somewhere between his laughter and his remorse, he felt an enormous surge of gratitude and love for this remarkable man. Risking a glance at Shaw, Dax was surprised and grateful to catch his wise, affirming nod – free of judgment.

Sporting that flowered hat as proudly as any captain in her majesty's fleet, Grampa Pat turned back to face the sea and piloted them home.

They got there well ahead of Scrub, because Grampa opened up the throttle and because a thick school of grunion caught the sea lion's attention. But a little later, Kai's beloved pet caught up. Finding his best friend waiting for him there on the beach, he tackled the lad with countless sloppy, whiskery kisses.

Almost to the backyard, Dax heard his little brother's buoyant laughter and turned to see him rolling in the sand with Scrub. Surprised at how good it felt to watch them playing together, his heart grew warm with newfound appreciation that their family had grown just a little bigger.

Distractions

The North Shore neighborhoods were sporting a lot of late October spooks, goblins, flickering torches and plenty of orange and black. The inescapable festive décor was comically at odds with the conspicuous and unsettling silence from governmental leaders about the recent alien visitation, almost as if it had never happened. The event, and the subsequent information 'blackout,' sparked countless exasperated conversations, heated conspiracy theories and pointed observations by comedians, journalists and politicians. Still, barely a week later, the Halloween spirit had proven a magically alluring and effective distraction to those otherworldly concerns. Many nations had embraced the holiday over the last fifty years, so much of the global community seemed to be obsessing more this week on exotic costumes, elaborate carnivals and ghoulish entertainment than any notions of impending conquest by extraterrestrial beings.

Dax and his brothers had not heard from their parents. They had no notion their parents had left the seabase either, much less traveled to Washington D.C. and the Pentagon. But Dax had kept his word. Though repeatedly tempted to share what he knew with Cody, he had managed to avoid sharing what his parents had disclosed, even though the boys had discussed the aliens (and what interest they might have in humans) in general terms. Cody and his parents suspected Dax knew more than he was letting on, but they also respected his family. In that spirit, none of the Vallabhs had pressed him for information.

Never very comfortable with loose time, Shaw had filled the intervening days by not only catching up on all his schoolwork, but also plowing through two books about marine biologists – one heady biography on Ruth Turner, the other a breezier photo-journal of the voyages of Robert Ballard. Shaw had also caught up on his pet project, a reef-seeding nutritional supplement intended to

141

stimulate repopulation of a species of tiny fish once rendered nearly extinct in the South Atlantic. Happily, the latest results were robustly promising; this looked to be his first notable contribution to conservation science. But now he was antsy.

It was the odd disconnect, the silence from his parents over the last week. When they called again on the twenty-fifth of October with a hastily-explained suggestion that the boys extend their visit through "maybe a few days after Halloween," Shaw was certain something had changed and he was being completely shut out. Four nights later, he couldn't keep his suspicions bottled up any longer.

"Grampa," he asked, helping clean up after dinner while his younger brothers carved jack-o-lanterns in the backyard, "you *know* something big's going on. And they're not telling us. *Us*. Family."

Patrick huffed, nodding but unwilling to weigh in. He loved having them near, but Shaw was right; something felt very 'off' about the whole thing, especially considering recent global events. Except for planned vacations like summer camps, Dayna and her husband had never been this cavalier about time away from their kids.

Dax and Kai, used to the more confining and specific boundaries of their undersea home, were quite content to hang around topside, accepting this unexpected shore leave in stride. After all, the prospect of celebrating Halloween for more than a single day was thrilling – in the past they'd made brief trips to the mainland early in the afternoon of October 31st. But this time, there were haunted houses and invites to parties with neighbors and old friends. Still ahead, they could look forward to scary movies, 'zombie pirate treasure haunts' and who knew what else – a whole fantastic season to experience. It all felt spectacularly *normal*.

Shaw, however, was not fond of Halloween or horror movies. As a child, prior to moving offshore, he'd been tricked on a dare by some older school kids into entering a darkened garage. Once inside, they shut the door, and he found himself surrounded by sticky cobwebs and rubber spiders. After a moment, Shaw steeled himself, gathered his wits and shouted defiantly that it was all so very fake – right before a huge, animatronic tarantula emerged from the rafters and crawled down the wall to block his exit. Though just a mechanical toy, it was an extremely hairy and persuasive one: while beating on the door, begging to be freed, Shaw had wet his pants.

Grampa put away his broom, reaching for a knife and some kiwifruit from a bowl.

"They might just be goin' through some middle-age phase; you know, they just kind of putter around and everything becomes a little more important than it should be."

"Grampa . . ."

"Let's give 'em a few more days. Maybe they can't say anything because . . . they can't say anything. After all, two ex-Presidents count your dad as a personal friend, he's played golf with President Wasserman twice since she was elected and I wouldn't be shocked if his buddy Easton ends up in the Oval Office someday. The things your dad hears, not too many people get to hear, so keepin' a tight lip's part of his job sometimes." He popped a chunk of kiwi into his eldest grandson's mouth. "Don't let a few secrets sour you on the people who love ya most."

With no desire to further agitate Grampa Pat, Shaw waved both hands in surrender, gobbling down a few more tasty slices.

Dax was brushing his teeth when Shaw came into the bathroom half an hour later and closed the door. Though there was no pretense of modesty between him and his brothers, Dax really hoped Shaw wasn't about to take a shower, much less do anything else.

"What?" Dax groused through foamy teeth. "Can't you wait till I'm out?"

Shaw rolled his eyes, his voice low. "Relax. Don't you think it's weird we're still here?"

"I don't care," Dax insisted. He swished a cupful of water in his mouth and spat. "It's great here. Sunshine, real food, real . . . everything. Dr. Lautrec has this crazy car! And I've already done two haunted houses!"

"Dax, something serious is going on. Why can't we go home?"

"Who's stopping us from going home?"

Shaw thumped his index finger against Dax's skull in frustration.

"Don't be a tark. They've never just abandoned us like this, and never this long. And I know Grampa wants to ask them about it, but you know he likes to keep the peace."

"This is seriously messing with you, isn't it?" Dax grinned. "Is it 'cause you hate Halloween?" Cupping both hands, he spider-crawled his fingers up Shaw's neck and face; his brother swatted them away.

"Quit it! Something just doesn't feel right."

"Fine! Let's call 'em. We'll tell 'em we want to come back and give Grampa some space – and you can go back but I'm gonna stay till at least Halloween – but then they'll say 'okay' and you'll realize you're just getting all undie-bunched."

Shaw released a long, slow sigh. Finally, an ally.

"Okay. We'll call in ten minutes." Then he opened the door and shoved Dax out.

"Whoa! What are you—"

Shaw just gave him a look and Dax blinked, backing away into the hall as the door shut and locked with a definitive click.

. . .

In the backyard, Dax and Shaw waited for their parents to pick up on the call. Soon their mother's face hovered on the floating screen. Though it was good to see her, both could sense a tightness and a careful, practiced cadence in her words.

"Hello, boys!"

"Hi, Mom!" Dax replied.

"Everything alright there? Are you driving Grampa crazy yet?"

"Funny you should mention that, Mom," Shaw answered. "I think all three of us at once might be wearing him out. And then there's Kai's sea monster . . . We were thinking maybe if two of us came back home, it might be easier on—"

Their father swung into view abruptly, his brow knit tightly with concern.

"Boys! There's a lot of . . ." Evan paused, careful with his words, "prep work going on here . . . with a few outside contractors. It's very . . . *loud*."

Shaw's face twisted up.

"A lot, huh? And it's loud? Dad, why would that matter?"

"It's just busy here right now, boys," their mother interjected, "and to be honest, you'll have a lot more freedom at Grampa's. Dax, what are you and Kai going to be for Hallo—"

"How long?" Shaw interrupted, bluntly. His parents glanced at each other.

"Well, let's say November fifth . . . eighth," his father answered. "Somewhere in there. You guys have fun till we call you. In fact, if you want to take a jumper to Los Angeles or San Fran, I'll load some more credit on your accounts."

"Banga!" Dax blurted out happily.

"Yeah, very banga!" Dayna added, so cheerfully even she cringed after saying it. "You boys enjoy your vacation. Dax, you're responsible for your schoolwork and Kai's. And if you go to any theme parks or fairs, don't let Kailen eat too many sweets!"

Jaw agape, Shaw stared first at his parents, then his brother. But it was too late; Dax had been successfully co-opted with an all-too obvious bribe. Their father waved a cheerful goodbye.

"You boys behave, help your Grampa with chores and we'll call you soon."

Their parents abruptly blinked out, with Shaw more irritated than ever. Dax, however, was already juggling imaginary trips in each hand like invisible coconuts.

"Los Angeles? 'Cause if we go *there* we can take in some swells at Malibu, maybe even a few days at Disneyland! But if we go to San Fran, NASA just set up this huge new space encounter thingy. They have these padded anti-grav chambers, flight simulators and—"

"Shut up now or I'm going to hurt you."

"Narf! What?" Somewhere in the latter half of the twenty-first century, 'Narf' – a frightened noise made by a long-since-forgotten cartoon character – had become a standard response to unexpectedly harsh remarks.

"You caved! Dad bought you off and boom, you turn into Bobo the dancing bear."

"Bobo the what? Look, you heard 'em. They're busy. It's loud."

"Dax. You saw what we all saw out on the boat. That wasn't some small operation. They're not doing some remodel there. Any conversion of our home into a museum or whatever wouldn't happen until we were all moved out. And we haven't even started packing."

Dax shrugged. "Well, maybe it's some military stuff they can't talk about."

"Gee, ya think so?" Shaw snorted. "'Hey, boys, take a vacation! I'll even load you up on credits. Just forget all about those aliens that said 'hi' to the entire human race – and whatever you do, don't look over *here*! Where all the big ships and helicopters are suddenly having a party!'"

Restless, Dax looked out past the boundary where Grampa's fluffy green backyard dissolved into smooth white sand.

"What do you wanna do, Shaw?" he chuckled. "Go home and spy on our own parents? Break into our own seabase?"

Shaw stilled, then turned slowly, a glint of daring in his eye so bold it startled Dax.

"You're crazy. No way! I bet they have patrols and stuff now."

"Chicken."

"I'm not chicken! I'm not stupid, either! Mom and Dad would kill us if we came back and interrupted some important stuff they —"

"More important than their own kids?"

"Shaw, you get on me for doing crazy stuff, and then you wanna do this?! Turn into a stupidhead just because you feel —"

"Feel what?"

"Never mind." Dax popped up to head back inside, but Shaw grabbed his elbow.

"Get off my yon, Shaw!" Dax shouted, jerking his arm away. "You get all burned when you think you're not getting any respect, like you deserve it just because you're the oldest! But you don't respect *me* at all."

"What's it matter?" Shaw replied, exasperated. "You're thirteen!"

The glare his brother shot back was searing; Shaw winced.

"I'm sorry, Dax. I *do* respect you. I do. But sometimes I think you're willing to just let life toss you around, instead of making decisions that might cost you something. And then other times, you do incredibly risky stuff for no reason at all."

Dax kicked at the grass.

"Not for no reason. If I think it's gonna be fun, I do it. Besides, soon I'll be fourteen."

"Well, some things are worth doing that are a long way from fun," Shaw countered. "With all that's happened in the last few days, you're not even a little curious to know what's going on? What's turned Mom and Dad into ghosts overnight?"

Dax leaned back against a wall. Shaw's pointed remarks were sinking in bit by bit. He glanced to the windows to see if Grampa was anywhere near. Finally he spoke, in whispers.

"When did you want to go?"

"Well . . . tonight."

Dax's face fell.

"Can't it wait a few days? You know, like after Halloween?"

"Are you kidding?" Shaw huffed. "Why?"

Though Dax was never one to beg, his voice cracked plaintively.

"Well, Kai and me – we never get to do this stuff . . ."

"That's a whole week!"

"Shaw, if we go there tonight, whatever happens, we are *grounded*. Probably forever. You can always go back to college, but I'm gonna be the one who suffers.

Kai too, maybe. So we'll be grounded and they won't let us come back onshore, and there won't be any trick or treating, no haunted houses, no parties or spooky stuff . . ."

"Why is that so important—"

"Girls!" Dax exclaimed, amazed he had to spell it out. "Wow! How can you just not *know* . . ." He fell back on the grass, exasperated. "I *never* get to meet girls."

Dax went quiet, flushed with embarrassment. Stunned for a moment, Shaw chuckled gently and sat next to him. Sure, Kai was still pretty oblivious to matters of romance, but Dax was nearly fourteen – an awful age to be cooped up in a home so far from land and so hidden from the sun. Still, Shaw couldn't let himself be seen as caving so easily.

"Okay. I'll give you a random biology question. If you answer correctly, I'll go to Miami, catch up on schoolwork and you can take the rest of the week and soak in Halloween."

"Wait, what? What if I don't—"

"Nope! That's the deal. Let's see if you've been studying."

Dax rolled his eyes. "Fine."

Shaw thought for a moment, squinted, looking around. He held up a finger, staring at it as if a butterfly had landed on it. Dax grew impatient, releasing one of those heavy sighs teenagers seem to practice to perfection.

"Okay. Cellular biology."

"Come on! I'm barely in eighth grade!"

"Too bad," Shaw responded, pleased with himself. "What are the stages of mitosis?"

His brother's head dropped, as if stumped. Then he straightened up again, smiling.

"In order," Shaw added quickly, after which Dax nearly bit down on his tongue. He took in a deep breath, staring straight ahead.

"Prophase. Met—Wait. *Pro*metaphase. Then metaphase."

Shaw nodded, catching that strange glassy look in his brother's eyes again. It was always just a little unsettling.

"Anaphase . . . and telophase," Dax finished proudly, lifting a mischievous eyebrow.

"Okay, brainiac," Shaw said. "And you better meet some cute girls after all this. Because if you chicken out, I'm gonna bust you."

Dax beamed an appreciative grin.

"'Kay. Thanks. But what if I'd gotten 'em wrong?"

Shaw put an arm around his shoulder. "You didn't," he yawned. "Anyway, I kinda need a few days in Miami. My professor wanted me to check on a lab project and the remote feed's not showing everything. And by now I bet Bardy's wondering if I'm ever coming back."

Dax smirked. "And Hayley . . ."

"Yeah," Shaw said, fondly, "and a few days back east might get me feeling close to normal again, too." He stood and reached to pull his brother up. Heading back inside, Shaw lowered his voice. "I'm gonna set my alarm, but if I'm gonna go I want to catch an early jumper. So if I sleep through it, wake me up by six, okay?"

Dax nodded, a daring nugget of a thought popping into his head. His wicked snicker drew a suspicious glance from Shaw, who incorrectly assumed what it was about.

"My little brother going to parties with girls. The world actually *is* coming to an end."

"Yeah, maybe!"

And with that, Dax strode into the avocado-monkey room and slipped happily into the cool sheets of his bed. Kai was in a deep sleep, but Scrub's head rose up like a thick, whiskered periscope. He sniffed, staring at Dax, his eyes shining like big black marbles in the dark.

"Go back to sleep, Scrub," Dax whispered. "Go on."

Scrub puffed out a cleansing breath, then settled contentedly back into his pile of pillows on the floor, as Dax set his own alarm for a few minutes before six.

. . .

Far below the billowy white clouds, floating in an impossibly bright blue sky, Shaw was holding Hayley's soft, freckled hand as they skied the cobalt and diamond surface of the Atlantic Ocean. A school of dolphin broke through the waves on either side. Hayley's scarlet hair, pulled back in a tight little net, bobbed in the wind as she gazed over with those sparkling Irish eyes.

And then Shaw lost his footing and plunged into the sea. Flailing haplessly, the water enveloped him and a hairy black octopus slammed against his chest – just as he awoke in bed to a horribly salty, pungent scent and a large pink tentacle lashing at his cheeks, stringy with drool. He was conscious for about two seconds before realizing this was the sum meaning of his brother's strange laugh of the night before.

"SCRUB! Get OFF ME!" he roared, as Kai, Dax and Grampa exploded in laughter.

The animal kept licking his face in long, rapid swipes, its whiskers trailing across his ears, neck and nose like a coarse, damp broom, until Shaw used every last ounce of strength to heave the animal off his chest, sitting up with a ready glare for the others in his room.

"You told me not to let you sleep in," Dax said innocently, ducking when Shaw flung a saliva-drenched pillow his way.

"You're so dead!" Shaw grunted. He bolted out of bed and gave chase all the way to the beach until Dax collapsed in the frothing surf, laughing so hard he was wheezing, pointing at his older brother. Baffled, Shaw finally looked down to discover he was completely naked.

He made a mad dash for the house, ignoring the stares of sunbathers and surfers down the beach and catcalls from Kai and Grampa Pat, and didn't stop until he was in the shower. Fortunately, Grampa had a hot breakfast ready by the time he'd toweled off, so soon he was able to laugh right along with the rest of them. Within an hour, he was on his way back to Florida, to school and hopefully some time with Hayley.

. . .

Seated together in his study, Evan and Dayna were both staring at a floating image of Easton Russell, his large form filling the frame. He looked haggard, his voice hoarse and low.

"There won't be an announcement about anything for a while. We have dozens of heads of state clustered in a very big room, trying to agree on what to tell the world, and when."

"Better to offer something preemptively, General," Dayna suggested, her husband nodding in agreement. "Conspiracy theories can lead to irrational conclusions. Desperate acts."

The general coughed, then took a sip of something from a steaming mug.

"Sorry. Too much talking for this old man. They're turning me into a diplomat, Evan."

Evan laughed. "That'll never happen!"

"Speaking of desperate acts, we're tracking some intel on a few —" he pursed his lips, searching for a tactful term, "—unscrupulous types, who would love to get their hands on alien technology, or . . . *biology*. Some of them pretty ruthless and well-financed."

The captain and the doctor absorbed this and nodded grimly. The general saluted.

"If we don't stay frosty," he finished, "this could go south fast. But you have my implicit trust, and the trust of many leaders around the world. I'll talk to you soon."

His image faded, and Evan blew out a long gust of air. His wife stroked his arm encouragingly, but there was no hiding her own tension, either.

"Well. That's no pressure at all," Evan said.

"It'll work out, darling," she replied, quietly. He offered an appreciative smile and stood, staring at the dark sea beyond the ports above his desk and the mysteries unfolding out there.

"I know," he whispered, though quite aware he was not at all convincing.

Blasts from the Past

Shaw pushed open the heavy door of his dorm-room in Miami and froze. Bardy was gone! His clothes, artwork, some mementoes from home – all gone. The one item he'd left was an oversized, reclining chair they'd christened 'Suzie' for no particular reason, filled with a gel that made for the most rapturous naps one could imagine – and Shaw had regularly made himself comfortable in it. There was a single, folded piece of paper on the chair. Shaw set his small travel bag on his bed and picked up the handwritten note.

Shaw, something great came up and I had to jump. Can't speak on it now, hopefully soon. Suzie's yours. Don't ever forget, the world changes, but I'm your shoul', always. – Bardy

Shaw sat, sinking into Suzie's compliant embrace, completely bewildered. Bardy was methodical, careful. He wasn't merely immersed in the scientific method for the sake of science – it colored his whole thought process. Not that he couldn't be spontaneous, but in the time they'd been friends Shaw had never seen Bardy do anything important without careful deliberation. Usually, he'd come to Shaw for a second opinion when considering a trip or a new class. For him to not even mention an opportunity that would take him away indefinitely . . . Bardy was starting to act just like his mom and dad.

Shaw stilled, and for about eight seconds he entertained the notion that somehow Bardy and his parents were connected; then he caught his reflection in a mirror and burst into laughter at the sight of his intense expression. Having become so invested in conspiracies, he was seeing them everywhere.

The windows to the room were open, the air rich with the smell of hibiscus trees just outside. Shaw loved Coral Gables, and more so all of Miami. It shared just enough color and visual texture with Hawaii to feel comfortable but had a much more diverse, cosmopolitan vibe. The ocean was ever present, and there were beautiful girls of every stripe and—

Hayley's face came to mind and he called her right away. Happily, she was glad to hear from him and available for dinner. Shaw selected a nice set of clothes, hung them in the steamer closet and jumped in the shower, humming. Coming back was a good idea. For the next six days or so, he would just put away all thoughts of hidden secrets and alien visitations and block out any scenarios of wherever that might eventually lead.

And he did manage to lose himself: in schoolwork, in Hayley's warm companionship, in a couple of dives and even one day of surfing up at the Sebastian Inlet. The swells were nothing like they had back home, but the sunrises were breathtaking.

On his last day, he and Hayley took a monorail 300 kilometers north of Miami, to a quaint little spot, Indian River Lagoon. They joined some very welcoming strangers for a party on the shore, convening around a big, blazing fire pit. But Shaw was coy about his *real* reason for bringing Hayley here. About an hour after sunset, they went for a walk, discovering a kayak directly in their path, unattended, with a small tag labeled 'Zander.'

Hayley laughed.

"What's all this now?" she asked, in her perky Irish brogue.

"A little nighttime sightseeing tour."

"But it's dark. There's nothing to see . . ."

He grinned, pushed the kayak to the waterline and held it steady as she stepped in. After snapping a floatation vest around her neck and shoulders, he did the same for himself, pushed off with his paddle and they drifted out with the gentle tide.

They glanced up at the moon, back to its old self, and both remained quiet. Like many people, they felt a slight twinge of apprehension about the moon, anxious something new might appear, and that this time it might not be good. Hayley opened a little bag and pulled out a small round shape.

"You didn't get any hushpuppies back at the party, so I stole a few."

Shaw cringed. He'd not warmed to some of the more southern dishes Florida had to offer. Hayley, though Irish, was a country girl, fearless in exploring local delicacies wherever she traveled. She held the tiny ball of fried cornbread to his lips, but he leaned back, pretending to paddle harder; fried foods were not his thing.

"You big baby! Try something new!"

She huffed, then dipped it in a little ketchup and waved it again. Maybe it was her big shiny eyes, but he gave up. Shaw opened his mouth and took in the whole hushpuppy, discovering the taste and texture unexpectedly delightful. Hayley swaggered triumphantly.

"See?"

"Yeah, okay," he muttered, chewing. "Sold."

She giggled. "Want another?" Shaw shrugged, and she popped another in his mouth.

"It is nice out here," she sighed, "with the moon and the little quiet sounds. Peaceful."

He just smiled, looking around. Then his eyes fixed on something, and he subtly turned the kayak in that direction.

"You never said anything about Bardy," Hayley said. "D'you know where he went?"

Shaw shook his head. "Do you?"

"No," Hayley said quietly, "he just found me in the library and said 'goodbye' and 'give Shaw a kiss for me.' And then the next day he was gone."

Shaw grunted morosely, paddling on.

"He'll pop up before you know it," she said, without a shred of doubt.

"Nothing new. You get used to it when you grow up in a military family."

"Aye. My Auntie was always getting shipped off here and there. And she was so good to her kids when she was home, they'd miss her somethin' awful. The whole house, my cousins, would just fall prey to this gloom. So my mum was the sort to say, 'Let's go buy some balloons an' a cake and bring some happy to your cousins.'" Her dimples creased sweetly with the memory. "And we would."

Shaw chuckled. "I don't remember many balloons. Till I was seven, we lived on the mainland, and Dad would just disappear for months. Then he was promoted and a few weeks later we moved . . ."

"Underwater," she finished for him. He nodded, continuing to paddle.

"That far out," Shaw said, "with troops ready to launch at a moment's notice, made great sense. Great *tactical* sense. Dad and his patrols could sneak up on the bad guys in a flash – they'd never see him coming. And those seabases made the difference. In about five more years, it was over. So for everyone else, it was great. But moving the Zander family wasn't an easy transition. Mom says I cried at least once a day or night our first full month there. I'd go to the window, and usually you go to a window and you see clouds and trees and sunlight. If you're lucky, some pretty birds flying by, singing, and you want to go out and play." Shaw's eyes stared off, his voice a tiny flutter. "But it was always dark. Big shapes would drift by, and I'm a little kid, so a big dark shadow, a few meters away, with only a viewport between us . . ."

"That would've terrified me," Hayley admitted. "I don't think I would've been able to sleep." She noticed the lights of shore were tiny now. They were surrounded in black.

"Where are we going, Shaw Zander? I'll brook no shenanigans, young man."

"Trust me. You'll like it."

"Aye, aye, Captain. But be fair warned," she balled up a fist playfully, "I'm not some wilting violet falling prey to a kidnapper. And the Irish know how to land a punch."

He laughed, acknowledging her bravado. Eager to spring his surprise, he put more effort into paddling.

"I played music to sleep. For a while. And still above it, you could hear strange, empty noises, like ghosts. Over a lot of the next four-and-a-half years, till the war was over, Dad was off somewhere looking for bad guys. He'd call in and we'd see him and talk, but I didn't get to hug him at night. Dax was too little to know the difference, and Mom always kept us busy in all kinds of creative ways. So every time our dad came back it was like Christmas. And every time he left for a long time, I'd keep quiet about it, but inside I was always incredibly afraid something would happen to him. 'Cause you can't help it. You'd hear stories, we'd catch news reports and see some of the conflicts going on at sea. Whole armadas of ships Dad's troops would run up against."

"But he came back, right?" Hayley asked, in a bright, lilting tone. "And now you're a proper marine scientist, bringin' fish back from the brink. So obviously, somewhere along the way, y'must have learned to love the sea."

"He always came back. Eventually I just stopped being afraid. Somewhere in there Mom said I needed to be strong for Dax. Keep him distracted and happy. What I didn't realize is, that was her way of distracting me from missing Dad. She was helping me."

Hayley rested her hand on his knee.

"Now, I really want to meet your mom. I've always thought of her as this fine-tuned mind, an intellectual invested in physics and energy and developing new alloys. And yet she was tender enough to raise her boys to care for each other."

Shaw laughed. "Well, I've pounded Dax's head more than a few times. We've scuffled over the years. But . . . yeah." His grin grew wider. Catching that, she smiled suspiciously.

"What?"

"We're here," he said, pulling the paddle out of the water.

Taking her eyes off him, Hayley gasped.

All around them, in hazy little patches, the ocean was glowing. Softly afire with a bluish-green light, as if billions of microscopic fireflies had gathered to welcome them.

"Ohhh," she cooed with delight, "bioluminescent plankton! Right?"

"Right. You didn't think I brought you 300 kilometers from Miami to crash a party and eat hushpuppies, did ya?"

"Well, I had no idea! Oh, Shaw, it's lovely. . ."

She held out a hand and tapped her wristband, recording the phenomenon.

"And here I thought it was my job to cheer you up about Bardy," she said.

He raised a playful eyebrow. "Well, you know what Bardy said. Technically, you still owe me that kiss."

It took no more persuading. Sitting there under the silvery moon, in the aquamarine glow of gently lapping waves, their lips met, and Shaw knew that returning to Florida had been a good decision. For a while, he forgot about the nagging feeling deep in his gut, the sense that his dad was drifting away again, and that some dark, unknown tide might carry him very far.

. . .

The last days of October were about as perfect for Dax and Kai as any kid could wish for; it helped that Grampa loved Halloween. In addition to getting the boys involved for days with his decorating, he had prepared a menu of diverse activities for each morning or afternoon. Secretly he aimed to take their minds off of home, but ball games, aquariums, treasure hunting and volcano trail hikes were pretty effortless distractions for young men. Somewhere in the middle of all that, Dax surprised everyone.

Slipping inside a little before noon on the 31st, Dax was counting on Kai and his grandfather being out on some adventure. But no sooner had he entered the living room than Grampa popped out of the kitchen, dressed as a rather portly, shockingly white-faced vampire.

"Greetings, my child!" he exclaimed in a thick Transylvanian accent. "Vwat do you zink of our—"

And when he actually *looked* at his grandson, his fangs popped out.

"Holy hackin' buzzsaws! You chopped it all off!"

A queasy feeling squeezed Dax's stomach as he wondered if he'd made the right decision. Grampa picked up his pointy teeth and stepped closer, running a hand across the remaining shock of hair atop Dax's head. The sides and back were little more than fuzz.

"Wow. I'm glad you left a little there, at least. Otherwise you'd pass for a kiwifruit."

"Yeah," Dax said uneasily, "at least I won't need another one for a while."

Kai ran in, dressed in a quaint suit of velvet, pointed ears, a rather extreme widow's peak and his own set of oversized teeth, which he gnashed together with gusto. Scrub galloped at his heels, a set of webbed wings and a long dragon tail bouncing along with every buoyant step. Seeing Dax, Kai's enhanced, very bushy eyebrows lifted a full centimeter.

"Wow! You're so bald!"

"No, that's what we call tastefully coiffed, Kai," Grampa corrected. "The big question is why the change?"

Dax was already anxious to change the subject. "No reason," he fibbed, "but what are you guys supposed to be?"

"We're Munsters!" Kai exclaimed, tapping his wrist emitter. A floating image of several ghoulish-but-cheerful characters, apparently a family, appeared above his arm.

"Does he mean monsters?" Dax asked.

"Nope!" Grampa replied cheerfully. "*Munsters*. It was a show way before your time. Heck, way before my time, but I found it as a little kid in reruns; made me laugh and laugh. I'm Grampa Munster – who's kind of a vampire and a mad doctor – Kai's my grandson Eddie and Scrub is Spot. We've been gobbling up episodes this week for research."

Dax looked Kai up and down, then Scrub, absolutely mystified.

"Spot's a dragon! He blows fire under the stairs! And I'm a werewolfie!" He snarled, then turned to Scrub and snapped his fingers. Scrub's whole snout shook as he blew a long gust of hot breath; apparently, they had been practicing. Dax laughed.

"Okay, tap me a few 'Munsters,'" Dax said. "Maybe I'll watch with Cody."

A few minutes later they enjoyed a lunch of fruit and barbecued turkey wraps. Now out of costume, Grampa nonetheless soaked in the festive sights. It had been years since he'd gone to this much trouble; there were ghosts hanging from trees all around the house, a few corpses lunging out of and then sinking back into freshly dug 'graves,' a skinny, pumpkin-headed figure tiptoeing across the roof and faux candles everywhere. At night, a series of tubes would flood the outdoor walkways with a low-creeping fog. He always decorated a little, of course, but having the boys with him this time offered an excuse to go all out.

"I think we should leave it like this for a long time, how about you?"

Dax laughed; Kai nodded enthusiastically.

"Can I turn on the smoke tonight?" the tyke asked.

"It's fog, buddy," Grampa said, "and yessiree, you sure can." His brow furrowed, considering Dax. "Going to Cody's tonight? Are you guys dressing up?"

"Cody doesn't leave the house much. So we were gonna watch some scary wraparounds and his mom said we could eat bad stuff all night."

"But you gotta dress up!" Grampa pleaded. "It's Halloween!"

Dax seemed restless, but didn't argue. His grandfather sighed, looking him over.

"Well, we gotta do *something*."

Despite wanting to experience the holiday more thoroughly than in years past, Dax hadn't put much thought into a costume. So a little later, rummaging around the house, they found a perfect solution. In the garage, Grampa kept a box of old, torn cotton rags meant for cleaning *The Empress Lilly*. They were regularly laundered, but after years of stains and bleach, they looked ancient. With a little bit of patience, fabric adhesive and some black greasepaint around his eyes and cheekbones, Dax made quite a striking mummy. Kai watched the whole transformation, giggling occasionally as some wrappings would fall off and have to be reapplied. At one point, a large flap peeled off his backside, revealing Dax's bright blue underwear. Kai laughed hysterically for three minutes straight.

"I can fix that," Grampa offered.

After Dax shed himself of the mummy outfit, Grampa took it to a desk in the corner of the garage. He retrieved what looked like a pen from a small clip and drew a line around the section of fabric now hanging loose like a trap door. Carefully positioning the whole thing flat on the desk, Grampa unfolded a counter-balanced arm with two little nozzles at one end. He lowered the array over the fabric and flicked a switch. A soft blue laser traced the line he had drawn, followed by a fine stream of what looked like silken plasma, welding together the ripped fabric with a barely detectable seam. Dax was impressed, but Kai's eyes were wide open; the boy loved anything that moved like an animal.

"It looks like a giraffe spitting snoodies on Dax's pants!" he said, entranced.

"Yeah, I haven't used this in a while. Your Gramma would make all kinds of neat things with this – hats, sundresses, even a costume once in a while. She was a real seamstress."

There was a faint, pleasant smell as the overhead array went dark and folded itself back up. Grampa lifted the mummy-pants with a flourish, whapping them once to ensure they would not split again.

"Okay! You can stand proudly with the pharaohs now! *And* bend! In any direction!"

"Thanks, Grampa!"

Dax slipped them on and admired himself in a mirror, turning side-to-side. He pulled over his raggedy hood and lunged at Kai, grunting as if awakened from a long, accursed slumber. His little brother screeched and ran out of the room. Scrub snorted protectively, but Dax growled again and Scrub yelped, bounding out of the garage. His Grandfather nodded with approval.

"If I was an archaeologist, I'd be running, too."

Dax stilled, then turned to his Grandfather with a gleeful, wild look. Inspired, he glanced around the garage; all kinds of tools, collectibles and things that made no sense at all to Dax hung on hooks or filled shelves. There were two long rows of hats – baseball caps, mostly, but a few others more exotic in nature. Dax stepped quickly over and plucked a pith helmet. It was spotted and faded with age, but that seemed all the better.

"Grampa, could I borrow this? And . . ." his eyes zipped around, definitely looking to fill a mental list, "maybe some of that rope and your air-sled?"

"The sled? Sure. It's all charged up. You don't want to take your scooter?"

Dax looked up and grinned.

"Not tonight."

Spooks

An hour later, Dax was a few blocks away, riding the sled at a moderate pace along the embedded sidewalks, the turbines providing gentle forward thrust. Dressed up as an ancient mummy, he made for a funny sight—several of his stray bandages trailing in the wind like streamers, the Pith helmet strapped to his head, some folded-up cardboard boxes and rope stashed beneath him. Every astonished look fueled his zeal to go 'full ghoul.' As he approached other pedestrians, he'd stretch out a shaking arm as if to capture them and slow his approach. Usually they would catch the hint and step clear so he could zip on by. It was Halloween, after all, so most people were in the spirit and had a good laugh as he passed.

Halfway to Cody's, he got a call, but his receiver was covered up by layers of rags around his wrist. He stopped the sled and pulled some slack in the rags, irritated that he'd messed up his costume. It was Shaw – and Dax had not heard from him since his departure.

Shaw blinked, processing Dax wrapped up in all those stained rags. He laughed.

"Where are you? I just got back to Grampa's. Nobody's here."

Dax was a little surprised. Shaw seemed uncharacteristically chipper. Relaxed, even.

"On my way to Cody's. Doing Halloween. Everything okay?"

"Yeah, I had something for you," Shaw began. "Cody can't trick or treat, right? Going outside's a bad idea, I would think."

"He can't walk real far. But Grampa gave me an—"

"I made something for you guys. Well, I got it from a friend. Something Halloweeny."

"Seriously?" Dax asked, wondering about this sudden generosity. "You hate Halloween."

"Yeah, but you don't. And Cody's our friend, so . . ."

"What is it?"

"A custom X-Pince: *Zombie Swamp*. Neither of you have to walk. You can just sit there and it's like you're on a boat, going through . . . I don't know," Shaw rolled his eyes, "a bunch of zombies and I guess other things. Bats, crocodiles, swamp squids, all that."

Dax was absolutely shocked.

"You got that for us?"

"Yeah. Don't get all weepy on me. I have a friend who does haunted houses for fun and he always does an X-Pince version for anyone who's sick or special needs. He's pretty good."

"That sounds great! Hey! You think we could hook it into the air-sled? I brought it with me, and that could be our boat! Maybe we could synch it up, so it rocks like it's in real water!"

Shaw nodded. "You can try. I'll tap it over to you now, so just hit play whenever you want and it'll be ready to go."

"Shaw, this is crazy banga, man. Thank you."

Shaw winked, his cheeks flush with pride.

"No problem. And don't forget . . . We're going tonight."

"Going? Where?"

Shaw's relaxed tenor suddenly tightened up. Dax laughed.

"Relax, I remembered. What time?"

"Late. After Grampa Pat's in bed."

"It's like, ninety clicks to home. How do we get there? Please don't say *The Empress Lilly*. I don't want to take any more chances with Grampa's boat."

"No," Shaw assured, "my friend Boone's got a mini-skimmer. He owes me a favor."

"Does it absolutely gotta be tonight?"

"C'mon, we had a deal. And Mom and Dad didn't call me once this week, Dax. That's very strange for them. Something's up, and it's time we learned what."

Dax replied, quietly. "Okay. I'll be back by 1:00. Grampa will just think I'm sleeping at the Vallabh's."

"Dax. Tell Cody—" his voice drifted, then, "tell him Pomaika'i hoaloha."

"I will. Thanks, Shaw."

160

Shaw chuckled again at his brother's goofy getup.

"See ya later, King Tut. Have fun."

He blinked out and Dax shivered for a second in anticipation of a very late night. He started up the sled again, whisking along the shimmering walks that hugged gently curving streets, and reached Cody's front porch less than five minutes later.

His pal was actually rocking in the large chair suspended from the porch overhang, reading. Dax shouted "Hey!" and Cody looked up, then nearly fell out of the chair laughing. Dax pulled the air-sled up the steps and unloaded the rope.

"That is great! Did you make that?"

"Well, Grampa helped. A lot."

"But why are you wearing the safari hat?" Cody asked, pointing up.

Dax patted his head and laughed, removing the helmet.

"Oh! That's for you! It's part of your costume."

"I don't think I can go trick or treating," Cody answered, trying on the hat anyway. "My legs aren't strong enough to go very far, and my glider doesn't like bumpy sidewalks . . ."

But Dax was busy unfolding the cardboard boxes he'd already cut into specific, complimentary shapes. He snapped them together with a few adhesive-backed hinges, and in minutes a whole outer shell popped up, surrounding the sled. Cody squinted, trying to figure it out, which was about the time his dad stepped out on the porch.

"Hi, Dax," Mr. Vallabh said, holding out two cups of juice. "What is that? A rickshaw?"

Dax nodded happily, gesturing for Cody to get in. He handed his friend two long ropes, slung around his armpits, then took a stance in front, as if ready to pull it forward.

"Wow, this is super comfy," Cody noted, finding a nice position inside. He tugged at the 'reins' attached to Dax and his friend grunted, pulling the air-sled forward a meter or so.

"You're a mummy pulling a wagon," Mr. Vallabh observed. "I get that, but what is Cody supposed to be?"

Dax looked over his shoulder proudly, pulling a ripped piece of rag from his mouth.

"He's the world's laziest archaeologist!"

They had a good laugh together, after which Cody's parents found him a khaki-colored jacket, magnifying glass, and several improvised ancient scrolls to stuff conspicuously in the rickshaw. After sunset, the boys were gliding down the sidewalks, where the embedded tracks made Dax's 'mummy pulling' practically effortless. Numerous people stopped to gawk or take pictures. There were plenty of vampires, zombies, princesses, pirates, fairies and superheroes going door-to-door for treats, but the archaeologist and his rickshaw-pulling mummy stood out.

They spent a good two hours trick or treating, the 'rickshaw' gradually loading up with goodies. After a while, Cody was quite literally sitting in a pile of candy. On their way back, Dax paused to stare up at the sky. The moon was full and brilliant, though now free of ominous symbols. Perfect for Halloween night.

"Spooky!" he said, his bandages now flopping off the whole lower portion of his face.

"Your face is peeling!" Cody laughed. In fact, Dax's costume was starting to itch and he was ready to shed the whole thing anyway, so as they moved on, he randomly tore off loose sections, tossing them back at Cody, who swatted them away in mock disgust. When he finally got to peeling the raggedy strips of cloth off his head, Cody's eyes popped, staring at him. He swiped a palm up the side of Dax's temple.

"Wow! It's like your head is naked!"

Dax chuckled bashfully, muttering.

"I don't know. I got stupid, I guess."

"No, no," Cody replied, wry amusement worming onto his face, "you didn't get stupid. And I bet Illone will like it a lot."

"No, that's not why —"

But his pal knew better; they shared a grin.

"Really think she will?"

"Oh, yeah," Cody said with a smirk, "but if she doesn't, it'll grow back in a year or two."

Upon their return, Dananjay had a platter of fish tacos ready on a hot plate in Cody's bedroom, and the boys devoured them all while watching an old 'flat' horror movie, as they were referred to these days. Once it ended, Dax stripped the sled of its rickshaw overlay.

"Shaw did something pretty chewy for us," Dax explained, uploading the program to Cody's X-Pince system. In seconds, the room darkened, filling with raggedy old trees draped in moss, a very still bayou, inky black, and strange, eerie sounds everywhere.

"Get in the sled!" Dax said. He opened Cody's closet and rummaged about, grabbing two X-Pince swords they'd not used in years. He sat down beside his friend a moment later.

"Is it scary?" Cody asked.

"Maybe. I mean Shaw got this, so . . ."

Within a few seconds, they were no longer in Cody's bedroom sitting in a sleek little air-sled, but a creaky raft plying a swamp peppered with countless perils. Squid tentacles broke the muddy surface, and they swung their swords, slicing up all kinds of calamari. Zombies emerged from rotting trees, hungry for them, only to be sent back in pieces to the oily depths. Shaw's gift proved scary enough for the two boys, capping a Halloween night they would both cherish, and the last time in their lives they would giggle and howl like carefree kids. A few times while fighting off various beasts, Dax recalled that in just hours, he'd be accompanying his brother in an act that might make his parents tremendously angry, a thought he kept pushing away. By comparison, no monsters in a simulated swamp could possibly be as intimidating.

. . .

About half-past 1:00 a.m., Dax tip-toed into the house through a side door, relieved to hear the gentle thunder of Grampa Pat's snoring two rooms away. The jack-o-lantern atop the dining room table had long since gone dark. A quick check in the avocado-monkey room revealed Kai cocooned in a jumble of blankets and stuffed animals, Scrub likely lumped somewhere in there as well. Shaw, however, was nowhere to be found. Moving into the backyard, Dax stared up at the sky. Heavy cloud cover now obscured the full moon.

A single word suddenly appeared, pulsing like a specter above Dax's sleeve:

BEACH

He looked out to the water, but it was very dark – just a rolling surf of silver froth and heaving swells of inky black beneath a murky, slate gray sky.

Finally a light flashed from out there – blinking a few times, a tiny urgent spark against a very uncooperative void. Certain it must be Shaw, Dax went to the garage, slipped into a clean, dry skinsuit, and headed for the beach. Even with his booties on, the sand felt cold under his feet. Night dives always brought a tiny thrill to his gut, a sense of greater potential for the unexpected. In the quiet, his mind drifted. Quite unexpectedly, he found himself rediscovering the violet-blue miasma of Illone's eyes, with an itchy but not unwelcome feeling there were adventures to be found there, as well.

The crashing waves, louder as he reached the shoreline, brought him back to the here and now. The silhouette of Shaw's mini-skimmer, holding position maybe fifteen meters out, was just visible against the muddy skyline. The night chill might have been an illusion since the waters off the North Shore almost always skewed warm, but as Dax waded in he was grateful for the insulating coziness of his skinsuit.

Shaw moved the boat to intervene and helped pull Dax aboard. He smiled earnestly, the light from the instrument panel painting his face in a way that seemed kinder than usual.

"You okay? How's Cody?"

Dax paused, genuinely touched that his brother's first question was about his best friend's welfare. Shaw noticed the clear waterproof duffeltube hanging off his wrist, holding a toothbrush and a few other personal items, Cody's baseball cap among them.

"Chicago Cubs. He give that to you?"

Dax nodded.

Shaw stilled, putting a firm hand on Dax's shoulder.

"That's tough, Dax. I'm sorry. I know you think I don't care, but if you ever want to just, you know, talk—"

He stopped, squinting a bit, gazing at Dax strangely. He reached up for the hood covering all but his brother's face and Dax lurched back.

"Hey!"

"Pull your hood down."

"Why?" Dax asked, annoyed.

"Come on . . ."

Shaw folded his arms, clearly unwilling to let this go. Dax grunted and peeled his hood away from his forehead and cheeks, rolling it down around his neck. Shaw's jaw literally dropped in shock.

"Whoa! The rainforest is *gone*!"

"I just got a haircut. Get off my yon."

"All of a sudden. Amazing. Why?"

Dax turned away with an awkward shrug, mumbling.

"I dunno."

"Come on . . . There had to be a reason."

"It was time, I guess."

But he turned back around and even in the dim light, Shaw glimpsed the pink in his flushed cheeks. That was all it took.

"You met a girl!"

"Shut up," Dax grumbled.

"You did! What's her name?"

"Start the boat! I am not talking about my love life!"

"Whoa! You're in love! Dax is in *love*!"

"I am not! Start the boat, you gobie!"

"Sniff, sniff. My wittle bruvver's all gwown up."

Scowling, Dax plopped into a seat, yanking his hood back up in one firm, defiant gesture.

"Can we go now?"

Shaw snickered, starting the motor. He was about to open up the throttle when a raucous splash to stern startled them both.

Scrub's loud, throaty bark came just seconds before Kai's enthusiastic call.

"Hey! I'm comin', too!"

Shaw groaned. Dax was even more upset.

"Kai! Why aren't you in bed! I saw you at home!"

Kai wagged his head, quite pleased with himself.

"You saw my pillows. HA!"

"He fooled you with a few pillows?" Shaw sniffed, not even trying to hide his amusement. "You know how old that trick is?"

Dax ignored him. "Grampa's going to have a heart attack if he finds you missing, Kai. Go home!"

"NO! Scrub and I are going with you guys."

"You don't even know where we're going!" Dax replied, exasperated. Undeterred, Kai climbed into the skimmer. Scrub leaned in, over the edge of the hull. Kai tapped him on the head, a signal to the sea lion to hold his position.

"You're goin' home to s'prise Mommy and Daddy, and I am, too."

Surprisingly, Shaw kept a cool head.

"Dax, if we send them away now, they might wake up Grampa Pat. If we're careful, we can check things out and have us all back before dawn without anyone knowing anything."

"You mean if we're *lucky*. Maybe we should wait, Shaw."

"No!" Kai pleaded. "Dax, please! You never let me have any fun."

"You're cracked! I take you all kinds of places."

Shaw set his jaw, pushing the throttle gently forward.

"Okay, we're going. He'll be fine. Strap in before I open it up."

Dax darted an aggravated look to Kai, whose big, self-satisfied grin stretched ear-to-ear.

"Strap in, droney!" Dax barked. Kai stuck his tongue out, reaching for his seat restraint.

"Come on, Scrub! Here, boy!" Kai called, and the creature scrambled into the boat.

"Kai!" Shaw exclaimed, "this is not my boat and he drools all over everything! Get him out of here, now!"

"Scrub's gotta ride with us! He can't swim fast enough to keep up!"

Shaw grumbled something under his breath; Dax settled back with a knowing smirk.

"Yeah, this is gonna be fun."

Chagrined, Shaw opened the throttle. Soon, they were skimming along toward home at sixty knots.

"Are we there yet?" Kai asked, about five minutes in. Dax and Shaw just laughed, after which Dax closed his eyes, convinced Shaw had the helm firmly in hand.

"What if those ships are still around?" Dax mumbled aloud.

"Then we'll anchor further out and it'll be a longer swim. I made sure to top off both our reserves and . . ." His brow furrowed briefly; he turned to Kai.

"Kailen, what's the reading on your N-pack?"

The lad touched his wrist and gazed at the display for a few seconds, then held it aloft to reveal they were 94 percent full.

"Plenty," Shaw said. "If Kai gets tired of swimming, he can hang on to Scrub."

Dax offered a simple thumbs up. The thrumming whoosh-whoosh of water rushing all around them, the balmy Pacific wind blasting his cheeks were all too perfect to not catch a nap. A random, fleeting image of Illone's fingers flitting through his hair brought a sweet smile to his face. And then sleep.

A rippling windbreaker zipped up over his skinsuit, Shaw kept his attention mostly to the sea ahead, glancing occasionally to the ever changing, glowing navigational panel hovering just above the wheel. Feeling something press against his side, he looked down to see Kai there, clutching his jacket. They shared a nod, but neither spoke, just enjoying the night air and that shared anticipation of a little adventure. Of them all, Scrub was probably enjoying the trip the most, gulping repeatedly at the brisk, salty spray as they cut across the midnight sea.

They had been traveling for fifty-two minutes when Shaw abruptly slowed the skimmer.

"Dax."

He glanced back; Dax had nodded off, his head crooked to one side, snoring. Shaw reached down and rapped his chest.

"Dax! Take a look."

Groggy, Dax stood up and leaned forward against the misty windshield. He squinted, expecting to see at least a few of the ships they'd glimpsed before, but there were none; no vessels at all. Instead, out across the surface a series of starkly blinking buoys marked the perimeter of a circle, perhaps half a kilometer in diameter.

"Where did those come from?" Dax muttered.

"You're smarter than that, Dax," Shaw answered humorlessly.

His brother gazed out at the dark water, the tiny lights. So small and obscure, but something about it was wrenching a knot in his gut.

"Don't make this a big joke, okay? But . . . I'm a little scared."

Shaw looked him square in the eye and put a hand on his shoulder.

"And that's how smart you *can* be, little brother."

He turned back to the endless black sea, pulling out his macros. Looking through them, he sighed, then handed the unit to Dax.

"Are *you* scared?" Dax asked timidly.

Shaw's low, anxious chuckle caught in his throat.

"Oh, yeah."

Invaders

K ai squeezed in between his two brothers, squinting at the dark ocean.

"Why are those lights there, Shaw?" Kai asked.

"Don't know, buddy. Maybe a signal to let people know there's work going on."

"What kind of work?"

"We're not sure," Dax answered. "Check your skinsuit and run a self-test to make sure it's charged up."

As Kai busied himself with that, Dax quietly conferred with his older brother.

"So we got a plan, Professor Arronax?"

"You want me to start using *your* middle name?"

"Don't! So? If that's a security perimeter . . . what if there's a net?"

Shaw had obviously already been considering this.

"We get close, go straight down, and once we reach the reef, we move in."

"And if we set off some kind of alarm?" Dax pressed.

"Then Mom and Dad will have to explain why there's a sensor grid around our home."

"Then *you* go back to Miami and they ground me and Kai for all eternity."

Shaw chewed on his lip, staring out at the buoys and their pulsing signals. Dax searched the skimmer for any equipment. If a grid had been activated around the seabase, it would be nearly impossible to evade detection. But there might be another possibility. Dax checked the helm console and frowned.

"Your friend bought a skimmer without a depth gauge?" Dax asked, perturbed.

"He won this in a contest. I think it was pretty bare bones when he got it."

Immediately Dax began to open cabinets, pulled up covers to reveal compartments under the seats, but found nothing.

"What are you looking for?"

"Any kind of com equipment, sonar, frequency relays, whatever. We could send out a little scrambled series of pings to confuse a proximity sensor long enough for us to slip through."

"You can do that?" Shaw asked. His brother seemed increasingly full of surprises.

"It's easy, if your boat actually had any tools. But I can't even find a wrench."

Curious about the opened compartments, Scrub shuffled near, sniffing around.

"Scrub! Get out of my way! Kai! Call your dragon!"

As Kai gently pulled Scrub away, Dax was struck with a possible alternative.

"Wait. You've been teaching Scrub some tricks, right?"

"Uh huh," Kai affirmed, "Shaw taught me some before he went back to Florida."

Shaw perked up with the idea and crouched on his haunches.

"Kai, do you think Scrub's learned enough where we could get him to swim to our base? Or even . . . swim around it? Like, snooping around?"

"You mean like a spy?" Kai whispered aloud.

"Yeah, exactly like a spy," Dax chuckled. With a single finger, he stroked the top of his hood and the upper half of his facemask slid down over his eyes, composed of bulbous lenses and a sloping nose guard. Though collapsible when not in use, a low voltage current instantly made the wafer-thin material rigid, strong and waterproof. Once in place, the bottom section slid up over his mouth and chin to meet and seal with the upper half. There was just enough room and play in the lower portion of his mask to permit speaking with ease, and the integrated communication system could network with any suit on the same frequency.

"This could work!" Shaw said, newly enthused. "His core temperature should read at least a little lower than ours, so if there's a sensor grid set for humans, it might not pick him up."

"Too bad we didn't bring a peeper," Dax said, his processed voice just slightly tinny. "Then Scrub could do some real remote spying for us."

Shaw chuckled with satisfaction, opening a mesh pack. He yanked out a tiny, straw-like device attached to an elastic band. Dax reached for it, pleased.

"You wanna risk losing a thumb, or should we let Kai put it on him?" he asked.

Indeed, despite the fact that the intended surveillance targets were their parents, Kai found the idea of spying terribly exciting, especially as his pet and personal bodyguard was to be the key operative. His brothers watched as he secured the strap around Scrub's slippery head with the animal's full and trusting compliance, and eventually they got the tiny scope pointing in the right direction.

Soon all four mammals were in the water. Networked communication devices were already standard in skinsuits, as were bright-beam units, integrated along the torso and just above the wrists, so there was little chance of them getting separated or lost. And their seabase was typically pretty well lit – impossible to miss once one was within half a kilometer.

Diving down to the reef, the first thing they noticed at twenty meters was that things were not typical. The entire seabase complex was dark, but for a few tiny perimeter lights along the roofline edges and then again marking the boundaries of the shelf, where the depth dropped precipitously. From the windows of the barracks and residential wings, only hazy patches of ghostly blue-green were visible within.

"Why are the lights out?" Dax asked, more than a little unsettled. Shaw just shook his head, grunting.

"Is everything okay? Where are Mommy and Daddy?" Kai asked.

"Don't worry, Kai," Shaw reassured, "they're asleep . . . it's late, right?"

Kai nodded, Scrub circling and twirling around his stout form.

"Think you can get Scrub to circle the whole base and come back?" Dax asked Kai.

Almost nose to snout with the creature, Kai spoke slowly, put his hand on his chest and drew a circle around it slowly with his finger.

"You go out there, all around. Then come back here."

Scrub nuzzled Kai's hooded cheek, and with one powerful kick of his tail, was off like a dark missile.

Dax and Kai crowded in around Shaw to get a look at the remote video display floating just above his sleeve. It was murky until Shaw adjusted the contrast, and then they were seeing, essentially, what Scrub was seeing.

"Well, he hasn't set off any alarms," Dax observed.

They all squinted, staring at the changing imagery. The windows were indeed dark; there seemed to be no activity at all until . . .

"Mom's lab!" Shaw exclaimed.

"Go back!" Dax said.

170

"Wait! We might miss something."

So they watched, getting more footage of dark modules. And then, for quite a few seconds, Scrub seemed to be following the exploits of a crab, crawling between some rocks.

"What's he doing?" Dax grumped. "Lose the crab!"

Almost as if by command, the camera's attention shifted from the crustacean to a few blurred, tiny fish that vanished an instant later – almost certainly into Scrub's gullet.

"Whoa!" Shaw said, enlarging the display so Dax could see better. Within the frame, a slender, cone-shaped rock formation came into view, apparently held in place vertically by a series of cables all around its perimeter.

"What is that? A new . . . rock?" Dax muttered, "I've never seen that rock before."

"That's weird," Shaw observed. "I wonder if that's what those helicopters dropped."

A blur of red and pink lights flooded the lens, and the screen went completely dark.

"Scrub!" Kai shouted, grabbing Shaw's arm. "Something got Scrub! Find him!"

"Relax, Kai. He's okay. I'm sure he's okay."

"You sure?" Kai's eyes were shiny with tears behind the goggles in his mask. Dax nodded reassuringly, but he wondered how big a sin it was for brothers to lie to each other.

The long flippers on his feet barely touching the sandy bottom, Shaw tinkered with the display mechanism that had just lost its image.

"Hold on, Kai. This is old tech. The battery taps might be worn down."

Dax, however, began to feel a chill, a foreboding sense that something was very wrong. For possibly the first time ever, he felt ill at ease in the place he'd grown up.

Shaw squeezed and tapped at the controls and sure enough, the feed came alive again, revealing: himself, Dax and Kai – small in the frame but rapidly getting larger. Shaw kept tapping, momentarily bewildered, until they looked up to see Scrub's dark form zooming straight for them. Kai opened his arms and caught him, rolling back with the impact, but holding tight. Scrub nuzzled the lad's neck and chest, but he was visibly trembling.

"He's afraid! Something scared him!" Kai exclaimed.

"I'm sure he's fine, Kai," Dax reasoned, even as he started to notice something odd. They were casting shadows. Lengthening shadows. He pointed to the ocean floor before them.

"Shaw, it's midnight, so why are we—"

The water around them, inky black mere seconds before, was getting strangely brighter, the particulate matter beginning to shimmer. Instinctively, they turned about, and the sight facing them chilled their blood.

Two of the three Delvans who had appeared at LAMIGA – one larger, the other considerably more compact – hovered in place before them. Staring back with softly glowing eyes, their colored markings seemed much more luminous at close range than in the footage the boys had watched over and over. They were sublimely beautiful this close, every limb and fin tapering in graceful curves. The larger of the two reminded Dax of the glowing stars on Cody's wall and ceiling – its dominant color was the same ghostly green, while the non-luminous pattern was closer to a pale teal. The smaller one had the hues of a ripening pomegranate – deep pink accented with a few gleaming patches of red. Something very calming about the gently pulsing light both beings gave off had the effect of soothing the boys' shock.

Scrub lunged forward, but the larger Delvan merely cocked its bulbous head and emitted something like a cooing sound, after which the sea lion retreated, settling down.

"Wow . . ." Kai sighed, appreciating the significance of this moment with raw innocence and purity.

Shaw and Dax shared a look. His older brother seemed at a loss for what to do, so Dax kicked forward, gently bobbing before the two visitors.

"Hello. Can you understand me?"

The larger of the two Delvans glided slightly closer just before the boys heard it 'speak.'

"We can," he answered, his voice masculine, but also oddly clipped and cold. "Please, do not be afraid."

What was almost as amazing as clearly hearing the words in English was that the creature's jaw was moving along with those words, as if simulating speech. But these movements were also not perfectly in synch – as if it was an improvised effort to approximate the way humans moved their mouths when speaking.

"I'm Dax. Dax Zander. This is my brother Shaw and our little brother, Kai."

"Hello," Shaw said quietly, far too overwhelmed to offer much else.

"Hi!" Kai waved amiably. "This is Scrub! He won't bite."

The two Delvans both seemed amused by this and very taken with Kai's energy.

"Salutations, Scrub," the smaller one said, in a distinctly feminine voice, followed by a few squeals and chirps directed at the sea lion that were clearly not of any human dialect. Whatever was articulated, Scrub responded with a little back flip, swishing his tail happily.

Dax nudged Shaw, whispering through his com unit.

"They speak seal. Or sea lion, anyway."

Shaw chuckled, as an image flashed in his memory of a pretty Dominican girl at the Miami SupraSeaquarium who had an impressive affinity for pinnipeds, and a similar effect on him as well. The Delvans turned their full attention again to the boys.

"I am Yol Beyyos," the larger one said. "Please forgive if we are not communicating with full clarity. Your language is inclusive of many idioms we still find confusing to construct."

Shaw chuckled. "Trust me. You're doing great."

"My other here is Ke'Yol Vren," the Delvan continued.

Vren waved a happy pectoral, her red whorls gleaming a tad brighter.

"That is myself!" she replied, with unmistakable enthusiasm. "Salutations! I am attendant to Yol Beyyos and —"

She stopped, suddenly pulling back to offer a deferential bow. Beyyos also stilled, staring past the boys, all of whom realized there was probably a new presence, just behind them.

Turning again to look, sure enough, the third Delvan, Prevek, bobbed there. The pattern of his hide was a stunning and nearly even complement of deep indigo and ultramarine swirls – the latter of which shone less brightly than the others, but in such a soothing manner the boys were absolutely mesmerized.

He didn't speak at first. Finally, Kai chirped up.

"You're the biggest."

Prevek's large head, which seemed to compose nearly a third of his mass, tilted to one side, considering Kai. The water all around him took on a magical blue hue as his luminosity intensified. Finally he spoke, his voice a velvety baritone so measured and resonant, the boys were taken entirely off guard. He sounded a little like their father.

"We were told there would be no visitors. But there is no question all of you are heirs—"

173

He paused, as if to reconsider his phrasing. "You are the offspring of Captain Evan and his spouse, the scientist Dayna."

"They're our parents. Yes," Shaw answered, in a purposely respectful tone.

Prevek's three-pronged tail swerved gently side-to-side, bringing him closer to Shaw, who found his golden eyes irresistible, like the hot, muted glow from a candle sheathed inside old, thick glass. All the while he sensed Prevek's eyes penetrating past his skin, into his thoughts. Could these visitors read minds?

"But your parents do not know you are here."

"So much for getting in and out," Dax muttered.

"You're not gonna eat us, are you?" Kai asked.

Beyyos darted to Prevek's side, answering crisply.

"It is not of our culture to consume sentient organisms."

"Dax? What's 'sentient'?"

"They're not gonna eat us, Kai," Dax said urgently, "okay? Shh."

"How do you speak?" Shaw asked, genuinely fascinated. "I know you're not actually talking, even though your jaws are moving. Is it telepathy? Because it *feels* like real sound."

Prevek nodded, and for the first time they saw a Delvan smile. Dax blinked; dolphins and quite a few other animals had what seemed to be a natural smile, but it was simply a graceful illusion of biology. The Delvans, however, apparently possessed more musculature in their heads and snouts, capable of indicating genuine emotional reactions. And when Prevek attempted this, it was surprisingly charming.

"We emit a series of vibrations calculated for reception throughout your skeletal mass as vocal sounds. It is a relatively simple thing for us to accomplish, though we have adapted the process for several specific languages, as the people of this planet use so many diverse tongues. We can accomplish this with little visible movement at all; but after studying your kind for a short while, it was agreed that approximating the visual mechanics of speech might provide for a more comfortable exchange of communication."

"Wow. You guys sure went to a lot of trouble before coming to Earth," Dax said.

"We have been to Earth before," Beyyos answered, "but there has been no need for communication with humans until now."

"Wait – what?" Shaw asked, astonished. "Who else would you have communicated with on your earlier visits?"

The three Delvans glanced at each other. Prevek flicked his eyelids at Vren and Beyyos, and they fell silent.

"There may be a better time to address these questions," Prevek offered, "as it seems we are no longer alone."

"Alone?" Shaw replied, just before the lights all around the compound abruptly flashed on, revealing a closing circle of over a dozen armed divers in uniform.

"Hold your position!" they heard through their com links. "Captain, are you there?"

While the Delvans remained calm, all three boys were in a panic, glancing around furtively, bewildered as to the sheer number of human divers now emerging to serve as 'escort.' Dax looked beyond them to the now brightly illuminated viewport looking into the Zander's living room. Their parents stood at the window, glaring out with a posture and scowls that left no mystery as to their mood.

Their father's voice, tight and crisp, broke a very brief, uneasy silence.

"I see them, Lieutenant," he said. "Boys, I know you can hear me. Inside and ready to talk in five minutes."

"Where'd all these guys come from?" Kai asked. Shaw slowly backed away with a glance at the surrounding troops, who watched without further intervention. Dax nodded to their new Delvan friends.

"I guess we'll talk later."

The three boys kicked away toward the nearest diver lockout chamber. They waited for it to fill with water so they could enter.

"Mom and Dad are never gonna trust us again," Dax said emphatically.

"Don't get dramatic," Shaw said. "I'll handle it. So, how about our visitors?"

"I think them being here means something we weren't supposed to know about," Dax answered, "and now we do. Which means . . . I don't know what it means. Kinda scary. But they seem nice. For aliens."

"Nice?" Shaw repeated, sardonically. The chamber keypad signaled green, meaning they could enter safely.

"What am I supposed to say?" Dax replied. "I've never met aliens before!"

The two older brothers followed Kai and Scrub into the lockout chamber.

"I thought the whole thing was pretty amazing," Shaw said, hitting the button that began to shut the thick metal hatch. "Until Prevek's last sentence, when I realized he's just a diplomat."

The hatch sealed with a hiss and a thunk; seawater began to drain through the floor.

"So?" Dax asked, too tired to be bothered with Shaw's unending preoccupation with second-guessing the motives of practically everyone.

"So a diplomat is basically a politician with no power at all. Which means they can be very nice, but you never know if or when they're even *allowed* to tell the truth. And you saw they weren't even a little surprised when Dad's scuba guppies showed up."

The boys began to pull down their hoods, breathing in fresh air. Dax winced, pulling hard at the rubbery material. Somehow this was easier when he had a much thicker layer of hair for insulation.

"Do you ever trust anybody, Shaw?"

"I trust Kai. And Scrub."

Kai grinned at both of them. Then his eyes widened.

"Whoa, Dax. I forgot about your hair. You look different."

Dax unlocked the entry hatch to the forward corridor and strode in, peeling off the top half of his skinsuit.

"You'll get used to it," he offered with a shrug. "And, Shaw, trust who you want. Just remember, next time you reach for your deodorant, I'm *great* with chemistry."

"What's that supposed to mean?" Shaw called after him. But as his brother slipped around a bending wall, the only response was a very loud, wicked chuckle.

Kai kept pace with Shaw, Scrub shuffling after them.

"I'm glad he cut it. He looks more like a boy again," Kai observed.

Shaw laughed.

"I really missed you, Kai."

A Family Talk

Dax entered the living room freshly showered to find Shaw and Kai nibbling on some buckeye sticks – one of their favorite treats, generous helpings of chocolate and peanut butter swirled around pretzels. Instantly something felt 'off.' His father did his best to look civil, but he was, after all, a decorated military captain who had led many men into combat and prevailed. It was no secret Evan Zander expected his boys to be model citizens and obedient sons. So Dax had prepared himself for a rough confrontation and some likely form of extended punishment. He turned to the kitchen, where his mother was setting a tray of steaming mugs on the bar.

"Dax, here's some cider for you and—" She froze, reaching out to touch his temples. "You cut your hair!"

Dax shuffled his feet. He'd been expecting this moment, too.

"Yeah."

"Wow. What finally possessed you?"

Dax offered a humble shrug, coupled with two big puppy dog eyes, and sighed.

"Well, you know. Hair in the salad," he said.

She considered this for about ten seconds, and her eyes narrowed a bit.

"Thank you," she said, but without the buoyant enthusiasm he was craving. "It looks much better. Would you please take these out to your brothers?"

"Uh huh. Sure."

Swooping up the tray, he glanced at his mom, very confused. She busied herself just as quickly, as if sensing his unease and purposely avoiding it.

Passing one of the observation windows, Dax scanned the water for even the most fleeting blur of light or color—nothing. No troops visible either. He set the mugs down before his brothers and slid to the floor, edging close to Shaw's knees.

"This could end worse than we thought," Dax muttered.

"Oh, yeah?" Shaw replied scornfully, "What's the so-obvious clue we're missing?"

"You're *eating* it. When's the last time Mom made buckeye sticks without anyone asking *and* served this late?"

Shaw nodded; Dax had a point. Kai stopped chewing suddenly, jumping up in a panic.

"Grampa!"

"I sent Fred a message," Shaw answered. "The instant Grampa wakes he'll know we're all here and safe."

Dax relaxed, though a touch guilty.

"He won't be happy about it, though. And after having all of us leave with no goodbye, I bet he's gonna be pretty lonely."

Shaw nodded, sipping on his cider.

"I have a feeling we'll be seeing him again very soon."

"Are we in trouble?" Kai asked.

"In trouble? For what?" Dax asked, feigning amusement.

"For 'vadin' the seabase and breakin' in."

Shaw took over, squatting down on his haunches.

"Kai," Shaw began, with a warm, disarming tone he employed for just about nobody else, "we're not gonna get in trouble for breaking into our own house."

Kai squinted. "It's not really a *house*."

Shaw laughed, shaking his head.

"Whatever!" Dax groaned. "It's where we live; it's home. We disobeyed, but we were worried about—"

"That's right, Kai." Dayna entered and sat beside him. "Your father and I know you were just concerned. But you have to trust that when we tell you to do something, we expect you to remember we have reasons and they're usually to protect you. And we're holding your brothers responsible. They know better."

Kai's eyes were wide and probing, searching past her to one of the viewports.

"But the Delvans don't look like they'd hurt us." He had to work hard at that word: *Delvans*. "And everyone said they're good. Even Dad said they're good."

"There's more to it than that, sweetheart. It's . . ."

She sighed, catching Shaw's gaze.

"What now, Shaw? This is a completely new situation! Not only for us but for—"

"Just level with us, Mom," Shaw insisted. "What's going on? The whole reef is on lockdown and your own kids aren't even welcome in their own home." He pointed out the largest window. "And, oh, look! There're three extraterrestrials, out for a swim in our backyard!"

Their father's shadow fell over them, his steps measured and slow, and Shaw fell silent. As he joined them, the captain's bushy eyebrows framed a forlorn stare, suggesting a man both a little lost and burdened with enormous concerns. Dax looked at his dad expectantly, waiting for him to wrap this whole thing up with a smart explanation. But he remained quiet.

"Evan. Just tell them," his wife said.

He took her hand, nodded, and then did something that Dax found curious. Without a word, he just *looked* at each of them, in turn, waiting to find their eyes. And then smiled.

It's almost like he's saying 'I'm sorry,' Dax thought.

"Dad, what's going on?" Shaw asked. "Why are the aliens here? Is that what all those troops are for? To watch them?"

Instead of answering, his father glanced again at Dax and blinked.

"You tamed the beast," he said, running a finger up his son's fuzzy neckline. "Looks good, Son. Let's keep it that way for a while."

Dax nodded slightly. After a few seconds, Evan took a deep breath and plunged right in.

"The Delvans have come to us from a great distance," he began, "because their world is in trouble, and they have asked for our help."

"Whoa!" Dax exclaimed in a low, whispery breath. In a few seconds, the world had just changed, even more than he thought.

"So they're *not* just saying 'hi.' Imagine that," Shaw responded dryly. "The government lied."

His mother bristled. "Shaw, you know that's unfair."

"The governments of many nations have agreed to move cautiously in disclosing details," Evan continued, "but there *will* eventually be an announcement. You can't risk scaring billions of people with a hastily-composed explanation. As an event, this is globally . . . unprecedented."

"Not the lying part," Shaw added, earning another scowl from his mother.

"Shawwww . . ." Kai whispered loudly, "you're making Mom all red."

"No, Shaw," she said, flatly, "they didn't just come to say 'hi.' Their kind – their whole planet – has been blessed with an obscure existence for a very long time. To anyone traveling through their system, and even to our most powerful telescopes, Delvus-3 just looks like a big icy beach ball."

Their father tapped at a small imaging emitter on the table, and a swirl of lights coalesced just above to form a translucent, icy, pockmarked ball, hovering there. The boys leaned in – the detailing was excellent; it even rotated slowly on its axis.

"It kinda looks like Enceladus," Dax observed.

"Yes," his mother agreed, "with some other similarities, but a little smaller in size."

Floating all around the circumference of the projected sphere were dozens of topographical notations, but in larger, bolder letters, 'DELVUS-3' glowed prominently.

"Whoa!" Dax said again, enthralled.

"Don't you have any other words?" Shaw chided.

"Off my yon, bro!" Dax retorted.

"Boys!" their father scolded. They fell quiet, and he enlarged the image, continuing.

"Here. This thick outer shell is the exosphere. It's a mix of ice and other frozen chemicals enmeshed in minerals and a lot of shed organic detritus – essentially bits of dead coral that float up through the liquisphere . . ."

He tapped a sensor on the emitter and part of the outer shell faded away, revealing a thick mass of ocean and a relatively small, solid core.

"This is the liquisphere – nearly eight-tenths of the entire mass – and then, of course, the core. This whole region was hidden for eons. Up until about ten months ago, the exosphere naturally prevented discovery of everything beneath from all sensors and deep space probes or any other prying eyes."

"Somebody went deeper and found 'em?" Kai asked.

Evan nodded pleasantly. His youngest was tracking it all pretty well.

"Yes, Kai. A race of alien colonists, who from what we've been told are quite ruthless and violent, have started to migrate into the main part of the world where the Delvans live."

He tapped at the vast middle region – a dense territory of blue-green ocean currents forming the majority of the planetoid's whole.

Dax was dazzled.

"The *liquisphere* . . ." Dax said, reading the terms floating on the image.

"What are the bad guys called?" Kai asked.

"We can't just automatically call them bad, Kai," Shaw interrupted before his parents could answer. "We have no idea if they're bad."

Dax rolled his eyes.

"Shaw, if they're coming in uninvited and messing up someone else's home, then they're bad guys! Come on!"

"That's so simplistic! We don't know anything about—"

Their father stifled an impulse to shout them down, keeping his voice calm.

"Okay – let's set that aside for a moment – whether they're actually good or bad. The Delvans don't yet seem to know what to call them, Kai. But they do know they're not prepared for an invasion of colonists and they're definitely not equipped to protect or defend themselves. They can travel the stars, but the Delvans don't have any native capacity for strategy, deception or violent resistance to any sort of intelligent, aggressive enemy. Especially a tactically experienced enemy armed with advanced weaponry."

A hazy image appeared of several hulking figures seen from a distance, with what seemed to be heavily armored torsos and long necks. They moved with fierce, deliberate precision through the sea, their muscular legs and thick tails (nearly the length of their arms) powering them along. The flesh of their head and limbs was a dull gray-green and each carried some sort of long weapon; a few were actively embedding devices in the rocky ocean floor.

"What is this? Recon footage?" Dax asked.

"Not exactly—" his father started to explain.

"They look big," Kai said, his voice betraying his awe.

"This is the best image the Delvans could provide us early on," Evan continued. "Essentially, these are memories, artificially reconstructed from a few on-site observers. But we know it's very close to photorealistic. And it tells us the invading colonists are organized and sufficiently weaponized to overcome any modest resistance."

"But no resistance effort has happened yet, right?" Shaw mused.

"So the Delvans want us to fight their battles, Dad?" Dax asked.

The discomfort with which their mother shifted in her seat, and the way her brow had been sporting a deep, troubling crease was not lost on the two eldest brothers.

"They purged most systematized instincts for strategy and combat out of their culture tens of thousands of years ago," their father answered. "For instance, while they are incredibly intelligent in other ways, something like a

181

football playbook would be baffling to them. So when this situation began, they had to consider options to reach out for help. Another race of beings that seems to know a little about us advised the Delvans that we could help."

"*We*. Humans," Shaw said. His father nodded.

"I bet it's 'cause they don't have hands!" Dax interjected. Shaw looked at him sideways.

"What?"

"Can't hold a gun, or fire a plasma-cannon or a whole lot of other stuff if you don't have hands. You saw Prevek and the other two, they just have those wooky-long pec fins."

"That is so unbelievably idiotic—" Shaw began.

Kai slid his hands up into his sleeves and waved his arms around, apparently to demonstrate. Dax cracked up as his little brother shuffled up to Shaw.

"See? I'm handless guy! Can't fight back without hands!"

"Kai!" their mother said, a little shocked. "That's enough."

Evan pulled Kai close, speaking softly.

"That's not nice, Son. There have been plenty of people who accomplished amazing things in spite of missing limbs or lack of control over their own mobility. Long before I was born, America was going through a terribly dark time. People were very scared. But our country had a President who, because of a disease that hit a lot of people in those days, couldn't use his legs. He couldn't walk. But that man didn't let it stop him. And he inspired an entire country to be brave, to accomplish things in tough times many thought impossible. These days, physicality doesn't have to be a limitation at all. Your Grampa Jonah lost a leg in combat when he was young and for years he did all kinds of things – traveled around the world and even helped build hospitals for poor people, and all that was *before* they finally gave him a new leg."

"I'm sorry, Daddy," Kai offered, sincerely meaning it. It had been quite a while since he'd last seen his father's parents, but he vividly remembered Grampa Zander's amazing cybernetic leg and how its powerful servos could lift him off the ground and swing him around. He'd never thought about the man ever being without it, however.

"Still, while it doesn't help to make jokes," their mother said, "the principle Dax speaks to is somewhat correct. Once upon a time, the Delvans might have been better physically equipped for self-defense. We know they developed other traits over time, like synchronizing the synaptic energy in their brains to stimulate molecular vibrations. I don't yet understand the process, but working together in groups, they seem capable of modifying matter on a quantum level, permitting them to travel through space."

"So all this . . ." Shaw said, his eyes narrowing. "Are we getting ready to send soldiers out there to fight? Is that why all those troops are here?"

"You might as well know," his father said with a sigh, "there are over 200 troops in the dormitory bunkers now. Another eighty arrive tomorrow from the mainland, and there'll be more after that."

Stunned, Shaw fell back into the sofa, shaking his head with a bitter laugh.

"Unbelievable. This is going to go so bad for us."

"They're all volunteers, Shaw. Not a single soul is going out of compulsion."

"No, just out of sheer stupidity and I bet some seriously heartbreaking speeches."

A hot flash burned in their father's eyes, but when Dayna's hand touched his arm, he bit down on whatever retort was about to leave his lips.

Kai piped up, his words soft and gentle, but cutting nonetheless in their naked innocence.

"Daddy, are you gonna have to go help 'um?"

The question was so perfectly blunt, Dax was overwhelmed with a sense of impending loss and grief, so powerful he just looked around. His mother was staring into her lap, and Shaw's stoic glare felt like a cold rebuke for daring to feel anything at all. So he looked to his dad, who had always been a straight shooter. Dad would answer truthfully.

"Dad. *Are* you going?"

His father looked up at him, and suddenly Dax wasn't so sure he wanted to know.

Assumptions

aptain Zander took a few seconds before answering, but to his sons, the intervening silence seemed like forever. Shaw closed his eyes, anticipating disappointment.

"I . . . have been asked to lead a protectorate force," their father began, "composed of volunteer military personnel from many nations, to establish defensive outposts on Delvus-3. The objective is to fully repel the opposing alien colonists and secure that world to the point where the native species are no longer at risk. Along the way, we would install robotic defenses that could be monitored directly by the Delvans, who would routinely correspond with military advisors on Earth. Over time, as we achieved our benchmarks, we would withdraw, reduce and eventually eliminate the presence of any human troops on their world."

"You've been asked," Shaw snapped bluntly. "What was your answer?"

"I haven't given them an answer, Shaw—"

"How long? How soon?"

"Soon," his father said. "We've already sent probes to collect samples of organic and non-organic material, do some mapping for the first territory designated for occupation. You probably saw the mineral sample tethered outside the barracks, to evaluate raw components available. And once there's a secure facility for housing, I – or whoever leads the mission – would be there for about three years—"

Shaw stood, frustrated, his tone harsh.

"Well, that's it, isn't it? Of *course* you're going. It's in your blood. You so miss it all, you've been going crazy here ever since the action died down—"

"Shaw, trank yourself!" Dax broke in, but there was no calming his brother.

"—and you just had to settle for 'dad,'" Shaw finished.

184

Dayna, Dax and Kai held their breath, waiting for Evan to counter harshly. But he just took it, a very brief flash of hurt evident, followed by a tired sigh. Dayna stood up between the two of them, her cheeks as flushed as her words were clipped.

"Shaw, sit down. You're wrong. He has *not* given an answer. He was asked by the Secretary of Defense and your father made him wait."

"Uncle Easton?! The Secretary of Defense is his best friend, Mom!" Shaw interrupted again. "What's he *going* to say?"

"Your dad already promised he wouldn't go unless the whole family voted on it first," his mother declared firmly. "What's happened to you, Shaw? After taking care of you your whole life, why would you assume your father *wouldn't* put his family first? How dare you even think such a thing!"

Shaw looked away, only to catch a similarly reproving glance from Dax.

During the heated exchange, Kai had been completely distracted by the sight of all three Delvans drifting far out beyond the window, hovering around something small and indiscernible from this distance. From here they looked like living, floating jewels, their colors iridescent and eerie. Kai stared rapturously, feeling all other anxieties slip away, despite the strident conversation around him.

His mother's rebuke still stinging, Shaw blushed in shame. He had no good answer for her question, and that made the pain in his gut worse. Maybe it was the culture shock of the last few months, living out in a different and noisier world, but he had judged his father harshly and far too hastily. Ashamed and more than a little angry with himself, he looked up to his father.

"I'm sorry, Dad."

Evan reached out gently, and the moment his palm touched Shaw's forearm, tears erupted from the boy's eyes. He wiped them away quickly, desperate to preserve his composure.

"I just – it's so far . . ."

"I know," his father responded, deeply moved. "But right now, all I'm doing is facilitating and supervising training of our first batch of troops for the mission." He put a strong arm around Shaw's neck and shoulders. "I want to say something else, too. Coming home after the wars ended – to you, your brothers and your mom – was a relief and a joy you can't imagine. I never 'settled.' Being your dad outstrips all other honors and privileges I have ever known or will ever know."

The two youngest boys watched in awe. Kai even tugged on Dax's sleeve and mouthed, "Shaw's *crying*!" Dax nodded without reply.

"I know . . . I know," Shaw went on, "but we need you. Kai's so little and Dax is just starting—" But he stopped, sucking in his lip until he finally felt he had control again. "It's a bad idea, Dad."

"Okay." His father pulled him close, realizing he hadn't seen his eldest son truly afraid in quite some time, and that fear, even if misplaced, came from love – for all they'd shared. Unsure whether his gesture had inspired any courage, Evan looked at Dax and Kai.

"I guess that's been weighing on your minds, too?"

Dax simply shrugged, not sure how to answer.

"Daddy?" Kai was staring into his mug of hot cider. He dipped a finger in and tasted it.

"Yes, Son?"

"What happens to the Delvans if you don't go?"

Evan and Dayna traded a look. He smiled, his tone soft and measured.

"Without me, there might or might not be a mission, Kai. General Russell made it clear there's just one other candidate for the post who carries any similar measure of their confidence, and that person hasn't yet indicated whether he's willing to go. Right now, they'd prefer he serve as my second-in-command, assuming he agrees to take the post at all."

"That's not fair, putting all that on you," Shaw observed.

"Dad, that's crazy. If there's nobody else," Dax asked, "they just won't go?"

"The entire Delvan civilization exists within an ocean, Dax. I've commanded troops both above and below the sea, and our skillsets are bullseye center of what this mission requires."

Shaw looked up. "Our? You said '*our*.' They asked you *both* to go?"

"Your father's a hero," his mother offered matter-of-factly, "this is a volunteer mission and he's a name the very best people trust. But I've also been working on the preparation side, helping with structures and design of certain equipment meant to ensure the safety of all the troops and their success. And I'll continue to do that, however things work out."

"So then you wouldn't be going, either," Shaw concluded.

"No," his mother answered, without much enthusiasm. "I would be staying here. With Dax and Kai. And, of course, you have your studies in Florida."

"Okay, good," Shaw said quietly.

"But, Daddy," Kai interrupted again, "what happens to the Delvans if they don't get protected from the bad guys?"

Dax caught the hard, sober look in his father's eyes, a tiny spark of fear there – less likely a fear of any potential enemy, than of destroying his youngest boy's boundless optimism and buoyant faith in good conquering evil. So Dax did his father a favor. He took the hit.

"The bad guys will move in, Kai. And a lot of Delvans could be hurt. No matter what, their world will never be the same."

Evan nodded, slowly, a reluctant affirmation of his son's simple yet painfully accurate explanation.

Kai's eyes shone with emerging tears, looking out the window again for the Delvans that had been there moments before. They were gone.

"They'll die? Vren and . . . and the others? And their families? They'll get killed?"

Dayna knelt on the floor, face-to-face with her youngest, her soothing, carefully chosen words tenderly offering what hope they might.

"We don't know, sweetheart. We'll send them whatever we can to help protect them – robots, other devices. But if we don't go, we might not hear from them . . ."

"For a very long time," their father finished, quietly.

Shaw had quieted, opening the part of his mind that tended to brood upon consequence, risk and probability. Having the soul of a scientist, permitting his brain to debate opposing sides had become a regular exercise in critical thinking. Unfortunately for him, it sometimes also caused him to stumble headlong into unexpected, sobering conclusions. A new one had struck him with such numbing power, he couldn't help but speak it out loud.

"So, Dad, if Earth does nothing . . . the first alien lifeforms to contact us . . . in friendship. We turn them down and shut the door. Or send a few robotic guns and then . . . shut the door."

As if a switch had been flipped inside his head, Dax sat up straight, calculating that equation further out.

"And if the next species that reaches out isn't so nice, what do we do then? What if the alien colonists find out about us, from the Delvans? If they – sorry Shaw, the 'bad guys' – think we were too weak or scared to help, what keeps the bad guys from coming *here*?"

"Okay, I was out on a limb," Shaw snapped, immediately regretting he'd inspired the thought, "but you're way out there on teeny little branches. You know that's not gonna happen."

"It could! You don't know! Who was expecting all of this? That they'd even come here?"

"Well, my boys," Evan broke in, "those are what we call the stakes. And the core subject of lots and lots of conversations between politicians and diplomats, and I don't know how many theologians from all over the world. Those are the questions that have kept us waiting to have a serious discussion with the three of you. Now you know why we've been so secretive. You know that up until a few weeks ago, we've tried never to be that way with you. The fact that these creatures live under the ocean, in deep space, instantly made all these busy people in Washington and Vancouver very interested in talking to your mother and me. But, yes, the simple answer is if we say 'no,' the Delvans might very well lose their home and maybe their entire existence."

Dax caught the clear message conveyed via Shaw's pointed glare: *Stop talking.* But he needn't have bothered; the truth was Dax had little more to contribute. He was, perhaps like his older brother, a little nervous about where the conversation was heading. Many questions had been provoked that seemed to demand a response, but in this case more talk might serve to put all their lives at risk.

For now, he kept silent, as all eyes drifted out to the view beyond the big window, where the objects of their discussion were glowing again with a sublime luster. The idea that such life, such beauty could be utterly extinguished forever had never been so poignant a possibility.

"There's a lot going on tomorrow," their mother said matter-of-factly. "In fact, it's going to be getting very busy around here for a while."

"Busy how, Mom?" Dax asked.

Their father sighed, clearly content to postpone the details.

"People will be coming in. Scientists . . . And others."

Shaw bit down on pushing for what 'others' meant. He was pretty sure he already knew.

"We're all tired. You all should clean up and get to bed," Dayna said, rising. She glanced at Evan and he just nodded awkwardly, rubbed Kai's head and followed her out.

The Zander brothers sat in silence, gazing at the vaporous licks of flame in the fireplace. Despite its warmth, they all felt a numbing chill. Dax wondered how long it would be before their parents let them venture back to the mainland. After a fantastic extended vacation with Grampa on the North Shore, he wondered when he would next see Cody. Or his newest friend, Illone – the slightest thought of whom gave him a happy, weird tingle in his belly.

"I don't want the Delvans to die," Kai pleaded, in a tiny, mournful voice.

"Nobody does, Kai," Dax said, "Dad's not gonna let that happen." He looked to Shaw for backup, but his brother said nothing. He just rose from the sofa, stretched his neck left and right, then headed for his bedroom.

"Night," Shaw said, never looking back.

. . .

Mid-morning the next day, Dax had prepared a surprise lunch for his mom; after spending half an hour carefully selecting and preparing an array of her favorite foods and dipping sauces, he sealed the container and headed out into the corridor to make his delivery.

Three modules housed the seabase science labs – one devoted to chemistry, a second focused on biological and zoological research, and the largest, where Dayna Zander spent most of her working hours, dedicated to engineering and fabrication. Occupying a good chunk of space in E&F were several large 'cookers' – machines that processed raw materials into alloys appropriate for printing whatever shapes and structures Dayna or any of her colleagues might need. Most recently she had been refining the designs on a series of struts and load-bearing beams intended as building blocks for existing and near-future settlements on planets or moons with native environments inhospitable to human life. With the Zander compound already located undersea, she had a near-perfect testing ground for such components. Until a few weeks ago, she had been focused on fine-tuning cookers that would accompany astronauts to Europa. But the target was different now; she was preparing a new class of machines flexible enough to 'bake,' on site, the foundations, framing and walls of structures that would house human troops on Delvus-3, using whatever raw elements that planet had to offer.

Dax stepped into her engineering lab to find it filled with dozens of crates, many stacked taller than himself. When had all of this arrived? He wove through the haphazard maze, noting three large cookers against one wall, humming quietly as they extruded long, gently curving structural beams. Stepping near, he could see patterns of shallow, wavy grooves embedded in the otherwise flawlessly smooth surfaces.

189

Hearing voices, he turned a corner and spotted his mother and a fit, olive-skinned man with short kinky hair and a goatee staring through the glass panels of a large, reinforced case.

"I was wondering if you were going to sleep all day!" his mother said.

"Could this be Shaw, or—" the man started to ask in a brassy, British baritone.

"This is our middle son, Dax. Sweetie, I want you to meet Dr. Jabari Narouk. He'll be supervising installation of the first living quarters and shipyard for the mission."

Jabari shook his hand so vigorously, Dax laughed in shock.

"A pleasure, Dax. Your mother says you're quite the thinkah!"

Dax chuckled. He never really gave much thought to his process of thinking.

"Here," Jabari said, waving a hand over an illuminated table, "a sneak peek for you."

A glowing grid spread out across the table's surface, rising to form the sculpted topography of some rugged terrain.

"This is where we'll build our first compound on the core of Delvus-3," Jabari explained, his eyes gleaming as several holographic structures materialized amid the rocky surface. The proposed compound wasn't unlike the seabase facilities they currently inhabited.

"Did the Delvans map all this out for us?" Dax asked, impressed.

"We have three survey drones there, mapping and collecting information," his mother answered. "The Delvans send back molecular data pods as they fill up and we've been analyzing those, but there's a dense number of files to process and the drones are collecting more daily. We'll be prepping until we leave, and then even more after the first troops arrive."

"Of course, we won't be in these finished structures at the beginning," Jabari said. He 'pushed' the landscape further away from the planned seabase structures toward a broad, rising cliff nearby, then moved *into* the cliff, revealing a system of enormous caverns.

"This is where we first land. Or transport in. We'll set up camp here until the first bunker modules are ready for habitation outside. It's a few hundred meters away, but right now we're sealing up three small tunnels with some welding robos. Before we arrive, the whole system will be pressurized and organic oxygen processors will come online. Then, *voila*! Basecamp. It's also where we'll build our shipyard."

"We'll send preprogrammed cookers into a large cavern, ahead of any humans," his mother added, "and they'll create the first necessary bits of infrastructure and actually form the components for even larger cookers. Those in turn will be used for construction of both our vessels and compound modules."

Dax marveled at the images, reaching to turn them about and explore the various spaces.

"You can do all this?" Dax asked.

"It all hinges on careful planning," his mother answered. "The real challenge will be psychological. About 380 people will be moving from our planet into the middle of a hollowed-out rock, and we're asking them to sit tight until we can safely forge a few stable lockout chambers to the ocean outside."

Jabari enlarged the interior of the cavern systems, revealing placement of hammock-like bunks, hanging off the walls, stacked atop each other four to six units high. They'd taken into account the best possible use of the tall ceilings.

"These aren't small chambers, but initial living conditions will be somewhat primitive; and with so many sharing the caves, it will most definitely feel confining and claustrophobic."

"No way! That would be awesome!"

Jabari smiled.

"Your mom also told me you can shoot the curl like a dolphin."

Dax perked up.

"You surf?"

"A little in Al Diffa on vacation, and I'm very much an amateur, but we have a few days coming before our schedule tightens like a vise, so I was hoping you and your dad might show me a few things back on the North Shore."

"Yeah, definitely!" Dax offered. Realizing he'd been avoiding his true reason for coming here, he turned to his mother, popping the cover from the bowl to reveal some seaweed strips, celery, carrot sticks and dip.

"Brought you some snacks! And there's plenty for you, too, Mister Narouk, sir."

Jabari's eyes lit up, betraying a stalled appetite. He didn't hesitate to snap up a few samples. But one quick look at the contents gave Dayna Zander all she needed to know.

"Thank you, sweetie. That's so thoughtful."

"I know. All the stuff you like, right?"

She laughed, kissing his forehead.

"Yes, but you're still grounded, dear."

Dax's face fell.

"You honestly think I just figured, 'Hey, I'll bring mom some veggies and she'll let me do whatever I want'?"

Watching them, Jabari suppressed a knowing chuckle.

"You know," Dr. Zander began with a smirk, "that would be too easy, wouldn't it?"

Dax squirmed, a whine infecting his response.

"But Cody's all alone, and I met this girl . . ."

Dayna shook her head, more than a little dumbfounded with that last word. The light that sparkled in her eyes suddenly gave Dax the cold gripping fear that his mother would be peppering him with endless questions about 'this girl.' To her credit, she just chuckled.

"Well. Behave yourself and I'll talk to your father."

Ebullient, Dax lunged forward and kissed her; Jabari laughed.

"He's just like my boy, Hasani. A little older than you. Fifteen. He's with his mother back in Paris. Smart, smart, smart. And can never sit still. But my daughter, Amira, *is* here, in Launch Bay Three, working on a project of her own. An engineer, just like her old man."

"And she's nineteen, Dax," his mother added with a wry smirk. "Sorry."

The boy shifted uncomfortably, then raised a mischievous eyebrow.

"Uh oh. Can't wait till she runs into Shaw."

"Dax!" his mother chided.

With a cavalier swagger, Dax lowered his voice for a very well-rehearsed impersonation. "Hey, I'm Shaw. Look at these shoulders. Wanna see some chin-ups?"

His mother cackled with embarrassment, shaking her head. Jabari laughed heartily.

"Dax, he is *not* like that! Jabari, I can assure you, Shaw is actually a very charming and responsible young man."

"Oh, yeah, Mom," Dax affirmed, "Prince Charming, with lots and lots of cologne."

"It's fine. I assure you," Jabari grinned. "I know how young men can be. But Amira is remarkably . . . self-aware. Not to mention quite mechanically inclined and very comfortable with power tools. So I offer my sincere sympathies to any soul who dares tangle with her."

192

Dax chuckled at the thought of Shaw meeting his match, then squinted, leaning over the dark glass case.

"Is something happening in this box?" he asked.

"Soon," his mother answered. "We're waiting on a special delivery from the Delvan homeworld. They're bubbling it in—"

Jabari raised an eyebrow, interrupting.

"Bubbling? That's what they call it?"

"Yep!" Dax chimed in. "They do it together, using their brains. Crazy."

Jabari chuckled thoughtfully.

"Of course, I'm aware of their capacity for manipulating teleportation, but I'd not heard that precise term."

"We're still waiting on a systematic breakdown of the process," Dayna added. "They've promised to explain it for us, but to be honest, so far there's been so much else to do. For now, we just have to trust them to do the driving."

For some reason, this struck Dax funny. "Driving. Nice, Mom."

Just then, Vren's voice rang out over the com system.

"Doctor, we have isolated three cubic meters of seawater from our lower liquisphere and it will arrive in your designated containment very shortly."

"Thank you!" Dayna called out, then whispered to Dax. "Which one is that?"

"Vren. Gee, there are only three of 'em, Mom."

"Thank you, *Vren*!" she said out loud, emphasizing her name.

"You are most welcome, Doctor! Ten seconds."

They fell silent with expectation and a pinging sound went off. Within the large glass case, a hazy glow materialized, swirling about as they leaned in. But as it coalesced, all three stared in utter confusion.

"Is this at all what you were expecting?" Jabari asked in an awed whisper. Dax leaned in, squinting, the same question on his mind.

Dayna looked at the object now floating in the case. If her hunch was right, this could very well change many of their assumptions.

"No," she answered, chewing on her lip, "it's *not*."

Uncertain Variables

In the direct center of the case, a translucent blue sphere had appeared, held in stasis. To the naked eye it was just a small, round globule of water, no more than six or seven centimeters in diameter. Dax could have easily held it in the palm of his hand.

"I thought you asked for three cubic meters," Dax observed. Dayna and Jabari frowned.

"Vren? I don't think we received the entire volume of what you intended to bring from your world. Is there more coming or did we misunderstand your figures?"

Vren swam into full view, gazing at them through a waist-high port window.

"That is the full volume, Dr. Zander. The atmospheric and gravitational constraints of your world have compressed it to these dimensions."

Jabari's brow knit as he stared at the little glob of liquid. He chuckled, more in consternation than amusement. In fact, he was chewing on one of his knuckles, deep in thought.

"The whole point was to test the molecular density and chemical makeup of their seawater and calculate its compatibility with our materials. I'm not sure what to make of this."

Dayna just muttered a little "huh." Dax was riveted on the sphere, gently floating there in the middle of the case. Then he turned to the port, where Vren was observing patiently.

"Vren, this is what you guys swim in on your world?" Dax asked. "This little bit measures out to three of our cubic meters out there?"

Vren nodded affirmatively.

"Ohhh . . . I get it. It's like thin-water," Dax said.

Jabari looked at him, puzzled, as did his mother.

194

"What?" Dayna asked.

"If they can swim in this stuff, then it's still got, uh . . . molecular tension," Dax said, his voice tinged with the electricity of pondering an unexpected, fascinating concept. "On their planet, between gravity and magnetic fields and whatever makes up this water, it's probably more like a super thick gas, right? But not as dense as water on Earth."

His mother was nowhere near as entranced, and Jabari could read her expression.

"Our physics for this world are going to need a new baseline, I think," Jabari said.

"On the plus side," she added, "the deep ocean pressure has to be a lot more tolerable for anything we build and—"

"And for humans as well!" Jabari blurted out excitedly. "We'll be able to move with so much more efficiency in that environment. Theoretically. Potentially to our great advantage. But if the physics on our planet compress their liquid like this, how can they function so readily within our oceans?"

Dax lit up. "That's why they shimmer like that!"

They both looked at him.

"You mean their colors? I don't think that's anything but a bioluminescent trait to ward off larger predators."

"No, Mom. When you get up close, you see this little extra . . . like a film. Like their whole bodies are coated in something invisible. Maybe it's some kind of energy field protecting them from our gravity, the atmospheric pressures, even our germs and toxins and stuff."

Jabari nodded, deep in thought. "If they can generate wormholes through space, something like a biological raincoat might be child's play," he said, softly.

"Your dad should know about this," Dayna suggested. "With lower density and pressure, our own ability to move through their liquisphere should be significantly more . . ." But her voice trailed off, lost in thought.

"Thin-water," Jabari said, as if trying the term out for a test drive. "Thin-water. I like it, Mr. Dax."

The boy chuckled; if he didn't claim it now, his contribution might be forgotten forever:

"Hey, if it goes in a book, you guys better remember I said it first!"

"Sweetie, Mister Narouk and I have a lot to discuss." She sealed the container again and handed it to him. "Why don't you take some snacks to your father?

He's about to lecture the troops. You know how he gets cranky late morning if he doesn't nibble on something."

Dax rolled his eyes; he knew quite well.

"Nice to meet you, Jabari!"

"And you, Dax! We'll surf together soon!"

"Hot-now!"

Jabari squinted, clearly lost by Dax's phrase. Dayna laughed.

"He means 'you couldn't be more right.'"

"Oh!" Jabari exclaimed. "Then . . . hot-now! Absolutely!"

Dax laughed, marveling again at the glob of alien seawater, then headed immediately into the corridors.

Cutting through the barracks, it took just a few minutes for Dax to reach the 'Commons' – an expansive, round module once intended for recreation and entertainment. Scores of men and women, all in standard issue, royal blue jumpsuits, were now gathered in tiered rows. All eyes were trained on his father, perched on a small platform at the center, an array of glowing schematics floating beside him, very similar to what Jabari had demonstrated. But these images were a mix of real video and an overlay of topographical grids, expanding beyond the planned basecamp into adjacent territories. Canyons and craggy ridges marked the surface of the core, adding up to a spectacular diversity of geographical features. The troops were fixed on the images, trying to make sense of them, while the captain turned every so often in an effort to acknowledge the entire audience, as he was completely surrounded.

"We are learning more about the aggressors day by day. Thanks to our drones, we now know at least one location where they're clustered."

A hand shot up in the back row. Evan paused and pointed at a man with an athletic build.

"Seth Walton, Captain. Corporal, medical unit."

"What's your question, Corporal Walton?"

"The term 'aggressor,' sir? Is there a reason we're not referring to them as 'the enemy'? And do we know if the Delvans have had any direct contact with them?"

Quietly slipping inside behind a row halfway up, Dax waited for his father's answer.

"These are our current protocols," the captain answered, "so until further notice, we'll avoid using the 'e' word. This rationale was developed out of respect for prevailing Delvan philosophy, expounded upon in your mission briefing, which you should have read by now."

There were muted snickers throughout the room as Corporal Walton shifted awkwardly in his seat. He nodded with a jittery, almost silent, "Yessir!"

"It's alright," Evan continued, his voice quickly muting their chuckles. "We all have a lot of catching up to do and the compiled mission brief is a long read and frankly, not that well organized. We will get better, I promise. As to the question of contact . . ."

He halted, as if pondering his choice of words.

"A delegation of eight Delvans representing their various . . . tribes . . . made an effort to meet with the aggressors at their first identified location. Four of the Delvans were killed within a few seconds, while the remaining four fled to report details of the incident. The aggressors never attempted communication. After much deliberation by Delvan leaders, a decision was made to find assistance. And here we are. Granted, this all comes from the Delvans, but we've processed a lot of information and are resolved their version of the truth is reliable. Accurate."

Dax felt a cold emptiness in the few seconds of silence that followed; if there had been any question up to this point, everyone now understood the aggressors were indeed 'bad guys.'

"Now, here," the captain continued, moving a hand through the large blue expanse composing most of the image, "at the center of Delvus-3 and its liquisphere, we have the core, divided into eight sectors – four north, four south."

He gestured broadly with his arms, reducing the virtual landscape significantly, until the entire core rotated beside him, about a meter in diameter.

"This bright orange triangle, in Sector Alpha, marks our first compound, shipyard and initial basecamp. All of our initial patrols will proceed from here. Seabase Alpha."

Like a feather-light beach ball, he turned the whole thing upside down to locate a brightly pulsing green marker, situated on the edge of a long series of ridges.

"Underneath *this* terrain in the Epsilon sector," he went on, "in a region we call Goliath's Ribs, is where the aggressors – now known as *Ogribods* – have been seen coming and going."

Dax blinked, repeating the word soundlessly: 'Ogribods.' So that's what they were called. Though it gave him a deep chill, now he desperately wanted to *see* one.

"We're planting our base nearly 180 degrees opposite on the core," his father added, "well beyond line of sight and far enough where our troops should enjoy an element of relative obscurity, for at least a little while. The Delvans have assured us that any sound we generate will be muffled by currents, geothermal venting and other native activity in-between. The Ogribod troops are embedded beneath the surface of the core, and to be candid, we have no idea yet of their numbers or how to quantify their weaponry or vessels, if any. Thus far, they've only been glimpsed as individuals or in troop formation, not in any kind of watercraft."

A hand shot up and from his angle, Dax could hear a young man's husky voice, but couldn't see the actual person asking.

"CPO Finley Coyle, sir. Have we identified any kind of spacecraft in orbit around the planet? Or maybe a fleet?"

Dax noticed the captain clenching his jaw; a telltale sign of his father's discomfort.

"As yet, we have not determined a good method of deploying and positioning orbital recon devices for that purpose, so as not to be detected by the aggressors. Long-range robotic sensors on the exosphere have identified localized heat signatures that would seem indicative of exhausted particulate matter from some sort of engines. Much larger in size and configuration than any unmanned satellites. But that's it so far. We are wrangling many uncertain variables, but again, we *will* get better. The situation and accumulation of intel is constantly accelerating."

The captain looked around the room and caught a conspicuous flash of colorful clothing topped in platinum blond hair. He and Dax locked eyes for a moment, but another hand went up near the front – a tanned, attractive brunette. He nodded for her to speak.

"Lieutenant DeLaRosa, Captain. I pilot Sub-Darter One. So are we going in blind, sir?"

As the captain absorbed this, an unsettling wave seemed to ripple out over the troopers closest to the seemingly fearless lieutenant, as if she'd just invited lightning to strike.

"We're learning more every day," he answered plainly. "The risk with remote recon is in tipping our hand; if our drones search underground, they're likelier to be discovered, and from that point on, we've lost any element of surprise. Same thing in space, especially considering our technology on that front is almost certainly inferior to theirs. Once we've set up basecamp, we're all sitting inside a giant rock. It will be at least a week before the lockout chamber to the sea is complete, so nobody's engaging the aggressors for quite a while. In fact, given the Delvans' unique mode of transport, the Ogribods won't even know that we've arrived on the planet. In that intervening time, I'm convinced our broadened recon efforts will have us much better prepared."

Dax felt his chest swell. As the captain began to pull up diagrams of six-passenger submersible vessels, he had the full attention of every man and woman in the room, their trust and confidence, even their eager anticipation to follow him into destiny. And this was his *father*.

"So, Lieutenant DeLaRosa," the captain said, pointing to the new images, "I'm glad you brought up the Sub-Darters. Some of our greenest patrollers will be riding with you, placing their lives in your very capable hands."

DeLaRosa swallowed, visibly pale. Whatever she'd hoped to gain by questioning the thought process behind their mission, she was about to be made an example of.

"The Darters are fairly new tech, based on prototype vessels we developed toward the end of the pirate engagements, but until now have never been designated for combat. Why don't you come down here and give everyone an overview of the navigational upgrades."

DeLaRosa, having no idea what she could offer beyond her expertise in navigation, or possibly from sheer stage fright, was trembling – until the captain broke a mischievous smile.

"Relax, Lieutenant. I'm kidding. I've seen footage of your runs through the Nansen Abyssal. It's why I sought you out for this mission."

The whole room burst into much needed laughter as the lieutenant's shoulders sank with relief, several friends poking at her in jest. *Score one for Dad*, Dax chuckled, enjoying the pleased grin on his father's face. Laughter, he had often told his son, could be as great a means of instilling camaraderie as the prospect of facing a common foe.

"Alright, let's break till fourteen hundred hours. We are at T minus twenty-three days before the first of us venture into the great unknown. That will put human beings on their world one month to the day from when the Delvans asked us for help."

The captain paused, his voice noticeably raspy. He took a sip of water.

"No one is denying that's a very compressed interval to a mission unlike any we've ever faced. History may label our actions as hasty, but time is critical in responding to what is no less than an extinction-level threat to their kind. So expect your daily itinerary to intensify and fill with a diverse array of preparation drills. On a personal note, I would urge all of you to take whatever spare time you have over the coming weekends to reach out to those who love and care for you. Once our troops are entrenched on Delvus-3, it might be some time before you're able to make contact with home again."

Dax looked across the mostly young faces, a mix of expressions, some just wide-eyed. It was hard for him to tell if they were scared or simply too 'green' to know their lives were about to be placed in almost certain jeopardy. He could see his father wondering if perhaps his words weren't entirely hitting home. Nevertheless, he pressed on.

"In this afternoon's session, we'll be addressing how troop rotations will be organized and outfitted, and we'll review our initial strategy to push the aggressors off the planet. If you're prone to food comas after lunch, bring coffee. Dismissed."

The troops broke apart, filtering through three different exits, most heading for the commissary and a hot meal. Dax hung behind, waiting for a moment alone with his father, even though the distant aroma of what might be Italian meatloaf was palpably distracting.

"Corporal Walton!" the captain called. The young officer turned attentively as others brushed past him on their way out.

"At ease, Corporal. I had something else to discuss with you."

Halfway to the platform, Dax stopped, realizing a new conversation was underway. He sat down at a respectful distance, giving space for his father and Corporal Walton to chat. But the large round room had very accommodating acoustics and he had pretty great hearing, so while he didn't stare and though they spoke quietly, Dax heard absolutely everything.

"Yes, sir," the corporal said, seeming fidgety, despite the captain's disarming manner.

"You know, I have a son a year younger than you. You're twenty, right?"

"That I am, sir. Yes, sir."

"Corporal, your bio is one of a very few in a folder of candidates under review for a delicate task critical to our early mission objectives."

The young man looked up, mystified.

"Me, sir?"

"Your evals portray a man who takes risks, routinely puts the welfare of others ahead of his own. To a degree that's true of every person who just left this room, but you're an elite breed among specials. Your delivery on mission objectives, real and simulated, has been outstanding."

"Just doing my part, thank you, sir."

"More than your part." The captain paused, a hint the pleasantries were done. "You also have no family to speak of, at least that I could find in your files."

The corporal's brow creased a bit, his voice low.

"No, sir. I was an only child, raised by my gramma after my parents died. And she outlived almost everyone else. Till last January. So I'm it. There's nobody else left."

From his distant seat, Dax couldn't help but look up. He was drawn to the corporal's eyes, which though a piercing crystal blue, seemed sad and accustomed to loneliness.

"That your son, sir?" Corporal Walton asked.

The captain turned slightly, nodding subtly to Dax: '*I'll be with you soon.*'

"Yes. My middle son. You'll probably get to know him at some point."

"Depending on how this task goes, correct, sir?" Walton pressed. "I mean, I'm guessing that folder's slim because the men and women in it are all pretty short on family."

The captain looked him in the eye, a solemn nod affirming Walton's suspicions.

"Yes. But also people who, to my thinking, carry the most leadership potential."

"I don't know what kind of leader I am, sir. But if you've got some dicey territory and you don't know if there's any coming back from it, then I'm your man. Walked through a lot of doors in my life. Kicked down a few others. Guess I don't fancy a closed door."

Evan soaked this in, then cleared his throat with a little grunt. Dax knew that sound; he'd first heard it at the funeral for his grandmother, when his father got up to share his last thoughts.

"Interesting way to put it. Alright, Walton. We'll talk more, but I'll consider you my man in front. Report to the med lab tomorrow at zero-eight."

They both stood; the captain offered his hand and they shook, this time eye-to-eye.

"Thanks for your confidence, sir," Walton grinned, so proud his freckled cheeks gleamed.

The captain watched him stride up the rows and out the door. Finally, Dax started toward his father, who spoke before he turned around.

"I guess you heard most of that? Sound bounces like a racquetball in here."

Dax shrugged, embarrassed to admit he was eavesdropping.

"It's okay, Dax. It's a good day when you get a glimpse of a brave soul. And he's one."

"So Corporal Walton's gonna do something dangerous?"

His father didn't speak to that. Instead, he sat, noting the container under his son's arm.

"Whatcha got there, Son?"

Dax lit up, opening it. "Snacks! Thought you might be hungry!"

The captain looked at the array of veggies with a little 'hmm,' and then closed the lid.

"You made these to butter up your mom and she sent them on to me, right?"

Dax's jaw dropped and his cheeks flushed red with shame.

"How do you *know* this stuff?"

"It's what I would've done at thirteen." Seeing his son deflated brought him no pleasure. He rubbed the back of the boy's neck. "I think they've got pizza today in the commissary . . ."

"Let's go!"

And they ate lunch, just the two of them, Dax relishing what for now was a rare hour of his dad's company, with no one daring to distract them from their meal, or their laughter.

Sparring

By 3:00 in the afternoon of the next day, the second of November, four troop transports had arrived, delivering a total of forty-two more volunteers, adding to scores of others already strolling around the barracks and support installations, studying mission briefings, swimming laps and speed runs around the perimeter, undergoing endurance tests and more. While Dax was mesmerized with all the new energy, Shaw found it unsettling, as if the world were moving far too fast toward a waterfall with an untested drop. So he had hunkered down in his father's small library, hoping a little reading for school would settle and distract his thoughts. He didn't get much done, however; Dax found him there mid-afternoon, his attention fixed to the view out a port window, watching dozens of troops running through an assortment of undersea drills.

Shaw sensed his brother's entrance without ever turning around.

"Guess you've been buzzing around the whole place today, huh?" he asked.

"Mostly the docking bay," Dax answered. "They just kept comin' in – and as soon as they walk out of their shuttles, they all have this look . . ." He bugged out his eyes, dropped his jaws and Shaw started laughing.

"Well, *we're* used to it, but this is still a very special kind of place. You try to explain it to people out there and . . . you know. It's kinda like we grew up in another world."

Dax nodded, by now also absorbed with the view outside.

"And soon, they'll actually be in another world," he whispered with evident awe.

"A hair over three weeks," Shaw offered. "I found out from Maz. They're leaving the day before Thanksgiving."

"Wow." Dax felt sad for them; he loved Thanksgiving. As much or more than Christmas, he identified the holiday with countless joyful memories, and these volunteers would be denied this.

Out there in the reefs, squad after squad of new troopers were put through their paces, outfitted in the latest diving gear, swimming in formations of six, routinely engaging in mock-combat with several different types of weapons, most of which Dax had never seen.

"Looks like they're learning fast," Dax observed.

"There might be some greenies," Shaw mused, "but it's not the first field assignment for most of them. Dad already said the Americans are from every branch of the military, with troops from thirty other nations so far. And he screened every single one."

"So he took the most experienced, right?"

"Best and the brightest, blah-blah-blah . . ." Shaw mumbled.

"We have some non-military as well," their father's voice boomed from the doorway. The boys spun around as he entered, already suited up for a swim. "Some shiny apples from NASA and space agencies of other nations, mostly for scientific positions."

He joined them at the window, resting a hand on each of their shoulders.

"And every single one is a volunteer. When they asked me to help organize this, that was my line in the sand: Not one person would be serving against their will. And this mission is full of uncertainties, so the Mission Command Alliance gave little resistance on that point."

Dax looked up and down his father's skinsuit; it was obviously a fresh model, sporting a unique pebbled texture over the chest, shoulders, arms and legs.

"That suit is banga, Dad!"

"Glad you like it. I ordered a couple in your sizes. Suit up. You guys could use some exercise. Unless you'd rather fall asleep here by the window."

"Are we being drafted now?" Shaw asked dryly.

Evan pulled a single bar from a long sheath along his outer thigh. He twirled it like a baton and it split apart into two prongs. Short crossbars snapped out at one end and in the middle to connect both batons. Not averse to showing off a bit, their father swung it around in a wide arc, demonstrating its potential as a weapon – defensive or otherwise.

"Whoa! Can I, Dad?" Dax exclaimed.

Shaw rolled his eyes; his middle brother was such a pushover for anything new, fast or shiny. This was all three. The captain handed it over, demonstrating for Dax how to grip the center crossbar and steady the length of the baton's twin bars against his forearm. Two prongs extended half a meter beyond his grip.

"Okay, now spread your fingers out on the crossbar."

Dax did so and the prongs telescoped another meter, tapering toward the far end.

Shaw perked up, intrigued; it *was* an impressive instrument.

"Hot-now!" Dax exclaimed. "Can I have one?!"

"We'll see. We need every available unit for training till the next shipment arrives. Now squeeze the handle like . . ." He pressed his son's fingers in the middle and Dax felt something give. Suddenly the tips of both prongs lit up with a fierce, bluish-white light. Dax cooed with fascination, a tingling, fiery power felt from the tips of his fingers to all the way up his arms.

"Careful now," his father admonished. "These are set for sparring, so they can't do much more than discharge a little static electricity, but you always show proper respect for a weapon."

Dax spun around, waving the baton with broad swishes toward his brother, who raised an annoyed eyebrow, but didn't flinch.

"Why don't you just sign up now?" Shaw said. "I hear the food's great."

His brother swished the baton twice more, then brought the prongs to hover just above the top of Shaw's head. Dax and his father began to chuckle, provoking him to glance up; sure enough, his hair was standing on end, attracted to the static energy.

"Ha ha," he said, dryly, holding out a hand to examine the weapon.

"Whoa – wait a second," the captain said, grabbing Dax's arm, "let's turn the stingers completely off, just to prevent any accidents." He squeezed the handle to deactivate the power, then handed the unit to Shaw.

"I don't get it, Dad," Shaw murmured, feeling the weight, "these seem designed for individual combat. You really think that's gonna happen? Who fights man-to-man anymore?"

"We want to be prepared for anything. The early intel we have on the aggressors attempting to colonize the planet is that they've been spotted swimming freely and in swarms. We'll have other weapons at our disposal, but versatility is key when we're going in this green."

Shaw squeezed the handle; the prongs collapsed to their original length. He turned it over in his hand, impressed with the solid but lightweight construction.

"It's kind of like a double Sai baton," he observed. His father raised an eyebrow, seeming both pleased and surprised.

"You know about martial arts stuff?" Dax asked, surprised. Shaw just chuckled.

"Good catch, Son. We call it a Dusai . . . dual batons."

Shaw handed it back to his father, who snapped it back into one solid piece and holstered the weapon so neatly it almost disappeared.

"We do have units you can use for sparring, if you want to suit up and follow the instructor off to the side. Or you can stay here. Just didn't want you to feel left out."

"Shaw," Dax urged, "c'mon."

"First session's about to start," the captain added. "If you dress out real fast, you can make it. Skinsuits are already in your rooms."

Shaw made a noncommittal grumble and Dax elbowed him, eliciting a louder grunt.

"Owww."

"Come on, bro. How often does Dad give you permission to knock me sideways?"

"Who said I needed permission, Goldilocks?"

"Excuse me," their father corrected. "Yes, you do, and technically this is just a little light sparring. No hard 'knocking' – sideways or in any other . . . way."

Shaw needed no coaxing; the prospect of taking Dax down a notch was too tempting to ignore, even if it meant getting temporarily cozy with the military or risking a few blows himself.

. . .

Fifteen minutes later they were floating just a few meters away from two squads of six each, the first decked out in padded, iridescent-green skinsuits facing off against another squad in a shimmering gray-blue. Each man or woman held a Dusai in each hand, crossing them like a sleek 'X' before their head and shoulders.

Wide-eyed, Dax remained a spectator for the moment, though he had a strong impulse to just sneak into the near-flank of the green squad and join the fray.

As their father swam into view on the opposite side, the troops straightened in posture. He offered a chest salute, a common but clear undersea gesture for troops to carry on.

His gaze shifted beyond, to his two sons across the short expanse where the drills were about to commence, and he gave them a little nod. Dax felt a little twinge of pride, quickly stepped on by Shaw's low, snarky aside on their private com link.

"Hand-to-hand combat in a liquid environment is pointless. There's no way to build up enough speed to take your opponent off guard."

"Well," Dax countered, "maybe things are different there. You should study up on the thin-water."

"*Thin-water*. Sure," Shaw said, in that casual, throwaway tone that always served to rankle his brother. Dax huffed, but was too annoyed to engage Shaw further, and it was clear the first set of drills was about to start. Several tiny drones lit up, hovering around the perimeter to record the session. Two officers backed away, one hovering above the twelve divers, the other taking a squarely even vantage point with their field of combat, more like a referee. He flashed a light above his head, then pulled it *down*, and the green and blue teams CLASHED.

Dax and Shaw watched with breathless fascination. Initially, the troopers were matched one-on-one, slamming their batons against the other's with a calculated series of blows. The combat went on fiercely until the 'arena ref' signaled a pause with an orange, strobe-like flash.

"They already need a break," Shaw said, elbowing his brother in the side as he said it. Surprisingly, Dax felt his new skinsuit tighten, and Shaw's elbow felt like a distant touch on his ribs. What? He poked his chest, abdomen and the tops of his legs, noting a strange sensation in the material. It seemed to toughen upon contact, as if the suit somehow 'knew' it was being challenged and, like muscle, intensified its own density to absorb an impact and prevent penetration. Feeling at his hood, Dax gently caressed the insulating, pebbled texture around the back of his head. With gentle pressure, it felt soft and supple. Then he jabbed it with his forefinger and an area several square centimeters in diameter constricted tight, like armor. He felt a very dull thud on his skull, but not a stitch of pain.

"Whoa! Shaw, you gotta check this out! You think Mom worked on these suits?"

"Shhh! We're supposed to be observing. If we end up sparring later and you come home with a big headache, it's gonna be because you didn't pay attention."

"Fine, okay," Dax grumbled, fed up with his brother's brooding angst. He was just about to hurl his own insult, when a fleeting inspiration made his eyes flash wickedly behind his mask. "After all," he said, "I know you're just grumpy because all your friends are so far away."

"Keep mumbling, Dax," Shaw shot back.

"Cheer up, bro. A lot of the troops here are your age. Maybe you should make more friends. There's a new engineer working on a project in Launch Bay Three, and—"

"Dax, what would I have in common with some engi—"

The 'referee' in the underwater combat arena flashed a harsh blue-white light, bringing the troops back to their start positions. He eliminated two sparring opponents on each team, reducing the number to eight – four-on-four.

The second round of sparring began and the troopers showed no signs of flagging.

"Well, she's nineteen, just like you. So you're the same age . . ."

Shaw perked up at that single magic word.

"She? What's her name?"

"Amira . . . Egyptian, I think, or maybe Moroccan," Dax said, as if he'd not been waiting for a moment to spring this on his brother, "and I bet she could use a friend, too."

Shaw nodded thoughtfully, rubbing his chin through his hood. That subtle reflex wasn't lost on Dax – for his older brother, this was as good as saying, '*How fast can I shave?*'

"Well, maybe when we finish here."

"Okay. And Shaw, thanks. I'm glad you're around to set me straight when I need it."

Shaw looked at him, not quite sure how sincere that felt.

"Sure, buddy . . . anytime. And you know, I only mean to help."

"Oh. Sure," Dax replied, smiling innocently, "I definitely know that."

Shaw was too lost in the powerful compulsion to clean himself up to second-guess the practiced, oh-so-contrite flavor of his younger brother's change in demeanor.

Now down to just four combatants, the arena ref flashed his light again and the fighting became even more aggressive, with the skills and instincts of each trooper coming into play, making for a much more interesting skirmish. Now, besides a series of blows and defensive blocks, they began to jab at each other with the prongs, their padding lighting up with each successful impact. Once . . . . twice . . . when the third successful strike lit up the tally pad, that opponent's Dusais went dark and the 'dead' sparring partner reluctantly swam to the edge of the arena. Finally, two were left, facing one another in liquid space. Though a safe distance from the action, Dax and Shaw and the eliminated-but-happily-resting troopers felt vibrations from the heavier blows; the last pair made for some good entertainment.

Dax smirked, talking out of the corner of his mouth.

"Those two are movin' pretty quick for a liquid environment . . ."

Shaw didn't take the bait; instead nodding slowly, intrigued.

"Yeah, well they probably did some weight training so these things would feel light."

The match ended with the smaller-framed, blue-suited combatant pinning her green-suited opponent against the reef floor. The arena ref signaled all the competitors together and Captain Zander joined them as they assembled. Dax and his brother stayed where they were, but the com system carried their father's voice as he addressed everyone present.

"That was some excellent work. We'll hold drills every day, and your squad leaders will be responsible for making sure you get at least an hour of combat time in. Not simulated, not in the gym – you need to be training out here. Now for some good news – our early analysis from the Delvans, assuming we're getting this correct, tells us that the liquid density and gravitational forces on their world will be nowhere near as extreme as on Earth. So we'll still be swimming – in fact most of our extro-vessel patrols will involve long hours in the water – but physical exertion will be far less demanding."

Dax glanced over to his brother with an 'I told ya so' grin. Shaw pretended not to notice, fixing his gaze upon their father.

"These Dusai will move a lot faster for you," the captain explained, "and *you* will move a lot faster wielding them. That alone will require some adjustment. The point is, if you can master these drills here, you're going to be all the more prepared and potent a force when we make the transition to their world."

He smiled behind his mask, but he could read their body language – the troops were overdue for a break.

"Okay, I need two sets of Dusai batons please, and you may all resume your afternoon itineraries. Dismissed."

The final two challengers to face off lingered, offering their batons to the captain, who gestured to Dax and Shaw to swim over and collect the weapons.

In the optical display of his mask, Dax could already read the names and short bios of both: Akei Watai and Caden Jaeger, she formerly a Japanese paratrooper and he a Marine 'gearhead' from Hoboken with one very distinctive passion. His father turned his attention to them both, demonstrating the breadth of the homework he'd done.

209

"Second lieutenant Jaeger. You played goalie for the USMC hockey team?"

"Three years, sir!" Jaeger responded, with a heavy but grin-inspiring New Jersey brogue that left no mystery about where he'd grown up.

"Well, there's a lot of ice on Delvus-3. Maybe you'll get a chance to play."

"I heard, sir! First thing I'm cookin' up when we get settled is a new set of blades, sir!"

The captain laughed, as did his sons; this guy had spirit.

"Lieutenant Watai. You did well just now. Your father was an Olympian archer, yes?"

Her cheeks flushed behind her mask, but her shoulders straightened a bit, chin out.

"Yes, a silver and a bronze. Thank you, sir. And may I say, it is and will be an honor to serve under your command, Captain Zander."

The captain glanced briefly at his sons, his tone atypically halting and uncertain.

"Well, we haven't quite . . . decided on the hierarchy of command yet. You may very well end up with a different field commander."

Watai and Jaeger both blinked, but he was first to speak.

"Sir, beggin' yer pardon, but . . . I signed up because a' you. My C.O. told me solid, Captain Evan Zander was leadin' this thing; so I said, 'Gimme a pen, I'm goin' to outah space!'"

The captain had clearly not wanted his boys to hear this exchange, and his throaty final words seemed carefully chosen so as to end the conversation.

"I have other obligations to weigh, lieutenant. But thanks for your confidence. You're dismissed."

Watai and Jaeger nodded, slightly perplexed, then swam back towards the compound. After a few seconds, Evan Zander turned around to face his sons. He held up the Dusai batons.

"Okay. You wanted to spar. Here we—"

"Uhh, on second thought . . ." Shaw said softly, "I'm not feeling it right now. *Captain*."

"Shaw . . ." his father pleaded, but he was already kicking away, a tiny swirl of bubbles in his wake.

"Shaw, come back!" Dax called insistently.

Sill watching his son swim off toward home, the captain's shoulders sagged.

"Let him go, Son. It's okay."

Dax resisted calling out again, but more than ever, he *really* wanted a chance to spar with his brother. Preferably without a referee.

Defying Expectations

Where dozens of trainees had been facing off just moments before, now it was just the two of them – Dax and his dad, who seemed more wounded by Shaw's departure than by any attack some mysterious aliens could inflict.

"I'm sorry, Son," the Captain said, turning to face him. "I know it looks like I already accepted a call to lead this mission, but you have my word, I didn't. There are people assuming I'll go without any assurances on my part."

Dax looked at his father with genuine sympathy. This man, so revered by biographers, military historians and countless young soldiers of all stripes, could still be rendered vulnerable by the thought of losing trust with his sons. In Dax's eyes, that wasn't weakness – it was a quality that made him all the more a hero. He knew – and deep down Shaw had to know – that his dad would never lie to them, even if he had shielded them from a few facts for a while. There was absolutely no question in his mind what his dad held most dear – and it wasn't a title or leading any mission. It was his wife and three boys. It had always been that.

"I know. Dad, you're the most honest guy in the world. You're the whole reason I wanna do something great someday. Well, you and Mom both."

They looked at each other, the cold ocean briefly seeming a little less so. A new voice buzzed in on the com link. Already patched in on his dad's channel, Dax perked up, listening to someone speak in a crisp, but mature, unmistakably Asian dialect.

"Captain Zander?"

The captain tapped his sleeve, responding crisply, "X.O. Zander here."

"Captain Zander, I know I'm not due until tomorrow, but I squeezed into an earlier transport to take advantage of—"

"Joon! Welcome! Check in with Seaman Todd. We have quarters prepared for you."

The captain gestured slightly for Dax to wait, but it was unnecessary; his son knew impromptu interruptions were part of his father's job, and he kept silent.

"Commander," his father continued, "let's connect for dinner. I'll see you at eighteen hundred; we'll take a little tour around and then grab a bite."

"Very well, Captain. Thank you. Song out."

"Dad," Dax prodded, hoping to get the scoop on their new visitor, "who was that?"

"That's Commander Joon Song, a highly decorated Captain of the Korean Republic."

"Okay . . ."

"He's the man who leads the mission when I tell Easton I'm passing on the job."

Dax suddenly felt a wave of solemnity. Maybe it was the wistful tenor in his father's voice, that salute of farewell to a last chance at adventure.

"So you've known about him all along? As your replacement?"

"I was told a few hours ago he'd said 'yes' to the mission, whether as executive officer or as my second."

"So now you can tell 'em 'no,' and the whole thing still goes forward, right?"

His father nodded quietly, but even through his mask Dax could see the way his eyes had lost their light. His dad looked older somehow.

"I'm gonna tell Shaw, okay? He owes you an apology."

"Your brother's a little scared, Dax. He's seeing the world drift into a new place, and after tasting things out there, he wants this family to stay together, to avoid change. I can't blame him for that, even if it makes for some misunderstanding. His heart's in the right place."

"Yeah, well he doesn't have to keep knocking you around while he figures stuff out."

"It can take a while to find your footing as a man. Until then, it's up to others to give you a little room. And I've had a lot more practice."

"At what?" Dax asked.

"Sparring," his dad winked. He hoisted his Dusai, eyes sparkling. "Think you can take your old man?"

Dax grinned broadly.

"Dad. All I gotta do is pretend you're *Shaw*."

Both laughed and secured their protective gear. They faced off as the captain counted down from five, and at *one!* they began to bob and weave around each other. They landed some blows, to be sure. But mostly, they laughed.

From a considerable distance, the three Delvans watched with great curiosity.

"They fight. The parent against his progeny," Beyyos observed, with considerable consternation, "and yet they seem to *enjoy* the conflict with no damage to their relationship."

Prevek merely grunted, unwilling to make any conclusions.

Vren smiled, in her way.

"Can't you tell? They're not trying to hurt each other. With each blow, they offer and receive respect and trust."

Beyyos snorted dubiously. "They offer respect by harming one another?"

Finally Prevek spoke up.

"You would do well to read their ancient wisdom writings, Beyyos. One of their sages is quoted thus: 'Faithful are the wounds of a friend, but the kisses of an enemy are deceitful.'"

Beyyos was stubborn. To his credit, he would admit when he had fallen short. Still, the concept frustrated him. He watched the father and son continue to strike and counterstrike, their Dusai batons flashing with each hit.

"It is hard to conceive that one would ever provoke injury toward an object of affection for a noble purpose."

"And that conceptual difficulty with which we so struggle," Prevek noted in his deep, gravelly tone, "is exactly why we are here. We will need these beings to survive and prevail against the shadows that have overwhelmed our kind. They love, and yet they do not experience our level of hesitation with conflicts where more dire action is called for."

Vren allowed herself a tiny rush of pleasure. Though she greatly respected Beyyos, he was often unwilling to listen to alternate views – especially hers. And then, he stunned her:

"Vren. I apologize for demeaning your interpretation of these events. You are very clearly evidencing an evolution of thought to an admirable capacity."

Apparently Vren's expression caused the deep rumble that was Prevek's chuckle. She jittered a little and finally responded.

"Thank you, Beyyos. You honor me."

Beyyos nodded, and all three knew it would likely be a long time before he ever offered another compliment like that. But Vren felt such gratitude for this rare show of esteem, she glowed noticeably brighter for the next nine hours.

For his part, Prevek was both amazed and amused that Beyyos had displayed any humility at all. But it pleased him to think that after so long, they were all still capable of growth. If that was true, then the future – should they survive it – was full of promise.

. . .

Freshly showered, shaved and wearing the best shirt he'd brought with him, Shaw slipped into the launch bay, only to be quickly disappointed. There was no girl in sight, but there *was* a beautiful vessel, the shape of a squashed egg, wrapped in a strangely intriguing, chameleon-like hull. From outside, he guessed it might accommodate a crew of up to four, and as he walked around its perimeter, the surface seemed to mimic the lighting and colors of its immediate surroundings. *Out in the reef*, he thought, *this thing would be great for observing marine life.*

"Yes, it would," a smooth, feminine and very British voice confirmed, "and I can't wait to see you cataloguing lots of alien life from inside it."

Amira Narouk's lithe figure popped out from an almost impossibly small compartment in the rear of the vessel. Her big, dark eyes perfectly complemented her olive skin and long, ebony tresses pulled back over one shoulder, neatly held in place by a turquoise barrette. She had thick, dark red lips, already curling up in amusement, as the look on Shaw's face was a mix of shock and newly-triggered, nineteen-year-old hormones.

"You can read minds? That's super rare!"

"Yes, it is, but no I can't. You were speaking out loud."

The way she says 'can't' is so chewy, Shaw thought, too beguiled to be embarrassed, and completely unaware his jaw was hanging open.

Amira chuckled, unspooling herself from the hatch, landing with a slight hop just in front of Shaw. She held out a hand, then realized it was dripping with some sort of transparent red fluid. Shaw started to shake it anyway and she pulled it back.

"Oh! Sorry!"

Grabbing a towel, she wiped her palm clean, nodding in lieu of actual contact.

215

"But to your earlier comment," Shaw said, "no, I can say that I'm pretty sure I won't be joining the mission."

"You won't?" Something like disappointment briefly flashed across her face.

"It's unwise. We can't possibly prepare for a conflict with an alien race we know nothing about, especially when it means risking so much for a civilization we barely know at *all*."

"Oh. So you're xenophobic," she said, flatly.

"What?"

"Never mind. I respect your right to . . . whatever creed you find most comfortable."

Within seconds, she became engrossed with the gaskets lining the main hatch. Despite the awkward silence, Shaw hovered nearby, but she barely looked at him. Finally, she spoke.

"You're the eldest. Shaw Zander, yes? I can see your father's nose, and your chin is unmistakably your mum's."

Shaw grimaced. He turned to catch his profile reflected in one of the dark port windows.

"I have my Dad's nose? Seriously?"

She patted the hull like a beloved pet, seeming satisfied with her cursory inspection.

"I just replaced the fuel lines, so I think we can take this fellow out for a bit of a tour. Since I don't know the reef, would you care to come along? Seeing you're intent on staying safe and cozy here on planet Earth, it might be your one chance to take a spin."

Though pretty sure he'd just been the recipient of an emasculating sideswipe, Shaw was nonetheless too smitten by that sonorous accent, that lilting voice, to mind.

"Yeah . . . sure. You bet."

"Alright. Jump in. Port side, please. I'm British. We still navigate on the right."

Shaw nodded happily, walking around the cab. Amira pursed her lips.

"Nobody ever thinks that's as funny as I do," she mumbled to herself.

She got in and the top of the cab came together in three segments, locking tightly. Amira engaged the controls effortlessly and the ramp upon which the seacab was mounted tilted up. Shaw yelped in surprise as they rolled backward down the ramp, into a launch silo. The doors closed behind them, isolating and sealing them in. Amira shifted in her seat uncomfortably; a quick glance over confirmed Shaw was just staring at her.

"I thought you were in college," she said, plainly flustered.

"I am. U of M. I'll be going back soon."

"They don't have girls at the University of Miami?"

Shaw laughed, not following.

"Yeah, of course they do!"

Amira rolled her eyes, pressing a button.

"Boys," she said, as seawater started flooding the bay, "are the same, dry or in the wet." She glanced over again and tapped his chest.

"Restraint, Mr. Zander."

"What? What'd I do?!"

"Your seat restraint," she clarified, patting his chest gingerly. "This vessel is intended for combat readiness, so the restraints are engaged *manually*."

Wondering how red his face actually looked right now, Shaw reached up and pulled the harness down over both shoulders, flashing a serious look once his couplers clicked.

"Okay. All set."

"My, won't this be an adventure," she observed wryly. "In five. Four—" and then she paused, sniffing the air.

"What's that smell?" she asked.

"Umm, cologne, maybe?" Shaw answered meekly, sinking deeper into his seat, then adding, "It's called Black Cobra." But even as the words left his lips, he regretted saying them.

She blinked.

"Cobra," she said, flatly. "Because I'm Egyptian. Of Egyptian descent." It was more a sober deduction than a question. Shaw nodded slightly, secretly wishing he were anywhere else. Inscrutable, Amira took a slow breath, then put her hand back on the controls.

"I see." She cleared her throat and stared ahead, the brief silence grueling. Finally, she returned to her countdown. "In five. Four. Three . . ."

But there was no 'two.' Instead, Amira hit 'launch' a split second after 'three,' prompting a wail of sheer terror from the depths of Shaw Zander's lungs as they roared out of the silo with such powerful thrust his tongue slapped the back wall of his mouth. Seconds later, they evened out, and for the briefest of instants between, he felt a tinge of weightlessness. Shaw stared over at her, his forehead beaded with sweat, her lips pursed into a tiny, satisfied smirk.

"Well, we know the thrusters have some oomph," she said, dryly.

"Yeah. Powerful," he muttered, loosening his grip on the armrests.

She giggled as they began to skim over the compound bunkers to the outer boundaries of the reef. Shaw gradually sat a little straighter, thinking perhaps he'd just made a new friend.

Dissonant DNA

Despite the fact all three Zander brothers were back home, they didn't get extra family 'together time' with their parents over the next few days. Aside from breakfast and dinner, Evan and Dayna were only occasionally glimpsed, each attending to what the boys correctly assumed was a very dense workload in preparation for a mission launch less than three weeks off. Though Commander Song had arrived, Dax's father was still the executive officer and therefore responsible for a host of tasks. How well the men and women were prepared for an unpredictable, alien environment and hostile opponents would most definitely enhance their chances of success, and preparation was far less costly than death.

It was getting late, and the galley wasn't far from his parents' quarters, so Dax was careful to keep his late-night snack preparation as quiet as possible. He knew how to create one of Grampa's fizzmotics, but that would require some fruit blending. Too loud. So he settled for half a grapefruit and toasted one of the banana-stuffed waffles his mother had prepared that morning, eating in the galley so as not to wake Kai. That wasn't so much about not disturbing his brother's sleep, as having no desire to share his hard-earned meal.

As the sea around the compound whispered and groaned, Dax settled into a comfortable chair, the events of recent days coursing through his ever-active mind. After they had finished sparring and cleaned up, his father had introduced him to Commander Song in the commissary. He was a charming, slender man of very few words, sharp features and a head of thick, short-cropped hair, so shockingly white that Dax wondered if the fifty-year-old officer had simply had it colored that way. Could they do that in the military? Maybe if you were important enough, he reasoned. In any event, it gave Dax great pleasure to tell his older brother later on, that right after he'd abandoned their intended Dusai drill, Commander Song had arrived to take their father's place as mission leader to Delvus-3. Shaw had retreated to his quarters for about half an hour, apparently taking that time to suck up his pride. Whatever he did in that interval, it worked; he found the captain, apologized quietly and sincerely thanked him for putting the family first, as always. They embraced, his mother kissed him, and then they all gathered to enjoy an old movie in the sunken living room, with several big buckets of garlic popcorn. Almost as if by magic, it had turned into a very sweet night for the Zanders, as if nothing had changed and nothing was going to. They knew better, of course; but for that one night, they rediscovered how splendidly they all enjoyed each other's company. Their mom even let Scrub sit in on the movie with them. The creature was remarkably still throughout, snorting or sneezing on seven occasions over two hours – which made for several group belly laughs, as Kai's head was resting on the sea lion's stomach and would bounce up each and every time, startling the boy.

Since that night, they hadn't enjoyed time together as a family, but the boys weren't going to complain; they knew once the mission was underway and the last of the troops had made it to Delvus-3, things would settle down. They would adjust once more to a fairly normal life. Perhaps they wouldn't even move to Houston or other parts unknown, in order to maintain a permanent transit hub for the troops and supplies. If nothing else, everyone had settled back into rhythms, and for now there was peace.

A fairly pervasive peace, in fact. As far as Dax knew, they were all asleep.

While strolling a perimeter corridor of the seabase, heading back to the far wing that held the quarters he shared with Kai, he spotted a Delvan through one of the floor-to-ceiling windows. It was Vren. She had something hanging off her left pectoral fin – Dax's clear duffeltube. In the unceremonious arrival days earlier, he'd dropped the thing and forgotten about it. Vren turned, apparently summoning Beyyos, who swiftly emerged from the darkness, followed by Prevek. They all swam toward the windows as Dax made eye contact, obviously attempting to get his attention, pointing forward. He moved to a darkened module extending out from one wing and the lights glimmered on. This was his mother's 'office' – a private, smaller lab, currently filled with an array of exotic mineral ores, powdery substances and what looked like algae samples, probably all from Delvus-3.

At the far end, there was a sort of 'blister bubble' spacious enough for one or two persons to step into, completely transparent and two-thirds surrounded by seawater. It made for great observation and sometimes Dax curled up here to do his homework. In this moment, it allowed him to convene with the alien visitors in privacy, with mere centimeters separating them. Vren held up the tube. Thanks to a microphone permanently mounted just outside the module, her eager, fast-paced words came through loud and clear.

"You dropped this. I believe it was when we first came upon you. Perhaps resulting from shock at our sudden proximity."

"Perhaps, yeah." Dax grinned. "Thanks. Do you see the specimen lockout?"

He gestured to a double-walled chamber with a tray, currently open to the ocean.

Vren let the tube slip off her fin and it dropped into the tray. Dax tapped the controls and the chamber instantly sealed off and drained of water. As the boy waited to retrieve the duffeltube, Prevek moved close, his voice resonant and measured.

"Something has provoked our curiosity, Dax Zander. May we discuss this?"

"Sure, I guess so," Dax answered, mystified.

"We noted two dominant genetic signatures within your container. Yours are embedded in several objects, including a small polymer device – a tool used for dental hygiene."

"My toothbrush. Yeah."

"But there is another object saturated with samples of genetic material very different from your own. It appears to be a decorative head covering . . ."

Though it was obvious he was referring to Cody's sweat-stained Cubs cap, a more disturbing thought struck Dax almost as quickly.

"Wait, how can you tell my genetic makeup from Cody's or anyone else's? Or at all?"

The three Delvans glanced at each other. Beyyos glided up alongside Prevek, his tone simultaneously deferential and instructive.

"Humans value privacy across a broad spectrum of domains and define boundaries for such," Beyyos opined. "It is possible that in scanning their sequences, we might have compromised those boundaries."

"When did you scan us?" Dax asked.

"It is an immediate event for us. We think nothing of it, as in our culture it is a method by which we mutually evaluate one another's health, mood and general well-being. We do not interrupt a discussion unless something is amiss – if the other seems unhealthy and unaware of such. At which point, it becomes a service."

"So when you guys get together you just give each other checkups?"

Prevek looked confused. Dax realized that Delvans might be slow adapting to 'people humor,' much less his own offhand quips. He tried again.

"When you meet, it's a normal thing for you to scan each other's DNA?"

Prevek seemed to brighten briefly, but then his large brow tightened again, as Vren leaned forward, eager to help.

"Dee En Ayy is an abbreviation for their term referring to formative genetic composition."

She looked to Dax for affirmation. He nodded, impressed, offering a thumbs up.

"Yeah, pretty much."

Pleased, Vren's red luster brightened noticeably. She tried replicating Dax's thumbs up, but the segmented portion of her pectoral fin wouldn't wrap around very much, so it looked more like she was scooping at invisible fish.

"Vren?" Beyyos murmured, and she straightened, her fin dropping to rest at her side.

"If we have crossed a protocol boundary, you have our apologies," Prevek said, "but it was in scanning you that we became aware you were not to be feared – that you were clearly biological offspring to Captain Evan and Dr. Dayna and therefore likely non-threatening."

"And you and your siblings are currently healthy, as are your parents," Beyyos added.

"However," Prevek continued, his tone taking a more serious quality, "the dissonant 'DNA' samples are indicative of an individual with a severe illness."

Dax stilled, amazed at how readily they had gleaned such a thing.

"Cody. Yeah, he's sick." He pushed close to the glass barrier, his breath fogging up the window. "You could tell that just from some old dried crusty stuff in his hat?"

Prevek seemed almost sad. He glanced at Beyyos, who obligingly filled in the details.

"What we've extrapolated is a damaged neurological system, anomalous to the norm for homo sapiens. It is as if the cells responsible for basic immunity have a tool set . . . How would you say . . ." Beyyos turned to Vren, switching his sounds abruptly – emitting a series of high pitched clicks and tones. In turn, she answered with a very brief but similar chirp. Beyyos glided in between Vren and Prevek.

". . . Switched off," Beyyos clarified. "The defensive tools responsible for his immunity have been switched off within cells in that system, as if originally triggered by some element incorrectly interpreted as an allergen. Whatever the activating agent, it is not present, and this needs to be repaired, otherwise his other vital systems will degenerate further, eventually resulting in death."

Dax felt a chill – at first seeming like intense fear, soon turning into a wonderful tremor, as he realized something wondrous and good might be within reach, an opportunity he must not squander. He was so nervous, so excited, he could only whisper his question, hoping beyond hope what their answer might be.

"You mean – you think . . . Can you fix him?"

The Delvans looked at him curiously. Prevek again had that quizzical look.

"Fix."

He looked to Beyyos, who turned to Vren, who perked up.

"Restore. Repair to wholeness. Orient to order from disorder."

Prevek and Beyyos each brightened, both in demeanor and in their 'glowy' patterns.

"Yes," Prevek said. "If we are provided coordinates to his location, we can 'fix' him."

Astonished, Dax sucked in air, every square centimeter of his body prickling with goosebumps.

"Wow. Wow! That's – that's amazing . . ."

Immediately jubilant, his breathing turned hard and fast as they explained the rest, but he got most of it.

"So long as there are even a few uncorrupted cells within his neurological system," Prevek continued, "we can provoke accelerated germination and duplication of those cells, while the damaged ones die off and are flushed naturally from his body with other expiring tissue."

Vren moved closer.

"Your circulatory pulse rate has accelerated . . ." she began, concerned.

"I'm okay," Dax laughed. "Honest."

Beyyos continued where Prevek had left off.

"After we begin this process, there will be a sustained middle period where he will likely enter a deep sleep, perhaps for many days," he said, "after which he will emerge with natural patterns of consciousness and in full health. There will be no trace of the effects in his system, nor will any of his offspring —"

Vren seemed determined to get a word in edgewise:

"Should he choose to mate, of course."

"Yes," Beyyos assured, with what to Dax seemed a slight trace of annoyance. "Should he sire any offspring, no trace of his malady will be carried on to them, nor to any generations following in his bloodline."

Gratitude surged through Dax with such irrepressible power, he couldn't help but open his arms flat to the glass, as if to embrace them all.

"You guys!" he said, tears on his cheeks – tears he didn't even think to wipe away. "Thank you!"

"Your appreciation is noted and honors us," Prevek replied, "but it is in our nature to nourish and enhance life when it is within our power."

"Dax Zander, we will need coordinates," Vren added, "so that we may treat your friend."

The boy blinked, overwhelmed, and his whole body tightened. Several thoughts hit him at once, the biggest being that his parents would never agree to any plan that had the Delvans visiting residents of the Oahu mainland. He hesitated for a nanosecond.

"Can we do it now? I mean, like two hours from now?"

"Two hours is acceptable," Prevek answered. "We are about to bring a quantity of water from our homeworld for study, and must retrieve several robotic survey devices already sent there by your scientists to compile data. Do you wish your parents to come along?"

"No!" Dax chirped back, so loudly he shocked himself. Instantly adopting a more casual demeanor, he smoothed out the response. "You know, they're asleep. I'd rather surprise them with the good news myself, after they wake up. You know, after it's all done."

Prevek was quiet, his huge head angling just a bit to the side. Dax felt a chill deep in his bones – was this alien on to him? Could they read minds? And would it matter?

The silence was brief, but Dax grew anxious. Finally Prevek answered.

"I agree, Dax Zander. We will leave it to you alone to enlighten them to these events when you are ready. Best to redeem the opportunity as it avails us."

Dax sighed with relief, nothing forced about his smile now.

"Great. I'll leave here in a few minutes. I'll let Cody and his parents know you're coming. 'Cause, no offense . . . You guys are pretty and glowy and all, but I think you might scare them if they didn't know in advance you were coming."

Prevek nodded, seeming amused.

"Very well. When you are ready, call for us, and we will commence a visit to restore your friend to wholeness."

"Awesome. Thank—" Dax stopped, remembering a better, fuller word. "Mahalo."

"A regional expression of gratitude!" Vren chimed in. "Mahalo to you, Dax Zander!"

"Oh, all of you – just call me Dax."

"Dax," Beyyos declared, trying it on for size. "Very well . . . Dax."

Prevek started to turn, then looked back with a gentle nod.

"Ma-halo," he said, carefully, but with unmistakable warmth.

And then he glided away, the others following. Dax slid down against the glass until his backside hit the floor. A small giggle welled up, his whole body trembling with wonder and anticipation. He punched the air.

"YES!"

Fortunately, he didn't wake anyone.

. . .

Twenty-two minutes later, Dax's singled-minded sense of mission had so fully flooded his every capillary with adrenaline that the lateness of the hour hadn't fazed him in the slightest. He managed to steal out of the seabase using a lockout in a corridor well beyond the residence compound. No chance that anyone in his family had heard. Actually, Scrub had nearly exposed him, but he'd anticipated this, distracting the animal with a bag of half-frozen sardines, buying time to slip away. But he still had to somehow slip through a sensor grid and the eyes of round-the-clock sentries. It was at this point that his many hours spent forging a friendship with Maz and Brooks over the last two years, helping relieve their boredom, proved fortuitous. With no real security threats, Brooks had taken the time to teach Dax all kinds of interesting details about how perimeter sensors worked, how they were programmed – and how they could be distracted by certain phenomena, naturally occurring or otherwise. Before leaving the seabase, he'd hacked into the perimeter alarms to ensure that upon his return, a simple frequency emitted from his skinsuit transmitter would prevent the sensors from going off. Then he found Prevek and the others to provide them with precise coordinates to the Vallabh household. The Delvans explained they would create a 'bubble' within the home from where they would then combine and direct their energies to treat Cody close at hand. Dax gave them an arrival time and from that point, he had to make the minutes count.

One lonely sentry saw Dax swimming about, but as the boy's manner was very casual and he wasn't anywhere near a perimeter boundary, the sentry hadn't reported in. Dax swam right by with a friendly, lazy wave.

"Hi!" Dax called.

"Evening," the sentry responded. "Can't sleep?"

Dax paused, hovering there, shifting the pack strapped to his side, hoping the sentry wouldn't find it of interest.

"Yeah," he replied, stretching, "sometimes it helps if I wear myself out a little."

"Okay," the sentry replied. "Have a good swim. I won't wake up your dad, but please stay within the grid."

Dax waved again, kicking away. "Night!"

The sentry kept watching until Dax slipped into a dark, deep shadow between two buildings in the compound – where one of the lockout chambers was located. Of course, Dax had no intention of going back inside. Instead, under cover of complete darkness, he opened his pack and removed a small pouch, set it on the sea floor, and watched as the thin, gel-like membrane of the pouch rapidly dissolved. Within seconds, small fish began to gather around it.

"Come and get it!" Dax whispered gleefully. He jetted off, keeping low as more fish darted past him, swarming to the contents of the pouch. Dax saw the tiny blue lights of the perimeter boundary and kept advancing until he was just a few meters away, hiding under a cluster of large rocks. He waited, and watched, as the few sentries in the area began to move toward the remarkably active cluster of fish now competing for whatever delicious snack Dax had left for them. It was an odd buzz of activity, and as he'd correctly assumed, the sentries would investigate.

Unwanted attention successfully diverted, Dax triggered a tiny signal and none of the sentries noticed the tiny shudder in the perimeter beacons – a brief 'numbing' of the grid's sensors, enabling the boy to slip through undetected. Fortunately, the late hour meant he was swimming in a black sea. Once safely past the security boundary, he shot straight up to the surface. Topside, he found the mini-skimmer very close to where they'd left it days earlier, the self-adjusting, retractable buoys preventing any significant drift. And as Shaw had no reason to lock out the ignition, it started up for Dax on his first attempt. Cruising back to the mainland, he willed away any anxiety about the Delvans making contact with his parents before the rendezvous could take place. He knew they could be trusted, but there remained a very real challenge ahead: Kiri and Dananjay. Knocking on their door alone in the dead of night, however fond they were of him, might brand him as a highly imaginative, possibly disturbed teenager raving about aliens from another world preparing to enter their living room. They might even call his parents before hearing him out. He couldn't risk facing them alone.

And this was why his grandfather never finished a pretty wonderful dream that had him feeding pandas and reindeer from the palm of his hand.

Rude Awakenings

The old man stirred with a cantankerous grumble worthy of a very grumpy gorilla, one hand pawing about at empty air – until it found Dax's chest. "Fred, lights."

A warm glow lit up the room, gradually intensifying as his eyes adjusted, then blinked, as Dax's head looked considerably more tamed than before.

"Ya chopped it all off . . ." But as it dawned on him they'd had this conversation, his thoughts turned darker. "What's wrong? Is Kai alright?"

"Yeah, Grampa, he's okay. But we gotta talk. And there's not much time. Can you just trust me?"

Grampa Pat sat up in bed, unsettled.

"Dax, tell me what's going on."

"I'll tell you everything – I promise. But can you get dressed? We need to go to Cody's."

"At this hour? You gone totally bonkers, kid?"

"Grampa, please trust me. I really need you."

Despite the weariness in his bones, staring into those pleading eyes, his grandfather could see something had gripped Dax's heart with a singular, intense purpose. He didn't dare dismiss or casually scorn the impulse.

"Okay, I'll be ready in three minutes. Have Fred make me a tall mug of coffee to go. The hard stuff."

Relieved, Dax snapped around on one heel and was out the door.

"And I mean *caffeinated*!"

Patrick turned and caught his haggard reflection in a mirror. He flashed a big toothy grin and then let everything sag again, heaving an exhausted sigh.

"Ohhh, boy."

Stretching his arms, he rose to find a clean shirt.

228

. . .

Grampa's coffee was still too hot to sip when the taxi glided silently up the driveway. They boarded, facing each other in the spacious, somewhat spartan, compartment.

"Requested destination is the residence of Dananjay and Kiri Vallabh," a disembodied but pleasant voice rang out. "Please confirm."

"Correct," Dax replied. There was a slight whir as the vehicle started on its way, and then just a low, almost soothing hum. As Grampa took the first gulps from his steaming mug, Dax released everything in a torrent – from the moment they ran into the very same aliens who had appeared at LAMIGA, discovering the nature of the mission his mother and father had been asked to consider, the heated family argument, the incoming troops already preparing for an engagement and the arrival of Commander Song.

Grampa Pat listened to it all, sitting in stunned silence. It was a lot to absorb. Dax managed to wrap up the bulk of it by the time they were a few blocks from Cody's house.

"That's incredible," his grandfather mused. "No wonder your mom and dad got so strange, with all that going on. And then . . .?"

"And then after all that happened," Dax continued, "I ran into the Delvans by myself and they said they could help Cody."

"Help. You mean . . . treat him? Improve his condition?"

"*Cure* him, Grampa. Fix him. Completely."

His grandfather let out a long whistle, his eyes wide as saucers.

"Well, I guess if they can travel space without ships and look into our DNA like it's nothing . . . maybe they have some other skills, too. So Cody's parents said it's okay?"

Dax sat back, his head sinking into his shoulders. Grampa nodded slowly.

"They don't know what's about to happen. So you need me to back you up."

Dax began to wonder if he had misjudged his grandfather's empathy for underdogs.

"You realize you're asking them to trust you on the spot," Grampa said, "with aliens from a distant world about to pop into their home, unannounced, in the middle of the night. And you're asking them to *trust* those aliens with their only son, who they've got for maybe another few months."

"I know. You gotta make 'em understand."

Grampa Pat released an uneasy grunt.

229

A ping announced their arrival; they looked out the large windows. The street was empty, the sky pitch black, awash with stars. A single light shone over the Vallabh's front porch.

Patrick Redtree looked across the cab interior at Dax with a gravity he rarely let show, a little easier now given the hour. With no idea where this might lead, his gut quivered anxiously, aware he'd soon face these creatures up close. And there was nothing to fully convince him they meant well, aside from his grandson's starry-eyed opinion.

There was also nothing to convince him they meant anything *but* good.

"If your grandmother were here . . ." His voice trailed off, as if he wasn't sure just *how* she would advise them right now. Dax waited, not interrupting, and then Grampa chuckled gently, shaking his head. Whatever had come to mind, it had brought some clarity.

"You know . . . seeing you this minute, she'd be so very proud of you, Dax."

Absorbing this, the boy's heart soared.

Another ping. The door slid open, inviting them to disembark.

"This taxi wants to get rid of us. How much time do we have before the Delvans arrive?"

"Thirty-one minutes, I think," Dax said.

"Hoo-boy." He pulled himself out and stretched. "Okay, let's go knock on their door. Hey, is it Delvan or Delvans?"

Dax shrugged, uncertain. They ascended the steps to the front entry, and Grampa Pat found a doorbell. Pressing it, he cringed a little, as the chimes from deep within the house were quite audible. He waited a few seconds and rang once more. Dax fidgeted nervously.

"This could get awkward, Daxer. But we'll figure it out. It's worth it."

"Thanks, Grampa."

The door opened to reveal both Dananjay and Kiri, in their robes, squinting against the porch light, bewildered and a little annoyed. But they were not people quick to anger, and Grampa's presence immediately lent an air of validity to the confrontation.

"Patrick. Dax. It's very late – has something happened? Do you need help?"

"It *is* late," Grampa Pat agreed, with a reassuring glance to his grandson, "but can we please come in? We wouldn't have approached you at this hour if it weren't urgent."

"But why not call beforehand —"

"Because we're not supposed to be here," Dax broke in, "and we couldn't take the chance that Mom and Dad would find out. Or . . . the government."

A chilly silence followed, the eyes of all three adults falling upon the boy in reaction to that last word. Fortunately, Grampa Pat had anticipated this subject would rear its head.

"I know how that sounds, Kiri," Grampa Pat offered, "but Dax isn't crying wolf. And I came along because there's a very real chance to help Cody, if we move immediately. We had to act now because at this moment, nobody else knows. And if he's going to get their help, it has to be without any undue attention. Without any fuss."

Dananjay's dark brow furrowed.

"*Whose* help?"

"That's what we have to explain. But we have to explain *right now.*"

Despite the concern deeply etched across their faces, Kiri and Dananjay opened the door and ushered them both inside.

. . .

They spoke in the kitchen, Grampa still sipping his coffee. It would've taken but a few minutes to explain the big points, had the Vallabhs not repeatedly asked for clarification on details that weren't all that relevant to what was about to happen. But they did get through it, and soon Cody's parents were reeling with the startling information and with a decision that seemed impossible to make wisely with mere minutes to ponder its implications.

"Have they ever performed a medical procedure on a human?" Dananjay asked.

"I don't know. They have been to Earth before," Dax explained, "but I don't know when or why they were here."

"How could they know so much about us?" Kiri inquired.

"From what Dax told me," Grampa said, "their culture is deeply devoted to the sciences, physics, biology, geography, energy, and, of course, exploration. If that consumes their race, and if they've visited us before, then maybe they've learned a lot about us."

Kiri looked to Dax for reassurance; he nodded earnestly.

"They could tell something was wrong with Cody from just a few hair fibers and dead skin cells in his hat."

Kiri was shivering so much Dananjay reached into a closet and placed a second wrap about her shoulders.

"I don't know. I just don't know. He's our little boy. You ask me to trust you, to trust these beings we've never met. And you invited them here without asking us first . . ."

"I'm sorry!" Dax said. "They said they could and I knew if we waited, my parents would say we couldn't risk the world learning about them yet. You know, all the military stuff that could get in the way. And Cody's getting . . ."

He swallowed, feeling Grampa's thick, strong hand on his back.

"He's getting worse with every day," Dananjay whispered gravely. "Yes."

"I know I'm just a kid," Dax conceded, "but you've known me since forever. And you know I don't make stuff up. Please believe me."

The Vallabhs looked at Grampa Pat, a glint of hope emerging in their eyes.

"We believe *Dax* believes the aliens can do what they claim," Dananjay stated, with utter sincerity, "but do *you* believe there is reason to trust their intentions?"

Grampa took in a long breath.

"I believe there is reason to meet with them, and give them a chance to convince you."

There was a heavy silence for a few seconds, and finally Dananjay gripped his wife's hand tightly. He looked at her, and she nodded.

"We will welcome them and hear them out," she said, with resolve.

Their heads all turned to the time displayed above the large oven.

"Won't be long now," Dax said. "We should wake Cody."

They were halfway down the hall to his bedroom when they heard Cody's scream. Rushing inside, each of them gasped at the sight.

Instead of three individual floating bubbles, one irregularly shaped mass of liquid filled the center of the room, holding Prevek, Beyyos and Vren. Fortunately, the lofty ceiling afforded considerable space, and the Delvans had positioned their containment 'blob' above Cody's bed, permitting Dax and the adults to walk beneath with about half a meter of headroom to spare.

Anxiously eyeing the strange forms above, Kiri rushed to her son's side. He was wide-eyed and trembling, but something clicked as soon as his parents, Dax and Grampa Pat entered.

"It's alright, Cody! Don't be afraid," his mother said, stroking his back. She looked urgently to Dax, who did not disappoint, stepping forward with a warm, reassuring wave.

"They're my friends, Cody," he said softly. "They won't hurt you."

Dax looked up; the underside of the containment bubble was so close he could reach up and touch it, but out of respect and a slight concern he might contaminate their mobile habitat or maybe even spring a leak, he refrained. Grampa Pat and Cody's dad knew well enough to observe in silence, but each could hear his own heart beating at a fast clip.

"This is Vren," Dax said, gesturing to each, "and Beyyos and Prevek."

The visiting aliens nodded quietly, in keeping with the delicacy of the moment, while seeming strangely captivated with the space mural that covered the huge back wall.

Awestruck, Cody just stared, the gentle light emanating from all three Delvans mesmerizing and drawing him forward, any sense of pain or weakness lost as he slipped from his mother's arms and stood, his hand rising to just beneath the shimmering boundary.

"Cody—" his mother whispered, but then she fell silent, rebelling against every instinct.

Dax was also inclined to stop him, but he could see the Delvans were unconcerned about the boy's approach, so he waited and watched, like the others. Prevek bent his body toward Cody, so that his large blue head was just centimeters away. The boy lifted his fingers higher, touching whatever made up the outer perimeter of liquid, an opalescent ripple flitting out from his fingertips across the jelly-like surface. He paused briefly, and then a crooked little grin washed over his face as his hand went *through* to touch the senior Delvan's snout.

The broad, curving pattern spreading across most of Prevek's upper head glowed brighter as Cody's hand lay flat against it. And together, he and the boy shared a smile.

Kiri moved to her husband's side, both astonished. Like Dax and Grampa Pat, they were rapt with wonder.

Cody glanced over at Dax, grinning broadly, his voice a whispered giggle.

"So banga!"

Dax nodded, and an odd little thought popped into his head, watching his friend, knowing that suddenly, Cody had a future. In this space - once an unofficial waiting room for what had seemed a certain and inevitable darkness - now there was hope. And a tiny voice in the back of his head quietly affirmed, *'It was worth it.'*

And it was – sneaking out, sabotaging the perimeter sensors, risking his parents' confusion, frustration and potentially severe punishment, confiding in

Grampa, waking the Vallabhs. It had all been scary, but Dax felt certain Cody would live. Even if fate threw them a curve somewhere down the road and something went wrong, he had brought his friend an unforgettable, incredible gift – a chance to reach past the boundaries of his contained world and touch a bigger universe. Best of all, he knew in his gut they would both regard this memory, like their friendship, as precious and rare for the rest of their lives.

With all five listening attentively, the Delvans carefully explained what would follow. For the better part of the next three hours, they would encapsulate Cody in an 'energy pouch,' safely facilitating their work – though to anyone watching, the process might prove disturbing. Cody's body and all his vital systems would be suspended in a sort of phased state of being, where the potentially debilitating and decaying effects of time, gravity and momentum could be stalled. Under these circumstances, while Vren and Beyyos exerted their attention on maintaining the energy pocket, Prevek would commence 'corrections' to his neurological system, replicating enough healthy cells to dominate, and in the ensuing days of his recovery, overwhelm those cells responsible for his deteriorating condition.

Much like their own kind on Delvus-3, human parents were quite emotionally attached to their offspring, so Prevek, Beyyos and Vren were sensitive to the potential trauma of witnessing firsthand a procedure unlike anything practiced in human medicine. At certain points, they revealed, some of the boy's major organs might require temporary separation from the rest of his body, where they would 'float' nearby in suspended animation. Kiri clutched tightly at Dananjay's arm, her fingers digging in so deeply he had to gently pry them out.

However, Cody, Dax and his grandfather were fascinated that this was even possible.

"So will I be dead for a while?" the boy asked.

The Delvans looked at each other. Vren bent near, her voice sweet and comforting.

"You will not experience death. But similarly, you will not be fully *alive*, either. It will be more like all of your cells entering a very deep sleep."

She looked over to Kiri and Dananjay, reading the worry on their faces.

"We give you our word your son will not be harmed. When we have completed our work, he will sleep for a very long time. During his recovery, he will require long periods of rest as his body resets, rejuvenates and finds new strength. But make no mistake, this process *will* make him well."

There was a long quiet in the room, where Dananjay and Kiri whispered to one another, her voice cracking slightly once with something like despair. Dax and his grandfather stepped to the doorway to give the family some privacy and watched at a distance as Cody's parents summoned all their courage and knelt before their son.

"You are your own person. We are uncertain and that comes entirely out of our love for you. But this is your life, and a path fully your own to choose."

Cody's eyes glistened, absorbing their affection and realizing how difficult and scary this step must have been for them both. Strangely, their words served to quell his own undercurrent of fear and replace it with a new boldness. Anticipation, even. He beamed warmly, embracing his mother and father.

"I want to do this. I know it'll be okay."

They hugged him tight, weeping.

"You will sleep now," Beyyos explained, in a voice gentle and soft. "And when you awaken, we will no longer be present."

"Well, then, thank you in advance, for everything. Before you start, can I say goodbye to Dax and Mr. Redtree?"

"Of course," Prevek said.

"Thank you for coming and helping Dax help me," Cody said to Grampa, who grinned warmly, crouching on knees that didn't take well to crouching these days.

"You get better, young man. And come visit me once you're back to full specs."

As Grampa tousled Cody's hair, Dax's gaze was drawn to the space mural just beyond.

"Your stars worked, Kiri," he said, his voice touched with awe. "Every time I looked at them, I knew something special was coming for Cody."

Kiri smiled sweetly, but the comment drew Prevek's particular attention.

"The stars?" he asked. "We found this representation confusing. Could you explain it?"

"The . . . painting?" Kiri asked. "The one on the wall?"

"We are unfamiliar with this particular system," Beyyos added, "and we have charted many vast regions."

"It isn't a map," Cody offered, "it's just art! My mom knows how much I want to be an astronaut, so she made that to inspire me."

Prevek cocked his head, intrigued. Grampa and Cody's parents were bemused, wondering why the conversation had shifted from the boy's health to his room's evocative, if ironically relevant, décor.

"The pursuit of interstellar science. And how much *do* you wish to explore space?"

Cody gestured broadly to the wall behind him.

"Dax can tell you! It's all I think about!"

Prevek turned slightly to Beyyos and Vren, reverting back to the native clicks and whistles of their natural communication as the humans in the room stood by, mystified. Beyyos looked back at Cody briefly before again joining the impromptu conference of three.

"Can I tell him?" Vren asked brightly, in audible English, with unmistakable excitement.

Beyyos made a noise not unlike an impatient 'harrumph,' and nodded once. Prevek gestured gently with one pectoral fin, and Vren proudly moved to the center as all three turned to face Cody and Dax.

"We'd like to show you our world, Cody Vallabh."

The two boys stared up at the Delvans, trying to process Vren's words. Grampa Pat and the Vallabhs exchanged looks of utter astonishment.

"You can take me to your planet?" Cody asked. He heard his mother wince, but glancing over, Cody saw his father place a reassuring hand on his mom's.

"In a sense. Were we to convey you physically to Delvus-three, there is currently nowhere you could survive. Preparation of human habitats has only just begun, and within the liquisphere, you would need protective equipment."

"So what did you mean?" Dax asked.

"After your damaged systems are restored," Vren explained, "you will sleep for several days. So as a courtesy, and to provide thoughts more conducive to rest throughout your healing, the three of us can create an experiential bubble, compiled from our very specific, respective memories. This would last a few brief moments, but for you it would seem quite real."

"In a sense," Prevek added, "you would be the first human visitors to our planet."

"Visitors?" Cody asked.

"We can generate energy for a bubble sufficient to contain two of you."

Cody swallowed. He looked to Dax.

"No," Dax said, mustering every bit of selflessness he could summon, "you gotta take your mom or dad, Cody. Family."

Cody Vallabh looked across the room to his parents. They gazed back proudly.

"You *are* family, Dax," Kiri said, blinking away tears. "It should be the two of you."

Cody's jaw dropped; he and Dax slapped palms with exhilaration.

"Hot-now!" they shouted.

"Hot-*now*! Gonna blastoff to space!" Grampa Pat cheered, punching the air joyfully. Dananjay looked up to the Delvans.

"To be clear, they're not actually *going* anywhere, correct? Not traveling physically. This will be a type of manufactured, virtual illusion?"

Prevek stilled, but Vren leaned close and whisper-clicked discreetly. He seemed satisfied.

"Your assumption is accurate, Dananjay Vallabh. The boys will not leave this room."

Cody's parents nodded, offering their blessing.

"Very well," Prevek said, "if you are both ready, we shall begin."

Cody and Dax nodded eagerly, standing straight up.

The adults gasped as a portion of the large glob dropped down like a tube, just big enough to swallow up both boys and some airspace about them, pulling them up like an elevator. In seconds they were surrounded by the three Delvans – a bubble within the bubble – with but a thin, protective membrane as separation. Beyyos moved to within centimeters of that boundary, his snout so close they expected it to burst through at any second. Vren bobbed closer as well.

"What was that word?" Vren asked, turning to Grampa Pat. "Oh yes! *Blastoff*!"

And then, the world, the room around the boys . . .

VANISHED.

A Glimpse Ahead

"**W**HOA!" Dax and Cody exclaimed, as Earth fled their feet. They flew through space, the moon looming near, barely glimpsing the edge of the international compounds founded decades earlier, the blackness of the dark side of the moon giving way to countless stars. Mars approached, but just as it began to draw them in they took an abrupt turn, their dizzying, involuntary trajectory avoiding any more of Earth's sister planets altogether, as space itself seemed to bend and streak like a million shiny ribbons twisting and burning all around them.

Dax and Cody felt completely weightless, the sensation strangely at odds with the very convincing and incalculable speed with which they could swear they were traveling. Then, though he could not be seen, they heard Prevek's voice.

"Compared to your own, our world is very small, hidden within the gaseous clusters of the Large Magellanic Cloud."

Their rippling tunnel evaporated without warning, leaving them to soar in silence toward a spectacular nebula of pink and turquoise, while all sorts of interstellar matter, asteroids and gassy tendrils flitted by like ghostly rain. Their approach slowed as a huge round marble came into view ahead, icy blue and white, wrapped in an austere, rippled surface of pitted glaciers.

"This is our planetoid," Beyyos continued, "Delvus-three. Delvus-one is smaller in size, and Delvus-two no longer exists.

"Wow," Cody cooed aloud. "Dax, do you see this?"

"Everything," Dax replied, his voice barely a whisper.

They floated toward the frozen, bleak terrain of the exosphere, and so certain did it seem they would crash into the snow-capped peaks that the boys grabbed each other's arms, screaming aloud as they flew *into*, and then through dense layers of ice and sediment, boring deep into an outer shell that had thickened over eons. Like a hot spear piercing wax, they slipped deeper and deeper through murky strata, glimpsing crystal ores and massive fossils of strange beasts lost to the ages. Then, without warning, they broke through – effortlessly gliding through an ocean, serene, silent and so devoid of light it was a deep, purple-tinged black.

"Our kind live within the lower liquisphere," Vren said, "but these upper regions are habitats for those who never cease to forage."

The boys drifted past enormous sea beasts, some with forms similar to whales, eels or even dinosaurs; others were almost beyond description – a few just tangles of glittering membranes or tentacles. They also saw innumerable tiny animals that ran the spectrum from 'fishlike' to . . .

"Those look like otters!" Cody exclaimed, as a school of fuzzy purple animals swam close to their astounded faces. They reached out to touch them, but, of course, the boys' hands passed right through. Strangely, the ambient light began to increase, illuminated by wispy, drifting ribbons of something like gas, glittering with billions of bioluminescent 'somethings.'

"The Channi microorganisms permeate the currents of the lower regions, providing us with both light and a vital nutrient for our kind. They are not unlike the krill of your own oceans and thrive in abundance throughout the liquisphere. As they mature, they drift to the upper regions, where they become prey for other species."

The boys marveled, their eyes adjusting to take in thousands of these living 'currents,' swirling and flowing everywhere.

"It's like the aurora borealis," Cody observed. Dax nodded.

"Yeah! But – thousands of them. Millions, I guess. And they're alive."

"The entire life cycle of the Channi is about survival and sustenance. We classify them as lower life forms, but their presence is vital to the balance of our ecosystem, and as much as we are capable, we respect and nourish their existence."

Dax was about to ask if the Delvans' natural 'glow' was due to a heavy diet of Channi, but every few seconds there was a new sight to absorb, and he didn't want to miss anything. Soon the boys neared a sprawling plateau, mostly flat but for a wide, shallow crater, located just before the edge of a steep drop off – over which they subsequently plunged with convincing and exhilarating velocity.

"Even now," Prevek said calmly, "the foundations of your father's command center are rising upon this site."

Suddenly uneasy, Dax muttered a tiny, "Oh."

"Your dad's going to the planet? That's amazing!" Cody whispered excitedly, but Dax didn't answer.

Dipping over the precipice, they gawked at massive walls of rock below the ridge.

"The caverns within have been expanded and will be sealed and pressurized for initial human habitation. This will be your temporary home until the outer compound is complete."

"Wowww . . ." Cody cooed in awe, "you get to live in a cave!"

Fortunately for Dax, their tour kept them moving, covering a great distance in mere seconds toward a cloudy patch of light, the thumping of their hearts squeezing out the sounds of the sea. Rising out of the murky depths, the twisting parapets of a Delvan village came sparkling into view, busy with so many beautiful creatures, Dax and Cody gasped.

"We have many free-floating communities, but the vast majority are anchored to the planet's core. This one we call 'Quilita.'"

Their eyes danced wildly as they gaped at this thriving community, and to their delight Prevek, Beyyos and Vren let them linger for a moment. The boys found themselves circling in and about gracefully curving architecture, which seemed not so much built of interconnected bricks or stones but *woven* somehow – in some places composed of millions of threads and slender tubes, in others, rippled, webbed curtains stretching across great distances.

"These are beautiful," Dax whispered.

"We use the currents in building our habitations," Vren explained, "using a material produced by lower organisms. It is for a time very pliant, and can be guided into forms, layer after layer. Very soon, it crystallizes and thickens, creating sturdy walls and enclosures."

"The bigger ones look like huge shells," Cody said.

"Shells . . ." Beyyos murmured, as if the word were foreign, "as in protective husks grown by lower forms on your world. Yes. They do share attributes both structural and aesthetic."

The boys watched as large and small groups of Delvans clustered, as if sharing stories and meals, or in even smaller numbers, gently expressing affection.

"Those are Delvan . . . families, right?" Dax asked.

240

"Correct," Prevek replied.

Dax gasped, certain he had caught a glimpse of something incredibly interesting.

"Wait! Can we slow down for just a few seconds?" he asked. Instantly, the boys hovered, watching Delvans enter various dwellings, pass through meeting areas and engage in conversation. Over and over, as they came into contact, many made the same gesture to one another, warmly and respectfully, lifting a pectoral above their bulbous snouts and sweeping it in a broad arc. Dax and Cody cooed at the same time, knowing they had both figured it out.

"The moon," they said, amazed.

"The moon?" Vren repeated, quizzically.

"The symbol you put in the moon!" Dax said. "It's how you greet each other, right?"

"It is. For us, it conveys loyalty and enduring friendship."

Cody shivered, pretty sure they'd just learned something very special.

"Wow . . ."

As they drifted out of Quilita, the boys were sad to see it all shrinking away.

"Is that it?" Dax asked.

"This is all we can share for now. We must reserve our strength to properly remedy your friend's malady."

"Oh, okay."

"Wait!" Cody cried out, craning to see something just beneath them. "What's that?"

Below, along several long, wavy outcroppings of rock, were dozens of glowing stones, each embedded about a meter apart. A few Delvans hovered quietly over some of the stones, perfectly still, despite the current. Prevek, Beyyos and Vren all seemed to sigh.

"Tributes to our fallen. Since the arrival of the invaders, many have gone missing; so in their absence, we have created these monuments to their memories."

Dax and Cody watched as one small Delvan, probably a child, bowed to touch its snout against one softly glowing stone, radiating with a deep, lustrous blue. No interpreter was needed to make clear this was a soul trying to reconcile her own deep measure of heartbreak and loss.

"Invaders?" Cody asked.

Dax felt his gut churning with guilt for keeping his word. Nonetheless, he remained quiet.

"Yes," Prevek answered, "it is why we have asked your kind for help to preserve our species, our way of life. With Captain Zander's intervention, we now believe we will survive."

"This journey must come to a close now, so we may commence your restoration," Beyyos said. And as the world around faded like a blackening shroud, Cody turned to Dax.

"Dax! That's so banga! Are you gonna be going with your Dad? Is he taking you?"

His pal stared back, shuddering, aware now that the Delvans had not been told of his father's decision, and if he were to make that known . . . Would they still help Cody?

The aliens, momentarily distracted with 'closing' the sensory illusion, lowered the two boys to their original position. Cody sat on the edge of his bed.

"How was it!?" Dananjay asked, Grampa now standing alongside him and Kiri.

"I don't even know how to describe it!" Cody exclaimed.

"We are ready to begin," Prevek announced.

Dax swallowed, glancing at Cody, then avoiding eye contact. He could sense Cody knew something was amiss, and they were about to lose contact for quite a while.

"Dax, what is it?"

Grampa Pat, watching them, saw the quick, furtive look on Dax's face, and he read something there that felt a lot like '*help!*'

"Mister Prevek . . ." Grampa Pat called. The Delvans turned, curious.

"You have a question?"

"Well," Grampa started, offering a very subtle nod to Dax, "you're going to do this thing with Cody, but his parents need to know how to care for him while he's recovering, right?"

This time, Dax read the look on his grandfather's face: *Whatever it is you gotta do, do it now.* And while the Delvans interacted with Kiri and Dananjay, the boy bent to whisper his confession ever so softly in Cody's ear.

"Cody, my dad's not going. He wouldn't take the mission because it means leaving us."

Cody stared back incredulously.

"But they'll die! Dax, they'll all die!"

"No, there's another leader going. Dad says he's great."

Cody pulled Dax near, his trembling grip on his friend's arm, his words hushed but fierce, deliberate.

"No, Dax. It isn't just your dad. Don't you see? It's *you*."

"What?"

"*You* have to go there. I know it. I *feel* it. Whatever it takes, however you have to make it happen. You have to go. *You're* gonna be the one who saves them, Dax."

"I'm just a kid, Cody. We're both kids. I don't —"

Cody smiled warmly, shaking his head.

"No, you're not. You're gonna save their lives, Dax. Talk your dad into going and taking you along. I know what's inside you. You can save them. Promise me."

"I don't know why you think I can —"

"Promise me that you'll *try*."

The two boys stared at each other, while thanks to Grampa's little distraction, Kiri and Dananjay learned that Cody would wake often enough to eat some food, drink some water, use the bathroom and then sleep again. No special instructions at all.

"Cody Vallabh," Vren asked quietly, "are you ready?"

Cody stared at his pal, his eyes pleading desperately, and Dax was terrified that if he didn't give his solemn oath, Cody might just back out of this whole thing.

"I promise," Dax whispered hoarsely, upon which Cody embraced him, even though his tender ribs throbbed from the pressure. He let go and looked up, as his pal tried to process what had just taken place.

"I'm ready," Cody said calmly.

Prevek nodded and the Delvans moved closer, till they were hovering just over him.

Never taking his eyes off his friend, Dax walked back to Grampa Pat, who wiped a stray tear from his own cheek as he pulled the boy to his side.

"I'm proud of you, too, boy," he said. "You done good."

Emotionally drained from events of the last day and a half, Dax just knocked his head against Grampa's shoulder to acknowledge the tribute, but his heart swelled with pride.

Everyone watched while Cody stood and looked up expectantly. He glanced one more time at his pal.

"Thanks, Dax. You know you're my shoul'. Always."

Dax nodded, overwhelmed, finally mustering one word.

"Boink!"

Cody grinned broadly, then looked up. Without a word, the Delvans moved equidistant apart, and Cody's eyes began to flutter almost immediately. Standing there, his body sagged. Just as it went limp, it began to rise off the ground, tilting into a horizontal position, floating toward the glob. Just before touching the boundary, the boy's entire form glistened with a sort of bluish sparkle, encapsulating him from head to toe. Continuing up, Cody's prone form penetrated the bubble and hovered between Prevek, Beyyos and Vren. From this point on they focused solely upon him, as if no one else were in the room. The adults watched, but a long time passed during which it seemed as if nothing at all were happening. Occasionally, sections of Cody's body flashed or even turned transparent, briefly revealing sections of bone, tissue, veins and whole organs. It was quite bewildering, but perhaps the strangest part of it was that the Delvans never physically touched him – they simply stared at him unblinking, barely moving, occasionally chattering to one another in that tongue that only they could comprehend.

After a while, Grampa nudged Dax.

"We need to get you back. It's late, but if you can squeak into your bed before anyone's up, then you might avoid a rough conversation for . . . well, at least till you're rested."

They said their goodbyes to the Vallabhs, and Dax took one last look at his friend and the Delvans, this incredibly strange sight to which but he and three other people in the entire world were privileged to behold. Full of gratitude, Kiri and Dananjay hugged both, and soon Dax and his grandfather were on the sidewalk, still under the stars, waiting on another cab.

Dax didn't say much until the little driverless vehicle pulled up.

"I'll have to tell them eventually, Grampa."

His grandfather followed him in, happy to finally sit, his knees still a little upset over crouching earlier.

"And I'm glad you know it's right to be honest with them. But your mom and dad have a lot on their plate right now, a lot of responsibility, and people they answer to. They don't have to wrestle with this *today*. And maybe it's better if you don't burden them just yet."

"So it's *my* burden?" Dax asked, wondering about the right and wrong of withholding secrets when life and death were on the line.

"Now you got the idea."

244

"When do I tell them?"

"Well," Grampa mused with a sigh, "that's something you gotta figure out. Timing is part of all that growin' up stuff you deal with. But you've got more than a little wisdom in ya, and you've got a good heart. You'll know when it's time to explain things. And you'll also know to take whatever lumps come your way."

"I don't care about any lumps. Having you with me, knowing you believe in me – it's like I feel I can do anything."

Deeply pleased, Grampa closed his eyes to soak that in and store it deep. He wanted to sleep, but the ride home would be short, so he just rested for a moment.

"Yep. And accepting that is part of growin' up, too. But you might say a little prayer before you have that talk, just so you go into it strong."

Dax smiled, gazing out the window at the dark homes, trees and streetlights whisking by. They passed the park he had stopped in on his scooter weeks before, the last time he had attempted anything like a prayer. And his heart raced a little, recalling his humbly uttered words:

I'll do anything. I'll go anywhere. Just please fix my friend.

"What are you thinking about, m'boy?" Grampa asked quietly.

I'll do anything. I'll go anywhere.

He'd made an oath, and Dax had a strong hunch his resolve to keep it was about to be tested. The amazing thing was, though his heart should have been beating fast with fear of the unknown, it was instead swelling with excitement, anticipation, and most of all, gratitude. The road angled out and the tree cover vanished, revealing for Dax a lustrous indigo sky, speckled with billions of stars. In that moment, just that quickly, a new and powerful determination took hold of his entire being.

"We're gonna go there," he said aloud, dreamily. "We're gonna save these guys."

Grampa Pat perked up. "Save who? The Delvans?"

"Yeah. Fight for them. Drive out the bad guys. Whatever it takes."

Grampa sighed, his brow creasing deeply, but he did not comment, sensing a change in his grandson, a new sense of purpose as he stared up at the stars.

And he was right. From that moment on, Dax knew he would devote himself to ensuring the endurance and preservation of these amazingly wise and generous creatures. Before now, a voyage to space had been a novelty. It was a fine dream for Cody, but at best mildly enticing for a young man who found fast cars and speedboats both more thrilling and tangibly accessible. Tonight, however, his friend had charged him with a task, but the full experience had also awakened a new appetite, deep in his bones. He would keep his promise. While there was no question he relished his life, experiences, relationships and memories on Earth, Dax also knew that letting it all go, embracing uncertainty, unknown risk and great change, would now comprise the first steps of a new path that would define his future and the quality of his heart.

And in point of fact, *in his heart*, he had already taken the first step of that journey.

Shaw's Vote

B ack at home, breakfast was a quiet, somber affair. More than a few harsh accusations had been thrown around a few nights before, yet nothing had truly been resolved and despite the relative calm since, nobody in the family – not even Dayna – was 100 percent convinced that Evan still would not just decide to accept the mission anyway, or that some nefarious and faceless persons might not somehow *force* him to do so.

Dax had slipped back into the seabase, every bone and muscle in his body crying for sleep, just before 5:00 a.m. His hack of the security sensors had gone undetected, and it was a simple matter to slip back into the perimeter – even easier than leaving had been. But in order to safely pass through about sixty or so meters of open water nearest to the compound, he had to hunker down behind the reef for over fifteen minutes, until the sentry for that area had completed her sweep and moved on. Getting back inside noiselessly meant using an excruciatingly slow, manual setting to drain a lockout chamber midway between the barracks and the Zander residence. But he was so stealthy entering, Scrub barely stirred from his slumber when Dax crept into the room and back under the covers.

Unaware he'd been sleeping for less than two-and-a-half hours, his mother ordered him out of bed at eight, and as it took every last gram of energy to drag himself to the breakfast nook, keeping his mouth shut required no effort at all. In fact, his father chided him for a garbled request for milk. Deep down, of course, he wanted to let them know Cody was now on a path to full health – they all cared about the boy – but that conversation came with a lot of baggage, and he was too groggy to trust himself right now. As Grampa had said, the time would come soon enough, and Dax would recognize that moment. Until then, he'd hold his peace.

Shaw was the last to arrive. Alert and freshly showered, he pulled up a seat at the table next to Dax and began to spoon some scrambled eggs to his plate from a large bowl.

"Morning, Son," his father said, cheerfully.

Shaw offered a little wave and a grunt. Dax flicked the side of his brother's temple. "Your hair's still wet."

His brother gave him a cool, appraising look, then leaned over and whispered in his ear.

"Just like your skinsuit, cowboy."

Dax stiffened, averting his eyes. Shaw might have slept through his tip-toed return, but he was a budding scientist, always observant, and as a habit, annoyingly nosy.

"So? Who cares?"

Shaw leaned near again, his voice low but pointed.

"You think you're the first guy who snuck out to see a girl? If there's even a scratch on Boone's mini-skimmer, you're paying for it, Romeo."

The tightly-wound coil of tension within Dax sprang loose so completely, it was all he could do not to cut loose with a giddy laugh. As it was, he couldn't hold back the grin forming between his cheeks, which, of course, just served to irritate his older brother even more.

"I don't know what—" Dax snickered, only to be stopped by a kick to his shin.

"Later," Shaw muttered firmly.

"What's all the mumbling, boys?"

Both looked across at their mother.

"I just told Shaw to . . . leave some for the rest of us," Dax offered casually.

"Well, there's plenty. Here, have some bacon." She spun the lazy Susan in the middle of the table, revealing a large plate of thick, wrinkled strips.

"That's seaweed, Mom."

"It's delicious and loaded with good stuff. Eat it."

In fact, it was pretty delicious. Over time, thanks to skillful cultivation and the endorsement of several celebrity chefs, red seaweed had taken the world by storm, exceeding the popularity of lab-cultured bacon.

Kai reached past Dax to pull the plate over and swept a healthy portion onto his toast.

"I made a bacon sandwich!" he announced happily.

"See? Your brother loves it."

"Mom," Dax said, "Kai plays checkers with a *sea lion*."

"But I always win!" Kai protested.

Dax rolled his eyes, yawning loud and long, the hours of rest he'd deprived himself of now making his head, shoulders and just about everything else seem remarkably heavy.

"Did you not sleep well, sweetie?" his mother asked. Shaw smirked, but said nothing.

"Umm . . . could I have some coffee?" Dax replied, patting down his unruly hair. She looked at him quizzically, then reached for a steaming bronze carafe and poured him a cup. The boy practically swooned with pleasure in the first sip. Through the steam, he glanced across the table, noticing the pensive, slightly sad look in his father's eyes.

"Dad? You okay?"

Evan nodded, his eyes falling on Shaw, who met his gaze and slowly put down his fork.

"I meant it when I said I was sorry, Dad," Shaw said quietly. "I didn't mean to drop a bunch of guilt on you." He swigged down his own cup of coffee. "Besides, we all know you're not goin' anywhere, so—"

"He hasn't decided for sure yet, Shaw," Dax broke in.

Shaw looked at his brother like he was some kind of stranger, but it was the fleeting glance between his mother and father that suddenly made him ill at ease.

"What?" Shaw asked. "Commander Song agreed to lead the troops. So why would there be . . ."

"Son," Evan began, "there are still a lot of things to be weighed, variables your mother and I have to discuss."

"*Variables*?" Shaw replied pointedly, pushing away from the table in disgust. "I don't believe this. After everything we talked about? Everything you promised?"

Dax, still nervous Shaw would spill the beans about his own midnight voyage to the mainland, which would in turn open up a Pandora's Box he wasn't ready to manage, just kept eating. After all, he couldn't join in the conversation if his mouth was full, so he chewed with almost comical speed and gulped some more coffee.

"Yeah, stuff your mouth, bro," Shaw said. "Meanwhile, Mom and Dad are gonna go save the Rainbow Space Dolphins. Hope you and Kai enjoy living with Grampa till you're old enough to vote."

"That's enough, Shaw," their father interjected.

"We're not having a repeat of the other night, Son," their mother added. "When we say nothing's been decided, that's exactly what we mean. And despite what you inferred, nothing was *promised*, either. Please, let's just leave this alone for now."

Shaw grunted and dove back into his food, practically attacking his eggs, chewing so fiercely that Dax, the caffeine already kicking in, cracked up, dribbling some 'bacon.'

But Kai, who had been playing in seeming blissful ignorance with two triangular slices of toast as if they were dueling jets, poured some supercharged fuel on all that combustible awkwardness when he just looked up innocently and beamed a big smile.

"We could *all* go!"

Deep inside, Dax felt an electric tingle of opportunity; his chewing slowed.

"Yeah," Shaw snorted with wry amusement, "we're all gonna go to another planet and fight bad guys we've never seen and be stuck there for—"

Dax's eyes glazed over and he stopped chewing entirely. Suddenly, he could see it all.

"—Longer than it takes Dax to grow up. Hey! Breakfast's calling," Shaw finished.

"We're not going as a family," Dayna declared firmly. "We took that off the table."

At this, Dax *did* snap to attention, seeing in his sleep-deprived euphoria what seemed an opening delivered by fate, tailor-made for his new, all-consuming directive. In an impulsive rush of bravado, he pounced on the boundary fence of his mother's thought, and trampled it.

"If you took it *off* the table, it was *on* the table once, Mom. You guys *talked* about it."

Her jaw dropped; she looked away. Evan's eyes came up from his breakfast, shooting her an apologetic glance, knowing he was about to confess something to their sons that they had both conspired to keep secret. Shaw meanwhile, irritated by the insane rabbit trail his brother had just inspired, assumed his parents would simply quash the subject altogether. That was their duty, after all. So for the moment, he kept his peace.

"What's off the table?" Kai asked innocently. He ducked underneath, but all he could see was an assortment of legs.

In a flash, Dax had figured it out. He snapped his fingers and crowed. "They told you it would be okay, right? Uncle Easton and the government? That you could take the whole family if you wanted?"

Despite a fleeting, anxious look from his wife, Evan was done withholding the truth.

"The plan as originally outlined would have me promoted to Commodore. And in that rank I would hold authority over all decisions local to Delvus-3."

Shaw glared at his father, fed up with the evasive, ever-so-specific jargon Evan would invoke whenever trying to parse a few facts. Though their dad would never lie, his military training had taught him how to make the truth conveniently confusing when necessary. But at nineteen years of age, Shaw felt part of his responsibility as firstborn included that of deconstructing his father's powerfully persuasive shenanigans.

"Dad, your 'convincing' voice has devolved into your 'unconvincing' voice. That's my very nicest way of putting it."

"Thank you, Shaw," Evan answered, taking a generous swig of coffee before continuing. "Dax, Kai, what your brother is trying to get me to say is that, yes, we were given the option to bring you all with us, because of our experience and friendship with General Russell. And there are, in fact, a select few others so valuable to the mission that they've been granted similar permission – to bring members of their family along. But in the big picture, there's no way I could consider such a thing for us, for the five of us, at this point."

Shaw sighed with deep relief. "And Commander Song said 'yes.' Okay. Thank God."

"Why *not* consider it, Dad?" Dax asked plainly.

"Dax. I'm not taking this family to a place with so many unknowns, and so much pending danger. It's just not happening."

"Daddy, if we can save them," Kai began earnestly, "we should! It's already dangerous down here, right? And we live here every day!"

Evan looked to Dayna for help.

"Sweetheart," she jumped in, "here we know so much about our environment and the creatures we share the ocean with, and —"

"But we had a tsunami," Kai countered, out of the blue, "and that time when the power went out and it got really cold. And when Shaw's boat caught fire and he almost died . . ."

Dax raised an enthusiastic palm to Kai.

"Hot-now!"

Kai slapped it with gusto. Their mother felt her control of the situation slipping away.

"Do not 'hot-now' your little brother, Dax! That's the wrong kind of encouragement—"

"Exactly!" Shaw chimed in, "Kailen has no idea the scope of this—"

But Dax rolled right over his words, charged with momentum.

"And if Dr. Narouk is bringing his daughter, then there are probably other people bringing their kids, right?"

"She's my age, Dax!" Shaw replied indignantly. "We're adults!"

Again, his comment was ignored, as Dax's pleas took on an almost inspirational feel.

"Kai's right, Mom. Dad. We've gone through some scary stuff, more than once. Sure, this is gonna be even more dangerous, but you're a crazy brilliant scientist! And Dad—"

He turned to his father, who was, remarkably, listening to his middle son. Dax didn't waste that; he gazed deep into his father's eyes with the due respect of a hero.

"Dad, you're gonna have a ton of soldiers to build stuff, to protect us, to shoot things . . . if it ever comes to that."

"Not a ton. Little more than three hundred and twenty. And some civilian specialists. But that's still a very small compliment, Son."

"Yeah, but with robots *and* Mom's huge brain, too."

Shaw was getting angrier and angrier with his middle brother's cavalier sales pitch.

"Would you just stop? Commander Song already agreed to lead the mission!"

"So?" Dax replied.

"So? You're a *kid*," Shaw growled. "You don't get it. We're talking about jumping into a war! A war we're not ready to fight!"

"Dad *ended* a war, tark. And actually it's an *invasion*."

"I'm a tark," Shaw shot back, his face reddening, "*I'm* the tark!?"

"Dax!" his mother exclaimed.

"Sorry! Sorry."

Shaw stared about in frustration, as if watching some absurdist film produced by one of his pampered frat brothers in Miami solely for purposes of shocking the bourgeois class.

"Dax. Kai. Give this up," their father insisted. "We're not traveling to another world."

Dax stood up and stretched on his toes in an attempt to meet his elder brother eye-to-eye. Instead he just swayed a little, nearly toppling, furrowing his dark, thick eyebrows defiantly, adopting an aura of gamesmanship he'd learned from Grampa Pat, daring Shaw to oppose him.

"I say . . . we *vote* on it."

Shaw *and* his father were now both shaking their heads.

"No," the captain said firmly. "That's not an option and we're your parents. There's no 'voting' on this."

With that he left the table, moving to the sunken living room, where he began to peruse a list of impending arrivals, their images flashing one by one above the table emitter. Dax followed him out, as did his mother and Kai, who bounced into the plush sofa right next to their father.

"A few days ago," Dax said, standing just beyond the list of illuminated names and faces, "Mom said you'd let the family vote."

Evan set his jaw stubbornly, so Dayna answered for them both.

"Only on whether your father would go, not—"

"Okay," Dax conceded, "but if you tell them 'no,' and they ask you again, you should at least know if we're even *willing* to go there with you, Dad. Right? And for the record, I'm in as a definite 'yes.'"

Dax shot his hand up, and to no one's surprise it was immediately followed by Kai's. They looked to their mom. She rolled her eyes.

"This is silly, boys . . ."

"Two days ago," Shaw said, eyeing his brother with unmistakable suspicion, "you didn't want Dad to go, same as me. What changed?"

Dax ignored the question, gripped by a potential shift in destiny: Could he convince his parents to change their mind? To explore a whole new world?

"Come on, Mom," he urged, "would you go? You're gonna sit here while your sons go to another world? I don't think so."

Still holding his hand up, Dax got up and walked over to his mother, gently nudging her arm up, as if cranking it skyward for a full 'yes' vote.

"That's not real!" Shaw cried out. "You're pushing her arm up!"

"Yay, Mom!" Dax cheered. "Save the Delvans! See amazing sights!"

She kept her hand up briefly, though with a baleful glare that telegraphed an evaporating patience. Then she put it down and caught Dax's own disappointed face. So she put it back up.

"This is nothing more than a hypothetical 'yes.' And I'm starting to think you've been getting far too much sugar at Grampa's."

"That's not all he's gettin' at Grampa's," Shaw muttered, hanging in the doorway.

"What does *that* mean?" their father asked.

Dax felt a little chill, catching his brother's threatening glare, but he'd already defied a lot of real and imagined threats in the last few minutes. Might as well go for broke.

"Dad," Dax coaxed, "I know you wanna go—"

"Son, I have a pretty long day ahead. We need to wrap this up . . ."

"Come on. Mom's brave enough to put her hand up . . . Yeah, you know you want to . . . Come on, this is just an 'if it were happening' thing. A *hypothetical* yes. C'mon. Forget about it meaning anything. What do you *really* want?"

Evan sighed, finally lifting a weary hand of inevitable surrender. He'd already given up on whatever that list was about, tiring of pretense. When he finally spoke, his voice was hushed and tinged with awe, as if recalling a memory of some great battle he'd won, but barely survived.

"It would be . . ." he began, "a terrifying, incredible, once-in-a-lifetime opportunity."

"YAY!" Kai shouted jubilantly. Dax felt his pulse racing; *almost there.*

Then, the four of them looked at Shaw. He blinked, resentful and aghast – his whole family engaged in willful treason against common sense, and now, it seemed, against *him*.

"What? No. No, absolutely not."

He sat down with all the obstinate intensity of a child just robbed of his dessert. Dax chided him, trying to tickle him under the arm.

"Shaw. Shawwwww . . ."

"I will break your finger. Completely off."

Dax swiftly withdrew his hand.

"Well, Shaw's in college anyway," Dax pointed out, "so he *has* to stay on Earth. So technically his vote doesn't count."

"Doesn't count!" Shaw exclaimed.

"It doesn't. I mean you're gonna quit school? Who does that help?"

"*If* I went, I'd be doing it to help the family, tark."

"Don't call your brother a tark," his father admonished, with little conviction.

"He called *me* one! And why is your hand still up, Dad?" Shaw asked, his voice burning with annoyance. His father looked over at his raised arm as if it were a tree branch, but oddly, didn't put it down.

Dax kept pushing.

"So, Shaw, if we went, you're saying you'd be coming to help the family?"

"That's *not* what I said! At all! I said anything the family does, I'm gonna be there because I'm a *part* of this family. So . . . in principle, *yes*, I'm raising my hand! But this is entirely pointless, because you know we're not going. So there."

And remarkably, though flustered, though his every limb was tense from fighting, perhaps not even aware he was doing it, Shaw raised his hand.

Dax couldn't be more pleased. He and Kai grinned ear-to-ear, facing their parents.

"So, Dad, Mom," Dax declared jubilantly, "it's unanimous! Let's go save the Delvans!"

"Yipeee!" Kai shouted, so loud his mother giggled at the scowl it instantly provoked on Shaw's face. Burning, he quickly yanked his arm down, as if that would end the conversation.

"I don't know what just happened, but you're all completely crazy."

"Shaw, it'll be great," Dax said confidently, "and I know we'll be okay."

"How do you know that?"

Dax tapped his big brother's shoulder.

"Because you'll be there to keep us safe."

Shaw fell silent, his eyes locked with Dax, a hot itch crawling up his neck signaling his reserve of self-control was just about depleted.

"Don't count on it."

He turned abruptly and walked off.

Evan and Dayna plopped down into the sofa and Kai hopped into the barely-big-enough space in between. They shook their heads, stunned, weary and worn.

"Yay!" Kai cheered ebulliently. "We're gonna be pioneers!"

"Pioneers!" Evan repeated, amused, letting Kai snuggle into the crook of his arm. "Where'd you learn about pioneers, buddy?"

Kai pointed a finger at Dax, who had curled up on the other sofa and looked very comfortable. He offered a tiny wave, taking credit for Kai's history lesson.

"It's almost like we get to start over and do all this again," Dax suggested, gesturing around to the seabase, "but this time, it would all be new."

He yawned, the coffee's temporary jolt already wearing off, his body starting to feel like a sack of lead.

"We all have to go." His voice was taking on that aimless ramble, as he'd given up fighting sleep. "Well, Shaw doesn't have to go. But me and Kai . . . chance of a lifetime. Now you finally know how everybody feels. And Kai's right. We'll be the new pioneers."

He turned to the fireplace. "Fire . . . *on*. Medium burn."

In response, flames bloomed to warm life. It was just a hologram pumping heated air; a real fire would present a hazard in a contained, oxygen-rich environment. But it was plenty cozy for Dax, who gurgled happily in its glow, pulling up a large pillow and snuggling.

"Thirteen going on forty," Dayna muttered, provoking a chuckle from the captain.

"This is far different, Son," he replied. "We're not going to settle a world because we *have* to find a place to live. We'd be doing it for the welfare of beings we barely *know*."

Dax chuckled. Though his eyes were closed, his face was awash with an expression of deep pleasure that hinted at a much older, wiser man. He yawned again.

"Well, Dad, isn't that the best reason for us to go? 'Cause it's the right thing to do?"

His parents were rendered speechless with that. All curled up, Dax released a tiny snore as if to say, '*Mission accomplished.*'

Kai giggled, but he was falling asleep himself.

"Well," Dayna said softly, with a sense of resolve that seemed plain.

"Well," Evan echoed, nodding, "guess I need to have a chat with Joon Song. Not so sure he'll want to stay on as my Number One, but Lord knows he would add a lot." He searched her face for any hint of reservation. Dayna simply nodded, then rested her head under his chin.

"It will be scary," she said. "Terrifying. But you know, we'll have the best possible people with us, and . . . *you*. And my robots, of course." She winked and he kissed her. "So I honestly do think we'll be okay. More than okay."

"I'm still trying to . . . how did Dax do that?" Evan asked, not a little bit amazed.

She shrugged, then sat up with a giggle, biting her lip.

"Okay, this one really *is* funny."

"Okay, shoot!" he answered cheerfully, admiring her enthusiasm.

"What did the Carbon-8 isotope say to the Lithium-12 isotope when he proposed?"

Evan blinked, his jaw hanging open; he was pretty sure those were both radioactive elements, but . . .

Dayna was smiling so broadly her cheeks glowed.

"Sure, we're excited *now*," she began, "but our bonds won't last forever!"

He snorted, pretty tickled but also quite pleased that he got the punchline.

"That was a good one, right?" she asked eagerly, and he nodded, still laughing.

The captain and the doctor shared a happy little sigh.

"So I guess that's it?" he asked quietly.

"Guess so," she answered, sinking into his side as he wrapped an arm around her.

They stayed that way for a while, just watching the fire.

New Music

"**D**axer? Hey there, snoozy! Wake up!"
Still on the sofa, Dax twitched to life, smacking his dry tongue, confused. He rolled over to see the semi-transparent image of Grampa Pat, floating above the table emitter, on his knees in his backyard, weeding.

"Hey, Grampa," Dax said with a yawn.

"You gonna sleep all day? Your brother called me this morning. He was not happy. According to him, you conned the whole family into going on this mission."

"Shaw's always picking a fight, Grampa. You know how he is. And it's not like anyone ever listens to me."

"That's not the way he made it sound. From what I gather your mom and dad were all set to decline the post and then you gave a pretty persuasive oral argument."

Dax yawned again, a self-satisfied smile curling his lips. If he'd truly gotten them to reconsider a decision of that import, maybe his parents no longer saw him as just a kid.

"I don't know. Maybe."

"No maybe, Son. I just spoke with your mom," Grampa said, a mix of bitterness telling in the way he punctuated a few words, "and she said they've decided."

Dax bolted upright in amazement.

"Whoa! We're going?! Seriously?!"

Grampa was less enthused.

"Yes. You forget, buddy . . . She's your mom, but she'll always be my little girl. And now she's off to another world, light years away, where God knows what's waiting for you all."

Goosebumps crawled like thousands of electric ants all over Dax's body. A swirling, prickly mix of fear, amazement and elation swirled within as he realized they were all suddenly facing an incredible adventure. However, Grampa brought all those vibes crashing to a halt with a single question.

"You haven't told them about Cody and the Delvans yet, have you?"

Dax blinked, glancing around, leaning close to the emitter, his voice low.

"Not yet."

Grampa frowned, tapping down some mud with a garden spade.

"Well, it's up to you, but a thought hit me. Cody has a regular doctor, right?"

"Yeah, Dr. Lautrec."

Illone's face flashed into his mind. Would he ever see her again?

"Well, what happens when Dr. Lautrec checks on Cody and finds his whole prognosis has changed overnight? He's gonna have some big questions."

A cold wave of dread washed over the boy, realizing this was not a secret that would hold for long, and any search for answers would lead back to him.

"Dax. I don't think you can wait for a perfect time to have that talk with your mom and dad. Now we did a good thing, I'm convinced of that. But sometimes good things come with complications and you have to deal with them. That's what being a man's about. If you want me to talk to them with you, I'm here for you."

A chill went up Dax's spine. He had kept ignoring that nagging in his gut that started the minute the Delvans offered to help Cody – the strong sense that he should have told his parents of his plans. Now he would have to face their potential anger, or worse, their disappointment in his failure to be truthful from the beginning. And who knew if they might reassess their decision to lead the mission to Delvus-3?

"They're gonna be mad," Dax said, "but I'll tell them."

"After that happens, they should contact Cody's mom and dad. But Dax – talk to Shaw. He gets extremely passionate, and Lord knows he can be harsh sometimes, but it's always because he's looking out for you, and for Kai. Swallow your pride and let him know that *you* know that, okay? Let him know that all that passion means something to you."

Dax nodded.

"I love you, boy. I know this weighs heavy, and I know I vented a little, but I promise it's gonna be okay. Cross my heart."

Never cracking a smile, he wiped the dirty spade across his t-shirt, leaving a deliberately grimy 'X.' Dax laughed. His grandfather winked and waved just before his image blinked out.

Dax turned off the glowing fire and moved to the large observation window. From here he could see lights in several bunkers that had been sitting dark for a very long time and the shapes of quite a few individuals moving within their modules. An amphibious transit vessel, just a little bigger than the family's skimmer, dropped into view just above the launch bay; a torrent of bubbles surrounded it as the bay doors opened and it descended further to dock. A crooked grin formed on the boy's face, a small shiver of excitement taking hold as he sensed a new energy building in the compound. His steps quickened, heading for his parent's quarters.

"Dad?" he called a few moments later, leaning into their residential module. There was no reply, and when he stepped in to look around, his mother was also absent. But somewhere nearby, he could hear voices. Moving to the study, Dax leaned into the doorway and saw Shaw, facing away from him, seated at a large desk. One of their father's old books lay open upon it, the pages yellowed, but Shaw's attention was fixed on a floating live feed of Hayley's freckled face, hovering just above the desk. Dax could hear Shaw's voice, dry, hollow and terribly sad.

"I don't know when," he said quietly, "The way I feel right now, it's like I don't even belong in this fam —"

"Hello there, Dax!" Hayley cut in brightly, waving. Shaw spun abruptly, meeting his brother with a cold, hard glare.

"Hi, Hayley," Dax said. "Shaw, I'm sorry, I wasn't trying to listen —"

"No, it just conveniently *happened*," Shaw groused. He turned back to the floating screen. "Hayley, call you later?"

She nodded sweetly, and opened her mouth as if to offer something encouraging, but simply fell silent and waved goodbye. Her image blinked out and instead of turning to face Dax, Shaw bent over the book and tapped a page.

"Your place has been held at page sixty-eight," spoke a smooth, feminine voice. Shaw shoved the book aside and leaned back in the chair, sullen.

"It's only been a few hours, and they're all about the mission now," he said, without looking up. He gestured randomly out a small port to the hazy view outside. "Mom's in the cooker lab meeting with some structural engineer from Germany and Dad's talking to the first batch of eager beavers."

Dax was puzzled.

"Eager—"

"Recruits, Dax," his brother replied, his tone rich with sarcasm. "Grunts. The first soldiers or sailors or astro-scouts or whatever they're gonna call 'em."

"Oh."

Dax moved between him and a bookshelf.

"Dad loves all this old stuff," he said. "Some of it's pretty chewy, though."

Shaw sniffed, a small but unmistakable expression of condescension. Dax's first impulse was to take a jab at his brother's relentlessly brooding demeanor, but an unhappy possibility now seemed very possible: what if they went to another world and Shaw actually stayed behind? A life without him, without access or contact, would be . . . He was gripped with a new, not entirely unwarranted wave of loss, of remorse, and his words came a bit softer when he finally spoke.

"Shaw, I didn't mean to make you angry. I don't wanna wake up tomorrow finding out you went back to Miami all mad at me."

Shaw sighed, closing the book. Dax spied the cover: *The Martian Chronicles* by someone named Ray Bradbury. He wondered what it might contain; people had concocted many funny ideas about Mars for a very long time. Now it was just one more conquered stop on the slow-but-sure human diaspora into space.

"I'm not going back to Miami tomorrow. But, yeah, I'm mad at you. I thought we had a deal."

"Come on, Shaw. This is a chance to do something nobody's ever done before."

"Have you seriously thought about it?" Shaw countered. "We leave here and who knows what happens then? Or if we *ever* come back? Grampa Pat. Grampa and Grammy Zander. They're all old. Cody and his family. You're gonna leave your dying friend?"

His last few words hit Dax like an ugly punch to the gut, so much so he had to sit down. It was true. Even though deep-down Dax believed Cody would now recover, his friend had been very fragile the last time Dax had seen him. The memory still hung heavy in his heart.

Almost as soon as he'd said it, Shaw was remorseful. His voice dropped to a penitent, urgent whisper. "I'm sorry. But leaving all we know . . . that's what we're talking about."

"Why do you always wanna fight?" Dax asked, exasperated. "We have this great family and you always wanna bring things down."

"That's what you think?" Shaw replied tersely. "I love our family. All I want is to keep it safe. Kai's still a little kid, Dax. It's hard enough keeping an eye on him. He rescued a wild animal and nobody stops him. He just runs off and we always have to go search for him. What if he tries to rescue something on that planet with poisonous tentacles, huge claws or a really big appetite? If he goes just one step too far in a strange world – what does *that* do to the family?"

Dax pondered this, realizing there were many dangers no one could predict. But right now, nothing seemed so painful as falling out of favor with his older brother. Something distracted him out the port window. Dax squinted and saw that it was Vren swimming by, pretty far out there. If they were back, it meant Cody was asleep, his body now in the process of mending. A wave of deep gratitude swept over him, and then – a nugget of inspiration.

"Shaw, you know what that shape – the hand in the moon – you know what it meant?"

His brother cocked his head, thrown by the unexpected turn in the conversation.

"No. I don't think anybody ever asked. If they did, Dad hasn't said anything about it."

Dax held out a hand, angling the four fingers down, the thumb up, and gestured slowly and broadly, with a slight bow of his head. Then he held up his hand again.

"On their world, that's how they promise friendship to each other," he explained.

"They told you this?" Shaw asked.

"They kind of . . . *showed* me," Dax said, with enough gravity that Shaw just accepted it.

"Okay. So . . ."

"Their first sign to us was basically trust. And love. I want to help save them, Shaw. In my heart, I think we can do that. I know I'm just a kid, but—"

Shaw looked up, with something dangerously close to respect.

"You're not a kid anymore, Daxer," Shaw said with a sigh. "You're still annoying, but you're not like any kid."

Dax stared at him. He wanted to hug his brother, but they were sharing an awkward span of time in their lives when unbridled affection risked painful embarrassment. So, he just nodded and started to leave.

262

"So is she nice?" Shaw asked, genuinely curious.

Dax turned, not sure how to respond.

"I didn't go back to meet a girl. Honest. I had something important to do." Shaw's ready smirk faded, reading his brother's expression.

"I'll tell you what it was," Dax began, "but don't get any more mad at me, okay?"

Shaw sat up, his mind obviously jumping to the worst scenario.

"The mini-skimmer's good, right?" he asked. "Because I have to take it back."

"Not a scratch. Right where you left it."

Shaw settled back, and Dax explained everything. At first Shaw was incredulous that his brother had managed to slip out of their seabase without waking anyone, setting off the sensor nets or alerting the stationed patrols. He sat there, listening, leaning forward with keen interest the whole way through until Dax finished.

"Huh," Shaw grunted.

"Are you mad?"

"Mad?" Shaw shook his head, a rare touch of warmth to his voice. "No, little brother. I'm proud of you. You risked a lot to help your friend. Your shoul'."

He extended a hand, making the shaka gesture. Though commonly used as a friendly 'hang loose,' especially among surfers, Dax was confused.

"My shoul'? Cody just said that word and I didn't . . . what's it mean?"

"An expression Bardy uses. It means a friend you lean on, like a shoulder that's always there. They never let you down, and you always come through for them. And you did."

"My shoul'," Dax whispered quietly. It was a good word. He looked up. "Like what you are to me," he said.

Shaw stilled, his throat tightening unexpectedly. Every so often, Dax could surprise him.

"Yeah. Of course," he said with an awkward little nod, abruptly tapping the cover of the book. It opened on its own, to the exact place he'd left off. "But you know, you should tell Mom and Dad quick, and figure out what to do about his doctor, because . . . Wow, Dax. If it gets out that we have alien surgeons flying around making house calls, I don't know where that ends."

"You wanna come with me? They might be less mad if you're there."

Shaw sat back, thinking. The earnest look on his brother's face appealed to the part of him that always sought to bring peace to chaos. Still . . .

"What you did took guts, but you need to own this. Just you. Facing the music is part of following through, bro."

Dax felt that ugly, cold twist in his gut again.

"That's almost exactly what Grampa said."

Dax hung in the doorway a few seconds longer, hoping Shaw would reconsider, but he seemed once again entrenched in Bradbury's tome. Just beyond him, the port to the reef revealed a level of activity far busier than it had seen in many years.

"Better get goin', Dax. It'll be okay. I think Dad might even give you some points, after he does his whole meltdown thing."

Shaw chuckled quietly and turned a page, which made Dax feel no better, but time was slipping away. So he licked his dry lips and backed out of the room, slowly at first, navigating the main corridor that branched off to the research and military modules. Pausing at a viewport, he caught sight of all three Delvans hovering between the residence and the barracks. As if they sensed him behind the window, Prevek, Beyyos and Vren all turned around.

Dax waved gently, attempting his best version of their signature gesture.

In kind, all three bowed with grace and genuine respect. Then he gave them a quick little 'human' wave and they moved along, joining an awaiting formation of troops.

Dax was still. He took in a deep breath, then tapped his sleeve.

"Dad? Are you around?"

There was a brief second or two of empty air, and then his father's voice came through.

"Hello, Son. What do you need?"

"Do you and Mom have a few minutes?" Dax asked, plainly. "I have something I need to tell you. It's important."

"Sure thing," his father answered. "Meet us in your mother's lab in ten."

Suddenly Dax could feel the powerful drumbeat of his heart, and an almost deafening, brassy call inside – like trumpets urging him to come clean and take ownership of his actions on behalf of his friend in need. The concert of his conscience was demanding he turn a new corner into manhood, and in a flash the meaning of that old expression came into focus and gained meaningful relevance. With that clarity, he stood a little taller. Dax puffed out a little air, and started down the corridor. Whatever music might await, he was ready to join the band.

EPILOGUE

Beyyos and Vren followed close behind as Prevek glided past the cluster of seabase bunkers, out toward the edge of the shelf. Far below, dozens of troops were gathered around the mouth of a foreboding crack in the sea floor. Just as two divers emerged from it, another pair dropped in and vanished, their team leader gauging the stats of their descent on a small monitor.

"What are they doing?" Vren asked.

"Testing themselves," Prevek replied, "attempting to prepare."

High above that group, another twenty sparred with Dusai under Commander Song's watchful eye, occasionally halting to observe a fresh maneuver. Still more – scores of them – were swimming through and around a series of obstacles anchored to huge outcroppings of rock.

"You know what the Mazaal have warned concerning the humans," Beyyos remarked, ominously. Prevek nodded, pensive. Vren felt a shudder down to the tip of her tail.

"The Mazaal?" she asked. "Have the humans been made aware of their existence?"

The ensuing silence provided an unsettling answer.

"But if they only know about us, and so little about the Ogribods – is that fair?"

Prevek turned to her, his eyes glowing, stilling her with their intensity.

"We must survive, Vren. Our kind now hang upon a precipice of destiny, much like this plateau. If we venture into the darkness alone, it is sure to swallow us up. The humans bring us strength, a chance to preserve life, a light through such darkness, even if our joining brings great cost to both our civilizations. And they do not come alongside us blindly."

He directed her attention again to the troops in so many directions, testing themselves, training in multiple exercises. None were fleeing; no one was giving anything but their all.

"In their hearts," Prevek continued, "they crave adventure, though the price may be unknown. Even when danger is near and dark, threatening to steal all they are, like the currents of the breach. When persuaded of a just cause, they will leap with passion into the abyss."

His colors seemed darker than usual, much like his mood. Vren looked to Beyyos, whose demeanor suggested she not speak further. But Vren had been thinking on something for a while.

"Yol Prevek, what of the Zander boy?" she asked timidly. "His condition? Should he not be told?"

Beyyos shook his head in dismay, but Prevek sighed, gazing into the deep.

"We must learn more about their kind," he answered softly. "Then, perhaps, when we are absolutely capable of addressing his – rare and unique pathology, we will intervene."

"And until then?" Vren pressed.

Prevek turned to Beyyos, who instinctively completed his thought.

"Until then, we will watch the boy. Carefully. And, Vren, your compassion is admirable."

Sensing more activity, all three turned to catch sight of a new batch of troops emerging from the compound, hundreds now in the ocean around them, in all directions. Getting ready.

"We have asked so much of them," Prevek pondered, his voice tinged with something like guilt, "and yet so much more for which they cannot possibly prepare."

The ocean seemed inundated with humans now, all committed to a grand, unprecedented mission. Observing them, the Delvans seemed to have a single question on their minds:

Would it be enough?

The Mission Will Launch

in

DAX ZANDER AND THE OGRIBOD ASSAULT

ACKNOWLEDGMENTS

So many dear friends have nourished and strengthened my motivation and stamina over the years, going back to when "Dax Zander" was just a pilot script and pitch for an animated TV show. To those few whom I might forget to mention – I'll make amends in Book 2 (finished and coming soon, by the way!).

Joel Walton, my editor – with the patience of a saint, enduring my curmudgeony responses to notes, you've made my work SO much better. For years, you kept enthusiastically affirming this was something worthwhile to see through. For that and so much more – you have my deepest thanks, dear friend.

Russ Matthews – you've inspired ideas and plotlines that will weave through the entire series, God willing. What a great pal – your bold stride through life has inspired much "high adventure" in my own imagination. I'm glad we met that day in film school. You'll always be my personal Indiana Jones.

Steve and Emily Taylor – your many contributions of scientific articles, weird phenomena and other wonders provoked my curiosity and added fiber to new ideas. And *Brian Taylor* – you're a cherished buddy; your sunny confidence in my aspirations has been matched in action and generosity again and again.

Scott and Lisa Hutcheson – your affirmations buoyed my confidence at a critical point. For your initiation of an alliance that stands to fulfill my dream of making math and science exciting for kids everywhere, I'll always be grateful.

Michael Gordon Shapiro - I soaked in so much of your music while writing this, it's like you're an invisible character. To have a "court composer" and friend who also makes me laugh – wow. Thanks for every single note and chord.

Pernille Trojgaard – you believed in my crazy ideas - a patron up close and an angel from afar. Thank you for all you've done for me, for your love, light and enduring encouragement. Your new child will always be cozy in your glow.

Patrick Bradford – your gracious, sumptuous work on the DZ website *still* draws me to the homepage, to watch and smile. You're a soulful artist, a little brother I cherish.

Lorane Wasserman, thank you for being my big sister, for the depth of your generosity that literally kept me going when this poor writer's days were very dark. And for laughing at even my dumbest jokes. L'chaim!

Giorgio Grecu – your cover art blew me away! It transports and mesmerizes me still. You are truly gifted. Grazie, amico mio. Now about Book 2 . . .

Robbie Adler – your practical advice and constructive criticism have been so enriching – your daughter Vivien's smart observation made a wonderful difference, too! Thanks for being that friend with whom I can be a kid again.

To all those friends who believed in DZ along the way and risked something to keep me out of poverty while writing – I am committed to expressing my gratitude in appropriate and at least equal measure. So grateful.

Bryan Clavenna – when you told me the book was good, I think that was the moment I first believed my words would find readers. You lit my rocket boosters, buddy.

Kennan Blehm – thanks for your constant kindness, generosity, and substantive exhortations. I'm so grateful you're in my life.

Levi and Titus – your Unka K loves you very much. You regularly remind me why I'm writing these stories. Stop growing up so fast. And tell your mom and dad they're pretty dear to my heart, too.

Scott Blanding – I am so richly blessed to call you my brother. You really are my shoul'.

To my sweet Creator, who keeps pouring life, deep joy AND ideas into my humble, fragile little frame – because your *chesed* is better than life, my lips will praise you.

Noah Knox Marshall
Thanksgiving, 2018

Made in the USA
San Bernardino, CA
08 December 2018